Rare Earth Element

A Novel

G.A. Chamberlin

Titles by

G.A. Chamberlin

The Handmaiden Legacy
Cultural Attache
Rare Earth Element
Outbound
Somma
Unintended Consequence
The Particle
The Kneeling Woman
At Auction

~

Kathleen The War Years

Rare Earth Element

Printed in the United States
ISBN 978-0-9904027-3-2

Crown Eagle Publishing

Distribution by Ingram

Cover Courtesy, NASA

Rare Earth Element

climate, culture, commerce...Too important to ignore, too well written to overlook. And too technically suspenseful not to wonder about...

* * *

The Handmaiden Legacy

The Handmaiden Legacy is a contemporary thriller full of corporate interests, beautiful seas and ancient legacies...
---G.A. Chamberlin is an International Thriller Writer!

"International Thriller Writers ...that will surprise "
--Agent, Thriller Fest, New York City

* * *

Cultural Attache

"...Amanda Wells is lecturing on the historical integrity of medieval works at the University when she is informed that the original manuscript of a major work...has been stolen from the vault.

* * *

Rare Earth Element...

...an International Thriller

...Amanda Wells, sent by a Task Force to examine regional policy and cultural elements for market sustainability - is diverted to a rugged terrain rich with resources and open for exploitation...

"And on that soft scented night in India, while waiting for his call, she looked up at the stars - a diamond here, another there...
One, was not a star.

Rare Earth Element

A Novel

G.A. Chamberlin

Chapter 1

The sound of brook-water trickled, the night air lingering, scented, suspenseful, then a burst of floodlights filled the stage of color and costume.

The audience gasped. Shahjahanabad.

LADIES AND GENTLEMEN, GOOD EVENING!

The amphitheater was cradled on red soil tamped solid and swept clean like a clay tennis court. Designed to accommodate two hundred patrons, if was filled to capacity, and then some along the perimeter. A deep silk darkness had settled upon them, and they sat back in folding wicker chairs, silver sandals and leather slippers falling loose beneath them, like a warm evening visit with friends on a veranda.

Outside, chauffeurs waited against highly polished cars, a quiet cigarette their only torch.

Above them now a moon, bright as a magnolia, dispensed magic on Mughals of the 17th century. Here, within the walls of the fortress palace of the Emperor Shah Jahan, an aesthetic of Mughal creativity illuminated. As distant stone carvers pounded, an architectural edifice of serendipity unfurled for the Sound and Light show.

Stage-lights, reflecting off the faces of the audience, illuminated a scene of eager participants in quarters ruled by conquerors standing upon exquisite mosaics, their women wearing silk threads and offering gold cups.

Trevor, an Ambassador in the audience, leaned into his companion and squeezed her hand. Swept by the ancients, he had her all to himself he seemed to be saying.

Seated at orchestra level, Trevor and Amanda could see the players, masked and wigged, vibrant with intensity.

A baritone voice took command of the scene.

"THE FORT HAD MANY DEVELOPMENTS ADDED BY THE EMPEROR SHAHJAHAN..."

Blues and greens turned to red and orange. Warriors brandishing swords, swirled in mock battle.

"EARLY DEVELOPMENT CAME FIRST IN 1546 UNDER AURANGZEB AND CONTINUED LATER UNDER MOGHAL RULERS. IT WAS THE *SEVENTH* CITY BUILT ON THE SITE OF NEW DELHI OF TODAY..."

Trevor turned to Amanda, his breath warm against her ear, and he blew softly at a curl against her neck.

The lights changed.

"BY THE 19TH CENTURY, IT WAS MODIFIED AS A GARRISON FOR THE BRITISH..."

From the ramparts *Hurrah!*

"IT IS NOW A SYMBOL OF INDIA'S SOVERIGNTY: THE PRIME MINISTER OF INDIA RAISES THE FLAG OF INDIA ON THE LAHORI GATE OF THE FORT EVERY YEAR ON INDEPENDENCE DAY!"

Cheering.

"...AND IT IS TODAY DESIGNATED BY UNESCO AS A WORLD HERITAGE SITE FOR THE WORLD TO SHARE WITH US!

"THANK YOU, LADIES AND GENTLEMEN!"

The moment was quickly gone. The house lights came up and the show was over.

As Ambassador, the activities of Trevor MacDonnell were of as much interest to others as to his security detail. Dignitaries approached to shake his hand, some with their wives in silk saris, some offering calling cards for a later appointment.

Trevor stood taller than most, his brown hair and square face easily recognized. When discovered at an event, he was clearly a favorite.

The attention that multiple flash cameras suddenly directed upon his escort had not really allowed for much adjusting and rearranging. Not that she needed any. Standing up in a glimmering paillette-trim illusion shift-dress by Michael Kors, Amanda Wells made for an immediate sensation.

Trevor led her to his car, thanking someone here, waving to another.

"Hello Miss Amanda" grinned the driver holding open the door. It was Yusef.

Trevor's cell had numerous calls waiting. But he turned to Amanda instead.

"Care for a walk?"

She giggled. The suggestion was ludicrous with ten paparazzi behind them and Yusef communicating on his head piece with security. Even with the window closed, she knew they were watched.

"Find me a stone fort" she said, getting into the car "and we'll slay your followers with moon beams!"

"Will a sculpture garden do?" he said, sitting beside her on the rear seat and gathering her in his arms "There is one by a waterfall where only birds of paradise live..."

She smiled up at him "Oh? Would that be the one outside your window at your Residence, perhaps?"

"Absolutely!" he murmured, his words warm across her face "steps away... from a bed of white roses..."

She giggled.

The rear cab glass lowered. "Excuse me Sir. A message to proceed at high velocity through the city. An incident Sir!"

 Lurching into acceleration and dodging traffic with police tearing by, they burned their way through the city.

Trevor reached for his cell...

∞

CAPE CANAVERAL

She was a spectacle to behold.

Eagle rotated gently on her axis one hundred and twenty miles from the surface of the earth. She approached her pre-docking platform as if she were some organic species about to mate. As a mathematical exercise with zero tolerance for miscalculation her precision was her grace. Suspended in a dark universe, her thrusters made the only sound, and there was wonder in their eyes as they watched the monitors.

Bleep "Houston: At 18:15:54:15 into spaceflight we have visual contact with *Hydros*. Over."

Even Tom Cappachutto could not hide the pride in his voice. "*Eagle*: This is Control. Nice flying, fellas. We find you twelve miles above and nineteen miles ahead of target. Over."

Bleep "Roger. Reducing speed to 18,000. Gyro-synchronous orbit with target. Computer check. Over."

"*Eagle*, this is Control. Computers, check. Speed, check. Over."

Cappachutto leaned back into his chair. He took a deep breath and looked up at Bob Harvey and Jim Valentine. They grinned at him with wide fatigued eyes, not bothering with extemporaneous words but clearly in tandem with every heartbeat of their vessel. Like everything else in this labyrinth of complexities it was one controlled step at a time.

"So far so good" was all the Flight Director would allow himself to say.

Eagle's support data splayed across every screen and console at CAPCOM. Trajectory, time checks, spherical dimensions, graph projections, power consumption, orbital projections, rotation sequence, speed schedules, telemetry, temperature, fuel supply, life-support - at each data station the information was checked with methodical synchrony.

As Flight Director, Tom Cappachutto had assembled a compatible team of brains and iterative talent. They worked so well together that Tom frequently had to sit on their tendency for playfulness. Except on a flight mission. No one fooled around when Sam Weiss monitored the incoming data as transmissions and communications specialist. When it came to the permutations of fuel supply, Ted Dreysol, who came from United Technologies, could milk a cow for jet fuel. No one understood surface and structural temperature failures like Roger Blume. And John Valentine they said, could read medical life support systems by mental telepathy alone! For each of them every transmission began with a bleep. Its rhythm was anticipated in a subconscious way. They worked by it, they breathed by it. It was the ship's pulse.

Bleep "Houston..."

Flight Captain Rob Bonfield's voice was unmistakable. Even so far away, and with half the world listening, his accent was unabashedly Texan.

Bleep "*Hydros*, how about that little bugger? Done looks like it's grown itself a halo out here. Ah guess that's one thing the heavens will never do for me!"

Tom smiled. "We ready you. *Eagle*"

He liked the transmission. Things looked good. Bonfield was as solid an astronaut as they came. He and Eric West made an excellent pair at the helm.

As a matter of normal operating procedure, Cappachutto punched for life-support data on his console and scanned. Both heart rates showed normal, although Bonfield's breathing showed some acceleration.

Next, he punched in code 184 and two orbital trajectories were seen converging upon one another, each with its time dimensional sequence, the one having been re-tasked in the last two days from a longer elliptical orbit to correspond with a shorter orbit in gradual gyro-synchronism with the earth's rotation.

He leaned forward, careful to keep his voice even.

"*Eagle*: we see you closing in on target. Check."

Bleep "....ger. We are experiencing... Check.... Heat sensors...Systems...."

Cappachutto looked over his shoulder to the bank of consoles behind him. Sam Weiss shook his head and raised his shoulders. There was no immediate reason for electrical interference with the transmission.

Cappachutto turned to the merging trajectories. His eyes narrowed slightly. "Say again, *Eagle*"

Bleep "Houston...do you read electrical particle... Systems...Code...Repeat...."

Cappachutto called up 220 on his console and, looking at a graph of undulating sound waves in the atmosphere. The quiet voice of Sam Weiss was speaking on his headpiece.

"I can't find anything here, Tom. Nothing at all. There's nothing in the neighborhood to cause static. Keep asking."

The Flight Director's voice remained even. "Negative *Eagle*. Repeat readings."

His forehead beading with perspiration, his response was calm and disciplined as he reached for the "open frequencies" tab. Three others would now be monitoring.

"This is Control. *Eagle*, how do you read?" He flipped to Life-support and saw both pulses climbing.

"Some stress here" spoke Rogers softly for the open frequency.

"This is Control" said Tom, leaning into the speaker "*Eagle, do* you read?"

Bleep "Houston? *Eagle, Hydros* showing...brightness...heat increase of...degrees...temper...transmitting data..."

Cappachutto reached above and switched "Off" the tab for open public access to all transmission of flight progress usually monitored by friends, fans, commercial competitors and nations listening to US spaceflight intelligence around the world.

Now only family; contractors and a select board of approved press in their gallery were witness to the situation developing, their compliance agreements in place as per security clearances.

It was now an internal dialogue.

Cappachutto knew inhibition when he heard it. If he couldn't run a light show, he would draw the curtains.

The room of space flight technicians turned to their tasks in response to their ship's transmission.

"This is Control. *Eagle*, say again" Tom said waiving down the growing background noise at workstations everywhere.

Bleep "Houston, condition is deterior ...Readings...temperature. Data 00876.453...22...fast. Over"

Cappachutto ran through the countdowns of both orbits still converging, appearing it were a collision course in high speed data points.

"This is Control. *Eagle*, repeat data readings."

"Life support is garbaging," said Harvey, his voice now adding to the internal frequency.

 "Both heart rates are erratic" he said "...and rising!"

The seconds passed. Technicians were joined by others clustering at workstations.

"Decay, 184 windows," said Dreysol, fairly shouting.

Then out of nowhere, the next transmission came suddenly

Bleep "Houston...if...hear me..." It was John West, his voice stressed.

Hsssss

"One life support down!" squealed Rogers

Bleep "Condition ... Repeat. Red. Approaching...

"Say again *Eagle*."

Bleep "Satellite...entering...high levels...Concentration. Transmitting coordinates as follows: *Hydros* ...a halo. Silver...Disabled trajectory...094747630...orbit..."

"*Eagle*. This is Houston. Repeat Coordinates"

Bleep "Blind...brightness...Houston...transmitting data..."

"This is Control. *Eagle*, come in..."

Bleep "Hssss..."

"*Eagle*.   Static interference is corrupting incoming transmission of data. Say again, *Eagle*. Transmit code data...Come in, *Eagle*. Do you read? Over."

Bleep "Hsss..."

The point of distress recognition was never far beneath the surface. Engineers in the room knew the signs of critical failure, each plunging into options for resumption.

That dreaded judgment that every Flight Director knew lurked beneath every technical decision was ever present. But panic, in this business, was a luxury no one could afford.

Cappachutto gripped his pen, a tightening gut crawled through his inside and he stood up, throwing back his seat.

"Press Shutout" he barked "No official record at this time - a private conference in ten for their ears only - under privileged information. Premises is in lockdown!"

Slamming onto the Mission Controls of Australia, Spain and Madagascar he said "Open all frequency transmissions to *Eagle*...Attempt to make contact continuously."

Code 853 called up two hundred space manufacturers on standby alert for support information. Emergency Code 330 signaled ten NASA installations to place astronauts into spaceflight simulators for an emergency simulation program.

Tom would not betray his fears. "This is Control. *Eagle* come in. *Do you read, Eagle?* Come in *Eagle*. This is Mission Control at Houston!"

Cappachutto's voice remained calm as he turned on the internal intercom "All systems status Blue Code One: Standby."

He handed the CAPCOM to Vallentine indicating that he should take his place and continue hailing the ship. Cappachutto moved up and stood beneath the large overhead screens, his fists clenched as if defying their veracity.

Every monitor system came up as barren as the last. There was no incoming data from the orbiter, no feedback tracking. Dreysol, Weiss, Blume as well as a host of back-up specialists punched in for data links with *Eagle*.

Desperately, at the hands of expert technicians, they searched for rogue computations that might have severed their umbilical tie to the orbiter in which six souls were trapped.

The cross computing continued: checking, double checking - flight trajectories, projections, scanning, flight data, computers quizzed data with dizzying permutations.

The bleep did not come. Even static disturbances were absent. Their spaceship was falling into silence. They knew that for West, Bonfield, Bronte, and Smithson, hope for life was slipping away with the seconds. The influx of exigent data was relentless, and there was no way to moderate its message. They watched, captive participants, as the data described their ship.

"Harvey," barked Cappachutto scanning Retro data, "life-support?"

The orbiter's three main screens at Mission Control continued to roll from one system to the other. Each one presented a garbled image.

"Visuals?" he said with anger, perspiration now seeping through his shirt.

More static. "Replay last viable visual contract from cameras FA 6 or 7."

All eyes looked up. On the main screen two of the crew, astronauts Bronstow and Smithson stood suited for space work at the threshold of the bay hold. Their reflection visors were down. As the payload cargo doors opened slowly they raised their arms simultaneously. Even in the weightless atmosphere their movements were odd. What they were doing was an act of self-defense; a human reflex to shield their eyes. The screen's image broke up again.

"Jim," Cappachutto turned to Vallentine "don't let up for a second."

Vallentine nodded "This is Control. *Eagle* do you read? Come in *Eagle*. Over."

With the data screens up rolling like large hungry eyes searching for input, Cappachutto stepped into the soundproof office and dialed Washington D.C.

"I'm so sorry Mr. Cappachutto, but he's on the floor of the House, Sir" said the voice on the phone.

"I don't care if he's delivering the State of the Union Address. Patch him through to me immediately. Tell him it's about Tomorrow."

Cappachutto only had to wait two minutes. Stevenson never wasted words.

"Dammit Tom, I'm up to my ass in NASA's eighty million dollar budget. What in hell couldn't wait an hour?"

Cappachutto knew what the protocol code was. "I need to cancel Tomorrow's meeting."

"You're okay. I'm on a secured line. You can talk..."

"We've lost the *Eagle*. She was docking with *Hydros*. Routine procedure when we lost contact."

"Are you *serious?*" There was a pause. "Jesus Tom!" he squealed.

Tom waited.

Stevenson spoke, his voice composed "Explosion? Debris? Orbital silence? What?"

"It's too early to tell. Last transmissions showed signs of stress. But no warning. Whatever it was, happened very fast."

"Sabotage? Hostility?"

"Can't say at this point. Tremendous static precluded any incoming data that would tell us for sure. Possible jamming perhaps, but this was different. Her bay hold was just opening."

"What about her payload cargo?" Stevenson shot out.

"I don't know"

"Her cargo wasn't deployed?"

"Negative."

"Are you telling me she may be floating belly up with her Bay doors wide open?"

"It's possible," said Cappachutto flatly.

"Is her intelligence gathering secured?"

"She's vulnerable."

Stevenson's voice was deliberate and controlled. "Does anyone at the Pentagon know yet?"

"You're the first."

"Chances of resuming contact?"

"I can't rule them out altogether. We can't find any wreckage. We need time...The Media will be all over you... Though they did witness a flawless launch from here. "

"Blackout!" came the words from Washington. "Seal off your people. Keep the lid on. Understand? Give it 18, 20 hours. Get as much information as you can and fly your ass up here."

The Flight Director put down the phone and returned to his place. Not for nothing was Stevenson the President's pick for spaceflight defense systems, he thought.

No satellite had yet identified the *Eagle*.

"Give me a dump on the last twenty seconds of flight," said Cappachutto with the steely resolve of a crisis manager.

Cappachutto reviewed the data. West's heartbeat, something had happened just before they lost contact. He knew West, the man was not an alarmist.

"Sir, I have a visual" yelled one engineer. "Camera AF 3. It's still transmitting a signal."

Cappachutto punched it onto the main screen. Everyone looked up. Except for CAPCOM calling *Eagle* the room at Mission Control was silent.

Cappachutto stared at the screen, then stood up.

"My God."

∞

She stood there in a tan cotton tank-top and linen skirt waiting for questions, paper in hand.

None came. A murmur rippled through the room, all of them enjoying the moment.

She waited.

It wasn't every day the staff got a lecture from an international agency on local considerations. Usually, rank counted for everything in the hierarchy of an overseas Embassy mission.

Nor could anybody fathom Amanda Wells. She fascinated them. Plus she was wearing cool stuff. Nothing new or wild, exactly. Just clever and body bold without being inappropriate.

And that *je-ne-sais-quoi* quality as one girl put it...

"Yeah" whispered someone "The Ambassador!"

"Oh *hush!*"

"Please go on Ms Wells. We're on your side!" said Sandra Winters, accommodating.

Amanda was sent by the United Nations Task Force to examine new Environmental issues that might impact cultural elements within different regions. Hers was the duty of producing reports about policy adjustments for human sustainability, something that had international sanction but little local support. Something that local staff hated to meddle with.

Amanda smiled, leaned against the desk, crossing her ankles laced with canvas sandals on cork heels.

Trevor stepped forward.

"We are most fortunate to have MS Wells here to offer us insights into the new thinking on environmental issues as they affect regions rich in cultural history and social tradition" said Trevor.

"She is presently on a Sabbatical at the UN to assess global regulations affecting our regions" Then, evidently knowing his staff added "Specifically, matters that change land uses, agricultural methods and planning for health and social organization. Including the education of women in remote regions."

Amanda decided to step in. She thanked Trevor for his kind words and then quickly gave them a general overview of the questions that might arise, even as he was being called away by his executive assistant.

"Teach them to read you mean?" said one woman.

Amanda answered the woman whose hand was raised, suggesting that while reading was a skill easily learned, it was the processing of new values that was most at issue in regions less developed than the West.

The men in the room smiled at the admonition, and someone even gave her a discrete thumbs up.

"Now here's the tricky one" she said, digging in

"Item No 6: Taking into account Article 4, paragraph 6 of the Convention in the implementation of their commitments under this Protocol (other than those under this Article) a certain degree of *"flexibility* shall be allowed by the Conference of the Parties serving..."

She looked up, briefly

"...as the Parties to this Protocol etc. etc. undergo the *process of transition to a market economy.*"

She need not have looked up to examine the rate of absorption. The statement was met with audible dislike.

"OK..." said one staffer from the Commercial section "So how do we implement *compliance* and *policing...* with language like *that*?"

"What a joke!" another muttered.

"Ok people..." began Sandra Winters.

"And what of places in the hills we can't even reach... let alone check?" chimed someone from the rear.

"Yeah!"

"Or the combat zones..." added another.

 "I understand that this directive has its limitations... And they might seem unfeasible. But as the Kyoto Protocol suggests, its *developmental* through 2019" said Amanda. "That means it's a phased-in process. By then, they will have absorbed the new realities of climate change and communal health. Besides, it only applies to a quantifiable aggregate anthropogenic carbon dioxide...or, as it says here, "equivalent emissions of the greenhouse gases listed in Annex A"

"So what does that *mean?*" said Susan

"It means we start an Awareness Campaign" said Sandra, quick to sort the task.

Amanda unfolded her legs, and gave them time. She put down her papers.

"Look. It's not easy for an emerging economy struggling daily to come up to speed on global requirements. But remember, they are a nation that voted on these protocols in the first place!"

She paused. "Consider the consequences, after all. There is the matter of disease and contagion if contingency plans are made with inadequate planning."

She smiled and added "Look at the bigger picture. It's a civilized effort to open trade and commerce...which of course, is a vital interest to us all, right?"

They started nodding.

"Thank you Ms. Wells" concluded Sandra finally. "You open our understanding"

"Right!" muttered one disgruntled voice as the crowd dispersed.

Some of the staff came up to her and thanked her. "Hi...I'm Jeffrey" said one, extending his hand...

The wide halls of the High Commission in New Delhi were long.

Tim, from the Registry section, ran up to her and came close to colliding with her.

"Nice work. But we don't all agree. So you're telling me all this environmental stuff isn't profitable for somebody?"

They had reached the elevators. "What?" he persisted "There isn't enough misinformation about climate already? As in, God- playing climatological-politics syndrome?"

"Excuse me?" laughed Amanda.

"You know, so that *some* can get a free tax-ride while they compete with our industry, yes?"

"Surely you jest?"

He shot out his hand "I'm Tim"

"Whoa" she gasped "...One day at a time, Tim!"

"I'm sorry. It's a controversial issue. But I understand. Thank you for not addressing us with harsh judgments. I'm sorry if I alarmed you."

Tim invited her to join them for lunch in the Cafeteria.

She was introduced to several of his colleagues and friends. Others, who heard her speak, came over to sit with them as wait staff presented platters of spiced chicken, rice and vegetables.

Everybody wanted her attention, finding her social life of greater interest. She must have said yes to three party invitations for the next 24 hours, including two pool dips; one golf game and even a tour of the souk by sunset...

By the time Amanda returned to her quarters, she collapsed on the bed with exhaustion.

It was, in her mind, quite amusing to find Trevor's name on the lips of junior staffers. She had known him for so long...

Actually, it was Trevor who found her and asked her to advise his staff on environmental policies being developed by the world organization she worked for. He certainly had given her a glowing introduction as a working professional visiting the Embassy.

Still, she could sense their frustration. Embassy personnel engaged on the front lines with a host country were frequently caught between reality and untenable policy. And unlike the military who remained ever prepared for any eventuality with defense, diplomats could offer nothing more than trust.

Amanda went upstairs to the Ambassador's floor to say farewell to Trevor before leaving.

Through the glass doors a small waiting area allowed her to sit while his secretary, Erin Simpkins finished her phone call, one hand waving hello.

To one side a baroque stand held a tall vase of long stemmed white orchids with purple hearts; to the other hung a framed picture of modern London, *Fitness on the Thames.*

Finally Erin got off the phone.

"Oh Amanda, I'm so sorry to disappoint…but he's been tied up for hours over at the American Embassy. And I don't think he'll be back today!"

"No problem Erin. I just wanted to say Goodbye. And to thank him for his kind hospitality on station!"

"I'll tell him!"

She waited all evening for a call. But none came.

She walked out on the veranda and took in the darkening sights of the city, its perfumed blossoms filling the nigh air. Faraway traffic subdued, and somewhere a peacock settled to roost. India was a beautiful continent.

Soon she would receive word that her transportation was ready to take her to the airport. She looked up as the stars started to define themselves, one diamond here another there, endlessly tracking their way across the heavens.

One, was not a star.

∞

Time warps in a perverse way, thought Karen. So what if she was spinning through space at 18,000 miles per hour? She was weightless and must panic in slow motion, a nightmare from which there was no awakening.

More than anything, she struggled for orientation. Starting with earth time, she measured her day into orbits, looked for anomalies and tried to stick to a routine. But with capricious random, what should have been dawn over the horizon twice turned into an assault that rocked the Orbiter and blinded her with explosive light. Which dawn? What orbit? Back to earth time, that is, if her calibration hadn't been thrown off.

Right now all she wanted to do was prioritize, get a grip on the degrees of severity of the damage. How badly had she panicked? Karen prided herself in containing anxiety before it surfaced, especially during the roar and rise into orbit. Once aloft, settling into a routine onboard a spaceship was no different from any other ship. There were the same confinements, the same details, large horizons.... But something else had happened, something hours of relentless training hadn't prepared her for. Sitting alone in her anti-g suit with dark kinky hair raised in a gravity free corona around a pale face, she recognized it now as that phenomenon known to bond fellow voyagers for a lifetime. Camaraderie.

Which is why Karen felt so numb. She sat in the co-pilot's seat of one of the most sophisticated machines ever created by man, staring at a bank of switches containing dark CRT monitors, and the silence was overwhelming.

She shut her tired eyes; there were no tears.

Where had they lost control? She and Cindy had been decompressing for extravehicular activity for two hours. Nitrogen in the bloodstream was nil. It was agreed that Cindy would exit the airlock first since she knew what she was doing, Karen said. Captain West suggested Karen wear the portable oxygen "walkabout" unit, called POS, and Cindy plug into the Orbiter supply of air.

"Okay, girls. Time to suit up and earn a living!" came Benfield's drawl on the intercom.

Cindy rolled her eyes.

"You look beautiful," said Karen as Cindy climbed into the airlock wearing her liquid cooling and ventilation garment. "I'd offer you some lipstick but I see you've got a mouthful" she bantered, the tension mounting as Cindy shoved the oxygen mouthpiece into her teeth and the airlock hatch sealed with a terminal click.

Karen moved to observe her partner from the glass hatch, now isolated in her own oxygen supply.

Cindy climbed into the lower torso, bent down and reached into the upper torso of the extra vehicular spacesuit. She fooled around inside with the thumb loops before popping out and attached the undergarment cooling water tube to the backpack. It seemed to be a clean connection, and Karen gave her the "thumbs up" to join the suit halves.

Next item to be attached to the EVA suit was the communications carrier and Cindy adjusted the oxygen flow on her wrist computer. She pushed the dial back a bit, then forward, then back again.

Come on! Come on! thought Karen knowing the timing and sequence of events.

She felt the tremor beneath her feet and at her handgrips, different from the normal shudder of a ship in flight.

She now noticed the blue light. It had been in strobe for 15 seconds, the tremor now increasing to an oscillation.

Jesus!

With a portable oxygen unit supplying air to her lungs, she had no idea what happened to cabin pressure.

The Orbiter was fully vibrating and Karen fell backward to the deck in a slow swim. She spun off and was bounced off the ceiling before she could reach a handhold by the airlock where she could see Cindy.

A high pitched hissing screeched through the cabin and Bonfield was now barking for Emergency procedures.

Inside the airlock chamber, Cindy had taken a beating and her helmet was not fully in position. Her eyes were wide, her communications carrier gone, and Karen could see her saying "Oh my God" before reaching for the controls. She hit the AIRLOCL DEPRESS switch on panel AW 82A and had started to twist the knob to position 5.

"Don't leave the orbiter!" yelled Karen. "Stay put, Cindy! Stay put!"

Cindy, being shaken like a bean in a tin can was locking on her helmet, vibrations tossing the effort.

"Cindy! Don't exit!" Karen banged against the glass until thrown off her handhold to bounce off the bulkhead. "Stay with the ship!"

By the time Karen returned Cindy had fully decompressed the airlock chamber and was opening the hatch. She was in panic. Violating every rule of Emergency Procedure. And like a panicking diver surfacing too quickly, she was leaving the ship without thought to the consequences.

Karen swam desperately up the hatch to the flight deck. *How to help? How...*

 Bonfield was strapped in his seat gasping for air as if his lungs were on fire. West was floating above the co-pilots station, his face red, eyes dilated, mouth open.

Karen ripped off her POS and shoved it onto Bonfield's face. His arms lifted up.

She began to want air, her lungs screaming for repressure.

Bonfield's arms moved - weightless, lifeless? She glanced at the consoles.

Spikes on the cathode rays tore across data, sending Alarm thresholds begging for corrective signals from all five computers in mode 3 E.

Yet the orbiter was now vibrating less.

Bonfield was dead, she could tell.

She shuffled into the POS and inhaled deeply, her face in a corona of underwater myopia.

The blue light told her they'd lost cabin pressure.

Think!

 She dove down to the mid deck and found Williams strapped into his sack, eyes bulging. Cmdr. Retsin was floating. They were all unconscious, if not dead.

She had three minutes of air left on her POS. She returned to the flight deck consoles. The orbiter took a yaw to portside and she was bounced in slow motion off the bulkhead.

"Enter" she began on the computer, the consoles shaking in thunderous vibration.

CRT 1: MAIN FAILURE. BACKUP ONE. TWO. THREE FAILURE."

CRT 2: FAILSAFE SHUTDOWN 02.31:00

"God, no!" she screamed

CRT 3: AUXILIARY POWER UNIT, BOILER NITROGEN SUPPLY DAMAGE. HYDRAULIC FEED LINES. EXTERNAL DYSFUNCTIONS.

Dysfunction!

Dysfunction!

Karen looked at her monitor: One minute of air supply left on the POS. She'd have to extract a unit; attach a cylinder and put it on...

Stay on the console and re-pressurize! Work with the computers, save the others, *something*!

Less than one minute of air left. Or she'd join the others in a decompressed cabin.

She spun from the console and swam down to mid deck. Inside a wall locker she extracted a fresh POS with a new cylinder. She was already sucking for air when she switched her unit for the new, and returned to the flight deck. It took her longer than she thought, an eternity.

 CRT 2: FAILSAFE SHUTDOWN 00:10:00 COMMENCING NOW.

∞

The orbiter was vibrating with a vengeance. The decisions were now hers. She reached for "ABORT" and moved to depress the handle, but a flash explosion lit up the sky and sent her into a summersault off the ceiling where she bounced into West, his legs tangling with hers.

All CRTs went dark. Very imperceptibly, the orbiter's oscillations began to dampen out. She floated back down to the crew deck and extracted another POS. She tried to resuscitate Retsin and Williams. Then back up to the flight deck for Bonfield and West. She swam from one to the other sharing oxygen. They weren't dead. They couldn't be dead! They were here. All of them. Just minutes ago. Functioning!

And Cindy.

Where was Cindy? Karen swam back down to the mid-deck and looked into the airlock. There was no sign of reentry. The controls were still all amber. She pushed off back up to the flight deck, still no activity on its consoles. She turned to the aft crew station and saw nothing from the portholes, switched on the closed circuit television monitors, nothing; the payload control panels, nothing. Nothing! She banged on the rotational hand controller and decided to try the payload control panels again. She turned her back on the porthole. Outside, behind her, a silver glitter emerged. It hovered. Karen turned and screamed out in shock.

It floated up slightly, a silver-coated spacesuit, snagged, deflated and torn, labeled in bold print "Chapman, NASA.USA."

"Cindy!" yelled Karen. The spacesuit disappeared.

∞

Chapter 2

The central courtyard of the ancient monastery was open and paved with slate tiles. Hanging languidly in swirls of humid air, palm leaves told of a tropical storm soon to arrive.

DePhillipe submerged his statuesque body into the swimming pool. The men around the pool continued to talk amongst themselves. Discussions, like a good fiesta, went on for days. And these men were weighing their options carefully, if clearly, a decision was in the offing.

 Around the cloister, a procession of exalting columns rose to the sky, ever taking with them the implorations of men through the centuries who here sought refuge from devastating hurricanes. Or invading forces. Or local death squads.

Enriche Villas, slower for his age but still slim and shrewd, entered the courtyard followed by a younger man. He walked to the center of the courtyard and stood in the sunlight like a priest in a temple about to make a prophetic utterance.

DePhillipe rose from the water and toweled himself.

"The tracking stations have shut down. The *Eagle* is lost!" said Villas.

DePhillipe nodded imperceptibly to Villas before turning to his entourage. "Gentlemen, we have work to do. Call me in Chicago!"

∞

Just before 7 pm that evening, Amanda closed her suitcase and approached the phone in her hotel room at the Abe Hotel. She would make one last attempt to reach Trevor. She picked up the phone and dialed.

"Ambassador's Residence?"

"Yes. I'd like to speak to Mr. MacDonnell please. This is Amanda Wells."

"I'm sorry" said the voice, distinctly girlish. "He is not in. Shall I take a message?"

"No. No thank you." She hung up.

Her luggage was downstairs.

"A package for you Ms. Wells!"

The Concierge at the Front Desk of the Hotel approached, he was young and resplendent in his Hotel uniform. "From the Conference Center" he gasped.

She thanked him.

She would read it later on the plane, she decided.

Just as Amanda stepped on the shuttle to the Airport, she heard another call and saw a familiar face in the taxi line.

It was Yusef, Trevor's staff driver. He waved.

She approached him. "Hello Yusef!"

"Hello Miss Amanda" he said producing a white orchid. "For you!" he said "From Mr. Trevor..."

"Thank you!" she smiled. The Airport Shuttle tapped the horn for all passengers.

"Yusef, how can I forget that lovely trip to your home years ago? Your family, they are all well?"

"Oh Yes! Very well indeed, thank you Miss Amanda. My wife, brother, children. They all are growing up now!"

The Airport Shuttle edged forward to load her gear. She looked up.

"I am so sorry not to be taking you to the Airport Miss Amanda. Mr. Trevor, he very busy...!"

She shook hands. "Thank you. I appreciate the gesture Yusef."

She boarded her transportation to the International Airport where she would take her plane for a thirteen hour flight straight to her destination.

The orchid in her hand was taken from the tall vase of the lobby in Trevor's offices, she knew.

Yusef was kind.

Amanda also knew that the American Ambassador was a woman well recognized as a New York celebrity.

And single.

∞

On her flight Amanda opened the contents of her package from the Conference.

She had enjoyed herself. It had been a success for her.

The Dinner at the Adoka Hotel in New Delhi was a standard display of colorful artistry from Indian culture: Dance, music, food, drink and costumes were the culmination of a series of speeches; papers, and exhibits that marked three days of proceedings aimed at collaboration and consensus amongst regions.

The conference had been sponsored by cultural trade organizations. Academic institutions hailed it as a first step in the right direction. The WHO was strongly represented.

Amanda had made her presentation early in the speaker's list. Her topic focused largely on the preservation of historical heritage. And while it was quickly dominated by heavier topics involving global policy; economics, geographic infrastructure and climate-change, she was nevertheless pleased with her contribution. As were the sponsors of the event, she was told.

That was when Trevor had found her. He waved from the audience, grinning like a fan, and she almost lost her train of thought at the podium.

Nobody, she said later, warned her that he was attached to the Foreign Office in New Delhi as an Emissary.

He explained that it was for a short term... until a career officer could be made available.

And nobody warned him, he said, of her visit...

They laughed.

He badgered her through the event to come to the High Commission compound for tennis and a swim.

He insisted she make a small presentation to the staff about environmental impacts on regions of cultural tradition. But mostly, he insisted, he wanted to take her out to dinner in the City for a soiree at the Red Fort for a Light Show.

Tomorrow, they agreed, since her Conference Banquet dinner was tonight. And while he was unable to accept her invitation to join her, the soiree was one she would not soon forget. Nor the people she met.

She wore an Oscar de la Renta evening gown, simple and unadorned. It complemented her features. Amanda had a slender body and a strong face of blue eyes and natural blond waves that framed an earnest interest and natural beauty. She stood out, even surrounded by women in colorful silk sari's; glittering tiaras and jewels in abundance.

She found her place name at one of the many round dinner tables of white cloth and towering flower arrangements.

Waiters, wearing starched cotton turbans, served an assortment of delectable treats.

To her right was a woman, a doctor.

To her left was the "Elder Official" of a border village in Pakistan. He was young and well informed for an Elder, he said. Salem was his name.

Others seated at her table were government administrators, industry representatives and corporate leaders.

Salem asked where she lived, how she liked the food... They talked, and the band played as the Head Table prepared for Speakers to bring the Conference to a close.

The doctor chatted, and the microphones crackled with readiness for speeches. Amanda waited for further conversation on generalities. Then Salem surprised her.

"I long for the day of self-determination along the border regions..."

Amanda put down her food, wondering how to respond.

"Don't get me wrong. It's not that we wish to hinder progress..." he grinned.

"Progress...is a good thing in the greater scheme of things" she said.

"True" he said "But that's the problem. Everyone *else's* scheme of things ...in *our* progress!"

She had to smile at the humor of his phrase.

His eyes softened. He turned to her, placing his table napkin aside "Our region may be sitting on one of the richest troves of minerals in the world..."

"Oh?"

"Yes. Scientists value it as $1 trillion in monetary terms. Afghanistan, a nation torn by strife and inhospitable mountains, has mineral deposits geologically created by the violent collision of the Indian subcontinent with Asia, you see."

She nodded. "Yes. I have read of reports by the U.S. Geological Survey inspecting the region for industrial mining interests - if at some hazard to themselves..."

"Oh indeed! It's dangerous as hell. Especially since the U.S. forces drove the Taliban from power in 2004. But the discovery of minerals began with our *previous* occupiers, the Soviets, who kept geological maps and reports. Their surveys hinted at geological repositories of enormous wealth..."

"Very difficult terrain" said the Doctor.

"Yes" he said.

Amanda waited.

"It's a difficult terrain to mine" he proceeded. "I know they made airborne missions to conduct magnetic; gravity and hyperspectral surveys over Afghanistan."

Amanda smiled.

The Doctor leaned forward. "As I understand, the magnetic surveys probed for iron-bearing minerals down to 6 miles below the surface. Gravity surveys identified sediment basis filled with oil and gas"

Again he lifted his glass of wine to his lips, then spoke.

"Hyperspectral surveys examined spectrum of light reflecting off rocks that identified light signatures unique to each mineral. They're still searching..."

Amanda glanced up at the Head Table for a sense of timing. She was beginning to feel uneasy somehow.

He added "And they have found 60 million tons of copper; 2.2 billion tons of iron ore; 1.4 million tons of rare earth elements like lanthanum; cerium and neodymium..." He lifted his glass "Plus loads of aluminum, gold, silver, zinc, mercury and lithium: Khanneshin carbonatite deposits in

Afhganistan's Helmand province is values at \$89 billion alone..."

The music at the head table started.

"You have a home in India?" asked Amanda, intending to change to subject.

"We are on the border, perched close to the top of a mountain ridge. Some say the top of the world!"

"That's the Uplands?" asked the Doctor.

"Yes. We are above the snow line. Even the tree line. And we used to be known for harvesting the flora of the mountain for dyes, chiefly used in the artistic making of rugs... further down the mountain!"

"An old tradition?"

"Oh absolutely. Since the beginning of time, our lore says!"

"Sounds beautiful" she said

"It is..." said the Indian doctor to her right. "I have been there, twice!"

They turned to her.

"Yes. Once for a Study on the effects of work at high altitudes. And once to visit a friend two hundred miles north..."

Salem looked down at his food. "Then you have perhaps noticed the infant mortality rates amongst our women?"

"That ..." said the doctor, helping herself to more sugar for her coffee "is usually a health-related issue induced by neglect..."

"Let's agree labor-induced" he said "and I don't mean in childbirth!"

"Allow me to give you my card..." said the doctor cleaning her fingers and reaching into her bag. "Write me more, if you will..."

Amanda would have liked to ask more about dye-making, she wondered if there was anything duplicitous about their conversation. Had Salem and the doctor heard of each other before now, she wondered.

"You know..." said the doctor, "these resources being found in Afghanistan have the potential to lift the country out of poverty and terror! It could develop an economy, create jobs and build infrastructure as a world class contributor!"

"Not only that" said the young man "But in lifting Afghanistan out of poverty, there would be a chance at fighting crime and terrorism. Terrorists exploit the misery of local populations."

"Exactly" nodded the doctor. "Given the choice to feed their family and build a business, young men would put down the gun and turn to nation-building...Lets not forget, terrorists are very few in number..." she added.

They were interrupted.

"Ladies and Gentlemen" the microphone crackled.

It took a while for the room to settle down.

"...It is now the moment" said the Conference Chair "for the Presentation of our Award to the Nominee most notable for medical work amongst women. Dr. Saphira Sumptra."

Applause erupted.

The doctor stood up. She was invited to the Podium.

∞

"That can't possibly be true!" admonished Trevor. He moved his head from side to side and then looked at his Chief of Staff "how absolutely awful..."

"Yes Sir. Very grim"

"Is there any condolence or sentiment of regret that we can express on behalf of the staff here?"

"I'm afraid not, Sir. It's a matter for the police now. As you know, we cannot interfere with internal affairs."

"I'll call Mr. Sheriffe" said Trevor reaching for the phone "And show some concern from us all…"

"He has left the country. Precautions… as you know, Sir"

"Then I'll leave a message at least. Remember, I was sitting there… And at his recommendation no less!"

"Yes, Sir"

An actor had been killed, his body found at the base of the stage on the evening of the Show.

The incident, the police said, must have occurred during the mock battle scene where one stage prop was no make-believe: The weapon, evidently, was made of fine burnished steel.

The man had been beheaded.

The victim was discovered shortly after Trevor and Amanda had left.

Trevor was on the phone calling the Director of Cultural Affairs in India, Undi Sheriffe, a Sikh of some renown.

Chief of Staff Matthew Saunders knew better than to argue with the Ambassador.

Trevor MacDonnell was a man of conscience, no matter where the British Government placed him. And he had influence. Let it be a message then, he thought inwardly.

Still, protecting this Ambassador was a thankless charge for Security in a world thick with assailants who could pick their targets… and strike at will.

∞

On the Bay, shoals of silver alewives wheeled to the surface with tantalizing flashes. Jim Lloyd cast out his lure and reeled in. Two hundred feet away the water broke with a bluefish. Again he cast his lure. Over his shoulder an orange orb poured golden mercury over the water, and a circling crane screeched as it dove like a missile. This was the time of day he most loved on the water. Here he could forget a history of combat duty in deserts and jungles and terrorist towns that coursed through the family tree, he and his father before him...

But a distant sound penetrated the silence. It was not the sound of underwater propellers plodding up the bay, nor of wildlife settling for the night. It was that indefinable, high-pitched siren that grows into the unmistakable signature of DC10 turbines. And it sent Lloyd hurling into the past, his eyes sharp, alert, panic under wraps, his mind automatically reverting to his training as a pilot diving at high Mach speed for a bloodless attack at five to six Gs.

The past was the past. Enough!

 He shielded his eyes. A vague undistinguished profile was advanced from the sun. A ship on a mirage, approaching at estimated 50 or 60 miles per hour without touching the water.

There was only one vessel that could do that. So what was a PHM doing in the Chesapeake Bay? He did not have to wait long as he reeled in his gear.

The foil-borne twenty thousand horsepower LM 2500 reached within two hundred feet of Lloyd and sank suddenly to hull-borne buoyancy, its foils rising from the water like a bird of prey folding its wings.

The water swayed, and the air still rang with the resonance of turbines. But it was diesels that churned within the battle-grey hull, sealed tight, with only aft deck vapors of the foil-borne engine swirling over harpoon missile launchers.

And now Lloyd's boat rocked like a toy.

A hatch opened, and a US Naval officer followed by two seamen stepped on deck.

"Jim Lloyd, retired, captain, United States Navy, sir?"

"What if I am?"

"This is the U.S. Pegasus. Please make ready to come aboard, sir!"

"This is one hell of a way to get my attention, captain," said Lloyd, ducking his head to step into the pilot house "a phone call would have had me in Washington by 0700 in the morning - dressed!"

The officer looked down at Lloyd's shorts stained with crab bait and fish blood.

"I'm Vice Admiral Dressal" said a man moving away from the Dead Reckoning Tracer, his hand extended for a handshake. "May I introduce Commander Jefferson, Dr. Kalil Mutlu; Colonel Simpson, and you've met Captain Windsor.... Please, make yourself comfortable" He pointed to the ladder to go below decks.

Lloyd's unkempt six foot three inch frame filled the contour of the CIC hatchway, his expression showing the flint faced progeny of vanguard Welsh settlers, deep hazel eyes beneath a rouse of rusty hair, unyielding jawline and shoulders with arms aggressively slack at his side. His breath was slow, controlled, and they all stared at him.

"Forgive us for abducting you from your fishing, Captain Lloyd, but it was imperative you be taken in immediately without notice of any kind"

"Taken in?"

"Yes. You're on a list of personnel qualified in an area that's been badly damaged..."

Lloyd watched Jefferson's long and bony face stare into the radar screen before him. Mutlu was unmistakably Asian Indian. And Simpson was a woman wearing the insignia of the United States Marine Corps.

Lloyd edged around the plotting board and took his seat in front of the SPA 25B. He was handed a cup of coffee by a seaman.

"I'd like to inform you..." began the Admiral

"Hold it, Jim" interrupted Jefferson with smiling eyes. "Maybe he'll go easier on a fellow flyer!"

Jefferson leaned on the evaluator console and looked at him apologetically.

"We've had to take you out of circulation because of a sudden rush on jet-jocks"

"I'm flattered. But even the Iranians can fly FX15s!"

Jefferson nodded. "As a test pilot you trained on Apollo. For three years you covered every aspect of underwater weightlessness, donned every spacesuit and life support system, and sat at every simulator and control NASA has at its disposal."

"If that's a liability then you've got dozens of us on the loose" retorted Lloyd.

Simpson spoke for the first time. "Don't waste our time captain Lloyd. You've been reactivated for duty as of now. Your marching orders are to lift off the pad for a space flight in four days from Mission Control."

Lloyd stared at her then smiled.

Dressal shifted his position awkwardly.

"You may be Helen of Troy in your command ma'am, but your good looks won't launch me anywhere in four days! I am not in training for - neither am I in readiness for - orbital space flight!"

Simpson straightened up slowly.

"Lloyd" began Jefferson "we're going to have to jump start for emergency procedures. This is a rescue mission. You were personally picked for the mission by Cappachutto..."

Lloyd recognized the name well.

"Perhaps we've over-estimated him" interrupted Simpson "He may not be the man for the job"

Lloyd watched her cold eyes and didn't doubt her combat readiness for one second. He sipped his coffee carefully.

"Relax Lloyd. I realize we've approached you very suddenly. Your fishing boat will be returned to your dock.. "

Lloyd turned to Dresall. "There's a list of test pilots fully prepped for orbital flight at all times. The Colonel is right. I'm not your man. Besides, I resigned my commission three years ago remember?"

Dresden reached over to the SPA 25B and flipped on the monitor, then answered "And with an excellent military record I might add, except for the fact that you turned down a promotion to Vice Admiral and retired instead!"

He turned to face Lloyd "Look. Perhaps this will change your perspective. Here's the story. CAPCOM lost touch with *Eagle* 18 less than hours ago. We don't know *what* happened. We need immediate reconnaissance. A capsule was in readiness on the pad. We need some answers before we make our public assessments."

"What is the status of *Courageous* - if I may ask?"

"She'd take fourteen days to ready for launch. All we want is a visual on the condition of *Eagle*. If she's there. She seems perhaps lost in some kind of EMP pulse, bouncing off the top stratosphere. This could be more than just a spaceship, Lloyd. This could be a cyber disruption of untold dimension. We want a quick routine orbit for reconnoiter - that's all. The *U.S.S. New Jersey* will pick you up after splashdown in the Pacific."

"NASA is asking me because...?"

Dresall looked at Jefferson. Jefferson swallowed.

Lloyd turned to Simpson with some measure of anticipation. "I'll give you the privilege of telling me what's going on with the rest of NASA's highly trained astronauts."

Simpson glared at him, hands clasped. "Alright then. Too many have contracted a respiratory infection which suggests that each astronaut was targeted. This could be a premediated condition that was planned ..."

"Those that don't show symptoms yet may have a longer incubation period. Either way, the incidence of the infection amongst astronauts is too high for coincidence. We just can't take that chance. So we had to find personnel who were capable of the task but not on any active flying list. Cappachutto insisted you should do it. We pulled you out of circulation as a precautionary security measure."

"Are you suggesting its sabotage?"

"That's what worries us. Someone was working down a list of test pilots, and knew all of their whereabouts. Though most personnel were on the premises of various military installations, many afflicted were quite randomly dispersed. They all reported in within 72 hours of each other, globally. And until we know who did what, we're totally in the dark. All we know is that it was probably some inhaled bacterial agent that afflicted each pilot on active duty or on that list."

"I'd call that some act of terrorism!"

Captain Windsor clambered down the ladder from the pilot house. He looked at Dressal. "Making ready for all engines. Foil-borne sir?"

"Aye seaman. Foil-born." said Dresall handing a pair of headsets to Lloyd and placing his own carefully over his ears. Underway, the ship was too load to communicate in. So they communicated by headset, like an aircraft mission.

"Is it at all connected with *Eagle*'s disappearance?" said Lloyd.

"Highly probable," came Dresall's answer, his voice electronically modulated over the heightening pitch of the turbines. "And that's what we find so appalling."

The ship suddenly picked up speed and shuddered from the roaring turbines as three giant mechanical legs emerged from the hull and locked into place to put her on a foil borne hydroplane with the power of a jet engine. Across the evaluator console the radar screens scanned the horizon for CIC as it did on the bridge.

"What mission was *Eagle* on?"

"One of the missions was to investigating the condition of *Hydros* which was transmitting alarming information before it went dark."

Rome, Italy.

Dr. Fumosa was seated halfway down the center isle of the main auditorium of the FAO building in Piazza di Roma. Drs. Ricca and Foust were speaking in English. The house lights were dimmed for slides.

"The territory is subject to varied climatic conditions in which latitude plays an essential role. From the anti-cyclone of the Azores, a high pressure center, the trade winds blow towards the Equator and are deflected westward by the rotation of the earth. Last January, the cool dry wind of the Harmattan blew from the Sahara towards the west coast of Africa, from Mauritania to the Niger delta...."

Someone tapped Dr. Fumosa on the shoulder. He was a tall man, his close face grinning and shiny in the dark against the stage lighting.

"Uri Pavala" he said extending his hand, "I didn't expect you'd be here! They should save this propaganda for fund-raising!"

Dr. Fumosa was not amused but smiled mechanically, not having the vaguest notion who Uri Pavala was.

The man persisted.

"You think Dr. Fumosa that I could ask you some questions...about climate changing?"

"Questions? Yes. Yes. Of course. Please contact my assistant Ms Amanda Wells."

"Really?"

"Yes."

"What is her number?"

This man was not going to cease. Again Fumosa turned.

" She is attached to me from New York. Please ask her. She is very knowledgeable and supports me with everything. Now if you please..." he gestured to the podium of speakers.

Uri Pravda wrote down the name.

Later that night he copied the name in a Text Message. He sent it directly to Villas and Julian DePhillpe.

Tomorrow, he would know more.

∞

By the second day of the Forum in Rome, the topics were becoming serious.

As Director of the World Food and Health Organization, Mario Fumosa was a public figure. He picked this conference as one to attend because if there were one thing Fumosa had learned in his many years of public health, it was to address any problems before the press did.

Besides, Carina Bruneski was two seats away, and he could smell her perfume...

"...The annual rainfall is two to six meters along the coast of West Africa from Conakry to Abidjan and from the Niger delta to Libreville in Gabon; one to two meters in some mountainous regions of the Mahreb and south of the line from Dakar to Mogadishu; 500 to 1,000 millimeters in the High Atlas, in the coastal regions of Algeria and Tunis.

"In this schematic we see the aridity and evaporation rates showing the surface aquifers undergoing large variations in level owing to the imbalance between the evaporation and recharge columns. Here we see the amount of rainfall available to recharge ground water aquifers: namely the three factors of rainfall; its heaviness of the precipitation; and the value of the potential evapo-transpiration which is essentially a function of latitude, altitude and temperature."

Fumosa shifted position in his seat. It was close to lunchtime. Carina, Legal Counsel from the FAO office in Naples, moved her stiff neck and shoulders, sending her shoulder length hair back and exposing the silver earrings on her ears. Fumosa noticed.

From somewhere in the back of the room, another man noticed. Uri Pravda.

"...The problems we see in this diagram is typical of all zones of this latitude: Precipitation/evaporation balance is so low that crystalline formations capturing water are accessible systems..."

It never failed to amaze Fumosa how human suffering could be justified when narrated by the drone voice of scientific nonchalance. As a senior executive in Crisis Management, he struggled.

The Recess came not a minute too soon.

Outside, they were squinting in the sunlight, Carina slipped her hand under his arm and muttered provocatively "So what did the Rumanian have to say?"

"Chi sa?" he sputtered in his native tongue.

She laughed.

"Someone who couldn't see a thing outside his area of concern no doubt" she added in English.

They walked briskly through the throng and she stopped suddenly "What would you like?"

Fumosa looked down at her solemnly. "You know very well what I'd like. I'd like what we had before...you and me...those nights in Sardinia..."

She pointed to the counter behind him "Salami sandwich or pizza?"

His eyes softened, and they laughed.

∞

"Hydros?"

Dr. Mutlu spoke for the first time. He swung from his position at the Weapons Control Console. His words held the articulate intonations of an Indian national.

"Hydros is a weather satellite that we rely on at FAO for climatological predictions. The data helps us with rainfall projections, crop production, pest control - like locust swarms or other catastrophic phenomenon. Recent data showed unusual weather patterns that were at first considered isolated occurrences, even errors."

"How long had *Hydros* been in orbit?"

"About three years. There was no reason to believe any mechanical malfunction was imminent. Other regional satellites verified what *Hydros* was telling us but to a lesser degree. *Hydros* was on a higher orbit. Her eye was pan-global, she was reading atmospheric climate. We had to decide whether she was misinforming us. Then the field evidence came in and verified her data. Let me put it to you this way; when any aberrations occur that affect any electronic systems or economic models, we've got to investigate. Or rather we were about to... when *Hydros* went dark!"

"A capsule is on the pad for priority reconnaissance," reported Dressal. .

Lloyd pressed. "So. What exactly was *Hydros* seeing?"

"She was seeing temperature variations. In fact, a two degree temperature baseline drop is already having its effect," said Mutlu.

"Excuse me, sir" said a seaman to Dressal. "Another coded message off the teletype, sir."

"Carry on Mutlu" said Dressal taking the message from the seaman.

" What is puzzling is that this recent data seems to display sudden aberrations which without reason were displacing normal climatological readings. It could be catastrophic if we don't pursue it and give adequate warning. Unstable climates cause unstable governments. The FAO is the world's weatherman. Promise rainfall or sunshine tomorrow and people put away their guns. NASA is paid handsomely to do the weather-watching..."

"One dark satellite, one missing space shuttle, one decommissioned pilot in a capsule that was built for an once-around-the-block orbit decades ago... No, Dr. Mutlu, it's not a very comforting picture!"

"Sending you up in a capsule is a chance we can't afford *not* to take."

"Besides," came Simpson's voice, "under the National Emergency clause, you have no choice, Captain Lloyd. You're reactivated."

Lloyd looked at Simpson's face in tremor with the ships vibrations. "I'll need more time to the pad."

She opened her mouth to object.

"You've got it, Lloyd." came Jefferson. "But under tight security. No outside contact. Come up to the bridge. We're half way to Norfolk."

With Lloyd out of CIC Captain Windsor tussled down the steps and addressed Dressal.

"Should we transmit splashdown rendezvous coordinates to the U.S.S. New Jersey Sir?"

"No, Windsor" said Dressal looking up from the message to his colleagues, his face set. "The U.S.S. New Jersey won't be picking anybody up. The Tolstoy has just deployed a missile from the North Atlantic Ocean floor. Its purpose undefined, its destination is the *Hydros*."

"Armed?"

"Armed or not, it's a direct violation of Space Arms Treaty. Signal the New Jersey to join U.S.S. MacInerny in the Northern Hemisphere. Code Zebra Delta."

"But, sir, how long can he sustain orbit?"

∞

Chapter 3

Dr. Fumosa was greeted with overwhelming applause, and it was only a matter of minutes before his engaging personality captivated his large audience.

He spoke fast, with appropriate urgency and infectious enthusiasm.

The hour of his speech was met with rapt attention by the audience, and passed too quickly for many.

"The fact is," concluded Dr. Fumosa, "that these are nice 'text book' conditions... What you are more likely to see in the field may be very different. Prepare for the worst: infection, disease, dysentery, and errant behavior by natives - possible violence. Remember these are unnatural conditions with many unpredictable unknowns. These are desperate people whose lives are being severely threatened. Look out for each other! Plan for emergencies! Expect the unexpected! Please report your findings on a consistent basis. It will help us with distribution systems...

And now I wish to personally thank you, from the bottom of heart...for the work that you do!

... I wish you all good luck. May God be with you."

∞

At dawn, Jim Lloyd and Tim Martin began their rotation.

Breakfast presented them with a two pound porterhouse steak.

"What's this?" said Martin "Last meal for the condemned?"

"Relax and enjoy... Low-residue breakfast is not necessary on a short orbital flight. Your stomachs will be home for dinner and it'll take me all day to cook it..."

Joe Piper walked in"Howsya'll doing?"

"We're doing fine - at least better than you look. Have you been out all night?"

"I wish. We've checked and double checked all systems. Everything is OK"

"How's the countdown?" asked Lloyd

"Right on the mark. Cap says that if everything looks good, weather holding, it's a go for 8.30."

At the Ready Room in the medical trailer. Two medics examined Martin and Lloyd as if they were androids. They attached heartbeat and pulse sensors onto their long johns and slipped a ten-ounce amplifier into their waist pockets.

Two suit technicians took over. The helmet came over Lloyd's head with a resolute click, and he was sealed, alone with his breathing. He shut his eyes and swallowed hard.

"All right?" asked Joe, eyes square before the visor

Lloyd gave him a thumbs up.

"You're five minutes ahead of schedule. Nice feeling, no pressure. Everything looks good. You'll be right in your launch window on the mark"

By 7.00 a.m. Martin and Lloyd began the trip toward Pad 19.

"Reminds me of old times" muttered Martin.

Lloyd smiled.

 Six minutes later they were fed into the Gemini capsule by attendants, feet up. They were checked for strapping, feeds and helmet position.

Thumbs up.

The hatch was sealed. They sat, two units surrounded by the ergonomics of their vessel. As trained fighter pilots they would have liked to rip off their helmets and fly the damned machine like two men in control.

Jim looked over to Martin. "Just so long as some hormonal teenage geek hasn't discovered some new law of gravity since they built this thing"

It helped.

Martin raising his suited hand to the controls of the capsule. "We may be vintage but we can fly!"

Lloyd put his gloved hand on the copilot's arm "I know you can neighbor: I'm proud to be flying with you!"

 Under the circumstances it was necessary.

They were serving a mission of necessity: They had to think as one so that each man could anticipate the capabilities and limitations of the other. Together in simulators they faced one crisis abort situation after another, every detail a life threatening consequence. Cabin pressure dropped, fuel cells cut out, guidance systems failed, target vehicles moved. Centrifuge g forces spun them well beyond their expected thresholds and as the capabilities of each man complemented the other, it became apparent that they were well yoked as a team. Where Martin had experience, Lloyd had fast adaptability; where Martin showed caution Lloyd showed ingenious risk taking. Gradually a pattern emerged.

Still, nothing was left to chance: Continuously around the clock, with sleep carefully monitored, they trained. And trained. And trained - simulated spaceflight repairs underwater; remote manipulator systems; EVAs; payload assist programs, damage control, skin stress repairs. The results started to add up, recorded as digital and analog data and every judgment decision was analyzed, every choice plotted on statistical probabilities.

Briefings were fast and furious. Drills on orbital flight data, communications, computer systems, rocket propulsion. Lloyd learned to respect this veteran of the Gemini era, he even became accustomed to the California wit salted with air Force bravura. So Yes, Lloyd would trust him with his life. Despite his age. Sitting in the capsule now ready for takeoff was just another drill.

Meantime the U.S. Space Shuttle *Courageous* would be prepped for her launch as Rescue Mission SP 1500. On board would be a full crew of specialists and contingency support systems. Otherwise, like all other intelligence gathering missions, they knew the consequences of a space shuttle left unattended: *Eagle* would by default become the target of a full decommissioning. In this case by directive X 2000. Two thermo-nuclear explosions.

"Gemini. This is Houston. All systems OK. Looks like you're right on schedule. T minus 28 minutes."

Martin and Lloyd proceeded into prelaunch check systems.

Yet, cooped in a capsule that was about to be jettisoned into space, Lloyd had serious misgivings about the futility of the mission: One dark satellite. One missing space shuttle. One dated Gemini capsule built for short duration flight and a retired veteran who *once* flew the thing. It was unreal that this was happening! Were it not for the last briefing in the ready room, there was a strong probability that Lloyd would have told his Commanding Officer, Flight Director Tom Cappachutto, that their plan was bordering on fiction, and that he'd rather find reality on some Bahamian beach.

"Not when we'v got guts for brains" replied Cappachutto "...and you're it! If you can't pull this off, nobody can!"

"Now I know how you get volunteers to launch into space Tom!"

Tom shrugged. He offered the names of the crew on the *Eagle*. One name changed everything for Lloyd. He was stunned. Now he had his own reasons for the mission. The name was familiar.

"Pressurize liquid line 8," said Martin

"Check pressurized liquid line 8."

"Blockhouse doors sealed."

"Check Blockhouse doors sealed"

"T minus 15 minutes" interrupted Capcom

"Malfunction Detection System"

"Check Malfunction Detection System"

"T minus 9 minutes and counting" said the blockhouse voices. Cappachutto's voice was unmistakable. "We see all systems clear and raring to go. Monitors show undue stress load for launch. We wish Captain Martin and Pilot Lloyd good luck!"

Concentrate! With every heartbeat monitored at Houston he must put Karen Patterson out of his mind.

"Internal Power Supply"

"Check Internal Power Supply"

"Open Stage One Prevalves..." Martin was saying.

"Check Stage One Prevalves" said Lloyd, his voice constricted.

Hyperbolic fuels were on the point of meeting to ignite, they both knew.

"T minus zero! Stage One Ignition!"

Ninety feet below them a muffled thunder roared. In that split-second of time both men waited for the Malfunction Detection System to indicate a need to abort launch, each man had both hands on the ejection ring between their knees.

"Three seconds... Two... One... You have lift off!" said Houston.

The rocket started its furious hurl upward.

 "Start the clock" said Martin to Control Center

The sky began to tilt slightly through the hatch windows.

"There's roll program"

"Roger, roll" came back Cappachutto's calm voice.

"There's pitch program"

"Roger, pitch. You're on your way Gemini. Good Luck"

Then everything suddenly stopped. They had reached orbit, rockets ejected, and were floating through space as if captured by the heavens, mesmerized. Lloyd could see the earth crystal beneath him, a soft swirl of clouds laced the North African Continent with ethereal beauty, a tan Sahara implacably tame. Even the circular arms of a hurricane embracing Shi Lanka seemed harmless. Time hung with eternal indifference, the human condition silenced.

Inside the capsule, it took a moment to orient themselves. Lloyd took a deep breath "You OK?"

"Yes" said Martin and they proceeded through post launch checks with methodical care.

""Wonder what we'll find when we reach the ship" said Martin adjusting to the orbit mode "that is...if we find a ship, let alone survivors..." Lloyd turned his head away not to betray any expression.

"We'll find a ship!"

At the prelaunch debriefing Cappachutto had disclosed the record of missing crew. One name on the list was Karen Patterson.

"Yes: Flight Support Crew Lt Cmdrs. Patterson, K. E., United States Navy. First Orbital Flight. On standby scheduling. Why? You know her?" questioned the Flight Director, and all eyes turned on Lloyd. He knew very well what they wanted to hear. A prognosis as to her survivability.

"Yes I know her" was all he would bring himself to say, and without attracting speculation about her professional competence added casually "Damned good party girl!" He headed them off.

Their mission was absolute and justifiable, these things happened; mortality, as in casualties of combat, or, *if you were dumb enough to get your ass shot, you were no use to anyone anymore.* Cappachutto had eyed his two pilots momentarily before concluding that Lloyd was as ready as anyone else to go to battle.

Karen Patterson on board the disabled Shuttle! Lloyd wondered if she could have survived. She *had* re-enlisted! He remembered the last time they were together: Her curly hair thrashing in the wind of a race boat. She tacked the forty foot sailboat boat into the gusty wind, her very soul singing out with sheer unadulterated, exhilarated laugher. If she was a casualty on the *Eagle*, then he was the man who was responsible for her death. Or was he?

He disliked emotional ties to mission personnel. Keep it professional. Keep it real. Keep it impersonal. Those were the mandates of decision making commanders. The price of life was hard enough to weigh against the better good. Regardless.

"Come in Gemini. This is Houston"

Cappachutto had turned his seat over to Jim Valentine. He should have gone home. But he stood behind Jim, hanging on every transmission from Gemini with dark fatigued eyes.

Forty five minutes later the next communication came in and when it did, Ground Control watched hard. Bad enough to lose a shuttle at your hands. Worse to watch the damage. Or was there an *Eagle*? Tenuous, at best.

Bleep:" Houston we have a visual...on ...*HYDROS!*"

"Roger, Gemini" Valentine kept his voice calm

Bleep: "Houston ....Repeat...We have a visual on *HYDROS*."

"Roger, Gemini. Confirm visual on *HYDROS*"

Cappachutto's ecstatic face clouded for just an instant.

Bleep: "Houston. We have Electrical Particle.... Readings to transmit. High counts of Carbon Particle. Temperature radiation high."

"Roger, Gemini. We read your data. Prepare for Retrograde Impulse. You approach second perigee 87 nautical miles distant. Telemeter 87-137 nautical mile elliptical orbit, apogee 137. Check."

"Roger, apogee 137. 87-137 elliptical orbit."

"Prepare to maneuver system to 87-45 nautical mile ellipse. Check."

"Houston.......Trajectory....impulse –"

"Hold it!" interrupted Cappachutto, his face set. He put his hand on Valentine's shoulder. "Skip Retrograde!" he barked. "I don't like the sound of that static interference..."

Jim Valentine looked at his exhausted face. He was trembling. "Tom..." he began, "you're over-reacting..."

"No, gut reacting! Let the log show I'm taking over. Harvey, compute for once again around the block."

Bill Harvey stared at him.

"Tom, another orbit doesn't leave Gemini with much rope..."

"Compute!"

Cappachutto took over the Capcom. "Gemini, everything looks A-OK. We have data and we have decided a small change in orbital program. Check"

"Check. Change in orbital program"

"Gemini. We don't want you any closer to *Hydros*. Abort Retrograde Impulse. Repeat present orbit, 87-135 elliptical orbit."

"Houston, we copy. Abort Retrograde Impulse. Repeat present orbit. 87-135 elliptical orbit. Check." Martin's voice was unmistakable, "Err...Houston we hope there's someplace to buy gas up here....We show lines of limitation on any long range plans. The weather is fine up here but we don't want a forever vacation."

"Roger, Gemini. We'll bring you home okay!"

Cappachutto buried his face in his hands. He got up and walked out of the room. Everyone at Mission Control stared at him.

Jim Valentine took his place. "I hope the hell he's going to be able to answer for his actions!"

Cuba

Julian I. DePhillipe moved his body forward to peer out the plane window. It had already begun its descent.

Coming here, deep feelings might surface and threaten his well-groomed veneer, which explained why he never flew home with companions on his arm.

His eyes, normally arctic blue and staring from glossy magazines across supermarkets, were moist. It was hailed as a stroke of genetic good fortune that with all his Latin coloring he had inherited the blue eyes of a German grandmother.

Beneath him an island surged from the sea into tropical mountains and fertile flatlands. He could already imagine the smell of humid air mixed with orange blossom and sea salt, and he shuddered like a child, either from excitement at the prospect of returning to his equatorial playground or escaping the bleak Chicago cold. Either way, he tugged at his necktie, and he took a long, deep breath.

He earned it, he decided. The week had been long.

Monday's press conference went well, especially when he announced the new site for his major league sports arena, but he had pushed things a bit when he told a reporter from *The Financial Times* that he would keep his corporate center in Chicago, and would build a 164 story glass building atop a museum which would house the most lavish collection of Spanish colonial artifacts ever assembled in one location.

Shortly after the interview however, he got a call from Mike Peck ham in Texas. The price of oil was going to hell and the group he'd invested forty five million dollars with were going Chapter 13 in less than three months.

Not for long, he knew.

Tuesday, the stock market had dropped 30 points less than an hour after opening, and the Superfit Athletic Club chain, of which he owned twelve percent, was taking poison pills of bad debts to keep him from taking over. DePhillipe sipped at his drink demurely.

The only decent thing that happened on Wednesday was a midday tryst with Jeanette at the penthouse. But he had been too free with her… She was the best damned masseuse he had ever known.

By Thursday, when the FDA informed him officially that his health product line was misrepresenting itself, he yearned for a weekend break.

That night he went to Sally Lamar's studio where she was finishing up a sculpture for a hotel lobby. He never fully appreciated artwork, he knew, mainly because he thought most of it was hype, but he enjoyed her professional abandon; it was much the way he himself worked.

"Want to see me make seventy thousand dollars in twenty minutes?" she said.

"Oh yeah?" he answered, curious at her style more than anything else.

She took off all her clothes and put on a work overall. She threw two buckets of clay on the table and rolled them like dough, then upended the roll, bent it over, took a towel and massaged it over until she formed an oval donut.

'Voila!'" she said "It'll be sold by next week!" and she went over to him and threw off her overalls. "Any takers?"

Within two weeks, he decided, she would be reported missing.

By then Villos called him to invite him down to Cuba for the weekend to "wait out the program". Twenty minutes later, he had already sent word to fuel up the jet at O'Hare. In fact, the call from Villos was the signal to Julian DePhillipe to execute his coup-de-grace before flying down, and the meeting with Giannini was confirmed for 9.00 a.m. the next day.

The plane approached the runway to land.

Julian was born on this island, voracious seas lapping at its edges, incarcerated from a world teeming with opportunity. He recognized the flatlands along the west coast, once owned by his great uncles. He could see the paved tight streets of Havana where he had played. He remembered how is mother would be waiting along with his two brothers and sister. They would embrace him.

Andres Villos, the man who first put a tennis racket in his hand, and showed him how to hit bounceless balls off graffiti walls, would be waiting in the background. Villos often reminded him of his Spanish ancestors who created the old world and conquered the new with God, gold and a good arsenal.

 He grew up, after his father was arrested during the Castro regime, feeling like one limb were missing. But Villas had waited a lifetime for the boy. Villas taught him to survive, first with the body, then with the mind, and finally with the funds and contacts in America, waiting for their sons who would outlast the Castro regime.

Julian had developed into an extraordinary athlete. He won his way into the international heart at age 18. And as if to celebrate the post Castro Cuba, the world embraced him wholesale. Winner of the U.S. Open at age 19, French Open at 20, Wimbledon twice at age 21 and 22. He began his corporation in Chicago by advertising tennis shoes. Then using the agility and athletic prowess with which he stormed the world of sports, he focused on making money.

The sun outside his private jet shone onto his godlike face though a porthole. With its smooth olive forehead and lupine jawbones, he shut his eyes, basking in the remarkable events that transpired in the last twenty four hours. The complexity of his strategy was gratifying in itself, but the sequence of his strategy, in retrospect, now seemed to be a natural evolution of all that he was, all that his background could best suit him for.

He could still see the look on Marco Giannini's face when he realized what he had happened. Instead of walking into a board room to discuss the merger of Crop Credit Bank - the largest credit bank in the mid-western crop belt of all things - with Julian's Sterling Banks, he had just exposed the full holdings and liabilities of his company to DePhillipe, who had absolutely no intention of merging whatsoever. Never had.

Giannini's lawyers, preoccupied with the paperwork, had underestimated their competitor. Only Giannini looked directly at DePhillpe and understood. It was all over for Giannini. They had bargained all morning. All Julian had to do was go directly to the creditors and assume Giannini's bank without cost. It was only a matter of months before Giannini would be in foreclosure.

Instinctively, Julian DePhillipe knew the smell of adrenalin in the veins of a beaten man; the gestures of the large eyes and defensive posture, the lack of control as negotiations approached the flashpoint of fear, anger and loss; like everything else it was a testing of patience, and Julian had the patience of a temple-carved god.

∞

At 08:20:45.15 into the spaceflight, Lloyd recorded navigational reckoning against speed. An altered flight plan had been copied into the computers and checked. Methodically, he computed through each system for Reentry Trajectory. He examined the data. The figures were sobering.

Houston's change of plan threw Martin. Lloyd's computations only exacerbated his fear. A capsule on a fixed supply could not accommodate much flexibility in orbit. The margin of tolerance was slim.

"I hope they know what they're doing..." he muttered "*Hydros* turned them off altogether. I don't get it"

"I don't either," said Lloyd sensing Martin's tension. He kept his voice relaxed. "How about we tell'em that the next time around we either take a good look at *Hydros* or go home empty!"

"Yeah"a sighed Martin. "It was probably the readings that scared them. Reckon they got the same readings from *Eagle*..."

Lloyd turned to the rendezvous radar. "I'm going for some amplifications."

There was no question in Lloyd's mind that what they encountered in atmospheric readings was precisely the same as what *Eagle* read. The temperature puzzled him. On the dark side of their orbit there was no excuse for the heat radiation. Thermal radiation readings were even more bizarre. It was as if they'd flown right into the sun. But a sun on a *reverse* axis? It was unexplainable.- Acquisition and Tracking Radar was useless. It was completely garbled now. So, clearly there was interference.

Lloyd looked up at the Closed Respiratory Gas System of the spacecraft and realized that time would soon become a factor. Cosmic Rays: High, Transponder: Interference.

Lloyd rubbed his face. He had to locate the target vehicle.

If *Eagle* were there, it had to show up on the transponder. He reset it back to *Hydros* and tried again. Space was like a good mountain. Echoes bounced forever. They could have heard anything, provided there was no interruption. He waited for any identifiable signature. But it was as if he were dragging a metal detector through a copper mine. The garbage was unjustified.

They approached *Hydros* on the second orbit and Lloyd detected a powerful double signal.

"Did you hear that?"

"Sorta. a double bounce. An echo maybe?"

"No, listen. It's got to be *Eagle*"

"If it is, then she should be visible by now. She is not!"

"It's gotta be. I'm going out to take a look!"

"That's..."

Without warning all onboard readings flashed into a jump of static and electrical charges: Fuel cells failed, communications showed zero, the capsule took a wicked yaw.

 Lloyd tried to compensate, knowing that Yaw thrusters were burning precious fuel.

 "Forget it," said Martin. "We're spinning 360 degrees a second and we're going to have to jump into a slower orbit."

"Brute force requires a Change-of-Plane. It'll cost us!"

"We have no choice. We can't take the stress loads indefinitely."

"We'll switch off and restart."

"Primary propulsion is down, secondary may be gone. Damn it, Lloyd that means no fuel for reentry..."

"Not if we EVA and dock from the outside to *Hydros* for a free ride on a geosynchronous orbit!"

With the thrusters still burning, Tim took less than one second to decide. "Do it!"

Lloyd punched navigational changes to lower orbit. Slowly, in the black silence of space, gentle thrusters maneuvered the capsule in tandem with *Hydros*. Without wasting any time, Lloyd began to suit up for extra vehicular activity.

Everything he attempted put a heavy strain on the life-support capabilities of his spacesuit. He moved aft to the adapter section and began to don the astronaut Maneuvering Unit. His visor began to fog. He was overheating. He continued to rig the AMU but its arms were bulky and slow to maneuver. His visor continued to fog up and he decided that a rest period would cool the suit.

Hydros was one hundred feet away, her arms forever extended to the heavens in an eternal posture of supplication.

Lloyd left the capsule, his suit not cooled and his visor still fogging, a total blackness surrounded him.

Fifty feet away from *Hydros* Lloyd turned back and could barely see Gemini.

"Tim. Whatever it is that I'm swimming through, it's a substance that wants to crust on my visor. Visibility is poor. Hot!"

"Roger. Lloyd. You're approaching the 20% mark of your trip. Look for an appendage to dock to. Gyrations synchronized."

Lloyd stopped for a split second. He suited was now heating up unnaturally. It occurred to him in this motionless state that he and the two vessels were hurling through space at a speed of 18,000 miles per hour. It seemed unnatural somehow, and his concentration wandered. He pressed forward.

By the time Lloyd reached *Hydros* he was panting. What he saw made him gasp with disappointment.

"Well I'm here, Tim!"

"Roger"

"The docking collar... is, totally crusted with some kind of crud, dust, carbon-like. Whatever approach, everything seems coated by something in the atmosphere..."

Tim's answer was not immediate

"Tim? Do you read?"

"Yeah...Roger."

"Tim, let me think a minute..." Lloyd's face was pouring sweat. He scraped the dust off his visor and looked around him.

"Lloyd, you'd better come home. Orbital sunrise in 30 minutes."

What Lloyd could not get out of his mind was the signal. The signal, he decided, had to be *Eagle*. It came close to the signal from *Hydros*. But in this particle density it was hard to see anything.

"Tim, I'm here. And I'm going to look around....Stand by."

"Roger."

Lloyd floated in a sea of particle dust. He inspected the satellite and saw evidence of burn blisters. Whatever carbon and electrical substance was present clearly conducted heat. That explained the high temperature readings. It wasn't a constant heat, though probably a spike or flare impact, he decided.

Inside his space helmet, his breathing was hard. The visor was becoming a real problem. He had to concentrate. Visibility was limited to maybe twenty feet.

Decision. He must decide! He heard Tim.

"Standing by..."

Lloyd shut his eyes, his concentration wavered....*Source?*

What was the source of the encrusting substance? Something was wrong! Lloyd looked carefully. The substance undoubtedly would have to contain a high cosmic ray count, and the satellite was clearly inert. No, the satellite was definitely *not* the source. So, the source, Lloyd realized, must be... the *sun?*

"...minutes before orbital sunrise, counting..."

 From inside his glass bubble, Lloyd turned to determine the position of the sun relative to the orbit. As he did, a small glitter caught his eye. He cleared off his visor from the outside and looked carefully. He strained through the blackness resembling a praying mantis suspended in space, and he made his decision.

"Tim, I'm taking a short walk. Standby"

 "Roger. Orbital sunrise in...minutes. Repeat. 15..."

So, transmission frequency was corrupting already!

He aimed for space, ostensibly in the direction of the glitter, a come-hither call. What he could not forget was the signal he heard bouncing off *Hydros*. In all the garbage, it was still a loud signature. Sometimes it read like a double beat. An echo perhaps? Possibly two signals blurring. - Could it have been *Eagle*? In this mess he couldn't see a thing. Where was the glitter?

Jesus!

"Lloyd, you are...approaching 40%.... EVA...activity. Return. .Gemini... "

"Roger."

What if *Eagle* were less than fifty feet away? He looked around, he couldn't even see *Hydros* let alone Gemini. He was alone --and steaming up inside his suit. Should he return? Another glitter ahead caught his eye. A reflection of a large substance, perhaps a small...He moved forward.

"Lloyd...50%   ....Return....Immediately ...Repeat, EVA ...Do...read?"

Lloyd stopped, he was panting. He knew what Tim was telling him. He had consumed 50% of his extra vehicular activity capability. He'd need the rest to get back to *Eagle*. Decision time!

"Gemini....Read? Immediate...to base..."

Another twenty feet ahead and he'd probably know what it was. Then again, he might be twenty feet short of Gemini when he would stop breathing.

And what if he did get back on board? *Hydros* proved useless. So with the ship's limited capacity it was only a matter of time there, too.

He looked around him. Where the hell was the *Eagle*? If he found *Eagle* they'd have a chance; if he returned, there was none. He made a decision.

"Tim, I don't know if you can read me. But I've got to investigate a signal light ahead. It could be *Eagle*. I'll keep you informed. I'm proceeding forward. I read your command to return to base, but I'm on my own..."

Tim's response was not immediate. When it came, Lloyd understood. They had had some discussion about gesture and priorities. They both knew the odds of succeeding.

"Rog...luck...friend..."

The heat was intense and Lloyd paused periodically for measured inhalation. *How long did he have before his life support gave out?* He forced himself toward the signature. His mind was whirling, intense, he gasped for air. He thought of Karen, and swallowed hard. Had he made the right choice? Too late now...*Concentrate!*

The signal emerged suddenly at his side with overwhelming clarity. Larger than life and just feet away he saw along fuselage *The United States Space Shuttle Eagle*.

Lloyd was looking up at the underbelly. Dark heat-resistant ablating materials hid the profile of her superstructure. In the darkness she remained invisible!

Lloyd wanted to tell Tim. He couldn't. His EVA coolant was beginning to fail, he knew.

Slowly he worked his way upward. The glitter that had beckoned him was little more than a UV reflectant off a space helmet visor. He approached, his heart pounding. On the spacesuit of an astronaut held to the bay-hold infrastructure he read *CHAPMAN. USA.NASA.*

Lloyd raised the visor with some difficulty, its metal hinges stiff.

Astronaut Chapman, her spacesuit intact except for metal attachments, and her boot snagged in a foothold of the wingspan was dead. Her face was swollen.

He clasped himself to her and looked up. The cargo bay hold was open. Also open was the aft chamber.

He clambered in, strained in almost breathlessness to press the panel to seal the doors for decompression. The doors closed slowly. He slid to the ground, his lungs on fire, waiting. Whether his spacesuit life support could sustain him through decompression was not even a question. He did not care. His eyes rolled upward. He felt himself slipping out of consciousness.

∞

She stared a him incredulously. He was in her Orbiter!

On his space-suite flight arm was his name and mission.

Jesus!

She offered aid with a POS device, his breathing stabilized.

She waited. He has scared the hell out of her!

Karen wondered how she could explain what had transpired since that day in Annapolis. So much had happened since then! She had wanted to call Lloyd a dozen times, but never did. But that was a century ago, a world away, although the memory of it was fresh in her heart. And here he sat!

She checked Lloyd's pulse, waiting for him to regain consciousness.

 That someone had been able to approach the orbiter, let alone get inside the decompression chamber, defied reason. But there he was, the same resolute chin and suntanned face she had known, she wanted to pray with thanks!

 His eyes opened briefly and she suddenly felt self-conscious. She averted her eyes, bloodshot eyes, chapped and inflamed lips protruding from a white face like some monstrous ghoul...

Karen closed her eyes. She remembered the first time they met in Annapolis. Lloyd put her back on her feet.

How could she forget that? According to the tour buses parked beneath the cherry blossom trees at the Smithsonian, it was May in Washington DC.

The radio clicked on and a soft lyric filled the sunlit room. *You belong to the city ♫*.

Karen turned and crushed her pillow. Clocks were useful, if not as persistent as the clock within her head. She had overslept and an old panic nearly took her by surprise. Saturday, she sighed.

She had been sent to Washington DC for three weeks. Lizzie had arranged for her to stay at a friend's vacant house in Georgetown. And except for the maid who appeared, Karen had every possible accommodation, including a limo at her door each morning.

Outside, a siren screeched down M Street. She stood up, another beautiful day in the city.

She ran her hand through a mass of shinning hair and shut her eyes. Was she angry at her instinctive reaction? She thrust off the covers and sleep throbbed in her head. Champagne at the Eastport Clubhouse...*Oh yeah!*

She turned on the shower and stood, warm water cascading over her body.

She should go to the office today and collect more information for her final report. Or she should go jogging down the Potomac. Or she should have lunch with Therese.... *Anything, just get out of the house before Lloyd showed up.*

What was she thinking? He had invited her to go sailing...

She reached for the shampoo and massaged with all the enthusiasm of a car wash.

She thought of Lloyd standing at the doorbell, ringing without an answer. The soap drained off her face. In forty-five minutes he would be there, his Jeep packed with a cooler and all the other paraphernalia men liked to think won a race.

She got out of the shower, rubbed her hair and with a towel cleared off a misty mirror to examine the effects of a hangover on a face that ached for two extra-strength Tylenol painkillers.

Karen was kidding herself, actually she was searching for the invisible scars of stress and fatigue, the kind that comes when you've been away for weeks from familiar surroundings and you keep assuring your hosts that you're fine....

Karen had blue eyes, if swollen, naturally thick eyebrows, an angular nose and a mouth that could sustain long periods of silence without betraying a thought, let alone an emotion.

Yet, nothing could change the upturning at the corners of her mouth, that lilt that could be interpreted as a smile, or as she had often heard, a smirk in the face of a threat. "Where are you, Karen?" said the face that glared back at her.

A car pulled up. Was it Lloyd? It pulled away...

She turned suddenly and flung open the closet, smashing her resolve to play Hermit the Crab.

Hidden on a hanger was an ankle length tunic dress. She touched the fabric and thought of Lizzie. *Wear the damn skirt and go!* Lizzie would have said.

"Did you pack any shorts?" yelled Lloyd in the open Jeep as she tried to anchor the skirt that billowed like a sail. Karen expected such a remark from a man. But it was not insulting. It was the voice of a skipper gathering crew.

Without warning the Jeep peeled off into Annapolis and on down to the fisherman's harbor where a teeming crowd of tourists, sailors, cycle taxis, and United States Naval Academy Midshipmen had brought traffic to a crawl.

"Welcome aboard the Bonaventure!" grinned Lloyd standing in the cockpit of his racing Swan, sheets, sail bags and winches ready to go. She stood there rooted to the dock like a child, unsure of embarking on any venture that used wind as a source of locomotion.

"Come on!" he said. "If we capsize I'll rescue you I promise!"

Her fear of a good time was quickly realized when Lloyd barked, "Go below decks and change into something practical, I'll need your help out there!" He looked back suddenly and grinned, "It's blowing a small gale on the bay!"

Great, she thought. Serves me right for indulging a sailor over happy hour. She should have stayed at the boathouse and sipped wine.

But as he explained it, crew for the races off Annapolis Harbor should always include an Englishman...or an *Englishwoman*, if you were a man worth your salt.

The 15 minute Race-Gun blasted and racing yachts from every river of the Chesapeake appeared on a gusty horizon. The wind was blowing out of the south, bringing a long and wicked sea fetch with it instead of the customary short chop that big boats could slice through, explained Lloyd.

Karen needed few instructions.

Abbie and John, Lloyd's other crewmen, had come aboard by Launch, and they were busy feeding the spinnaker through the Shute on the bow for the downwind leg when Lloyd insisted she add some heavy weather clothing to her sweater, and find a pair of sneakers in the locker below deck.

It was hard to keep a footing in these seas and they were all soaking.

"Fillie" was baring down on them. "I'm going below!" said Lloyd suddenly "Take the helm!"

"What?" yelled Karen incredulously.

His eyes twinkled with mirth "Fillie wants to cruise on our air...Don't let her in! If she crunches us, she pays the damage!"

"Where are we going?"

"To cross the start line and win a sailboat race..." Lloyd looked at her steadily, "You're a big girl!"

"Sea room!" bellowed "Fillie".

Karen was appalled, but she took the helm and maneuvered the Swan to give "Fillie" some sea room.

Ahead was "Tenacious" a stunning vessel carrying huge sails and a very tall mast.

"They're on a port tack..." explained Lloyd relieving her of the helm.

"Fillie" was still hailing, or rather, the skipper yelling, until he spotted Karen.

"Well, well, well! What have you there Bonaventure? A new helmsman on a Swan no less!" He luffed up his sails for a longer exchange between them. "A woman who thinks she can sail!" He blew her an amorous kiss, and his crew joined in "Woosey- woosey-woosey!" They pushed closer. "We'll sail you to finish Lloyd, you and your female crew!"

Ebbie was counting down "eight...seven...six..."

"Fillie's" thundered within feet of their stern "Tack! Lloyd. I'll ram the stern off your god dammed hull!" yelled LeGates

A hard gust hit the boat and Karen lurched the helm into the wind with a "Tacking" order, and steered the Swan to a nice clear finish. Third was their place in the class.

It wasn't until much later that day that Karen said much.

They were moored in the harbor. The wind had calmed down as if finished with her wild rage and pleased to leave the sky cleansed of her ills.

Abbie and John were on shore partying, and Lloyd was turning tuna stakes on the stern grill.

"You turned the helm over to me on purpose didn't you?" she said finally.

"Of course!"

Karen looked up and took a deep breath at an expansive blue sky where a few timid clouds ambled over the seaport town and hovered in front of the mellowing sun, casting pinkish hues of light and shadow upon the rippling wakes of a harbor. From anchored boats there was a tossing and tinkling of halyards against masts. It was the music of Annapolis.

A long time passed and Lloyd "Boats have been sailing into this port since the first settlers arrived from England. In fact, it was the burning of the Peggy Steward, a vessel carrying a cargo of tea, which set off the Revolution down here..."

"You're a Naval Academy man are you not?"

"I am. This is where it all began for me. Life was simpler then. Now we sail out with a small nuclear arsenal at our disposal. By God we need to train well for it!"

She smiled. "We still prefer grog on our ships of the line!"

"Do you know what my favorite sortie ever was?"

"Age 12: Boy Scout Troop on the Sassafras River. I ended up cooking because no one else knew how to heat beans. Until then I was a nobody. Then suddenly everybody loved me! So, the cook I was!"

Karen managed a smile.

For a long time they sat there in the cockpit of the Bonaventure, swaying quietly beneath a sky full of stars, and the sound of a tune drifted softly from the Hilton.

"I am a stranger in Paradise... Take my hand "

Lloyd put down his drink, stood up and offered her a hand for the dance. She laughed at the gesture, looked up and added,

♫ *If I stand starry eyed*

He chuckled and they sang out, ♫ *If I stand...out of the commonplace...out there in space"*

With all of two square feet at the helm to dance in, they swayed to the tune as he sang in her ear, *"I hang suspended, until I know...that there's a chance you'll care...and have answer for the prayer...of a stranger in paradise...."*

Karen closed her eyes. And it felt good to be held, so very, very well. Her back stiffened, and from her far away world of political frays and global disputes, she responded to Lloyd's warm breath on her face. Life was sweet in the colonies...she decided.

∞

Lloyd had put in too many hours on a shuttle not to recognize a mid-deck when he regained consciousness.

He was looking into the eyes of a pale woman he barely recognized with her arms eerily extended in the neutral body position of weightlessness.

"Patterson?" he managed to say.

She stammered awkwardly reading the label on his spacesuit "Thank God for you for...for..."she began, unable to finish the sentence.

Lloyd nodded, and looking down at his straps he said, "So. Do you always nail down your patients?"

Oh! Oh!...Sorry!" she fumbled, clearly trying to come to grips with the situation. She cleared her hoarse and dried throat. "How else can I babysit a warm body if it's floating around the cabin. Hold still..."

"I take it you don't get too many patients up here?"

For an instant her eyes lost their panic, but only for an instant. He rested, waiting.

"My God, it was terrible!" she blurted suddenly "They're all dead! Dead! It happened so fast. I thought I'd be up here forever alone. It's all I can do to stay alive. It was unreal. They're all dead except me. Just like that. All dead. And me alone in this tomb floating in space forever..."

Lloyd extended his arm and touched her, a survivor.

She was visibly traumatized, the signs of dehydration and jaundice etched around her eyes and drawn cheekbones. Her breathing was shallow, uncertain.

From inside his helmet a sound crackled like an intruder alert. She recoiled.

It was signal from Gemini.

"It's OK. Karen It's OK. My transponder signal...ok?"

"Stand by Gemini..." he said. "EVA Successful."

"Roger..."

"Water? Any fluids? Karen?"

She nodded. "Yes...Yes, of course!"

It took a while, but she became lucid, apprehension ebbing.

He reassured her that he and Tim had come to help and that everything was under control. She smiled gamely. What he needed now was her cooperation, such as an anti-g suit, but she was selectively hearing, he noticed. And she was squinting for vision. Signs of long duration space flight distress were everywhere.

"I found you in the...um...in the airlock tunnel. Your suit was down to two, to two... psi. Thank God you err...the presence of mind to close the hatch and pressurize!"

"I see you've changed canisters okay"

"Sorta. Enough to maintain... With only me I've been changing once every 48 hours..." the thought of the others brought her hand to her face, uncertain. "But... But I'm on the emergency oxygen system 'cos nothing else would work..." she paused, still casting about for an explanation.

Then she looked sharply at Lloyd and, as if reading his thoughts, she spluttered "Yes I did reenlist for duty, but not to be a NASA astronaut okay? I'm here for acoustical research! I don't know squat about spaceflight, and I am *The Only Survivor!*"

"Karen! Karen! You're OK. You did OK. Breathe! Breathe for comfort and assurance now. We are a rescue mission. You did ok. You got that?"

She nodded dubiously.

If Lloyd was taken aback he didn't show it, he went down on his knees, opened the access panels for the life-support system and pulled open the stowage locker. He hefted out one old unit and replaced it with a fresh canister of lithium hydroxide. He disappeared up the flight deck access ladder and stood behind the commander's seat.

Martin was hailing again.

"Where are the bodies?" Lloyd asked Karen.

"I secured them... all... in the sleeping bags"

"Let me take a look?"

The pilot had blisters on his face and was severely bloated, the copilot showed signs of asphyxiation from sudden decompression.

He so noted in the voice ship's log that the crew was dead.

He communicated with Martin. Together they would orbit the earth holding their present telemetry. It would keep them close. For now.

Lloyd leaned over the Commander' seat and reached for a bank of panels to the left. The atmospheric pressure controls were not lit up. He flipped from Emergency systems to primary systems. Nothing happened. He flipped to secondary. Still nothing. He sat in the Commander's launch position and assessed the status of the panels that surrounded him.

There were no electronic displays, no cathode-ray tubes. He turned to the computer keyboards to his right and asked for access. Nothing came running to him, so he punched in for a general status.

He sat back and reassessed. The flight deck consoles of this remarkable space machine lay silent as it orbited the earth

250 miles above the surface. For the moment it would continue to orbit the earth. He knew that it would follow a path of gravitational forces that pulled relentlessly through space, heedless of the species that would tamper and tinkle with its unyielding power.

As Lloyd's mind raced through the options, he saw through the window the blue flawless planet of earth glide by, gently and without conflagration, vulnerable to the same relentless rotation as he. Yet here he was to fix a problem.

He wanted firstly to reestablish a link with Capcom.

That was out of the question. Obviously, some trauma had occurred to cause the computers to shut down in one fell swoop. The orbiter was in Zero Mode Failsafe Status, which explained why they were on Environmental Support State One. So, a very elementary decision was made to boot up the computers from zero. And like five arguing neighbors, they came up with an avalanche of data.

The last program code was 201, On-orbit Coast Mode, and there was nothing to indicate any stress except for strong electromagnetic activity. Overhead, he was relieved to see that the Cabin pressure was reading 16.7 psi - so he reinstated Primary Environmental systems on his left and punched in a transmitting signal to Gemini.

 It was quickly acknowledged. He switched on the overhead panels to Gemini's air-to-air frequency.

"This is *Eagle*. Radio check, over."

"Rog..."a came the unmistakably relieved voice of Tim Martin

"Gemini, switch to check channels 10. Over"

"Rog....Repeat frequ..."

"Gemini, switch to Channel 10. Repeat, 10. One zero. Over"

"Roger, switching ..."

"Gemini, this is *Eagle*. Radio check. Over"

"Roger, *Eagle*, loud and clear. Thank God! Receiving channel 10. Over"

"Report: All hands dead except one passenger Systems Status down to Zero Mode Failsafe State, now Program Code 201 resumed. Over"

"Roger, I copy."

"Gemini, this is *Eagle*. Do you see me at the following coordinates. Over"

"I see you now on TV, like snow. Please advise docking cap...ilty"

Lloyd wasn't pleased with the decay in frequency. He'd take no more chances. The options were not the best, and he had to rule out an elaborate docking procedure. The mating couplets and gaskets might have been compromised and it would cost Gemini too much thruster fuel. He made a quick decision.

"Gemini this is *Eagle*. Docking unfeasible. Advise you close in on coordinates for a tow on the happy hooker. Request you EVA transport to *Eagle* ASAP. Over"

"Roger, ETA possible 45 minutes if all goes ....ell"

Lloyd turned to the aft crew station, and engaged the remote manipulator system and controls. He clasped the rotational hand controller. Neither the shoulder, the elbow nor the wrist would extend. He turned the backup control and switched to direct drive. The closed circuit television monitors were on but would'nt rotate.

"Is there anything I can do to help?" said Peterson from behind.

"Yeah. Let's prepare for a complete list check of external systems while Tim is doing his EVA. Everything outside the hull clearly has a severe case of arthritis of the joints"

He returned to the flight deck console

"Gemini, this is *Eagle*."

"Roger *Eagle*..."

He kept his voice even "Gemini, we're having some difficulty with RMS, advise you come in close for synchronous orbit, take a tether walk and attach to airlock on tunnel adapter. Perhaps you could look over the shuttle skin. Over"

Lloyd knew that the risk and precision of such a maneuver would not be lost on Martin. But to NASA's redeeming credit, Gemini capsules, if dated, were maneuverable and self-sufficient. Martin's answer, when it came, put a smile on Lloyd's tired face.

"*Eagle* this is Gemini, coordinate orbit, engine shut down, take a hike, check the baby, piece of cake. Over"

"Gemini this is *Eagle*. Standby to receive program 202. Over"

With that command the shuttle computers transmitted in-flight maneuvering data that would put the capsule within yards of the orbiter.

"Check program 202, commence engine shut down,"

"affirmative.t

"Chapman?" asked Lloyd turning to Karen.

"She was in the chamber...she exited the ship...She may still be on the outside of the orbiter...." Her voice faded.

"Hey, hey...you're doing okay. Everything is okay!"

Lloyd looked at her, then slowly held her. "It's ok!"

"She will have to remain outside for the time being...We'll bring her in later."

"Okay. I'm okay. Thank you... I'm fine now" She pulled herself away.

"You look beat" she added. When was the last time you napped?" It was not a question worth answering, but he smiled. "I'm fine."

∞

These conferences were becoming routine.

He was one of the attendees at the Conference. They mingled for cocktails in the Hotel Lobby at the end of the day of forums. Each wore their badge and institute name.

 Uri Pavala enjoyed conversing with Carina Bruneski. He was a veteran.

 "Afghan revolution" he said casually, looking down, and Carina smiled sympathetically.   Somehow, she was surprised he worked for the Wazir akhbar Khan Hospital, a Czech-built institution that served as the aid distribution center for the American CARE-MEDICO team which included the Peace Corps, WHO and UNICEF during the Afghanistan revolution.

"Medical Unit "he said with rushed words as if sensing her doubts. "Life was abysmal in Afghanistan. Life expectancy was only 33 years; infant mortality 200% during the 80's. But food was not too bad" he added with a cynical smile. "Caloric intake was 124 percent of minimum requirements and protein intake at 95 percent. Not bad for tribal ingrates..." He looked suddenly at his watch "It was a land of frustrated ambitions for sheep herders not worth dying for. No wonder they turned to Marxist and Islamist parties when it was all over!"

"If I remember rightly" volunteered Carina quite uncharacteristically "This not the war initiated because the Soviet Union aspired to own a warm water port?" She immediately regretted revealing her perspicacity which might well have come from intelligence reports. Uri looked at her carefully and smiled.

It was midnight before they all turned in to their hotel rooms. Carina had let Dr. Fumosa in and he softly shut the door behind them.

Uri was one floor below them. When he reached his room he sat down by the bed and picked up the phone and made a call to Cuba. It was a short conversation. Maybe half a dozen sentences about things going well, dinner, schedules....

"They have made no connection. Climatic aberrations are still viewed as natural phenomenon and they are preparing for crisis management. Unseasonal changes in tundra have gone unnoticed. I will watch my party closely. If Fumosa gets any intelligence it will be from *her* though I think she may be out of the loop. In any event, I can prevent that if need be. So far, the Americans have said nothing" He said goodbye briefly and hung up.

∞

"I know what you're wondering. I was suiting up for EVA when it hit. In fact I had just put on the helmet when the shuttle began a small yaw. Then every damn alarm let rip and a surge of light and power hit the ship like a supernova explosion." She wanted to go on but a signal called Lloyd up the ladder to the flight deck. She followed.

"What's up?"

"I'm seeing this but I don't believe what I'm seeing" he muttered.

"Gemini this is *Eagle*, over"

There was no answer. Martin would by now be readying to transport and was on his headset but had not yet left the capsule"

"Gemini, this is *Eagle*. Do you copy? Over"

There was no mistaking the screen. He punched in for a trajectory and the computer answered. He hailed Martin. He would have to abort.

"Gemini, this is *Eagle*. Come in, Tim. Over"

"...ger, Eag... hatch opened, commencing EVA"

Too late!

"Your ETA is approximately twenty four minutes and six seconds" said Lloyd calmly. He would tell Martin what he saw.

"Gemini, this is *Eagle*. We have an oncoming foreign object intersecting our orbit in 24 minutes. Over"

"...ger, committed to EVA. Over"

"Computer identifies foreign object as armed rocket. Walk fast and get in here before possible impact."

"Roger...fast jog through space....ETA 22 minutes..."

"My God," muttered Paterson peering at the screen. "What is that thing?"

∞

Amanda Wells opened the report in the package. It came with a letter from Dr. Saphira Sumptra.

I hope you don't mind she said in a note *But I am most concerned about the party to whom you were talking at dinner. He is an unknown. But his region is not! Please look up your geographic analysis of the area when you return to the UN.*

My sources tell me that all is not well with this region. In fact, some data and findings baffle me. Let me know if you find anything that might shed light on this situation, will you?

Please keep in touch. I'm flying to London next month. Please let's get together for a meeting. Dinner, my treat!

Best

Saphira S.

PS: If you're ever in the region, I'm at the Lahore General Hospital.

Amanda read the complete document. There was little she could not understand, but plenty to leave her with questions. Chiefly, all the medical data collected from hospitals in both Pakistan and India that recorded patients from the Punjab Plateaus registered one complain. Pulmonary infection.

Amanda knew enough to understand that if sufficient numbers of people at that altitude, like the Ayahla Indians of Peru, contracted pulmonary infection, the community was dying.

For a society known by "lore" as have survived collecting "flowers as dye" for centuries, then something was wrong.

And nobody even heard of the Kush plateau!

Funny.

There was one other analysis that left questions. It referred to the mental health of the community. Some said they noted alarming differences in their responses to events of their traditions. Unexplained, it said.

∞

Lloyd switched altogether from hailing Ground Control to Tim's air-to-air frequency. His options were closing.

"Tim, this is *Eagle*. Oncoming target is closing, armed and will detonate in 2.8 minutes. Do you read?"

Martin did not answer immediately.

"He won't make it" said Paterson, her voice quiet.

Martin's words were chosen. "Roger *Eagle*...I hate to cut my spacewalk short on account of a missile and I'm standing just outside your door to boot. Guess I will see ya in heaven if you'll pardon the pun."

"Tim, this is *Eagle*. Proceed entry by airlock tunnel."

"Roger *Eagle*... So long, my friend. It was one hell of a ride..."

"Tim. No way I'm leaving you out there man. Stand by..."

He turned to Karen. "The payload doors, are they functioning?"

She nodded.

"Tim, this is *Eagle*. I'm going to close the bay doors. Do you read, Tim? Only way, no other way. Do you read?"

"That's Okay *Eagle*. You gotta do what you gotta do. I understand."

There was a chance that closing the bay doors would protect Tim from the impact of the explosion. Lloyd lurched over to the aft crew station and, with trembling fingers punched the keyboard with instructions to close the bay doors. Tim was already settling into the bay, his umbilical lifeline still attached to the Gemini. How long he could last if his umbilical were crushed by the doors was anybody's guess.

The large bay hold doors began to move, awkwardly. Thirty two latches were meeting resistance at the metal joints.

"Come on! Come on!" muttered Lloyd as the doors hesitated. They moved closer, but it was taking an eternity.

One minute to impact, the computers recited.

Paterson was donning her EVA spacesuit. "Err . . . Officer Paterson?"

"I'm going out there to help!"

"Patterson!"

Thirty seconds to impact.

"Tim, this is *Eagle*, keep moving!"

"Roger"

The bay doors were still closing when the missile exploded. Impact throughout the orbiter was immediate. The vessel shuddered. Being blown to bits would be the good news; Lloyd feared that they might be slammed off their trajectory and sent spinning through space. Lloyd held his breath for a further impact. It didn't' come. Nothing. It took several heart pounding breaths before Lloyd was certain the orbiter survived. The ship yawed. Readings on the flight deck consoles flared. Electromagnetic-impact hit maximum; communications peaked out; carbon readings and radar spiked out, and general static scratched every sensing device on the spaceship.

 Yet with astonishing speed, all five computers adjusted, compensating... Overrides, remedial reactions. Damage control, they stabilized.

Lloyd rushed aft to the crew station and hunted for Tim.

The bay doors had failed to close completely but the airlock hatch was closing from the inside, which meant that Tim was inside the airlock and still kicking.

Paterson was okay. Lloyd was surprised that all systems were stabilizing without serious damage.

Tim came up to the flight deck, the crisis was about over, but strains of fatigue and stress etched all over his face.

"You okay buddy?"

"Just a few good bruises. Next time just roll out the welcome mat. This is hard work for an old man!"

They needed to rest. A rehydrated meal would be good. But they talked.

"So, we got a load of fireworks - but no explosion. Thank God we sustained!" said Lloyd as he sank gratefully into the pilot's seat. "But I don't like the readings one bit. Carbon, radiation.... We're sitting in a sea of microwaves and God knows what else crudding up the skin is out there. I have this feeling we're being trussed up like a chicken for a barbecue."

"By what? What wiped out the others?"

"Extraordinary and unexpected heat and radiation burns, I think - of a higher order than what this baby was built for."

"My God."

"We need more data. I wanted a closer look at that missile before she lit up."

Martin was introduced. He had taken some time to work up to pressure in his airlock. Paterson had helped him into the cabin. But there had been other considerations and little time for introductions. So when Paterson now stuck up her head from below, Lloyd officially introduced them.

Even in his exhausted state, the prospect of sharing space with this woman obviously delighted Tim Martin. He was grinning like a schoolboy.

"Gentlemen, with all respect, you both look useless in your condition. Please come eat and get some sleep before we make any more serious policy changes. You might screw up my trip!"

Lloyd looked over the console for data. There was time allowance. He agreed.

Lloyd was being woken from a deep sleep of exhaustion, and he could barely believe what Paterson was saying.

The *Eagle* was receiving a signal from Ground Control...

Besides, she wanted his bag to nap in. He looked over at Tim and decided to let him sleep on.

It was a garbled signal and it took some doing to amplify the transmission.

He checked the orbit and reckoned it was the Pacific Tracking and Data Relay Station West that was hailing. This had to be the White Sands Missile Range in New Mexico.

"*Eagle*, this...Sands. Come...read."

How long they had been transmitting he couldn't tell.

"Control, this is *Eagle*, we read you like music to our ears!"

"*Eagle*, this is White...confirm transmit."

"Control, this is *Eagle*, confirming transmission, repeat, this is *Eagle* Mission STS 153"

"Welcome back! Glad to hear you're... Please transmit status..."

The signal was getting stronger as the orbit took them over the Pacific. They had a limited window, Lloyd knew. They would want a complete data dump from the computers for analysis and that there'd be no time for table talk.

The Orbiter sustained loss of all hands, except Paterson. Possible heat, radiation. Gemini crew aboard orbiter. Gemini in tow. Orbiter airframe 60% - repeat 60% - metal burns, particle encrustation, high electromagnetic content. Computer transmitting data code 22301."

"Receiving code 22301...long duration flight mode...missile launch Siberian Sea, origin unknown, report damage..."

"Damage to Gemini crew minimal, increase readings of carbon radiation. All systems OP 403 mode, life support sustaining."

"Ea....transmit...report...*Hydros*...override...communist..."

The transmission was already breaking up. How much they had received from the computers was anybody's guess.

"Control, *Hydros* seems okay. No visible dysfunction except for surface encrustation on unidentified substance. Next orbit for communication"

"Ea...Check...systems.

 Repeat...re-entry...all systems"

"Communications deteriorating" reported Lloyd. "Will check all re-entry system. Stand by for status of re-entry systems on this code trajectory next orbit."

Lloyd tried for several minutes, but he knew it was over. He had chosen to use the headset to talk, and now he took it off slowly. The rest could be recorded for replay later.

Paterson was standing behind him. He looked up and smiled reassuringly.

"Go get some rest while you can. At least they know we're here!" he added gamely.

She tried to smile, unconvinced. Her eyes darted.

"Relax! We made contact didn't we? They will be waiting for our next transmission. Everything will be all right." He reached for her hand and squeezed.

Paterson had been stranded up there too long. Her eyes gave her away. She swam backwards in a wavy motion.

She was struggling. Dehydrated, a few tears came anyway, tiny goblets that floated in the weightless atmosphere, each one carrying her despair.

Lloyd got up, and pulled her down for a hug.

"I'm sorry" she said, embarrassed. "I'm so sorry..."

"There's nothing to be embarrassed about" he said.

They floated together, and she clung to him.

She had not been trained by NASA. She had not been trained at all, he knew.

They floated, both suspended in a capsule of air-flight technology that circled the earth at eighteen thousand miles per hour. Her tears were allowed, he thought. Then, pointing to the mid-deck ladder he said "Get some rest! It's alright."

Lloyd sank back into the pilot's seat and began a comprehensive status analysis of all systems. He assessed all capabilities and dysfunction. Finally, he played back his conversation with Control.

Surveying the array of flight cabin switches above him, Lloyd let his arm suspend freely, and he took a long breath.

In the silence that attended this situation, he felt isolated.

Reality was offering little hope. There were too many unknowns.

"Do *what* now?" said Gottlieb.

They were on the road to the airport. He was perched, for all the commodious driving, on the edge of a soft fold-out seat of the limousine, laptop on his knees, papers strew along the deck seat facing him.

"Please pay off his bad loans. Look over all the farm mortgages and increase their rate by two percent! Then encourage refinancing applications with half as much money down payment!" said his boss.

"That's somewhat of a contradiction in terms isn't it? If new business is what you are soliciting here..." said Gottlieb, looking up.

But Julian, seated in the recessed seat of the rear, was far away with his thoughts and gazing out the window, ignoring him.

"... And only farms over 1000 acres need apply, including all those once turned down by the local banks for financing! Solicit their business. Waive crop insurance costs!"

"I hope you know what you are doing" said his attorney. "That's a hell of a lot of cash out there, plus reserves. What if they have another drought and can't pay?"

Julian DePhillipe looked at him.

It was clear in his face that he had nothing but contempt for conventional players. Too predictable, he once said, well-trained technocrats and policy-abiding administrators. But no imagination. No vision.

Gottlieb included.

"Precisely my point..." said DePhillipe with a nasal flair. His contributions to conversations came in languid sneers.

Not that Gottleib was far wrong, but his face remained uncertain. And Julien demurred just a second, attempting to calculate the distance between his inventive ideas and the judicial bar that guided Gottleib.

Gottlieb could have no way of knowing that it was *precisely* those drought conditions and subsequent foreclosures that DePhillipe was counting on.

In fact, DePhillipe already had prospective buyers for the depressed land which he could resell at a handsome profit.

"Don't worry Max! Talk to Ralf and his group. They've been working on this for days. And it looks good. Let's leave the accounting to the accountants. It's all I can do to handle everything else!"

"Right!" It brought a courteous smile from Gottleib.

They got out, and shook hands. Julien boarded the plane.

By the time Gottleib sank back into the rear seat of the limousine after the Jet took off, he dabbed his forehead with his handkerchief, feigning heat as he waved the driver on.

∞

In the last twenty four hours, they had stabilized two computers; re-established critical functions in the Orbiter's operations and surveyed all malfunctions. It was a beginning to containment.

They had eaten, rested briefly for rehydration, and entered a crisis report. Then with Karen's assistance, they respectfully tended to the crewmen who had perished, preparing their bodies to return to earth.

Another brief rest followed. Then most importantly, they collected sufficient evidence to demonstrate that they had been assaulted by sudden blinding radiation and heat, if not contamination...

One EVA was dedicated to an inspection of the exterior, and specifically, the payload.

As *Eagle* passed over the Pacific on her next orbit, White Sands New Mexico's signal started to come in. Lloyd was only too happy to deliver their first transmission.

"Houston. This is the *Eagle*. We read you!"

"*Eagle*, this is Control. Congratulations Gentlemen on your Attainment! Communications check"

"Roger Control!" said Lloyd with sanguine calmness.

"*Eagle*, this is Control, report status OMS, re-entry systems check, over"

"Roger Control" the static was clearing.

"Good to hear the voice of an old friend"

"That's a Roger" came the reply.

Based on their findings, and even with much of their observations already transmitted to CAPCOM, they knew they were on a short transmission. It ended abruptly.

"What I don't like" said Tim, "is that whatever this was that occurred, hit the Orbiter more than once!"

"Repeatedly!" chimed in Karen.

"I agree" said Lloyd. "In fact, I think its timed..."

"If so. Should we expect another?" asked Tim

"Assuredly" said Lloyd. "We need to prepare for it and defend ourselves as best we can..."

"How long do you reckon?" asked Tim looking at Karen.

"I'm not sure" she said. "I considered it a random occurrence..."

"Perhaps" said Lloyd. "But based on the spikes and electrical current signatures that showed stress points, I'd say it's periodic. If my calculations are correct, I'd say we have another one due in approximately one hour and thirty five minutes."

"Are you certain?" asked Tim.

"Pretty much. Here, look at the data."

"My God!"

They readied themselves with every possible precaution.

The onslaught came upon them without disappointment, wracking the Orbiter with vengeful oscillations blinding sunlight refraction that seemed spiked all temperature readings. They held on as they recorded the event.

"This is *Eagle*, at code 301, 17.23.8 Zulu... predawn experiencing high levels of heat radiation, similar to previous Failsafe Shutdown."

How much of this Control was receiving was anybody's guess. Lloyd knew there had to be extraordinary static. He would continue sending the transmission anyway. As long as there was life aboard the ship, they would be sending a transmission to earth. Their beacon signal might be picked up.

  "Whatever we have... is sticking around, with increasing temperatures. Out"

Two hours later, with Lloyd half asleep at the Control and the space ship evidently approaching an orbital position from which signals could be heard, a response came.

"*Eagle*.   Transm....unclear.   Repeat...readings,   systems status.."

Ok. They got the signal. They knew the ship was viable. Clearly, they wanted to know about re-entry before losing contact.

 "Control, this is *EAGLE*, re-entry systems Operations 302 confirm, APU check, OMS check, hydraulic exterior unconfirmed."

"...confirm status...over."

"We're experiencing increase in temperature, carbon radiation per mille-second into orbital sunrise."

Lloyd had submitted a full report on their finding once they came aboard, and assumed that Mission Control had processed the information and sequence of events. Only astronaut Karen Patterson was alive and well on board the Orbiter. He was about to say more when Tim, reaching across the computers, yanked at Lloyd's arm. He was pointing to the trajectory radar display. The evidence was unmistakable.

"Control, this is *Eagle*, we identify a foreign object within our path of trajectory, please confirm?"

There was no immediate answer, and with the window of opportunity for communications closing, Lloyd wanted to waste no time. Then something else caught their eye on radar modules.

They was passing quickly beyond the point of communication and would soon lose the link with earth on this orbit. So Lloyd jumped to a conclusion that sounded even stranger to his analytical mind than he realized.

"We're being tracked by a manned spacecraft, please identify."

Control didn't respond.

Tim flipped a switch to the onboard computer for identification. The computer came up with the requested identification, thought it took them a few seconds to confirm.

"Control, this is *Eagle*, we identify a manned spaceship tracking our orbit - computer identified it as Sarbo Class capsule. Please come in, Control."

"Roger, *Eagle*, this is Control. Sarbo Class is a Soviet made capsule. We need to know if intentions hostile. Code Orange. There is no schedule from Russia. Over"

"That's great!" laughed Tim Martin "And I thought the Cold War was over! Who in the world has dredged up a dinosaur like that - and for what purpose?"

"I don't know who that damned capsule is. But it doesn't matter anyway, 'because what we're looking at now is an orbital sunrise that could cook us if these temperatures don't stabilize."

"So what do we tell Control? 'There's a renegade capsule tailing us to see how long we last?"

"They must have made their own assumptions."

"What about asking them for help?"

Both men looked at each other.

"We're it!"

"Control, this is *Eagle*. Temperature readings approaching condition critical. Will attempt to communicate with approaching capsule. Switching to air-to-air frequency. Out."

"Do you think they heard?"

"Hard to say at this point. Anyway, here we go."

"This is United States Shuttle *Eagle*; Transmitting to Sarbo capsule, orbit 034854. Please identify yourself."

"Maybe they're little green men from Mars" said Martin, his voice tensing up.

"Little green men from Mars crossing your orbit at 17,000 miles per hour usually tell you they're coming long before you sees'em!"

"This is United States Shuttle *Eagle*, transmitting to Sarbo capsule, orbit 034854. Please identify country of origin. Please state your intentions. Over."

The light at General Purpose Computer mode five lit up on standby. The little numbers spewed out like nervous darts, changing, rearranging, and signaling. At this speed, in some proximity there was cause for alarm. It was clearly warning.

Lloyd hit Three plus One on CRT screen number three to display Flight System Guidance Navigation and Control Memory. There, clear as daylight, was *Eagle*'s projected path, with a tiny oncoming blip. He punched for the point of intersection.

The CRT number Two screen showed up: Position of 28 degrees, 36 minutes, 30.32 seconds north latitude and 80 degrees, 36 minutes, 14.88 seconds west longitude. The two lines would intersect in two minutes and 10.15 seconds, and counting...

"He's either sending us a message in a bottle -" began Martin

"- or... he's just launched a missile," finished Lloyd.

 He switched back to Control for what he knew was a fading transmission.

"Sarbo class capsule presumed hostile. Unidentified projectile to cross at 30 degrees north latitude and 80 degrees, 1.53 minutes, 13.99 seconds west longitude." Lloyd switched off.

"Nothing more we can do there." He looked at Martin "We can't sit here like ducks..."

Lloyd was already changing the computer code for orbiter attitude change. "We'll turn on the aft-burners. We've got to be able to move this sucker. Like now!"

"Are you serious?"

The two men stared at each other. The ramifications were enormous. Each flight was scheduled for a specific number of orbital changes and maneuvers.

 A burn attitude was usually reserved for de-orbit and re-entry. "We need the gas for later Lloyd..." began Martin.

"There won't *be* any later if we sit here. I need your support. Besides, there's plenty to get home with. Trust me!"

"Check your temperature peaks. They coincide with orbital sunrise! That's when you'll need maximum protection. Position for ample thermal protection from the sunrise!"

"14.59 to impact" said Tim to the numbers on the computer

It took Lloyd a second to decide. "Proceed with OMS. Arm for burn to position for maximum protection tiles allowing... Check: That bugger may burn us all alive...Shields up!"

"Roger."

"Check aft left and right RCS all four"

Martin reached for the overhead controls panel 07 and 08 "Roger."

"Check Tank Isol switches - all six"

"Roger."

"Check Cross feed switches - all four"

Lloyd continued barking commands lifting switches Left and right for OMS Engine Stats. " Vapor Isol all four"

"All go: Aux power unit prestart Check"

"Roger"

Lloyd pressed the bottom "Execute!"

 "So now that we're burning fuel, where to Skipper?" said Martin

"Computer check for elliptical sunrise position to orbit."

"Roger"

"Can we get HRSI in attitude to deflect heat impact from the sun?"

"What?" asked an incredulous Tim Martin. "Since when is a harmless sunrise a threat?"

"Since it killed the last crew!"

"You're not buying that theory?"

"I can't take that chance. Look at the data. It took them by surprise: Surges exceeded the Orbiter's thermal protection system, the sun and something else maybe - anyway, we're not sticking around to find out without some heat shield protection."

"Can we handle it?"

"Orbital Maneuvering Systems show a good supply of monoethyl hydrazine and nitrogen tetroxide for RCS. And all three engines are good. We can handle it. Attitude check?"

"It's too late for HRSI for maximum heat shield protection, perhaps LRSI before full impact. Surely the temperatures won't exceed 175 degrees...."

"Computer program OPS 304. Enter it!"

"Yes, sir!"

"Orbiter temperature rising to 100 degrees. Execute attitude to point of intersection. Enter"

"Roger"

"ADI shows roll zero degrees; pitch 28 degrees 39 minutes; yaw zero degrees."

"Temperature of orbiter 150 degrees...."

Low Temperature Insulation tiles was positioned on the forward fuselage, outer wing areas, pods and stabilizer. The Obiter was maneuvering slowly.

Too slowly.

The first glints of daylight peaked over a dark ball, and what should have been a normal sunrise turned into a blistering furnace, as if the craft were flying right into the sun itself.

Without protection from her ceramic tiles, the Orbiter would burn up. The question was, could the insulation tiles be positioned for protection in time. That is, if the assumptions were correct.

It was one hell of a gamble and Lloyd knew it.

"She's nosing up slowly" Amber lights went on.

"Temperature 165 degrees and rising."

Lloyd's voice was even. "TPS alarm activated, zone 3." He looked at the OMS burn rate and saw that fuel was roaring out the rear of his ship at a phenomenal rates.

"My God," muttered Martin. "We'll never make this...."

The computers tumbled through the numbers and permutations. On CRT # 3 the two lines were converging slowly.

"We'll make it Martin - just keep pushing!"

"Temperature 200 degrees, TPS alarm code 2," The alarm kicked on.

"Let's go, let's go," begged Martin as the lines closed - but not fast enough against the sun's unrelenting radiation.

"210 degrees..."

The Orbiter was functioning in temperatures beyond her design capability. Heat stress began to cook the packaging of payloads in the cargo hold. Paint started to peel off the airframe. Gaskets were buckling at critical joints.

"Okay. Okay" breathed Martin as the lines began to merge. "We're close...close....We're on!" he burst. "We're in LRSI mode!"

"Thank God." said Lloyd. "Post OMS burn activities, check"

"Roger"

"OMS burn complete!" said Lloyd triumphantly. "Now we wait and pray like we've never prayed before."

"The temperature dials showed 250 degrees

"My God," Martin whispered. "What's going on?"

"Temperature 275 degrees."

"It's like we've entered the earth's atmosphere without heat shields!"

"300 degrees..."

"Lloyd my friend," drawled Martin with deliberate obsequiousness. "You appear to be right about the sunrise. I've never seen anything like this in orbit before!"

"350 degrees...and we ain't seeing the sun yet! Visors down."

"I wish we had made it to RHSI...."

"There wasn't time Tim. Besides, we are on the point of being visited by our Sobra class missile...."

A sudden blinding light filled the Orbiter, and they shielded their eyes in a spontaneous gesture of self-preservation.

"Hold on!"

At precisely that time the sun, considered life of all life, fanned up over the horizon of the planet earth and flung the full impact of its rays across a dark universe to flash the Orbiter, flooding it with light.

The spacecraft glowed, a billion trillion sparkling diamonds glittering around her.

She was shielded behind her the low temperature abating tiles: A few more degrees of maneuvering would have given her the protection of her underbelly high temperature abating materials where she could have sustained temperatures of 650 degrees.

Would their present posture be sufficient against the onslaught of heat and light of the sun?

It was now only a matter of time.

∞

Tsung Hogun of the Republic of China was on the wired cell phone of his car.

They would come in wholesale mass packages, said DePhillipe from halfway around the world in clearly enunciated words via the interpreter.

"Very good. Good: Many acre-crop yield good crops for shipping down Mississippi River to Shanghai docks, yes?

"Yes"

"A Good yielding soil" reiterated DePhillipe indulgently

"Of course with capital to recondition if there were drought conditions, but of course you *are* buying at bank depressed prices" he added with a polite laugh.

"US Land as Toxic Assets, Yes?" came the Chinese response after a while to inform the vendor of his buyer's awareness.

DePhillipe smiled to himself. How should he put it?

"Well of course you know how efficient our farmers are in this country?"

"Of course. Of course. Yes... high technological productivity maybe 180 bushel of corn per acre. Very extremely good!"

"Yes!" He paused

"There are plenty of financial institutions to assist, including the Federal Government. But if God produces a drought -- and we are due a drought according to some atmospheric statistics, I would be in the unhappy position of calling in all my mortgages and looking for another buyer for the farms, you understand."

DePhillipe waited. The hook was baited. He held his breath.

"So we buy land if it fails...to make any payments Mr. DePhillipe!"

"Well of course this is all speculation Mr. Hogun..."

"Ah. No Speculation! We write back-up Contract of Sales in Hong Kong for all potential failed mortgages. You sign yes?"

"Yes" Julian smiled, the kill complete.

How many banks in the United States he wondered, had back-up contracts sitting in vaults in Hong Kong for all the mortgages they had underwritten? Nice work.

The irony of American grain lands owned by Chinese to feed Chinese was delicious: Title to productive crop land was something the Chinese would not give up without a battle in an international court, especially with their populations outgrowing their own food supply.

All he had to do was guarantee a drought in the Mid Western United States!

From the plane window he saw a horizon softly curved in the distance. What was it Villas once told him? The conquerors of ancient civilizations were gods! Yes, he thought.

It was cloudless as they touched down. Julian stepped out of the plane, taking in the tropical air, and strolled like a panther purveying his turf.

Verkho, from Moscow was on the line, said his assistant trailing up with a phone. It was an unexpected call, and Verkho was never an easy man to please. Julian immediately regretted his impatience on the line. But it did surprise him.

"Villos has invited me to Cuba for the wait..." he explained

∞

Chapter 4

St. Petersburg.

Not far from the new home of the Russian Stock Exchange, a big event was taking place.

Today, the Western world was holding its annual Economic Summit meeting on Russian turf, as if to amply the significance of the event, the World Bank and International Monetary Fund were also holding their annual meeting at the Palace of the Czars. Later that evening, a gala would be held at the Hermitage itself, a palace built by Catherine the Great in the 18th century.

Andrei Promisor left his small enclave at the Moscow State University and hopped the efficient subway that took him under the Moscow River and into the Kremlin. Almost everyone on the crowded metro was engrossed in a book or magazine.

Vladimir Petro left the academy of Sciences and took the tram up Dimitrov Street past the Church of Ivan the Warrior. To his right he could see the cupola of the Tretyakov Gallery. He crossed the river, vapors rising from the heated Moscow Outdoor Swimming pool which lay across the embankment from the British Embassy.

Everywhere the noise of power tools and construction filled the air. Moscow was a city on the advance, and modern apartment buildings could not be built fast enough.

When he reached the Kremlin the late afternoon sun shone off the golden towers and peaks of the five domed Archangel Cathedral where lay many tsars. He paused, even held his breath at this striking assemblage of historical events. He smiled to himself: If history was about to play another hand here, he was in it.

They met at the Soviet Writers' Union Club. Hardwood panels, beams and overhead galleries loomed over animated table talkers. Smokers laughed and listened; students hunched over dinner plates and drinks. It was a place of intellect. And coffee.

Andrei and Vladimir met in the entrance and were hailed over to a far table where Voznesenky and Lyubimov were eating. This was a celebration, and as the evening wore on, Lyubimov received several and sundry impromptu toasts and jokes about his latest film production.

He raised his class "The west has its Hollywood, but we have a cultural richness that surpasses all!"

They remembered, all of them, the effort that their people had made during WWII. Sons and daughters of returning Soviet soldiers, ally of the West, they struggled with the remains of a culture exploited and plundered first by their own countrymen in revolutionary fervor; then by the enemy over territorial boundaries, then by a world developing new economies...Bypassed, they were swallowed up in the maws of socialism. All of it manipulated by a Media war of words and propaganda. Words that robbed men of their lives; women of any joy, and aspiring young men a chance to compete in a global economy. Yes, they had their cultural richness. But their riches, once the envy of the world at the turn of the 19th century, had been sold for arms, guns and a cold war. How to reconcile the past?

George Andropolis arrived much later. He was heavier than the others, dark hair with black rimmed glasses, and looking every bit the Russian born Greek that he was. He was a man who liked to pick and choose the moments of his public exposure. It came as no surprise when George invited Andrei and Vladimir to his apartment for drinks less than half an hour later.

The apartment had very few furnishings for consumption. Only antiques clustered as warehouse. But there was no mistaking his inordinate wealth; every inch of his walls were infused with raw talent. Artwork in a crammed way. His home was a repository of avant-garde works of early 20th century Soviet artists - ignored or suppressed for years, and now on their way to a free market. And he would be the broker!

The room was prepared for a meeting. They took their places around a scrubbed oak table and Andropolis served them silver cups containing small glasses filled with sweet tea.

"My contacts in the financial world will begin to shift their investments from hard currencies into grains futures on our stock exchange by next spring. This gives me more influence over the financial institutions.

Andrei Promyslov shifted his position. "That's something the press should help with, and by the way, where's Peter?'

"He is working on a late edition. Never mind. Let him work. Together we will be meeting with Rubin tomorrow."

Vladimir finished his tea and put down his glass. "I am increasingly concerned about the international community. It's a matter of perception..." He took his time to fold his hands and face them both as if what he had to say was not a light thing.

"If we are perceived as unresponsive to the European community, then the flow of foreign investments into Russia might lose momentum, which of course would undermine our cause. Especially since Europe is following what the American's are doing and that is a shift of investments into specialized regional trends. This makes accountability of investments more highly visible. They will expect to know more of how we expend their investments.

They want to see regional "differentiations". Corporate generalizations will no longer be enough. Selling oil credits is not a small transaction...

"We *must* have DePhillipe change his track."

Joseph Rubin was dwarfed by the high-backed antique chair his position put him in. The desk had been the gift of Queen Victoria to Tsarovich Nicholas. Chairs, like all other furnishings and decorum, represented influence in the new Soviet order. A rising tide of tourists was pouring into the city. Soviets were overtly proud of their cultural heritage, having reconciled themselves with communism as being a "temporary aberration." Some even considered it a culling process, producing survivors of a nation destined to reshape the map of the world.

In this room, only capitalists gathered: This was a venture.

Like many of the survivors, Joseph Rubin had fared well. Of Polish parents, he had been taught to keep his head down and blend in. The sun will shine again, they would say amongst themselves in hushed tones over family dinners. Their values were vested in land ownership; trade and wealth as it had for over a thousand years. Regimes could be waited out. The meeting with DePhillipe was set up. The deal was on.

∞

DePhillipe walked into a room of gold and white renaissance splendor. The room was stuffy for Julian DePhillipe.

He smiled with all the generosity he could muster, even as he felt the sweat beading down the back of his neck. Opulence of this scale dwarfed him, and he was especially out of his league when it came to technical details.

The greetings were cordial.

He faced three of the richest men in Russia. They had influence. Between them, they represented most of the dominant sectors of Russia's social military and industrial complex. They also dominated the Russian space program.

"We must commend you Mr. DePhillipe on the successful execution of the mission!" said Colonel Vladimir.

"Thank you."

"May we offer you some tea?"

"Yes..."

"We are beginning to see subtle but significant changes in the climate of the tundra. We seem to be witnessing a steady melting of one inch per day. I did not think it was possible!"

Julian smiled.

"We trust that you are seeing drought conditions in the Midwestern United States?" said Vladimir, taking his seat.

"Yes" said Julian. He opened his leather briefcase and placed a file on the inlaid gilt-beaded desk. "In fact I have a Report on the precise technical data that may be of interest to you. My team prepared it for you. We are clearly in for a prolonged drought. The Americans are already experiencing massive crop failures and climatic aberrations."

"So our space program *does* serve this undertaking?"

"Yes, it does. As you can see from climate changes in the tundra. It is paying off well."

Julian was offered his tea. They paused, all of them sipping.

"We are concerned..." said Rubin sinking back into the high-backed chair "that in the event of those farm property failures due to arid conditions... there may be Foreclosures. Those...Foreclosures and financial failures, will you be tempted to sell those Depressed lands to the Chinese?"

Julian opened his mouth to speak. But the Russian raised his hand like an Imperial monarch.

They were one step ahead of him.

"Of course..." continued Vladimir "we would like you to know that if these lands were to go into foreclosure, we would be interested in buying them ourselves!"

Now they utterly surprised him.

"Being your partner" said Vladimir "we would expect first option...?"

Julian was silent. This was a turn of events he had not anticipated. *The Russians in the Midwest?*

His eyes flickered momentarily, his mind scrambling for an appropriate response.

"In the event of foreclosures..." he began "my bank would of course have to consider alternate financing options. And...err, I *would* need to consult with my investors and principles."

They smiled before speaking.

"...But Mr. DePhillipe" said Rubin "we *are* your investors - being as we are supplying you with the use of the Russian space program..."

"Yes of course..." said Julian, rearranging himself on his seat.

"What I mean is that we are talking about considerable equity since we hold several billion in asset valuations now, including the mortgages..."

Rubin got up slowly.

"What you are wondering Mr. DePhillipe is perhaps...*How in the world can we afford to pay you for these lands.*" He paused. "Is that not it?"

Julian smiled deferentially.

"Cash flow is the lifeblood of any banking interest..." he said magnanimously.

But Rubin would not be deflected. "It is no secret that cash is a crisis that Russia had struggled with for almost a decade..."

Rubin walked around the desk to face him directly, his hands folding decisively. "But we have Oil credits!"

"Oil credits?"

"Oil credits..." repeated Vladimir, taking his cue "are a commodity which Russia has in great abundance: Our wealth is still...*underground*" he said, relishing the pun.

Julian sipped the tea without responding, a tactic that had always served him well in tense negotiations.

They were patient.

"Gentlemen, I have no doubt that this is something which has great merit in the long term vision. However..." he took another sip of his tea and then fixed his bold blue eyes on them "I cannot pay my stockholders or my contractors with oil credits!"

They laughed and Julian's head nodded with them.

"Of course not!" said Rubin still smiling. "But you may well have a client who would pay you well for our oil credits!"

"Oh?" Julian put down his cup.

"The Chinese" said Vladimir, "they are in need of oil and we could be their supplier. But only if they agree to do so *with their interest* in your American croplands!"

Julian received the full measure of their intelligence. They knew about his contracts with the Chinese. They probably knew his profit down to the last hundred thousand dollars.

"I am not in the habit of being used as a broker" said Julian, his face reddening.

"But why not Mr. DePhillipe? Your brokerage fee alone would exceed the GDP of any small nation!" they smiled from their tea cups.

"Besides..." they proceeded "you have the Americans very upset at the loss of their shuttle, do you not?"

They gave Julian time to absorb the measure of their infiltration.

"So. Is there anything else you need from the technical side?" said Rubin bringing Julian back to the issue.

He said nothing.

"Our plans depend entirely on your continued success..."

"There are no problems?" asked Rubin.

Julian looked down.

"No? Alright then. The Americans have made no connection. It seems they will launch a second shuttle, the *Challenger* as a rescue mission. We will of course sabotage the *Challenger*...." He returned to the authoritative position behind his desk before continuing.

"But we may need to infiltrate NASA to a greater degree, and we may need more support against their intelligence gathering. Can you arrange that?"

Julian nodded.

"Then there is *your* government's continued denial of any involvement. Yes?"

They waited.

"So far, you have used our program to deployed missiles from the Polar cap, the Ukraine and Afghanistan...yes?"

DePhillipe looked at them.

"Further, we have operatives within the French *Arianne* space program. Perhaps we can make them available to you?"

"Yes."

"Is there anything else you need?" pressed Vladimir. Julian would have liked to ask them about security at the graphite mines, but he had been played...

"No. Everything is under control and on schedule!"

He shook hands then left the room abruptly with his fists closed tightly at his side.

Rubin smiled at his colleagues then walked out the door to deliver a press conference about the success of the economic summit. That night, he promised, the celebrations in St. Petersburg for all finance ministers gathered would be spectacular.

∞

Breezes off the Potomac River usually dissipated any humid haze hanging over the city, but Washington D.C. was sweltering in 91 degree temperatures. Tourists roamed around Corinthian buildings searching for icons that represented the democratic process.

At the US Navy Yard, three "greybeards" huddled over an intercepted message culled from Langley. Old hands, each retired from government, they'd been called in as a precaution. It took them an hour to settle down to business, their reunion animated.

The paper before them was not lengthy.

It was a routine personal message sent from the Captain of the Russian Submarine Tolstoy, un-coded, uneventful.

Further, it was classified as a non-military message and downgraded to secondary schedule of intelligence. It was almost dismissed.

The message was to the Captain's wife, wishing her a very happy birthday while she vacationed in Cuba at the home of her brother Julian DePhillipe.

The message transmittal was not the problem. It was the *Tolstoy*.

She was a dated submarine considered out of commission. The Russians had claimed the vessel mothballed, and all the evidence was there to verify that fact.

The probability of wrong identification was ruled out.

Yet the *Tolstoy* had just launched a missile from beneath the polar cap at 2200 hours GMT, 1800 hours Eastern Time.

The Whitehouse was not informed until daylight because the missile was considered unarmed.

Still, even an unsanctioned test-firing, albeit unarmed, was cause for alarm in Washington, even before examination of illegality or breach of any disarmament Treaty.

The possibilities had to be weighed.

Had the Chinese purchased the *Tolstoy* from the Russians?

That presented an entirely new spectrum of problems.

The NSA had informed the Pentagon that NASA's eyes were off-line.

The Navy volunteered the *U.S.S. New Jersey* to take a closer look: She could be diverted without alerting any observers of New Orders. It was a simple matter of expanding her range of her exercise maneuvers...

But there were technical problems with the ship just now. The *U.S.S. New Jersey* was in the middle of her Upgrades and Alterations, explained the Navy Yard...

"Options?" asked Stanley, looking up with eyes as blue and lively as they had been throughout his long career. Especially when facing a challenge.

Since WWII the British held Naval Offices in Washington DC for certain branches of operations. The three men emerged, briefcases in hand, walking around the Embassy Rotunda towards their parked cars, much as they had for decades. Nothing had changed. The British Embassy in Washington DC was familiar turf to these three men.

By thirteen hundred hours GMT, from the High Admiralty Command of Her Majesties' Royal Navy Offices in Britain, a coded message had been sent to the Rear Admiral in Command of a Trident Submarine, submersed.

Less than one hour later, her ballast spurted a few low bubbles, and she rose gently from her positioning at the China Sea.

"Mr. Ambassador, Sir" said Harry Wayson handing over the file "you have a Top Clearance communication Sir"

"Thank you Harry..." said Trevor, his eyes focused at the laptop at his desk.

Wayson saw the red button at the telephone console light up. He picked up at the side desk of the office and answered with a few terse nods of his head. He turned, the phone still in his hand "And, the American Ambassador called to see you Sir!"

The British High Commission in New Delhi India was one of the largest UK Delegations overseas, yet it was a security nightmare. It was a sprawling compound for community family members, one well infiltrated by local personnel. Not that the host country was not friendly, but there were some secrets best not shared in a temperate zone of high stress stakes.

If Allies had to talk, they talked face to face.

The British Ambassador read the file in the few minutes remaining before their meeting, he examined the wording. Trevor MacDonnell did not like the coded message.

Neither, evidently, did the Americans.

"The American Ambassador Sir!" said Harry by way of announcing

"Show her in" said Trevor.

∞

Julian DePhillipe was picked up at O'Hare by a grey limo. Within hours he was viewing the video of a conference of international experts on health, trade, and food aid.

By now, most had abandoned their professional posturing and were speaking with fretfulness and alarm. Others interrupted with wild speculations. A few were panicking as they watched graph projections of droughts, floods, cyclic changes in food production. Charts showed temperature ranges, economic indexes, and catastrophic incidents.

In the flickering darkness, Julian smiled. He waived his hand, he had seen enough. The lights went up and everyone turned to him.

"People are getting antsy..." said Rowens, Julian's first Vice President. "They want NASA to make a profound utterance - NASA, supposedly the ears and eyes of the stratosphere. Plus one dark weather satellite!"

"This is just the kind of thing that gives the Chicago Board of Trade the jitters," said Gottlieb.

Julian looked away from his lawyer. He was finding those comments increasingly predictable. "Especially stock companies holding large mortgages on farms that could see drought - to say nothing of the hit on crop insurance claims...."

"We are not in the crop-insurance business. And we don't need to generate capital from stock options!" said DePhillipe

"It is clear" continued Gottlieb "that NASA is frustrated with being unable to produce an explanation for their lost shuttle. It would help to answer questions about projections and for their space reputation."

They nodded.

"What is scaring investors now is the weather and the climate changes that can collapse fertile zones and render productive yields into arid land. Worse, melting tundra in Russia might surprise others! "

Julien smiled. "Yes."

∞

At the University of Maryland at College Park, Professor Jenkins tore off regurgitating data sheets from the printer. He had set up a math model that he'd entered yesterday.

And he stood there, a man in his 50's dressed not much better that the students he taught in his University classroom.

He couldn't decide a thing. His department operated on grants. Grants were government friendly. If there was one thing he did not like was statistical surprises. Surprises meant reporting to your authorities. So he stayed rooted to his spot, reading.

Surface water temperatures of the Indian Ocean and Pacific were warm; rain over the oceans, okay. Snow-cover in Eurasia was a massive good... So why did he feel like throwing up? He stomped over to the coffee machine and poured himself another cup.

The phone buzzed at him from deep within his office. "Shit!"

Marie answered the call and offered to take a message. He stomped passed her desk and she knew not to say a word.

"Call Dr. Fumosa for me will you?"

"Doctor...?"

"Fumosa. FUMOSA. At the FAO. As in Rome, Italy"

"Ok!"

Fumosa was not an easy man to talk to in Europe. With the split-second delay in satellite transmission, he was always talking over the words you had to say in response to what you had already said.

Finally Jenkins got to spell it out to the director of the World Health Organization.

"From the Alps to Siberia...a lot of rapid melting. We...No. no, *not* pre-monsoon drought effects. Just the opposite. Flooding, yes...I'll hold...hello? Dr. Fumosa...excuse me? Hello...yes, yes. Flood and potential disease...that's why I called—yes. No. I know you're anticipating drought..."

Formosa's voice was so loud that it could be heard across the room. So Jenkins put him on Speakerphone.

"....We're are already seeing an increase in locust reports and related disease....This morning I heard from your Atlanta Disease Control...twenty percent increase in malaria cases reported ...Brazil and Peru. What concerns me about Africa is that we've been so busy with drought operations that we have nothing in place for flooding if the dams are breached. And, as you know, on those plains there is nowhere to hide....However, at this point, I'm not alarmed...."

Jenkins hung up.

∞

Lloyd and Tim Martin hunched over the schematics like brooding witches.

NASA's Space shuttle *Courageous* was due in 24 days, surface time; *Eagle* could last that long and full contingency plans for the two shuttles were being defined.

Next order of business was critical and immediate. Orbital sunrise was due in 34 minutes. *Eagle* was positioned for maximum protection, and Martin had bought them three good bypass options for maneuverability. Even communications with CAPCOM was established, if sporadic.

The prognosis looked good to Lloyd. All that remained was an explanation for a foreign object on their trajectory.

But there was something else that burdened him.

"Look at this" insisted Karen tapping the keyboard to magnify a specific schematic. Tell me what you see, okay?"

"Sobra's trajectory...It's on an orbit. Unmanned. OK...?" followed Martin

"Now look at these climate anomalies"

"So?" said Martin reading down the list. "I'm looking for some kind of consistency, some...some...*what*?"

"Weather aberrations" she said simply.

"Meaning?"

"They are fairly consistent. This is a cyclical event!" said Karen

"Look at the timing of the catastrophes. They occur close on the heels of ...*what*?" said Martin thrusting an overlay chart of the Sobra's orbits "Maybe some frequency that... grows with the intensity of the heat from the Sobra pass?"

"But the heat comes from the sun, at each sunrise right?" she said.

"Right" he agreed.

"Maybe not..."said Lloyd "Judging from the damage to the shuttle, it appears that the greatest impact of heat damage was on the port side of the ship. Only, how many times did the sun rise on the starboard side?"

They looked at him.

"So what you're saying is that there is something *else* causing the heat ...?"

Lloyd paused. He pointed.

They glared.

"Well. Well. Well" said Martin. "Let's send down our findings. We're approaching our window of communication with CAPCOM. Standing by...in 45, OK everybody?"

"OK" said Karen.

She floated up to her harness bunk to use her time for rest.

"Let's look at what we've got:" said Lloyd to CAPCOM "Thermal buildup, possible deflection, orbital sunrise, and no definable point of origin..."

"We read you *Eagle*. We're on it! Over"

They passed over, and would communicate at the next orbit.

They looked at each other. The transmission, if brief, was effective. Thank God!

Back to the drawing board. Again they exposed the data of their research, then mulled their analysis for more thoughts.

Something was missing, thought Lloyd.

Karen was up. It was getting cold on the Orbiter. How many more assaults they could handle was questionable. Any small dysfunction might vary the internal cabin conditions for sustainability. Certainly, it felt like a sharp contrast to the heat beatings. Above all was the uncertainty.

She stood rubbing her arms at the elbows, perhaps feeling a little chill. Or was it fatigue?

Martin gave her an assuring tap at the shoulder. She smiled gamely, her eyes hollows and her face dehydrated.

Staring at the computer simulations of what had occurred at each sunrise, she reached down and typed for a wider schematic showing the vessels and potential directional flows in thermal charts. She wanted to show Martin possible parameters, a wider schematic of any earth effects.

Martin froze for just an instant as he noted an inflection in the thermal flow, a potential lag. But it was inconsistent. A wild thought crossed his mind. Highly improbable. He punched in for the atmospheric flows beneath them.

"There it is!" he spat. "Atmospheric ripples. Would you look at that?"

Karin strained. "Okay: So atmospheric ripples from what?"

"Us!"

He punched in for lower atmospheric ripples and asked for analogies... The computer dumped eclectic data. And there it was, a clear pattern of reflective thermal wave converging on one spot.

 They looked incredulously. How can that be?

"What's it saying?" said Karen

"There is a deflection effect going on. But it's thermal"

"My God..." said Martin "We're *are* it! The destination is this point: The sun is the source of the heat. But *we're* the refractor!"

"What? The *Eagle*?" asked Karen "But that's impossible! We are a moving target!"

"No" said Lloyd. "It would only need a fixed collection proximity. It appears to be concentrating in this site...like a cloud, Wait. Around us?"

"Hold it, hold it. What are you saying?" asked Karen

"What if the sun is heating up this cloud to deflect heat off aiming at one point of the earth's surface?"

"What for?"

"This! Take a look: We're on a near geosynchronous orbit with earth right?"

"Right"

"So we're looking at one concentration of heat. One refracted thermal impact upon the same spot at every sunrise."

"Right. But that would burn a hole in the ozone layer at the *same* focal point" said Martin.

"Exactly!" repeated Karen "And cook the earth beneath it if there were no even dissipation by the ozone layer..."

"But it would need a substance!" insisted Karen.

"Judging from the crud that caked the external body of the Orbiter, we have a substance."

 "What?"

"Some kind of ...of...Dust?"

"...Stand by" said CAPCOM when they explained it all.

"...We will run the numbers down here and get back, *Eagle*. If you are right, then we have a problem."

"And so look at this" said Martin "The geographic point of refracted heat is specific. Siberia!"

They stared, Martin Lloyd and Karen, trying to absorb the impact of what they were seeing.

This was too much speculation for Karen. "But it would eventually, like soon turn it into a desert...Right?"

"Not if you can turn the sun on and off at will." Replied Lloyd.

They looked at each other in disbelief. Finally, it came.

"The sun's rays turn upon this carbon particle cloud, which increases temperature and acts as a giant parabolic reflector of thermal concentration upon one consistent spot on the surface - geosynchronous orbit remember - and voila!"

"But that would play hell with the rest of the earth's climate...look at what it does to the jet stream over the Midwest during the projected summer path, it keeps if from flattening out; winter path with summer rainfall shifting to the east coast..." began Martin, dispensing with the rest of the sentence.

"My God. All that mess down there is no random act of nature. If it's a pre-meditated act of...of...what? Climate tampering..?"

"Who... *Why*?" began Karen.

"Whoever gains from these conditions," said Lloyd tapping into the computer for questions about temperature rises in that region.

The answer stunned them. Siberia would become "... a temperate zone ideal for crop cultivation"

"...and destabilization of the rest of the known food suppliers..." added Cappachutto at CAPCOM. Stand by *Eagle*. We'll be back to you!"

They waited. Something didn't quite fit.

Let's back up here" Lloyd insisted "As long as these carbon particles are heating up and acting as a reflector - but wait, - sooner or later this cloud would disperse wouldn't it?"

"Why? The damned thing is being replenished with routine deliveries by our friend that Sobra capsule!"

"*What*?" said Karen. "What is this stuff anyway?"

"But if the deliveries are stopped...Then this cloud is inert, something must be drawing *in* the sun's rays. Like a supplemental refraction point?"

Lloyd triangulated for sunrise, refraction from the cloud and tandem atmospheric concentrations upon earth. Like a happy child solving a puzzle, the computer came up with a simple answer.

They stared in disbelief.

"My God!" said Karen.

"*Hydros*!"

"Yup" affirmed Lloyd.

"Who's doing this crap?" said Karen.

"Them!" said Lloyd pointing to the data sheets showing the Sobra class capsule.

"And when are 'them' due again?" asked a skeptical Martin. "At maybe 1800 and some..."

"If *Hydros* is the thermostatic control, and re-appropriated by another party, then we'll take it out of the sky!"

"How?" begged Martin "EVA in that visibility is suicide and long shot without transmission capabilities, even if we knew which plug to pull."

"*Courageous*" smiled Lloyd."

∞

Lloyd had already reached some sobering conclusions. He wanted to discuss them with Martin after Karen Patterson turned in for her nap.

"I don't like this any better than you do. But there is no other way. Cappachutto has his hands tied. Nobody knows squat about what's going on up here, and there is no political incident that this can be hung on. I'm convinced that this is not an isolated problem, it's tied in with something else, and we've stumbled into it. Whatever's causing this thing is being manipulated from earth. And we're not solving a thing 'till we find the source down there."

"That's great!" said Martin. "So we come all this way to reconnoiter a ship, find one crew, press a few buttons, decide all is hopeless, and abandon ship and its sole survivor?"

Lloyd swallowed and waited for a few more assailing accusations. Martin's reaction was understandable.

"What do you say to Patterson? 'Thanks for the coffee, see ya!' That's not my way" growled Martin.

A sudden transmission interrupted them.

"*Eagle*. Come in. This is CAPCOM. Any thought about coming home soon? Over"

They ignored it.

Lloyd turned back to Martin "Not exactly. And that's not how it is. She'll be picked up by *Courageous*. She is trained for spaceflight. And she's stable. Martin. This isn't a natural phenomenon. It's man-made! We've never seen anything like it before." Lloyd let go of the handhold appendage and grabbed Martin's forearms so as to face him in the weightlessness of the mid-deck.

"We're it! We can't hide inside this technical machine. Look, if someone is tampering with environmental forces out here, there's a much bigger picture with awesome dimensions down below. Climate tampering isn't beyond our capabilities - you know it and I know it. Man has been fighting economic territorial wars since day one, using every technical advantage he can get his hands on."

Martin pulled free.

"Is this any different?" concluded Lloyd.

It took Martin several minutes to struggle with the reality. And Lloyd did not push. He knew what was going through Martin's mind. By training, they were astronauts, disciplined techno-gods. After all, 250 miles above the earth, they were performing admirably in the line of duty: It was easier to become preoccupied with a complex technical system which was more tangible, more solvable and a whole lot easier to die for, than some manipulating social cause of the day. Up there nothing lasted longer than one orbit anyway.

"*Eagle*..." asked CAPCOM. "Report findings...Over."

Martin let himself summersault slowly. When you train with an astronaut you don't have secrets. You have an obligation to be honest with the man you're flying with, he knew.

"How come she knows so much for a communications specialist?" he said finally.

"She had plenty of time for analysis. Besides, we were lucky. Our tiles shielded us from the source of heat. This is a safe posture to be in"

"She was the only survivor!" Martin was wrestling "So we leave her in the shuttle alone?"

"Yes!"

"CAPCOM" said Martin "Roger that."

"So where the hell do two able astronauts take on the enemy once we get back?"

"The trajectory of Sobra's reentry into earth's atmosphere would put her right here. She has a home Martin, and we're going to look in the windows!"

"Correction" said Martin "I'm going to look in the Window. You have bigger fish to fry in Washington!"

Lloyd looked like a man who'd been handed a sack of potatoes and told to start peeling.

There was no argument, he knew.

"Houston. Request for plan to de-couple from Orbiter. Over"

∞

Amanda didn't like her new mission. She worked for the United Nations in New York but, on account of the Climate policy changes, had to detach to Fumosa's office in Rome.

"I love Rome" she said to her family on the cell. "Don't get me wrong. It's just that the guy is...I don't know..." *Creepy* was the word she might have used, but instead chose the word "forceful". That was his style of management. And his effect on women.

"Yeah. Yeah..." she said with a sigh to the response about being in Rome and doing as the Romans....

But Rome, she later thought, was where you went when you were, well, in love! And the last time she felt love in the air was with the Moguls three centuries ago... Where parakeets flew and peacocks pierced the warm night air with faraway screeching.

She peered out the window. It was raining.

Europe could be drab in the rain she decided.

∞

The Summit had gone well. Topics of financial stability, sustainability, long term investment and global trade aired with specialists, panelists, policy makers and bankers alike. The final affair was a formal party in the ballroom.

Carina Bruneski wore a long black strapless dress. It contoured her body, the skirt slit to the thigh to expose provocative legs. Small diamond earrings adorned a face of angular features. Normally, it was her inclination to play down her appearance in order not to attract attention. Tonight however, was different. Tonight she was on a fishing expedition. With her blond hair coiffed in a braid above her head, Carina stood out like a Greek goddess made for a garden sculpture.

∞

The French ambassador was the first to engage in conversation. At his side was a colleague, Jacques de Touraine, Director of Special Projects at the World Bank.

Lord Halsingly of Great Britain joined them, the conversation had turned to the success of Summit, all expressing their admiration for the Russian economic contribution to the global recovery. Lord Halsingly's wife, heiress to considerable wealth in mining industries joined them, brining with her a staffer from the French delegation. He was introduced as a bright French economist Francois Bontemps with a proclivity for beach surfing.

"Oh really!" exclaimed Carina

"The only surf close to Washington is Dewey beach in Delaware, or maybe Assateaque Island in Virginia, if you call that a serious surf! "said the Frenchman, and he launched into a lengthy analysis of wave dynamics. Carina moved in.

"You must enjoy working in Washington, being an economist?" asked Carina, shifting gears.

"Econometrics! That's what I specialize in. Yes, I very much enjoy the position to identify aberrations where a slight tweak *here* affects consumers *there*...There is always a connection!"

"Or a storm *here* and the bananas *there*?...

"Oh definitely. You'd be surprised how seasonal conditions effect market economies" he said. "Analytics of benchmarks and trade balances can affect gross national products"

"Everyone is so very impressed with the Russian recovery; they seem to be a very dedicated...?" said Carina sipping her champagne. The Frenchman raised his hand to make points about their economy.

"Their stock exchange is very lively!" she nodded.

"Oh yes! And responsive. The Russian exchange for crop stocks occur almost simultaneously to variations of temperate climate changes, weather even upon some of the most hostile growing regions of the country!"

"Like the selling, acquisitions and mergers of the most fertile regions of the States?"

"May I have this dance? "interrupted Julian DePhillipe with his hand at her elbow, his long hair tied in a ponytail behind his head. They danced, she in her long dress, he in his tuxedo. A Foxtrot came up and he asked her "Shall we dare...?"

She looked him directly in the eye, a challenge. "We shall!"

The tall athlete and Carina made a stunning couple, and every head in the room turned to watch.

"What can possibly interest such a beautiful woman..." he asked with fixed eyes "in a Conference such as this?"

"Interesting men!" she replied without averting her gaze. She knew she was dallying with an alligator. He thrust her fiercely in a spin, then back onto his arm. They culminated to feverish applause.

Around them the finest art was available for sale, a collection, some said, of the finest new talent in Russia. And still the drink flowed ceaselessly to music and rhythm. Carina was losing control of the evening. Still, she asked the Cuban banker about his investments in the United States. It was a mistake.

Oddly, she felt mercifully relieved when Uri came up to DePhillipe and told him he had a phone call. He excused himself and asked her to wait for his return. Carina had an urge to retreat somewhere where she might regain her composure. But he was a compelling man, almost overwhelming this DePhillipe, and she thirsted for more. Just then, she turned and bumped into Fumosa.

"Carina" he said deeply, his eyes noting her flushed face and short breaths

"Mario!"

"Carina... What are you doing with this man? I want to talk to you!"

She stared at him.

"Shall we have a drink?" she turned, instinctively glancing for the face of DePhillpe

"Carina... you look so stunning!"

Her eyes turned stormy. "I need to talk to you later..." she began.

He stood in front of her, unmoved.

"Please. Mario!"

"It's all I can do to keep my eyes off you ..."he persisted.

A waiter passed by, and she firmly placed her empty glass on his tray.

"Please, Mario. Don't be foolish!"

He looked at her, puzzled.

She took her time.

"You are a distinguished guest here tonight. You cannot be looking at me that way..." She lifted her chin, smiled at a guest, then stepped back.

"Carina. There has to be a place for us!"

She turned to him and for a second, just a second, her eyes swirled with warmth before her expression changed. DePhillpe had just reentered the room.

She was stepping back.

"Where are you staying?" persisted Fumosa darkly

"St. Petersburg Hotel" she said. Anything to be rid of him

"I'll come to you there..." was all he could say before DePhillpe came within earshot.

Mario Fumosa blended into the crowd but did not take his eyes off her.

Later that evening, Carina left with DePhillipe in his limousine.

From above on the terrazzo, Mario Fumosa watched her bend her head to enter the limousine, the long legs and sequined black evening gown stepped into the car as the door closed behind her.

∞

∞

The morning was bright in the ancient city of Rome. Carina felt fully rested from the three day conference. She opened her balcony and took in the view of the old city, its domes white and its stone pink from the early sunrise.

Her flight was at 4 PM. Her team had left yesterday. Today was all hers. Perhaps she could take a walk in the city, or do some shopping before catching a taxi for the airport. She smiled...

 "Can I get you all to myself Carina..." had said Fumosa last night in the Hotel Lobby when finally she returned. Tomorrow? Perhaps a dinner in a quiet Ristorante, before you go?

Carina was surprised to see him there. She laughed and planted a big kiss on his cheek, rewarding his persistence with softness.

"You're wonderful Mario! How lucky I am to have you! Thank you for your kind hospitality to our Delegation this week!"

 "Lunch then?" he pressed.

Carina's room door called her inside from the terrace.

"You bags, Madam? At what time for your delivery to the Airport?" asked the bellboy.

She gave him a generous tip.

"Thank you, but I have a ride to the Airport with a friend!"

"Yes Madam"

She finished her coffee on the terrace and sighed.

Of course. Mario had found a way to spend a few hours with her.

He showed up early.

"Come on..." he waived, hailing his private chauffeur "I will get you to the airport in time!"

They pulled out of the lobby entrance and turned onto Piazza del Sole.

Behind them a dark green Mercedes followed.

She wore a white suit, a soft blouse and breezy hair, and he planted a small red rose at her lapel.

"There is a museum in town that only the invited can see.... and then, a lunch at a place where a friend of my family lives..." he was saying

"An Austrian Prince with a Russian vineyard?..." she laughed.

"La dolce vita, si?"

"Thank you. But no!" she looked at him directly "I have just enough time for a tour of the city, and then a quick lunch ...I'm a civil servant remember"

"O.k. If you insist" he said, settling back into his seat.

They toured a few shops.

"Nobody leaves without a Memento!" he said at a stall selling memorabilia. "Here...this one is made of fur, for your head to be warm."

They laughed. "Mario. It weighs a ton..." said Carina.

"Ok. Ok. This?"

He did make her happy. They settled at a lunch café shaded by deep blue umbrellas and gold trellised pillars. A family sat close by, their child was asserting his right to abandon his High-seat for a real chair. Tourists from Spain, they said.

"Va bene! Va bene!" said Mario to the parents "Che si siedi qui con noi!"

They laughed and he added "Ci sera anche piu un servizio di vino per il bambino!"

The boy looked up at Mario and grinned.

He wiggled off his seat, and turned to plonk his gelato at Mario's side, giggling, then sat with him and Carina.

The parents apologized, then conceded. They turned to their table, less than three feet behind their son.

"There is nothing more glorious to an Italian that the joy of a family" said Mario.

Carina smiled.

The waiter brought out their glasses on his tray, poured water and set the table with another two wine glasses and a few condiments.

It was warm, breezy, enough to flutter the fringes of the umbrellas. The boy slid off his seat and returned to his parents.

 For Carina, the ancient city was a cadence of people, traffic and motion swirling around them.

She was having lunch with Mario as he told tales of his family seated beside her in his blue silk cloth suite – striking a scene that no amount of shopping or tourist planning could compete with, she decided.

Carina placed her elbow on the table and raised her glass to take a sip. The boy turned from his family suddenly to stare at Mario. He then swiveled to retrieve the remains of his gelato from their table, and in so doing, reversed Carina's glass of water that spilled all over her white suit. She looked down and pulled back suddenly. It saved her life.

Suddenly in the ensuing hour, before she was rushed to the airport by Fumosa's chauffeur trained to do so in response to danger, she was too stunned to realize that this was no accident.

Two bullets had been delivered at their table from a car in motion. The first shot shattered the glass, the second missed its target.

It was the last time Fumosa would ever see Carina Bruneski.

Two months later a classified security message arrived on his desk. It was addressed from the CIA in Langley.

Her file status, it reported, had been stamped Missing in Action.

Her killer was identified as one, Uri Pravala.

∞

The last day that Amanda Wells saw her boss in Rome was the day he received a phone call from New York. Not that she meant to overhear, it's just that Fumosa was a loud man.

 "The Americans did *what?*" he said, standing at his desk with the speaker-phone On.

"They are using their military cover in Afghanistan to investigate the Pakistani border. For some reason, they are focusing on locals- turning-informants. So far, it has yielded nothing!"

"Tell them that we will issue a statement that is totally in opposition to that action" insisted Fumosa. "I don't care *who* we embarrass..."

"Mario, please! Put me on the phone with you only. .."

"Very well" Fumosa punched at his phone with such fury that it chattered along his desk.

He listened. "Ah!"

Nodding vehemently, he added "Non! Non! Non!"

Then again "Ah!"

"I don't care *what the Americans say*...It is not the way we can succeed at Outreach..."

He turned to look out the window, the phone still in his ear. "Very Well. Tomorrow then..."

He sat down, and the business at hand carried on at the office, if under new hushed and apologist tones. He seemed distracted, irritable.

Further, as Amanda noticed, the day progressed with less and less talk from her boss.

Clearly, he was agitated. His thoughts were subduing his outbursts and stealing his concentration. By the end of the day, he was downright somber.

The next day his office remained vacant, and he was unreachable by phone.

That was the last time she saw him.

It took a week in the office to absorb the fact that his absence left a vacuum. No explanation came from headquarters.

A void in leadership ensued.

No word on his whereabouts, nor his position on decisions could be ascertained as the office of Aid continued to meet its obligations and correspondence. In the absence of instructions as to how to proceed, they remained as consistent with past actions as they could. Pretty soon, the staff were making jokes.

Amanda had been in enough offices to recognize the symptoms of professional separation induced by sharp hostility somewhere along the hierarchy...

His personal belongings in the office suddenly had disappeared. Calls were re-routed. Personnel stayed away without offering answers. Eventually, his desk was cleared of papers and finally his office even remained unlit.

In the meantime, his e-mail traffic was redirected into their inboxes before they had a chance to delegate officially his duties.

Someone, somewhere, had enough sway in the chain of command to sweep away his impact, she observed. Fumosa had been a flamboyant Italian executive - chivalrous and gamely with the ladies, but a loudmouth nonetheless. And now he was gone without replacement.

She had waited a week for someone to call her in and issue new marching orders. But none came. By the end of the second week it became abundantly clear that she had taken his place by default. In the workings of non-profit organizations, that was rarely an issue since tasks tended to be deployed universally. But there were some necessary decisions.

And the true test came soon enough.

It had been a long morning already, and she wanted to go out to lunch. She invited the Accountant Mike Pulanski down the hall to join her, would he ready at lunchtime?

The situation was awkward as hell. Most of the files were still wanting to land somewhere if not in the Director's office.

She was more comfortable in her own office-garden around the corner, as she put it. But No! She had to sort through this stuff, and so it was that things fell entirely upon her shoulders to make the decisions for a phantom Department Leader.

Annoying as that was, she became less apologetic about sorting through his stuff with her own decisions: She rerouted to Communications all queries that needed routine answers. She appointed to Mary and Barbara items requiring some deeper research. She delegated to Andrea all matters of public relations. Some material was more significant than other... and some could wait, even if the pile was growing.

It was annoying her that she had to decide what was important, and what was not.

Increasingly she was viewing notifications that had patterns, like climatic aberrations. Or, just when she decided things settled down, statistics would come in by the megabyte, data that was copied to them by overseas delegations reporting on political governments; their organizational stability, policy and national leadership in regions under duress...

Today was such a day.

Twisters were ripping through Gulf of Mexico. Shri Lanka was appealing for flood relief. Zimbabwe was having critical drought conditions and already its 12 days of relief storage was in jeopardy; 15 million people were migrating...

Elsewhere, the mid-western United States was seeing drought.

At the same time, the Ukraine was enjoying unseasonably early spring rainfalls without explanation.

Further, the intelligence was coming in with increasing gravity.

Military shipments of food supplies were following large waves of military maneuvers, usually *outward* towards territorial boundaries... That was unusual.

  Finally, there was more Code Orange information coming into their office. Especially as it related to critical supplies of food globally and growing mortality...

Refugees maybe? More like terrorism opportunities, she knew.

And there was another problem.

Where was the source from which these images were coming?

A head popped in her doorframe.

"Where shall we go for lunch?" said Evelyn "Mike can't come! He's busy, so he sent me, ok?"

"Sure!" smiled Amanda, relieved. She would consult with Mike later.

"Oh God, let's go!" said Evelyn "Somewhere we can have a smoke and a drink!"

Amanda laughed. Evelyn was a tall English blond from Liverpool. And this was Rome.

"Well. Let's see…" started Amanda, their options few around their office corner.

"Nah! I think we take a taxi and go across town to a seedy little place of *real* Italian blood sausages?"

Amanda smiled and looked at her watch. "We don't have much time…"

"Bugger it… Let's go!" .

The city roared in traffic and noisy activity. They hailed a taxi, Fiat.

"Better than a Vespa…" chortled Evelyn as they climbed into the Mini, horns adding to the cacophony.

Lunch at the boulevard of Vittorio Emmanuel took them beyond their lunch range. It was worth it.

Not because of the food. Dinning amongst the venerated statues of Rome and Trastevere was extraordinary. Here, it was told, thirty thousand Jews had settled at the end of the first century, performing the wonders of Rome's greatest artistry and chiseled stone carving.

They chose a café where a "*un scritore*" wrote his words here, said the waiter, and in that corner… a famous painter his sketch…

Amanda began to smile. They sat down, she took in a deep breath as she looked around.

Until the sixteenth century these ghettos breathed the air of baroque workmanship. Here lived the underlying hands that worked the metals from filigree fretwork to tapestry, from gold to woodwork, from stylists' perfection to naturalism. Here, the skills of generations of Jewish artisans imbued Europe with imagination, casting fortunes for the Holy Roman Empire.

Emancipated in the mid nineteenth century, and ghettos long gone for *Uffici,* the contribution of Jewish people created the culture of the Middle Ages and the Renaissance, Amanda knew.

Nobody noticed the white car parked at the turn of the road. Neither the *Carabinieri* nor the tourists observed anything, not even the Traffic and Parking Monitors. Certainly not Amanda and her friend. It just sat there, silent as a tomb.

Amanda finished her calamari. Before them was fresh baked bread, warm dough holey and soft. Oil and pesto sauce lay in a white porcelain dish, black pepper and Parmigianino cheese in a bowl was for the pasta. A deep sweet red spaghetti sauce dribbled off linguini. A deep Chianti swirled richly in the glass. It was a culinary treat way beyond their per-diem budget.

Evelyn was grinning. *Lunch-hour be damned!*

The waiter approached with two cups of strong coffee and biscotti. He smiled widely for the two women.

As wine decanted from the straw flask, Evelyn become petulant, behaving more like an aggressive tourist than a friendly pedestrian. At least Amanda had persuaded Evelyn to sit outside and eat au-giardin. There was some sunshine. And people-watching was entertaining! In Italy it was all about high fashion...

"or *low* fashion" giggled Evelyn, pointing at walkers in flat heels; big hats, stern-suits. It was clear Evelyn was interested in looking at the men, especially those that looked back and...

The explosive blast ripped through the air and shot the street with projectiles. The shockwave burst through smoke and debris. Dust respired from every stone standing.

It was a full hour before they recovered. Dust and debris hung in the air. By then screaming sirens and the *Polizia* were pouring into the block.

Evelyn screamed out, if not in fear then in a stunned stupor. Amanda grasped her arm and they extracted themselves deftly from the street. That was Amanda's doing because more significantly to her, they were unharmed and safer to vacate the area.

Later, Amanda heard it was a car bomb. Two days later they offered the Polizia their witness accounts. By then, Evelyn had booked her flight home, and Amanda knew it was the right thing to do before she departed. However, as they told the police, they were little more than visitors in the area, and they could shed little light...

News got around. Within a week, she got a message from New York. She was being transferred. Non-essential personnel were recalled. Also, "Send up all Files"

As she boxed them all up, she wondered if there was any connection between the car bomb in Rome and the closing of ranks at the intelligence source material she saw. After all, Fumosa had vanished.

Probably not, she decided. Just timing. Except for some final tasks, her business would be concluded here.

Lloyd was on the phone.

"That sample you gave me caused us quite a thrill up here I tell ya!" said the Director of Materials Research, Ron Dylon.

"How's that?"

"You're right on one thing: it used to be known as space-dust. In fact it is space-dust!"

"Okay" said Lloyd.

"But it's one of the most beautiful things you can find on earth. A rare earth element"

"Beautiful?"

"Well, to a scientist. Some men define beauty in the arms of a luscious woman, others want more in- depth..."

"I get the idea" interrupted Lloyd

"Okay. It's a unique substance, an organic substance. It's a carbon - you know, as in the basic rare earth elements of life consisting of carbon, right?"

Lloyd waited.

"...But it's a *new* form of carbon. It has an interesting shape."

"Oh?"

"Yes. You own a soccer ball Lloyd?"

"I did once. Yes."

"It's the shape of a near perfect sphere - the highest possible symmetry allowed in Euclidian geometry! Each element contains 60 carbon atoms, arranging themselves in a pattern like a soccer ball with 32 faces composed of 12 pentagons and 20 hexagons."

Lloyd inwardly smiled at the enthusiasm of a scientist. "This elegant shape is stable, so *other* atoms can be attached to the outside ..."

"Do you mind if I share this information with my people at the Lab, Ron?"

"Be my guest...I'm glad to be of help!"

Two hours later, Lloyd left the lab with a ream of information. He took it all back to the office, and worked all night.

By the next day he was back in the lab. This time with a conference table of scientists.

In fact Lloyd invited Dylon to the meeting, and introduced the Director of Materials Research as he made his presentation about the substance analyzed.

Time was passing. Lloyd looked up at the clocks in CAPCOM. There was a ship in flight even as they spoke - one console actually showed the perfect waves of trajectories across the northern hemispheres. He needed to speed up his doting researchers.

"So what are they good for exactly, in space Ron?"

"What? Err...let's see. Applications.This substance, if described as particles is...What can they *do?* They are high temperature superconductors."

Lloyd consulted his watch and nearly cut him short.

"Actually, it's so simple, it's perfect. They're also a great lubricant - perhaps replacing highly refined oil on earth used in computer chips. Why? Because they can rearrange themselves with infinite and tight-fitting precision. We call it space dust only because we first saw it in space. Or buckeyballs."

 "An interesting concept" remarked Bill Finlay from the far end of the table "considering space was thought to be a vacuum!"

They laughed. "Vacuum my ass..."

"Can you simulate one in a lab?" asked Lloyd.

"Yes!" grinned Dylon "It's truly simple to do, and it yields promising properties. Take a rod of graphite, stick it in a vacuum chamber and run a current through it. So. The graphite vaporizes, producing a soot that settles inside the chamber. The soot is collected, run through a benzene bath and made to dry. Instant buckeyballs!"

"Instant *what?*" asked a Researcher at his elbow.

"Buckeyballs, we call them. Officially, after the architect Buckminster Fuller, who built geodesic domes that look like this diagram. Actually, they were initially identified by a physicist from Arizona, Donald Huffman and his German collaborator, astronomer Wolfgang Kratschmer of Heidelberg's Max Planck Institute. They were never seen on earth before! Now Rice and UCLA will tell you there's a source on earth. Apparently they are known to exist within rare graphite mines in Afghanistan, Pakistan, India - the Karakas mine maybe. High in the plateau regions of the Himalayan mountains. But we can't be sure quite yet."

"So to *vaporize* them, you'd need a vacuum, right?" asked Lloyd.

"Right."

"Then a current through them, right?"

"Right."

∞

Greenbelt, Maryland.

Washington was not happy.

"What I can't understand" said Colonel Brewer "is how NASA had no diagnosis for the symptoms *before* it became an issue."

Cappachutto was not surprised.

"Well, it's not a matter of diagnosis Colonel. It's a matter of determining the nature of something we've never seen before. We now believe this may be a very deliberate act of hostility"

"Hostility?"

"We've been all over that Tom" interjected the Admiral "And we can't identify the species of the beast let alone decide if it's hostile."

It was a long day.

Don Chairs was determined to quantify the problem in one simple dilemma. "What's more to the point Gentlemen, is that we've lost one shuttle crew; and we're launching a second shuttle into the same elements without knowing precisely *what* it is we're facing...It's the mission itself that bothers me. How to contain the damage and salvage the missions?"

"I understand. The question is, damage control? And how do we explain what we do?" Cappachutto looked at them.

Stevenson remained silent.

 The argument was going round and round aimlessly. It was time to jolt this bunch of boy scouts into real time. He put down his pipe, sat up in his chair and cleared his throat.

"We've looked at every possibility as exhaustively as we know how. God knows there are too many unanswered questions - and too little to work with. But work with we must!"

He had their attention, so he went on.

"Given that there seems to be economic turmoil at the uncertainty of things, plus climatic and atmospheric anomalies, we must assume that this is no accident. And until we have more feedback, we must assume that this is a hostile event and that we must take every precaution to protect and defend ourselves. It's that simple."

The room went silent.

There it was. The gauntlet was on the table! That assumption would put them on a risky footing, they all knew.

"That's great!" burst General Reynolds of the US Armed Forces. "Send in the troops to battle against an *undeclared* and *invisible* enemy? It's too soon!"

"Enough of that!" admonished Stevenson. "We'll have to brief the President based on our assumptions,.."

"And exactly *what* measure would you have us take to protect ourselves?" said the Admiral turning to Tom.

"Well," said Cappachutto, bracing himself for a full assault "we'll have to react as if something is threatening our spaceshield defense mechanisms."

"Oh, for God's sake!" said Brewer. "Send up nuclear bombs to disperse a cloud in space? That'll do wonders for our credibility!"

Cappachutto took a deep breath and delivered his final salvo. "Only if we assume that cloud is the source of havoc on earth and more specifically to our climate, temperature, food supplies, water level, and market viability...."

They all stared at him in disbelief. The correlation never occurred to any of them. The ramifications were sobering.

Reynolds spoke first. "Yep! That sounds like a threat to me. But we're only making an assumption. Besides, how do you fight a thing like that? With all respect Tom, I think that's a load of crap. NASA's going to have to come up with a better excuse than *that* for bungling two of our most expensive shuttles!"

He looked fiercely at each one around the table.

"If you'll excuse me, Gentlemen, I've heard enough. I've got another meeting." He pushed away from the table and walked out.

They felt stung.

Stevenson broke the silence.

"Is there anything you haven't told us Tom?"

Cappachutto hesitated, still reeling. He wasn't sure if he could take much more of all this...

He took a deep breath.

"Go ahead, Tom," said Brewer. "Reynolds is a crusty old soldier whose only interest is ordinance on target. You haven't given him much of a target."

"Okay: there *is* something else. A Sobra class capsule has been shadowing *Eagle* with uncanny regularity. She is considered inert, officially that is. We believe she's observing."

"She's transmitting a signal?" asked Stevenson

"Not that we can determine. Unless it's a very low frequency intermittent one. And that's something only *Eagle* could have determined if her systems were on line."

"A Sobra class? That's...err...let's see... vintage Russian you said?"

"Right. But that doesn't mean a thing. Those things could be bought on the open market!"

"What about the payload on *Eagle*. Her intelligence gathering?" interrupted Don Chairs.

"All down. But secure."

"Viable?" he insisted now leaning forward

"We can't rule that out entirely as a motive..."

"Observing *what*?" resumed Stevenson to Tom's line of enquiry, not one to miss a beat "What are you suggesting?"

"...the disbursements of carbon particles into the cloud near *Hydros*" responded Cappachutto

"Are you *sure* they weren't a random occurrence?"

"No. They must be observing the Shuttle. Two different occurrences" insisted Chairs.

"That's your opinion. Regardless. It makes no difference now anyway "said Stevenson. "It's a threat. So what do we tell the political leadership? That some 'scheme' is burning a hole in the ozone to heat up earth's surface somewhere?"

"That's insane" muttered someone.

"That's climate tampering "said Tom.

"This puppy is too complex to second guess. This is one thankless decision the leadership will have to call. I don't know what they will decide! They might break out laughing. Or they might arm a couple of nuclear warheads -- it's hard to say with these facts...."

"If there's *anything* more we can tell them from a technical standpoint?"

He looked around the table.

 "Gentlemen. Meeting Adjourned"

∞

The propitious call came in not a minute too soon for Lloyd. He wasted no time in re-establishing his credibility on the ground. He would deal with Oliver and Gates later.

"*Eagle*. Now listen up! We *are* going to bring you home."

Karen shut her eyes. Did it really matter anymore? "Roger" was all she said.

"*Eagle*, standby to receive Code 712. Information for your analysis."

She was tired. She didn't want to work. She didn't want to do anything. She was at that point known to sailors at sea who welcomed death as an alternative to continued stress.

"*Eagle*, this is Control. Do you copy data?"

She let the computer run the code and she wanted to sleep. It was hard to focus.

"A special crystal structure carbon, once known as 'space dust'. It has 60 molecules, hexagon in structure with various functions of form. Substance is formed in a vacuum. Dissipated by electrical impulse when heated and cooled suddenly. It changes form into a substance known as fullerene..."

"*Eagle*, this is Control. Do you copy?"

"Sorta. Kinda." she looked down in hopeless frustration. "...No!"

"*Eagle*, to change to fullerene it must be in a vacuum: Check. It needs heat: a nuclear explosion. Then it needs an electrical discharge: check. Then cool: return to space ambient temperature!"

She laughed out loud. This was too much. "How do you plan to introduce a bolt of lightning out here, gentlemen?"

"*Eagle*, remember aIC No. 6 of our mission?"

"Experiment to test static discharges in space? The Electronic Pulse Generator apparatus."

Karen was getting mad. They sounded like boy scouts playing with a tadpole.

"Control this is *Eagle*: First setting up such a chain reaction is well-nigh impossible even under normal operating procedures. Second, with two nuclear warheads on their way I'm not exactly in total readiness for much assault ..."

"*Eagle*, this is Control. Standby by for data."

Just what I need muttered Karen. The anatomy of a nuclear reaction.

The computer came up with a nice bell shape curve.

"Energy release mark. Light mark. 0.76 second delay. Explosion here. Release of Pulse Generator on the spin table, equipped with three photo electric cells which will be triggered by the light. Delay 0.76. Release electrical impulse simultaneously. "In other words, Karen, you can diffuse the whole damned cloud by changing its properties: One, heat from the nuclear explosions, two, electrical charge from Pulse Generator"

"Control, that's crazy!" she said

"Why? Karen, listen to me. Time is of the essence. It's a giant capacitor ain't it? It'll discharge an electric bolt like lightening once charged sending an electrical discharge through this fullerene substance, which will quickly reduce to cold space ambient temperature and dissipate into harmless 'space dust'!"

Karen laughed out loud and wanted to cry at the same time. "Nice dreamin' guys, but how do the nuclear bombs not blow me up?"

"Easy." She recognized Martin's voice. "You'll get a swift kick in the ass and fly in on slingshot elliptical!"

"And once I'm out of harm's way, how do I fuel up for reentry?"

Referring to Martin, Lloyd said "My co-pilot does it all the time, he likes to drive these babies home on a dead stick."

"Control she said indulgently and for the record "This is *Eagle*. I know you're all trying...and I appreciate you....But, you guys are crazy in the head"

It took some computing and precise triangulation on all five little piggy's to position *Eagle* for the impact of two chain nuclear explosions to slingshot her into a high elliptical orbit around the earth, an orbit that at one brief point might be close enough to penetrate the atmosphere, manually and without fuel.

 Martin had transmitted the programs for a change in trajectories and elliptical orbits, and it didn't take Karen long to realize what they were trying to do.

She'd give it everything she had. But not now. She would sleep.

"Do I have enough time to launch the generator for a good charge?" asked Karen

"*Eagle*, do it now!"

Karen glanced at the digits: 14:40:25.

That left twelve hours to decompress. One EVA left. That left one hour and 40 minutes to work. She would be outside trying to preposition the generator. Then, if she survived the explosion inside the orbiter, she'd be flung away from earth on an elliptical orbit, with enough momentum to dead stick it home, provided her heat shields could penetrate the atmosphere. She shut her eyes. It was such a long shot. Dear God....

Okay, she decided.

"Begin decompression mode" She called up Martin's programs and entered into the computers.

Her next priority was to get on the arm and put the generator on the spin table. The shuttle's Bay doors were open...

"OMS Burn check" began Karen out loud. She steadied her trembling hand and engaged Program 602

"Engage" flashed the computer. She pressed it.

Suited up and sweating from her exertions, she noted the blips approach on the CRT2.

"Here they come" she muttered. "Fasten your seatbelts and do or die, girl!"

One bomb detonated the other.

First light, then heat on impact, and, like a well behaved android, the giant capacitor's light cell simultaneously sent off a charge that, together with the explosions, lit up the sky and particle cloud like an atmospheric storm, rearranging the molecular structure of the carbon into fullerene. It cooled quickly in the vacuum of ambient space.

$$\infty$$

Chapter 5

Zahir was very pleased with himself. He managed with his son to pick his way across hazardous terrain.

Over the years, he had affiliated with precisely the right group of muhajiin for each territory. True, after the Russian invasion forces vacated Afghanistan, he was apprehended by local militia for "local questioning." Kabul.

Either by good fortune or a natural waning of interest, he and his son were cycled through a listless process of uneventful investigations. Neither he nor his son had any tribal affiliation, it was determined.

He was too well informed to betray his pedigree, especially since it was the ambition of the newly formed government to break tribal ties and disperse the population into disparate groups. This, while conceded as something necessary, cut at the core of Afghan integrity.

Like many, Zahir and Jabil would never forget the human suffering that they had witnessed. They were survivors. Zahir decided that it was more than good fortune, it was his fast-thinking resourcefulness and sharp wits that made him pass through each verbal challenge as he moved across the constellations of the jihad.

Still, for Zahir, nothing came close to the pride he felt right now. Here, in the same room, through humble implorations and ritualistic procedures, he had managed to assemble the leaders of many factions. They were of the old line Resistance.

It was the first time such an event had taken place.

They sat in the Chai-khana knowing that in spite of their diversity, it was a meeting whose time had come: In Kabul, even, at a tea house just outside a bazaar in broad daylight, all of them together.

Zahir assessed all who gathered here. At the far end sat the brutal and quick-witted if elderly head of the Hizb-i-Islami representing once the fundamentalists of various Pashtun groups.

Besides him was a dedicated mullah with a successful war record.

Next was the former Professor of political science, respected leader of Jamiat-i-Islami.

As far as Zahir was concerned, Rabbani was the most reasonable of all leaders. He depended heavily on consensus and coalition building, but his support had been limited.

Then there were those of the northern regions. Now there was the trouble, thought Zahir, grinning like monkey and pouring out drinks.

Across the table were the traditionalists, including former professors from the University of Kabul known for their resistance since the Daoud regime.

At the other end of the table was the leader of the Afghan society known by various local names and codes. Many were charismatic targets of the Americans seeking intelligence. Most were double informants. But nobody knew.

Zahir was suspicious of them.

 Others hovered in and around these men as they ate and drank, glancing at each other with the subdued respect of a higher order at hand.

Without a doubt, Zahir was responsible for the meeting and he kept his role most deliberately servile.

As the conversation proceeded he wondered how many needless killing might have been avoided had not these stubborn champions sub-vented their personal vendettas and formed meaningful coalitions.

Let Allah decide, he said repeatedly. If God had tears, then surely he must have a heart for the innocent.

The discussion remained chiefly on the topic of the latest outside influence in local affairs. They spoke of trans-border relations with Pakistan, geopolitical warm-water sea-ports achieved for commerce.

Here, commerce was the topic of conversation. Market activity and trade routes - as if they could stem the relentless flow through their country of goods. Centuries of passes, routes and passage of trade East to West had carved deep inroads. Yet here they sat, these old leaders trying to find common ground, brave men for reconciling their wounds of war. But business was business. And Jabil's ears were open. Technology had come upon them. Industry was being overtaken by global markets; Chinese manufacture now ruled, and energy buyers had diversified...

They talked of the sale of the Russian arsenal - piecemeal through underground routes, including nuclear capabilities.

He heard about diversion, corruption, hidden agendas. They mentioned mining, selling and commercial enterprises that fueled opportunistic gain and financial rewards for corporate Russia. Bullets seemed redundant, their scars long forgotten.

Afghanistan was a colony being exploited and stripped of every natural resource that could be hauled off in a truck. The Muhadeen were bystanders, he realized.

Outdated, tribal, old-warrior bystanders. Not even the Eastern ethic that once so happily served the Muslim while enjoying Western wealth was valid. Their God of the universe was the same God in a dozen languages and currencies.

 Money had one language, they all decided.

What remained unanswered however, when all was said and done, was Karakas: The graphite mine was still being heavily worked.

Zahir would post informants.

And he would be well rewarded for his intelligence by the American Embassy in Pakistan.

∞

The Sykere Pass, bazaar of the tribes, drugs, arms, valuables of ancient cultures and trading post of new.

It was hot, teeming with livestock, and everywhere the smell of food, hashish, sewage and sweat. Here, no government had ever ruled. Here, mountains, like immortal gods, circled to observe human legions play out their destinies.

 Martin had driven hard for three days and nights. A youth, Salim, was in the rear, slumbering, chattering, and showing off his agility of tongue as they moved up the Indus River from one tribal territory to the next.

At Landi Kotal, Martin and Uri Pravala followed the youth through bazaars, rooting for information. With the sun throwing long shadows down hot streets, Martin's largess waxed thin and he openly accused the boy of leading them on. The boy squinted and ran off. Suddenly, he reappeared around the corner.

"We go..." he said, gesticulating that he had found a man who would lead them to what they were after. His was a tenuous world of fear and faith all tangled up, as his eyes told them.

Martin and Uri sweltered through a labyrinth of stone streets and primitive structures. Finally the youth let them into the dark shadows of a building recessed into a mountain.

They were breathing hard, adjusting to the darkness.

"Welcome!" said a voice from behind.

"I am Zahir, the father of Salim. Please do not be alarmed."

"I didn't know the boy was hitch-hiking a ride home," said Martin.

The man walked forward, his face very much resembling the boy's.

"Forgive us for our ploy. We know what you want. We are your friends. We will help you!"

"Help us to do what?" asked a skeptical Martin

"First, please sit down and be welcomed. We will introduce ourselves. I am Zahir. Muhajiin. "

"You speak very good English" said Martin, probing.

"Yes. I was educated at the University of Kabul. When the Soviets invaded, those who could read, left. Those who stayed where shot."

"And now?"

"The Russians exploit us. As do the local terrorists from here...there, everywhere! We make money wherever we can."

"You said you knew why we were here?"

"Yes."

"What do you want from us?"

"First, I want you accept our hospitality and refresh yourselves amongst us. Our facilities are modest but adequate. Second, we wish to help you strike Karatas!"

Martin was stunned. How could he know about Karatas? British Intelligence in Karachi would have been appalled, to say nothing of the CIA who referred them to the Brits. Even as they insisted on sending their own man along, Uri Pravda, a trusted local informant, they said.

"You'll get along just fine with Uri. He's a former Soviet agent of Cuba who served in the Afghanistan war prior to his defection..."

"What exactly is....*Karatas*?" asked Martin.

"Karatas," said Zahir, spitting out the word with gutteral thrust, is a military installation that has been launching rockets containing a substance that they haul from the mines south of Kabul. We have known for a long time, though they deny it of course. We are not space scientists, but we see it as a threat. We do not trust the Soviets, in war or in peace."

The man shifted his gaze to Uri. "There is something strange..." he said

Uri rearranged his posture and averted his eyes.

"I have a feeling that I have seen your face before...perhaps I am wrong?" said Zahir. He returned to Martin.

"We know about your crew person called Patterson. Clearly she is a link to you, though we are not sure yet from where the source of information comes." Zahir moved toward the door.

The threat was clear. Play foul and we know someone who may come to harm. Not that Martin knew Patterson was beyond reach, but that this man had current intelligence is what concerned him.

"Today you rest, eat. Tomorrow we move across the border."

Uri leaned on the wall and lowered himself to his haunches. He breathed deeply and nobody noticed the perspiration on his face. This turn of events wasn't in the picture at Karachi he thought. His instructions were to kill his target before he did any damage at Karakas.

What he didn't count on was this Zahir.

Did the man recognize him?

∞

At six thousand feet above sea level, it was an inhospitable ridge on the mountain.

Martin and Uri Pravda were to locate the source of the graphite. Several mines had been identified within the Himalayas. Few produced the composition of the substance brought back as a sample from space by Lloyd and Martin.

While geological compounds identified were evident in the region, there was no mine located there, technically.

Only a Russian communications and weather observation platform was known. Presumed to be on the site of a former mine. But it had been decommissioned by the Soviets during their occupation of Afghanistan. Its code name had been Karatas.

Lungs heaving, they stopped. Everywhere the scars of weather at high altitude prevailed. It was barren, treeless with scrub grass writhing pitifully from littered clumps of snow; eroded boulders telling of bitter blizzards in frigid temperatures, and the wind. The wind shrieked relentlessly.

This was a far cry from the hot air of Karachi, thought Martin repositioning himself on the saddle.

He was alright with the decision to approach the facility from the North side. But if they were to travel in broad daylight, they must use horses.

Martin's face was barely visible within the fur lined Parka, but he was surprisingly warm and comfortable. Except for learning how to ride again, it wasn't such an outrageous idea after all; they seemed to be an insignificant pack of local nomads wandering the slopes of the Himalayas on horseback. Too bad he couldn't take a picture, he thought. If they were being watched, they were clearly not considered a threat. What he couldn't understand was why Zahir insisted they *all* go on this mission. Zahir could have sent his Guide alone.

What was essentially described as a mule train ascent turned out to be a mountain-climbing sortie into weather suited to summit altitudes where the air was thin and depleted of oxygen.

They paused, the wind howling as they surveyed the far ridge.

Uri brought up his horse alongside his.

"Looks harmless enough," he said, referring to the satellite dishes and radar antennas.

"Sure. For a weather station" said Martin.

Zahir pulled up alongside. "This is a major Russian military installation"

"Why? They can spy on whomever they want from wherever they want..." said Martin, his eyes searching for evidence of activity.

Zahir pointed to the northern approach "...There are perhaps 50 ICBM Russian missiles sitting underground and aimed at China from there!"

A gust came in hard and the horses stomped two paces.

"So what do you plan to do?" said Uri, his voice altered by wind "uncap the Silos and blow them up?" He shivered, his face blue and small inside his parka.

Martin eyed him with steel eyes.

"Look, I'm tired and I'm cold. Let's get out of this this bitch weather. Besides, there is nothing here we want..." pleaded Uri.

Martin, who had reached his own conclusions turned to Zahir. He nodded.

"We withdraw!" Zahir bellowed over the wind gust.

Zahir smiled, and Martin had the distinct impression that he was testing something. Or someone.

The descent was slow.

Martin was standing quite still when he felt the tremor. A few pebbles tossed lightly. Nobody else seem to notice. It wasn't until the next tremor came that the horses stomped uncomfortably and Uri and Zahir dismounted. An earth tremor.

"Comes often" confirmed Zahir "We've had bad earthquakes over the last three months. Severe damage in some regions. Mud and ice slides buried village houses in other places. Little loss of life, though. So far. But it has hurt the mountain passes where supplies must come with deliveries. We live a simple life. But we are still human..."

They remounted and continued their descent, passing along mountain ridges and ravines that dropped into dark shadows with no visible bottom.

Above them an angry mass of cumulonimbus clouds gathered. Rock and scrub lined their pathway as they treaded waving fauna, dry shrub and rock-coated crutose lichens – the promise of blossoms months away. Underfoot pebbles and small rocks dislodged with random frequency. The tremors were no longer alarming. But the horses were skittish.

It took a lot of effort to hang onto the horses and rely upon the beasts' surefooted treads as they lurched and jostled, descending a mountain path with their haunches dropping in sharp plunges at every step. They stopped at a wide clearing and all dismounted. Zahir and Martin took bearings on outcrops and scraped ledges below.

Martin consulted his chart which contained overhead reconnaissance mapping for aircraft spotters. He locked up and recognized their hamlet which, except for a few threads of smoke, might not have been noticed by a low-flying aircraft. The stone houses, roofed with reeds and dung cakes, blended into the mountain side beneath the terraced rice fields. He knew that water cisterns channeled into each structure; and only tiny apertures let in the sun. The hamlet was carved into the lee side of the weather with remarkable efficiency.

∞

The sun came over purple mountain peaks with all the glory of a predawn promise.

Outside, pack animals were already laden and ready to approach the Russian Installation by way of the north-west frontier of Pakistan.

They had been in Afghanistan for two days, but it might have been two decades. Crossing over to Pakistan was without hardly knowing.

As they rounded the shallow valley, Zahir pointed out a Railway line that contoured along the mountainside beneath them. It was virtually indiscernible.

"The graphite mine," he said to Martin, now consulting his chart for any cognition of its features by overhead surveillance photo. It marked only as The Shoehire Pass

Uri joined them. "Down there is where the road begins."

The journey seemed less formidable, until they rounded a rock outcrop and saw the sudden drop ahead. A gorge fell steeply off the mountain ridge that they held, and receded into deep shadows and cavernous darkness.

"Don't be alarmed," said Zahir turning to face them "You hold the reins loosely and the animals will take you safely across. Don't try to control them."

They threaded, the horses, accustomed and deft. Martin did notice that they were panting and salivating excessively. Zahir came up to Martin and explained that for short excursions, horses offered as much liability as beasts of burden. But they could not be used at night. The temperatures dropped too low for them to survive out here in the wind at night. Horses, up here, were too highly valued to be thus exposed. Ancient tradition form these parts had produced horsemen since the stone age, many of them travelling fast across the great planes that changed the settlement patterns of humans.

Uri picked his moment. He maneuvered his horse to follow Martin. The ledge narrowed, and Zahir's lead horse quickly disappeared from sight on the trail as it contoured the rock ledge. The pack animals went next, snorting and swaying and picking their way across loose pebbles. Then, as Martin moved onto the ledge, Uri gave his mount a sharp jab and it spurred into Martin's animal.

Martin's beast lurched forward with surprise and lost its front footing. There was no place to go. Even with its knees bent, it tried scrambling desperately to regain purchase. Martin yanked hard at the reins to pull back the balance of the animal's weight--but too late. The horse was already off the ledge. Martin let go and desperately leaped for ground as the animal fell away and hurled helplessly through the air, scrambling and screeching, making a horrifying echo. Martin watched the animal freefall until it was out of sight.

"An accident! *An accident...*" yelled Uri as Martin turned on him.

It took all of them, dismounted now, to pull Martin off Uri's throat.

The mission was scrubbed of course. A bitter silence followed as they returned slowly across the deadly mountain gorge.

Trust was the only lifeline between them--and it had been severed. Each man watched the other suspiciously.

Just below the mine the tiny hamlet emerged.

"Civilization!" said Uri, lifting his head.

Later that night they were served food on an oak table scrubbed clean by Push tan women.

 "Chicken cooked from in-ground charcoal pits," they said, grinning. Followed by chapatis bread and tea, they produced honey with nuts, and a home brew somewhat akin to whiskey.

All evening and into the night the tremors continued. The wind ripped into the side of the mountain, the flame in the kerosene lamp cowered, casting duels upon the cavernous walls of shadow and light.

Martin and Zahir remained huddled over the dimly lit oak table, talking, tracing routes, gesticulating. Uri dozed weakly from his bench against the wall rug behind him.

"Your man Uri..." said Zahir, leaning forward. "He is a Czechoslovakian. It is true he worked with refugees in Afghanistan during the Soviet occupation. But not as he says. He was not aiding the Liberation Front. He was a Soviet soldier engaged against the Resistance!"

Martin stared at him. "You can't be right..."

"Oh but I am! You see he very nearly took my life as a boy. But we escaped, my father and me. In fact it was he who led *us* to *you*. He is, in our code, a man marked for vengeance...He is not to be trusted..."

∞

The plan was for Lloyd to arrive in Landi Kotal. His armed unit had dropped him off at a nearby base camp by air drop. He had six US Marines with him fully trained in endurance and high altitude engagements. One was a specialist in communications technology feeds. Their arms were low maintenance, but effective and highly portable. The Marines would stay low key and out of sight. Their mission was to deliver ordinance on target to be marked by the advance party, Martin: Target was to be laser painted by overhead aircraft once transmitted from the ground with its exact position identified.

Lloyd played tourist mountaineer. They were climbers. And wired. For now, they waited.

And Lloyd was tracking Martin.

Martin and Uri were on their way to the airport at Rawalpindi by ten that morning, their mission accomplished.

Or so Uri thought.

The Taxi –truck driver chatted dutifully for the first twenty miles then fell silent. Martin was catching up on some sleep. Perhaps more than anything else, he was satisfied with the way things went the night before. What he didn't count on was the village at the mine being buried half by a mudslide following the earthquakes. This information he would have to reconcile....

Still, Zahir and his tribesmen had performed admirably. Possibly because they decided that Martin was a man to be trusted, as a covenant agreement between them, which in these parts was tantamount to law.

After the bus left the village Martin, Zahir and his men prepared for the night: Weapons, food, warm clothing, detonators, and horses. All night they labored against bitter conditions and wind gusts that pinned them down every few miles.

Advancing under cover of night allowed for more transport options that included rugged terrain vehicles which operated on diesel fuel. That helped a lot, cut down their time, and brought them close to their target, the installation from the South side approach, which had an entrance, a road and even a railhead for the moving train.

And only when Martin approached did he find the track not only serviceable, but recently delivered of large steel barrels, like sealed canisters, from the mine itself.

Moving like wounded bears in a blizzard, they cut through wire and security posts and set detonating charges at the base podiums of two specific ground tracking dishes at the Karakas installation. Two trucks scheduled to ferry canisters of graphite from the mine to the installation were decommissioned, and, after their return, what Martin valued most was the promise that no further shipments would be allowed to leave the installation. Zahir pointed out that it would be some time before parts and repairs could be made up these mountains, and in this weather.

"Erecting a new satellite dish," laughed Zahir "without the full assistance of small battalion of Army supplies would have the dish fly off the mountain like an umbrella" he laughed.

In parting, Zahir gave them a flask of alcohol to temper their descent, as he put it.

But as Martin tried to get some sleep in the truck, the driver decided to be a good tourist guide. No passenger of *his* would forget these mountains, he said... Nor was the Safed Koh Range forgiving, said the tour guide, as they travelled through the ancient kingdom of Gandhara.

Despite their timeless countenance, something curious had occurred on these mountains. Men had tampered with the peaks over the centuries and created sloped fields for cultivation-- entire mountainside ridges, cleared of rock, contoured slopes with rice, crops, plants, groves and with unrelenting terraced steps.

"These were here," said the driver, determined to quote Cook's guide book, "when Alexander of Macedon, King of the vast Achaemenid Empire, marched across Bactria to the upper Oxus and Kabul valleys 2300 years ago." He grinned at himself in the rear view mirror, two gold teeth gleaming. "He wanted to march across the great Hindu Kush to defeat King Porus of Peshawar. But his men refused to go on: The terrain was too terrifying!"

True, thought Martin, but not before leaving their undeniable Hellenistic imprint in the satrapies and Saka dynasties of the East forever.

Martin gazed out the window of this world of unreal proportions. Up here, everything was larger than life. The smell of raw growth seeped into one's pores. Moisture breathing trees, like slow moving monsters, spread over every crevice with a voracious appetite. Here was the nursery of misty clouds and the life-giving source of the great Ganges that he had seen as an astronaut from overhead for two, perhaps three fleeting moments.

Martin looked over at a slumbering Uri. He was out cold. But it left Martin to his thoughts. Was Uri a field operative planted beside him? If the horse incident was a failed attempt at his life, then why did Martin walk away? What was Uri up to? Martin laid his head back, sleep pulling at his thoughts. If so, who was he working for? Why? What was his agenda?

When Uri awoke, Martin passed over the flask. It would be a long ride down, he said.

Martin took a short swig, talking, asking questions. He answered Uri's questions about being a space aviator. Conversational questions. Martin led him on, even. Explaining some hair-raising experiences.

"So, how long between these orbital sunrises?" Uri asked.

Martin took another swig from the flask. "God knows!" he said "It was scary as hell…"

The car was warm, rocking gently. Rawalpindi was another hour away. Uri was out of it, his body was slack. The Checken had by no means shown any smarts. And if Zahir knew who he was, then why the put on? Especially in the beginning…. No! Uri was not stupid. He had kept a low profile on purpose. Who was his contact? Whom did he represent? But he *had* avoided being alone with Zahir and his men. He had even grown a beard. Hidden behind Martin. That was it! Of course.

The bastard was clever, and he knew exactly what he was doing and what the American response would be: Uri had gone to Chitral with Martin. If Lloyd rocked the boat at NASA, Martin would come to harm. Uri was holding Martin hostage! No wonder he walked away. God only knew what he had set up for NASA.

If sabotage was at the heart of the space debacle, then would it not make sense for the saboteur to send out a field operative to shadow the investigative intelligence on those on its trail? Especially if there were more damage to be done…

If Uri Pravda worked for the saboteur, decided Martin, then here was an opportunity to discover who that was!

Then again, Martin was fatigued. What if the man was a bonafide agent of the Government, as he asserted? This was all highly speculative. But there was something else. Something very subtle. Uri had asked him about the orbital sunrises.

No shuttle flew blind. Every moment of space flight was accounted for by five highly precise data collectors. Yet it rolled off Uri's lips as if he was privy to its connotations.

Who said there were multiple orbital sunrises?

The taxi slowed down for a herd of sheep being taken north to the summer pastures of Panjshir River.

"Zurgbas" explained the driver, apologizing for the delay as if it were a providential act of God. Martin guessed from the age of the boys driving the herd that they might be moving no more than ten miles per day. Martin looked ahead and saw the road breach a deep gorge by a fairly respectable looking bridge. He made two snap decisions, waiting two miles, three... Then, just before the bridge, Martin asked the driver to stop. Uri was awakened by the talk expended in getting the man to stop and get out of the car.

Martin walked about casually, playing the tourist who had to stretch his legs. He picked up a good size rock and ambled his way over to the driver. Without warning he brought the rock down on the driver's head who buckled and slid to the ground.

 Uri was outraged and said as much, until Martin, puffing and pushing the car toward the precipice, explained that he and Uri were lucky Zahir hadn't plunged a stake through their hearts during the night.

The car went over the side and down the gorge like a toy, crashing, burning and splattering debris over a half a mile of mountainside. Martin opened his wallet, left about 50,000 Afghanis in it and flung the rest in the dirt at about where the car had gone over.

Together, he and Uri sprinted across the bridge, left the road and hiked a mile around the mountain ridge until they were out of sight. It was a good half hour before an Iraqi-built truck pulled up. They vaulted into the rear and slid low as they passed the same herd of sheep milling and grunting around the taxi driver, now on his feet. He was gesticulating madly and wailing at the herdsmen, Martin's money firmly in his hand.

"I had a decent pair of boots in that taxi," strained Uri

"Good! With any luck they'll be found strewn in the gorge..."

"Damn it to hell, Martin. Must everything be such a mess?"

"Only if it's a good mess. The authorities will report the accident and the CIA will soon be informed. By which time we'll be back in Karachi, taking a military flight home."

"So NASA will think we're dead."

Martin turned on him with the gaze of a Texan who had made ruthless decisions at high speeds without flinching a muscle. "So will all your contacts! You're number has just been erased from the computers buddy. ..I'm the only enemy you have!" Martin licked at a sore on the back of his hand to let the words sink in.

Uri was staring in disbelief.

"... and you have all the way home to get to know me. So....Err. Who do you work for?" said Martin.

"And err...what happened to the woman Carina Bruneski?"

∞

Amanda Wells was puzzled at the message on her email. It was from Fumosa: "Deliver Relief Aid package to victims of Earthquake in the Shorehire Pass"

It struck her as unusual, since he had ceased to send instructions in the first place. Secondly, it presumed that she should find the place and deliver the supplies herself, neither of which were within her scope to accomplish. However, as a professional gesture she would attempt to refine the point of destination for the deliveries, even if for general logistical support and transport purposes.

The task proved to be almost impossible: She could not get a fix on the point of destination. She scoured the reports and files for a location. The "area stricken by the earthquake" was nowhere defined with any specific village named. Neither was the incident particularly well documented - the number of victims needing aid; the extent of the damage recorded; the natural conditions reported; emergency procedures that might have already occurred to aid the area, nor was the jurisdiction named which should receive the aid. Still, the Relief Aid had been ordered at the FAO, the funds appropriated, and the deliveries shipped from Europe.

Come to think of it, she could not even find the epicenter of the quake!

She consulted the various weather; emergency and catastrophic reporting agencies concerned, and ended up with a vague description that was high in the Himalayan Mountains at the Sykere Pass.

Only one man, an agent in India, gave her clearer information, only because he had family that lived in the area. This, he would forward to her by email.

The site of the earthquake was at a hamlet close to a Soviet military installation, now abandoned. It had formerly operated as a mine earlier in the century. Most of its workers were hired from the local village. The village, for unexplained reasons of health, was now almost entirely abandoned.

However, the site was bought up by a private company that re-opened the mine, and re-leased the site of the installation back to the Russians who kept equipment on the site for storage purposes. It was a quid pro quo arrangement, evidently.

Amanda enquired after the name of the private company that owned the site. They surely might be willing to accept delivery of the Aid.

It's a Chicago based company, owned and operated by a man called DePhillipe. His designated representative for the site is one named Uri Pravda.

∞

The Mine presented problems to operate at high altitude.

Primarily it was the equipment that refused to sustain its engine fluid viscosity. Industrial scrapers were replaced with strategically positioned dynamite blasts that could loosen the rock.

Other improvisations were met with ingenious solutions, if unsanctioned. Water cooling, now exposed to the air, could freeze, something that tunneling operations had previously accommodated. So fires in cast iron furnaces were Jury Rigged and pipe runs had to be devised to keep the operation open. However, that led to other problems.

The greatest impediment to operations was the mounting rubble pile that could not be cleared away as excavations deepened into the mountain. It had not been cleared by heavy industrial shovels for two months because of equipment failure. And weather.

Escarpments, thus far, allowed for adequate collection mounds. But only to a point. The rock should then have passed through industrial crushers and removed by earth movers. Even the excavation trucking of the mine deposits was a challenge. That meant that the diesel engines were never turned off for loading. In the poorly ventilated passageways of the vein, workers were periodically brought out incapacitated by inhalation of fumes, carbon monoxide.

Still, the trucks were hauling off loads of the deposit and wending their way down the rugged mountain side, even if at a crawling pace.

Local laborers knew of the dangers. But they agreed to work anyway, not that their economic options were abundant.

They made the necessary adjustments with little complaint.

It allowed little room for error however. And regardless the subtle signs of danger, the managers, most of whom were not local, did not understand the full impact of the conditions they were creating.

The clouds, for example, were known to the locals. Little discolorations, they said, could indicate the direction of the weather with ensuing cold winds. Small details that seemed harmless at first, but added to nightfall and its attendant hazards, could have catastrophic consequences.

And weather changes.

Usually, it began with small uneven puffs of wind indicating a deeper front of wind shifting. At this altitude, something with only a two degree variation in temperature could glaze the side of a mountain like a cake in under 45 minutes, freezing solid all it breathed on.

Survival however, was hardly the chief consideration of the mining engineers. Trained in Russia, their expertise was considered sufficient, if dated. And supplemented with new weather resistant clothing, they thought they could beat the odds of a lucrative mine operation. They did not call it the Shoehire Pass for nothing. A Mogul dynasty legacy.

"It is the breath of God when he is angry..." said one local shepherd in a brightly weaved cloak and cane, his herd of yak grazing. For him, it would mean gathering his herd by an outcrop of rock where they would hunker down with their eyes closed, he sitting in a leather sack under his cloak now pitched like a pole tent with his cane. Sunrise would bring melting.

In the operational scheme of things, delivery of the fine graphite shale had been transported down the mountain with some regularity - if tortuous inefficiency.

And although the locals could not fathom the sudden rush to mine the deposits found within the veins of their mountain, they understood the need for demands of their resource coming from advancing economies.

That is, if anyone remembered any official who last showed up with any serious convictions about nationalism. Only teams of doctors and contractors did visit periodically, mainly by helicopter. Otherwise, they had remained self-sufficient for half a century at least...sending down their supply of pressed flora for dye in exchange for key provisions which, increasingly, included more synthetic materials for survival and endurance. Even entertainment devices with basic communications, fuel and educational materials for the children, if any could read.

Hence when the Mine operation opened in earnest, that is, in keeping with labor intensive management schedules printed on paper, it look little before the community showed signs of duress. Not only did those profit- driven paradigms prove unsustainable at high altitudes, but the weather had been uncooperative.

It was perhaps the squall itself that became the catalyst for the catastrophe. Or perhaps the piles of ruble that reached critical levels. Some said it was a tremor felt within the mountain itself. But it had been raining, and suddenly the barriers were breached.

The mudslide came slowly. Almost imperceptibly. And it took several days to develop its own inertia. But it crept down the mountainside - laterally sometimes - but downward nevertheless, finding the paths of least resistance wherever it could.

And it was well underway before anyone in the village saw it, one thousand feet below.

Actually, it was the noise that alerted them. A small crackling rumble, like lava, heralded a force of grinding rock that alerted everyone. They fled to some caves nearby. But its progress, once the alarm was sounded, was so slow that many made the pilgrimage back into their abode to retrieve essential articles.

Once the flow struck the village, there was little evidence of life left in its wake. Even the caves threatened to fill up as pressure pushed in the mud at the entrance.

Remarkably, no one perished. But their village was engulfed. All evidence of the ancient site was buried by the mine debris. Roofs, mud brick, foot paths and stone carved foundations, some as old as two millennia, had disappeared.

Chapter 6

Paul Turner met her at JFK.

She was in a suit arriving from London. He was in sneakers.

"How was your flight?" he asked, tossing her luggage into the back of his Mercedes and putting on his baseball hat.

Not that she minded travel, but today's flight was packed, oddly, with Iranians. And babies. "Crying babies in cramped seats and no room" she explained. "Next time, I'm crossing the pond First Class!" she said, her good graces giving way to fatigue.

"That's what your father said...You know your penny pinching ways don't exactly make the Foundation look good either" he grinned.

"Penny pinching is my way of keeping life real" she said.

"*Yeah. Yeah. Yeah.* I've heard it all before....over Thanksgiving dinners, Christmas dinners, School bazaars and field trips! You're the philanthropist at heart, even with your Lauren boots on... "

She looked at him. They had known each other since elementary school.

"Not that you wouldn't look alright with your boots off..." he continued, pulling out of the Airport on Long Island.

"Ok Paul" she said "keep your thoughts for your chicks will you?"

He laughed.

"So how's everyone?" she asked.

"Everyone is fine ...And waiting for you. So we're going to the beach..."

"*Hey?*" she strained.

He stopped the car.

Her expression said it all.

They owned homes in the Hamptons - all of them. But she had planned to return straight to her apartment in New York.

Nothing was lost on Paul. It was true. They had plotted to divert her plans...

"Yes. So we do *need* you!" he said "...you know, for our Annual Garden Charity; for the Wine Festival, and for a family gathering to make decisions about Grandmother's estate. As in, Hello. We're here!"

"Sorry" she said "I neglected to ask..."

They drove in silence for a while. Then she asked "Kauffman will be there?"

"Of course! He has navigated this family's fortune for long enough to earn an Invitation."

The wind whipped through the crack in the car window and brushed her face.

"Look Amanda, chill for a couple will you? You're back in the States o.k?"

She took a long breath. True. It had been a long time. She sat back, the road ahead long and familiar. It had been a long time since she'd felt safe and on turf recognizable, home.

∞

She'd been in the Hamptons for two days and she slipped back into a life of girlhood with ease.

Last night, Fall weather or not, she had traipsed down to the beach in bare feet with pants rolled up and a minnow net in her hand.

Paul's flashlight sent shy beach crabs skimming back into their tiny holes, and by the time they had all gathered at the campfire, she and her friends were famished. It had been a long day of fishing and sun and swimming and crabbing.

Someone held up their catch of two fish and five loaves, as they put it.

"No. Its *Five* fish and *Two* loaves" corrected Susan.

"Plus a case of beer!" said someone in the crowd.

"And now... a *Lobster!*" heralded Casey and Paul coming out of the dark with a large bucket. Sharing the weight, they had threaded an uneven path from the house down to the beach.

"Where did you get that creature?" Louise asked when it finally got set down.

Casey took a bow. "Ahoy y'are Seamate! From Ye Great Atlantic Sea ..."

"You're drunk!" said his brother Andy.

"Of course! And *you* paid for this monster with your credit card" he chuckled.

"What?"

"It *is* steamed?" asked Amanda.

"Oh yeah..." said Paul, dropping to his knees at the camp fire, Heineken in hand.

"Come to *Momma* with that thing!" lurched Amanda, all of them collapsing with laughter.

Thus, with a dark sea-surf swelling over the beach of London Island Sound, it was the heavy, damp, beach-sand mushed between her toes that made the world melt away for Amanda.

From childhood this bunch had gathered on their beach - a place of renewal and refreshment in a world growing up around them in city courtrooms or boardrooms. It was as if Amanda had left her little grey cells, as her friend Emily once called them, checked at the door. There was only one rule. *No thinking allowed!*

Certainly, it took most of the morning to sleep off the hangover the next day. But it was a big day of excitement, they knew.

Amanda was setting up the tables for the garden party when her Aunt came out on the porch.

"Someone to see you dear" she said.

He stood there, the tallest and most blue-eyed man she had ever seen, just standing there at her doorway, waiting to be asked in.

"...Call me Lloyd" he was saying. "From Washington DC" he said, producing identification.

NASA actually. Yes, he would love a Coors Light thank you very much...

In the kitchen, she fussed like a flustered school girl. Something the old kitchen had seen on numerous occasions through their childhood days.

But this was ridiculous. *Those blue eyes!*

She leaned into the counter, counting, and breathing... her feet still gritty with sand in her flip-flops.

He had spoken for ten minutes, and she never really heard a word. *Gorgeous!* (And unmarried she supposed, the way he went on about fishing and boating...)

"I was wondering - that is, if you don't mind my asking since Mr. Fumosa sent me here..." he dug into his denim jacket "if you ever saw this guy?"

Amanda nearly choked on her beer.

Business didn't belong here. It jarred.

He had produced an image of a man wearing the headdress of a Muslim Imam.

"No!" she said quickly. "Never saw him in my life!"

He said nothing, but he held the photograph, scowling somewhat.

"Why?"
"That's funny" he said "because here..." and he produced another photograph "you are pictured having dinner with him!"

She stared.

In the photograph she was talking to a man seated at the dinner table of the Empire Hotel in India. There was Dr. Sumptra on her right. And there was Salim to her left...

 "That's...?" She looked closely. "Of course...Err"

"Salim?" he said finally. "We're looking for him!"

She went cold.

It took Paul to bring her back to an even keel. Something he had done many times before in this very house.

"He's a *what*?" Paul later asked her.

"Astronomist" she said, vaguely.

"Astro...?"

"Astronaut!" she corrected.

"Sure. I'll bet! With that accent?... The closest he probably got to being an Astronaut was a Lego-set of play blocks issued by Mattel toys..."

"Whatever!" she said, shutting down her stay at the beach.

Less than four hours later, with the party in full swing, she was found upstairs packing her bags to return to New York.

"Need me to give you a ride?" said Casey from her door.

He was Paul's son, at home from college.

"Nope." She looked up at him and smiled nonetheless.

He left a set of car keys on the bed. "You o.k?"

"Yup!"

"So the Jeep is in the garage" he said, "I just drove it down from Yale. Needs gas! Bring it back by Christmas yeah?" She nodded. Down here, they dealt with transportation issues on a *whoever-needs* basis.

Casey knew the impact of an intruder on family down here. He understood her anger.

∞

By week's end, she was back in her office in New York working as hard as ever.

There was catch-up work. New work: Reading, memos, issues, policies, enquiries, complaints... The world was going crazy, she decided.

Dr. Fumosa was still without a Replacement.

She was to receive instructions from an Administrator in London, who was presently absent for another month.

After that, she was to prepare a report for the World Bank's Annual Meeting in Seoul.

Once again she was carrying his trade, so to speak.

She ignored Lloyd's calls several times.

He had taken her by surprise -caught her in a vulnerable condition. She was at home, resting and on vacation, as Paul put it. She did not want to talk about it, not now, or ever... The trap he had laid for her snapped like a bowstring. So what if she knew Salim? Besides...*Oh hell*

Her own stupid fault, she decided. And as the weeks went by, with New York for a city, she forgave herself for her childlike stupidity, attributing her self-deprecation to weeks...no, *months* in the field without a break.

Only one thing bothered her still. How did this total stranger know of her whereabouts? Worse, how was he in *possession* of an image that she never even knew existed.

Who *was* Salim, anyway?

It wasn't until the Secretary of State, a woman, showed up in New York to cast a UN Vote that Amanda found out.

The Secretary invited Amanda in for a meeting in her office.

Amanda never anticipated such attention, and this was way beyond her status.

"I am told" she said "that the Department of Defense has approached you with... an enquiry?"

Yes, she had to agree.

The Secretary was very nice about it, neither armed with a working suit nor a mindset training to inflict any mortal wound, nothing here was alarming. Still, Amanda remained uncertain.

"He is a subject of interest to our government..." is the best she could supply.

"Salim?"

"Yes. I think that's the name..." she shrugged with insouciance.

Amanda wasn't fooled. This was no casual questioning.

"We have heard from a Dr. Mutlu in the Space Agency about a condition that might have connections to this man's err - activities...? They can have serious consequences, and we don't want to be caught unprepared, that's all. May I ask that you pursue your leads with this man, if any, Ms. Well?...and to keep us informed?"

"Yes of course! Though I know very little. It's just that we were introduced at a dinner in New Delhi. I made acquaintance with him and a Dr. Sumptra..."

"Yes. We know of Dr. Sumptra. Very wonderful lady!" she said. "Please let us know if you can make any connections to him! And ...with frequent reports, if you would please. Addressed to *me* of course!"

"Yes, of course!"

"Oh, and err... if you need any assistance you might derive it from Captain Lloyd. One of our most able space experts" she said.

Amanda looked down at her hands. Then decided that yes, she would ask.

"How...how did err...this connection come to be made with *me*, exactly?"

"Oh. It's Captain Lloyd's associate, Martin. He met with the man's family...in the mountains of the Hindu Kush. Something suspicious is taking place. We don't quite know what yet...But we don't ask *lightly*. So anything you know, Ms. Wells, or get to know, please tell us!"

Amanda left the room a little stunned that the Secretary of State might be appealing to her for help.

Clearly it was the focus of highly concentrated attention by some very serious people. She just happened to be seen with him. Which made her wonder about being followed. Probably something National Security would know. If not the Defense Department, which Lloyd was...*attached to*?

Jesus!

What *had* she walked into?

Perhaps she could reach Trevor?

The funny thing was, she had just received a letter from Dr. Sumptra.

∞

Trevor MacDonnell was under the sea.

At 2,000 feet below the surface, the *HMS Inverness* submarine had been underway beneath the North Pole on a transpolar course.

At the Control and Command Center of one of the world's fiercest boats, stood Trevor MacDonnell. If pale and lightheaded, he was blue colored in the subdued ultra-lighting of a ship at war. The vessel barely purred.

Actually, he was uneasy.

It was the best he could do, considering the last three days. Plucked from the tropics; Air-lifted halfway around the globe; briefed in Germany then delivered to a surface combatant warship en-route to Iceland, he met special agents aboard the ship in turbulent seas. A chopper then had to deliver him to the Bering Straits - at night, in frigid temperatures - to meet with a beast of a submarine that came up for air like a whale...

Bloody Hell! Is what he wanted to say.

Worse. He felt sea sick!

But some things, he knew, were just too important. And he could not get in the way of this, let alone indulge his discomfort: When it came to duty, every man should find a way.

Still, while the crew buzzed about with crack efficiency and happy camaraderie, the weight of the task suited him little.

The Captain consulted the numbers handed to him by Executive Officer, his hands firmly on the chart table, his voice audible in the ship's inter communication system.

"Proceed ahead at bearings North 25 degrees latitude..."

"North 25 degrees... Aye" came the response.

"Turn Two Zero Two Degrees, Left Rudder."

"Turning Two Zero Two Degrees, Left Rudder, Aye Captain..." said the Engineering contingent.

"All Engines, steady!"

"All Engines, steady Aye"

"Stand by" said the Captain, stepping back and inviting his Executive Office to carry on with the exercise.

"Standing by,

 Aye" came the response.

The Captain turned to Trevor.

"I don't like this one bit" he hissed.

Trevor was watching and stood behind him.

Together they stepped off the platform and moved away towards the aft hatchway where a Sergeant of the Marine stood guard. The Captain nodded with a salute and the Guard unbolted the sealed door from the inside then stepped aside with a salute.

Trevor followed him down the passageway.

 "Standing by to launch an intercept missile is not what we want to do with an arsenal like this out here! It exposes us to too many probabilities in these conditions..." he turned his head briefly.

"I understand completely your position. But as a Flank fleet, it must be serious. The Americans don't ask often for our help. We just happen to be in the right place, that's all…"

"But not for this task!" admonished the Captain, looking back at Trevor following. "Comm'n! We'll talk in my quarters."

On the way he found an ensign and said "Bring me coffee and some sandwiches please, will you?"

"Aye Sir!"

It was two hours before Trevor could retreat to his own quarters, and he stretched out on his bunk, gaunt and fatigued. He closed his eyes. But in his mind he was already formulating the report that he would have to submit.

London held him in trust. And the Russians had agreed.

So here he was, in uniform as Special Assignment Commander of the Royal Navy, coffee in hand to assuage his sea-sickness, on a mission to guide the hand of a Skipper at the helm of one the world's fiercest Attack Submarines. Although they were far from detection, he knew the eyes of two Space satellites were watching.

And he wanted to throw up somewhere.

∞

"It's the things we *don't* see that bothers us!" they had said at the briefing.

"… There is little warning, no fixed target or projection or signature. Mainly because it camouflages itself with light from the sun, heats up in the stratosphere, and hides in the cool darkness from the earth's curvature" said the Commander at the board.

"Like a cloaking device" said Trevor, thinking aloud.

"Like a cloaking device" they repeated.

He looked down, apologetic for the paucity of his knowledge in the field. But as embarrassed as he was, the idea that... *whatever* it was... had been launched from the continent of India - and right under his nose - outraged him sufficiently to lose any self-consciousness and immerse himself with technical understanding.

Not that Trevor MacDonnell was uninformed exactly, having trained in the Armed Forces as a Cadet and specialized in light weapons, but his Attachment to the Royal Navy began not so long ago. Beirut, really, with a British Ship in port under his care.

"Actually, it's very simple really. The SM-3 Kinetic Warhead (KW) is designed to intercept an incoming ballistic missile outside the earth's atmosphere. It began as Joint Venture with the Americans quite recently. And as Raytheon has engineered two prior generations of LEAP designs, it's a bit of an old friend"

"More Coffee Sir?" asked the Lieutenant.

"Thank you" said Trevor, adding two sugar lumps with a tiny silver claw.

"Mainly, there are two elements that sing for us: The first is that the Seeker's pointing and intercept guidance are supported by a production IFOG Inertial Measurement Unit of the SDACS propulsion capability.

...And the other is that the KW includes a fully encrypted data downlink capability for full engineering evaluation of the KW performance as it goes, which will be monitored by NASA to support rapid kill assessment."

"But if we can't determine *what* we're shooting at...how do we tell when we've made impact?" asked Trevor

"We program with increasing refinement all the right ingredients that we *do identify* as pre-existing conditions..."

"That's flying a bit blind isn't it, like a scatter shot in a virtual cloud?" he asked.

"Well yes. And NASA is feeding us data all the time. So we're increasing the threshold of probabilities by the minute. But you are right...It's *not* certain with pinpoint precision"

"I see. And how do we deliver this thing?"

"The HMS Inverness. She's under the Bering Straits and best positioned for delivery."

"What? A Trident Submarine? Won't that set off defensive alarms ...?"

"True. But not only is she in the right place at the right time for the next orbital impact. But she can modify her vertical missile launch tubes for a four-pack KW"

Trevor looked at him askance.

"That's the...err little package clustered in four-bangers within the standard missile deployment tube" explained the Commander.

"And how do you propose to persuade the Captain Melison..." said Trevor.

Then it dawned on him.

He handed them back their coffee. Thanks very much, but no thanks he wanted to say. Instead, he said "I see. Of course. I'll stand by his side to assist with your orders any way possible."

"Thank you Sir!" said Commander Perkins.

Not that a British trained Captain of a Royal Navy ship or Executive Officer of a Trident submarine could not carry out orders without an onboard political officer, but the mission was so strange, so sudden and under conditions so oblique that any skipper would welcome support from a political officer if one were available.

For one, the ship's Captain would need to deviate from his orders in the extreme. For another, his nuclear warhead missile tubes would have to be modified and refitted while still submerged. And finally he'd be setting off every offensive alarm system across the world once he launched his delivery missiles.

And Trevor MacDonnell was available.

Before leaving he had to ask. "Does the Prime Minister know, Commander?"

"He is being briefed, even as we speak."

"And I should like to consult with the Royal Family about the operation.   Patch me through with a secure call if you would please?"

"Absolutely Sir!" said the Commander. Then with a salute added "Thank you M'Lord ,Sir!"

"You're welcome Commander. Good job. Let's pray all goes well..."

"Yes Sir."

∞

The Fumosa Foundation in New York City was well known as a privately funded organization. It carried both the aspirations of a man that shaped the global missions of hunger relief, and the vision of the World Health Organization - of which he was its Director in Rome.

Now concerned with environmental issues, the Foundation garnered support from many notable world organizations including the United Nations, headquartered in New York, and many other entities world wide.

In fact staff shuttled between his Foundation office, a small townhouse on West 26th Street, and the offices of the United Nations where he was frequently in attendance as Director of World Health.

Some said his Foundation enjoyed too great a bite out of the US Department of State Foreign Aid budget, often forgetting the interests of the United States, in its fervor, in aiding the wrong groups with the wrong intentions for the wrong reasons.

"Not at all!" he would say in his large Italian way, "It is the accusation of those who want nothing to change!" Such comments he reserved for those on his staff, and for those he trusted. But for a wider audience where he knew he would come under public scrutiny, he chose his words carefully, politically, and without rancor.

Still, his critics demurred on his legal authorizations that might overstep the bounds of US commitments overseas - at the expense of other initiatives; forcing policy that was normally reserved for government mandate, or Congressional approval let alone financial appropriations... Some even went so far as to say he had a collaborator within the Department of State that steered his requests into more coffers than the Treasury knew it had.

The Foundation could raise funds. It was a corporate favorite for tax-deduction donations. Especially from corporations sitting offshore. They did not question The Foundation's motives.

Fumosa had asked Amanda Wells to Administer the Foundation as his senior office operations manager. It was a desk job. She knew exactly what his aims were, and how to appeal for the support he needed. She was especially delicate with his responses to matters that involved political finesse. Even if it was always "Amanda, My Darling this..." or "Amanda, My Darling that..."

"You can stand that appellation?" asked Barbara in her New York twang that she could turn on and off with her level skepticism.

Amanda shrugged "Why Not? If it makes him happy...Besides, it's not that I have anyone else calling me *My Darling!*"

"As long as there are no more demands to *my darlings*" twanged emphatically Barbara.

"No. It's an English term of endearment really. He is quite the gentleman with me, thanks!" assured Amanda. "And who else could cope with all of this load?" she added at the array of papers, files and notes in her inbox, let alone the dictated letters and speeches that Fumosa left on her recording devises for official typing, uploading or delivering. He was one, especially, for writing research reports. And they could be copious. Hence with long hours of work dedicated to the Foundation both at the Foundation and in her home, Amanda was pretty much able to call her own hours. And her own fabulous salary.

"Well, you know what it is..." conceded Barbara with the final word as she took to the steps. "It's all those connections you have in Washington DC that he particularly likes!"

Amanda laughed.

Being of Italian birth, Fumosa was gregarious and engaging, able to couch all that was germane in kindly expressions and bold vision. But to his critics, his opulence seemed incongruous with humanitarianism; his gregariousness contrary to seeking hope for the lost. Not that such drawbacks stopped him from achieving the goals intended. But there was one thing that people knew. He was a notorious womanizer, even if to Amanda there had been 'no more demands' as Barbara put it.

Clearly, Amanda Wells commanded his respect. It was clear that Fumosa had passed the management of the Foundation to Amanda entirely. Whatever staffing requirements she needed, they were hers to have. Attorneys, accountants, statisticians, analysts, researchers, receptionists. Even the facilities of the Foundation were lavish.

It was an ample town-house. Offices upstairs, complete with waiting-lounges, kitchen quarters - all furnished appropriately for servicing conference privacy when needed, and all spaces interconnected with high technology and even higher security surveillance.

Amanda kept her office downstairs near the main conference center where she had access to ample storage. There she made arrangements for her receptionist and Interns. Across the foyer from her office an elevator of brass gate and glass doors ran like a golden bird cage on soundless pneumatics.

Amanda kept the offices simple, unpretentious and impeccably clean. Not that she had much to embellish, the architecture was of the beaux arts tradition built for New York City dwelling.

Against white silk walls Amanda chose sparse modern photographs of solitary places with great possibilities; an ancient white roof top from which simple steps led to the sea beyond. A beach of arched caves and natural carvings; green fauna that moved with the climate.

Clearly, the Foundation made for a happy place to work where everyone enjoyed their surroundings. Here, the hours were flexible; trust in abundance, and the work performance highly productive. Especially when preparing for Annual Meetings requiring enormous effort on speeches, research and reports to be delivered often at a conference located half way around the world.

Actually, it was more than once pointed out to Amanda that half the meetings held downstairs at the Foundation could be served better at the United Nations if not the World Bank in Washington DC. These sentiments she would pass on to Fumosa. But he would hear nothing of it "Bring them here!" he would bellow, if rarely in attendance himself.

Frequently, he held large parties at his apartment off Central Park, or at his place on Long Island. But as long as the Foundation operated flawlessly, he was rarely troubled by much.

Still, Amanda wondered what he was up to. She was sitting in her office when she noticed an inordinate list of donors for the year. She wondered what propelled the sudden interest - other than concern for the year's end fiscal calendar and the normal tax related donations.

She smiled. Perhaps the Foundation's mission was visible. Their hard work had paid off...

∞

Rome.

"The problem with the report is that is isn't specific…" began Charles Wainright, chief advisor.

"No. The fly-over didn't record a thing!" said Francois.

"Actually…" he added, standing up "It's too high for normal low altitude reconnaissance flights. And choppers are reluctant to get up there. To say nothing of the snow problems and the weather in that region." He stood at the head of the conference table, his pointer leveled at the blackboard behind him.

"But we do have mortality reports?" insisted Fumosa in his blustering way.

"Yes!" said Carina. "The village has been buried… We don't know how many have died. And in any case, at that altitude, it's uncertain how long they can survive in the open without relief…"

"Then we send up supplies!" said Fumosa.

"Well. It's airdrops, at best. Tents, blankets. Food etc." said Francois.

"But without a call for help from the sovereign country we *cannot* dispense anything…" said Charles Wainright.

"Oh. You mean money?" thundered Fumosa

"Yes. I mean budget. But more importantly, authority to intervene. We have to be *invited*. We must stay within our protocols to dispense world disaster aid of *any* kind."

Fumosa knew enough not to argue further.

His assistant walked in with more information sheets in her hand and gave them to him. The room remained silent.

∞

"The problem is, the locals are engaged in regional warfare, we can't get the Government to *acknowledge* this incident...It's considered a political liability! " said Charles. "No. The problem is we can't just ride the planet with our sense of justice and screw the locals..."

"It's not like that..."began Carina.

"We would need more data" advised Charles. "An Emergency situation must be declared. An invitation to receive Relief must be on file. Contacts must be established. The money for the Aid accounted for...A contract with neighbors, like the Pakistani Government for God's Sake!"

"So. What do you suggest?" thundered Fumosa "We show up with a file and say "You hold your dead baby until we get the right *signatures* for our files?"

Charles was frozen by Fumosa's combative posture. He looked down.

"Sure we sympathize" said Charles quietly. "We can offer to render Relief Assistance. But we have no clear *mandate* for this action, or for the expense!.."

"Don't worry about the expense. I'll raise the funds!" said Fumosa.

"Mario. This is an unauthorized "event" according to the local governments. It is NOT sanctioned for Relief Aid. It is dangerous territory! It could be considered something else...It's even considered illegal to interfere!"

"Maybe. But there is a **need**" said Fumosa quietly.

And that was the last word, they all knew.

Charles Wainright was a New York Attorney trained in International Law. He was worried. Later that night he got a call. He was alone in his apartment, in the dark. He drained his Scotch.

Catastrophe was one thing. Climate another.

∞

Amanda was looking for a suitable gift.

From her offices in New York, there was little about global anomalies that they did not hear about in daily Press Releases. In her case, if it affected a cultural resource, it was her bailiwick: Global anomalies and local culture should meet somewhere in the middle for solutions, she knew. At least that's what the policy papers suggested.

However, her focus today was on one of the catalogues for travel. And she was smiling, if puzzled. Here was something that was neither a cultural resource, nor an anomaly. But definitely strange, she decided.

"What's up?" asked Barbara sitting in her office on the side with a laptop.

"Since when have we seen a Beer Fest; a Thanksgiving celebration and a Carnival Grape Festival all at the same time...In *Russia*?"

"Sounds like a party to me..."

"Yep. But in December? In the Tundra?" she asked.

"You got me there..." chuckled Barbara. Then she added as an afterthought "Wouldn't you be putting people at risk for such an event? I mean, don't they roll out their Huskies and Sleds or something at this time of year?"

"Precisely!" said Amanda, her thoughts almost lost to imagining a Winter Wonderland... Yet there it was. An open invitation to an open Festival. Right in the middle of the tundra in mid-December. A party indeed!

She was about to Text Andy, one of her neighbors, and agree to go to a Concert tonight, but her eyes remained fixed on the brochure.

Then she got a call from Fumosa.

Then a message from a name she would rather not see again. *Commander Lloyd. US Navy* said the message slipped on her desk by the Receptionist.

"So... what got you looking?" asked Barbara, later.

"Oh?"

"The Russia thing...?"

"Silly, really. I was looking for a bottle of wine to give to my Uncle for Christmas from a lovely spot. This tourist brochure touted wines from Russia, one called Chateau d'Ukri, in the Ukraine. Sounds so *Lara-like* and musical, all that poetic white snow and vast landscape..."

"Right!" said Barbara "Only that's bullshit... Cold as hell! More like an ice age in the Tundra...And now doing *grape festivals*?"

"They must have been imported from somewhere warm or something. Do the Russians have somewhere warm?"

"Who knows?"

"Vineyard DePhillipe!" said Amanda peering carefully at the label in the brochure.

"Right then. Let's get some food. It's cold here too!" griped Barbara.

"I'm Hungry!" said Amanda.

Dave stuck his head in her door, his professorial red bow tie impeccable crisp under his short beard and eye classes.

"Lunch? Care for New York's best pastrami and Swiss on rye?"

Amanda inhaled suddenly. "Hmm. sounds good! Your favorite?"

"My mother's finest upbringing!"

"Yes. I am starved. Fifteen minutes good?"

"Make it ten..." he disappeared.

Barbara opted out. "Bring me back something!"

"So what are you up to these days?" he asked, his face happily framed by a white table napkin tucked into his collar.

Amanda sipped her red wine and returned to her French role and onion soup. "Nothing much, outside catching up with an endless list of requirements for the Rome Conference."

"No Memorial Day Weekend at the beach?"

Amanda's mouth was full, Swiss cheese melting in her mouth over a sweet onion. "No. I've got too much to do, and I'd just like three days to myself to get it all done!"

"Tony coming down?" he asked, his hand holding an oversized sandwich stuffed with sauerkraut, jalapenos and oozing mustard over pastrami and cheese.

"No. He's staying up for a few days, then coming down for the summer later. He's giving a paper at school that adds to his grade, apparently..."

Dave smiled. "Smart kid, your brother..."

"How about you?"

Dave looked down at his sandwich, his face draining of appetite.

It had been eight months since Sandra his wife had left him, and Amanda was getting concerned about his disposition.

"No. My family are in Chicago, and it's just...well no one's here anymore. Sandra's going to Ft Lauderdale with her *nouveau*, and wants to dump our child and dog Twinkle on someone so she can take off in two days. Imagine!" he said. "There is no *us the family* anymore."

Amanda put her hand over his. "Can't you have Ursula and the dog at your place?"

"Not for another four days. I'm on a tight parent visitation schedule. I get her for the weekend only. Sandra just wants to show off about how free of obligations she can be for this new idiot she's dating...Its bullshit!" His voice trailed, he pushed away his plate. "I'm supposed to collect Ursula from a babysitter at Social Services..."

Amanda noticed his eyes fix quietly on the edge of the table, his thoughts causing him deep sadness.

"I'll take her! She can stay in the Hamptons at our place and wait for you... There's Aunt Alice. Do you think your wife will accept?"

Dave stared at her. "Damn right she'll accept. We used to love coming down to visit you at the Hamptons as a family. She'll take your invitation as a huge social compliment. Thanks...But no! You don't need to..."

"Why not have Ursula stay at the beach for a few extra days?"

"Take her to the..." said Dave

"Why not?"

"I'll call Aunt Alice, and she'll have a couple of rooms fixed up with a ton of kid's stuff on hand. I promise you! I'm serious. My family doesn't roll in for another month or so. Please!"

Dave looked around. "Really?"

"Then you can join her for the Weekend: Take Ursula sailing at the club. Get her in a Opti. Fish out of Ketched's pier - Tommy will make a short trip for you guys, pay him fifty bucks for the gas. Then eat out and chase crabs at night on the beach with a flashlight... Go!"

"You're not going?"

"No. As I said, I need some time here without the interruptions. Look. I'm serious. Aunt Alice will love some company for breakfast... Barbara can driver her up there, she's going up in a couple of days: Ursula knows Barbara, right?~"

"Sure she knows Barbara! Two months ago I had Ursula for the weekend when you all camped at my place preparing for Malta's Annual Conference. I had Ursula on visitation rights for the weekend, remember? Actually, it was good...the kid had a blast and was spoiled by all of us! Especially by Barbara!"

"That's settled. I'll call Sandra and make my offer this afternoon. Is that ok?"

Dave's face said it all. He was thrilled with a solution to entertain his six year old daughter at the Hamptons for Memorial Day Weekend. He was grinning all the way back to the office.

"Oh, I nearly forgot to tell you..." he said. "Fumosa has me on loan to New Delhi for some research at the American Embassy. Statistics and what have you for demographics. He's got us all going in every which direction these days. Lucy Melanie is off to Pakistan. Bart and Sand are going to Ceylon. *Jesus!*"

"Well. That's a surprise. When did this come up?"

"Yesterday. He was leaving Washington and he asked me if I could accompany a team out of the World Bank looking at aid for public health programs..."

Amanda looked down at her watch. Fumosa would be calling her tonight after he got back to New York. They walked up the front steps of the building. "Maybe it's all this new cash he's getting for the Foundation."

"Yes, I know...How about it. Did you see the numbers? Fantastic amounts of money. Huge jump! Geese, we should be running a small corporation..."

"How about a *large* corporation" laughed Amanda

"Or even a small national sovereign budget!" he added

"He's definitely an ambitious man when he has the means. He's determine to make a difference"

They walked in together and smiled at the Receptionist preparing to hand each of them a list of messages.

Dave turned to Amanda "Thanks for the invite. I'd love to take Ursula and Twinkle out to the beach."

He looked down. "I'll be gone for a couple of months on travel. And it'll keep Ursula chatting to her friends about going to the beach on Memorial Day! That would be fun for her... Thank you Amanda."

"It's my pleasure. I'll call Sandra first. I will assure her that you will not be leaving the city until the weekend, and the child will be staying at our place with Aunt Alice. Then I'll call the house... and email you with the details. Enjoy!"

∞

Amanda was smiling.

She had been at her desk for six hours and here came an email from Dave that utterly relaxed her. It would have gone into her spam had her code address not be so fully correct by the sender. And it only contained three words.

We ate crabs.

Clearly, Dave and his daughter Ursula, withTwinkle were having a good time at the beach for the weekend. Nothing gave Amanda more pleasure. She made herself more coffee, went upstairs to the office kitchenette and opened the fridge. She kept juice up there, and a sandwich. She brought them both downstairs ate at her desk.

The thought of a young girl chasing around the pond with a crab net in her hand filled her with joy.

Of course Aunt Alice would have provisioned them fully. Crab net. Sunscreen. Sun hat. Camera. Shovel for the sandcastle. Bucket for the shells. And of course a netted bag for bludgeons and muskets from pirate ships that might just have washed up on the beach. A water bottle for drinking, just in case she got thirsty in the sun! Today, Dave was clearly having fun with his daughter.

Aunt Alice always had the right idea about priorities, decided Amanda. Life was not about having friends when the going was good. Life was about having friends when the going was rough.

Amanda reached for her coffee and returned to her spreadsheets.

One hundred and twenty more donors to catalogue, and their donations to calculate, along with their missions, tax identifications and Foundation affiliation.

By now her eye had calibrated to spot the majors who normally gave to the cause of the Fumosa Foundation, the regulars and then the newcomers. Chiefly well-endowed companies of European cities that gave generously in the past, if with greater intensity this year. But others included names that had come upon the business world with force and function, especially in communications, technology and internet markets.

Amanda was amazed. Their generosity this year had been phenomenal. Fumosa must have spoken to them all, at some point, with personally or in conferences that attracted their attention.

It was Amanda's responsibility to make sure they were each properly represented as donors for the upcoming annual meeting, and so she took the time to look them up and deliver in their listed presentation a small item of great pride that each donor offered in their mission and commercial success. It was the least she could do as recognition of their generosity. Fumosa would expect nothing less of her.

Most remarkably of all, she noticed how well subscribed they each were by users and cross-markets. Revenues were impressive too. Then Amanda logged their boards of investors, being sure to thank them in the recognitions. Some boards had members that served on multiple corporate boards. Finally, Amanda observed the asset base, and their portfolio managers. Occasionally, she noted the financial institutions that kept their accounts and clients in order. It was a massive task, especially since she was able to reduce the picture into palatable quadrants of donors. The financial numbers of course, required intense concentration, and before long her eyes were glossing over the amounts with some rapidity with repetition.

We ate crabs. That was so cute! Dave clearly put her up to the computer and had her write the email to Amanda. She appreciated his thoughtfulness. Clearly, the child was having fun!

Amanda reached for her coffee. In fact, she appreciated Dave's *thoroughness*! He must have spent hours setting up all this data for her to view. He was a meticulous financial accountant. Nothing, but nothing went passed him, short of computer generated computations.

She took another sip of coffee and sat back. Her arms needed stretching, and so did her back, and legs. She got up again, paced about, and stopped. You'd think the world was linked by networks, she mused. If she drew a map, all donors came from city hubs, European capital centers! Puzzling, really. Especially since so many people lived outside the cities, you'd think the corporate centers would be more evenly distributed?

She was getting tired. She looked at her watch. One more hour of work at the office and she'd wrap it up for the day.

But then it struck her that not all European capital cities were alike: Some financial districts within certain Euro centers had a concentration of donors to the Foundation.

Others less so. She made a list. Did Italians like the Foundation more than, or less than Parisians, for example? As for Londoners, well, they were always most generous, no surprise there.

It wasn't until she was putting on her walking shoes to leave that she thought about some of the figures. Not all corporate donors were equally sized, yet many were equal in their donations. Especially those in same proximity to each other! Perhaps they were all friends, the boards of directors, or perhaps Fumosa clustered his campaigning that way...Oh well.

She pulled down the blinds and switched off the computer systems, the security codes and was turning to activate the electronic alarm when she saw a note at the bottom of page 10.

She wasn't sure, but she thought it was penciled in by Dave during his work on the donor lists. Certainly the data points were copious. But it was an odd thing that caught her attention.

ECB.

All the way home she wondered about his note. And that's when she felt it, an odd... coincidence? Something beneath the long list of donors surfaced only marginally. But what, exactly, she wasn't sure.

What was it?

By the time she got home she was exhausted. The apartment was sparsely furnished, stark even, but clean and simple. Rather, uncomplicated for a professional coming home to a need for a sanctuary, a space of peace and calm. Amanda switched on some tunes, pulled out a lasagna and put it in the over for her dinner.

She answered her iPhone messages, prepared for shower and decided to cancel the movies with a friend for the night. It had been a long day, and possibly more work tomorrow! Besides, there was a good book; a new edition magazine that came in the mail, and even a couple of shows on TV she wouldn't mind watching.

She ran on her treadmill and decided an early morning run in the morning would better clear her head, let alone her muscles. Then into the shower she went before dinning. She sipped at her wine, finished her salad and leaned back in her chair at the mahogany table. She was sitting there gazing at the three small table center ceramic bowls made for flowers. Pottery class I, made by her niece. Amanda thought them charming.

That's when a thought occurred to her. She opened her laptop, and within an hour discovered what ECB was. All the major donors came from financial centers closely linked to the European Central Banks!

In fact, if she looked again, not only were the donations the same, but the names on the boards were each connected to the central bank of each Euro nation. Oddly, some with the greatest European Sovereign Debtors were the biggest donors! How strange was that?

Either Fumosa was one terrific fundraiser, or she was missing something ...In fact, the Foundation seemed to be the recipients of donations from particular banks that enjoyed major LTRO 1 and 2, Longer-term Refinancing Operations.

How odd. Perhaps they hoped for stimulus jumps in the economy?

She wondered about that. How did that work if it failed to produce the inflation expected by gold buyers?

Regardless, definitely not an economist she was. She'd ask Dave when he got back.

In fact, what was truly puzzling was the lack of assets available to those making donations. Come to think about it, what were their reserves if the banks were using...what? Assets of all member states of the ECB as reserves, right? Like, Southern European banks depended on the steady flow of subsidies coming from the ECB?

But what assets, exactly, if they were inheriting Sovereign Debts...How did that work?

A cold chill went up her back. The donations...were solid, right?

So if the politicians couldn't figure all this out, how was it that she could sit here and wonder about these issues? She felt so inept. What if it was a positive financial position on holding bonds or something?   Her suspicions were groundless, right?

Except that the sharp deterioration of public finances was not secret. The IMF said the global fiscal landscape was over 100 percent of GDP.

She wrote a note to herself, mainly to ask. I'm not a monetary expert, but surely the only way to solve all this debt ratio is a massive tax, like a levy or something. Were the donations aimed at avoiding such a levy? If so, who'd be paying that levy?

Taxing by voluntary census was hardly new. And anyway, since nothing was changing it would take decades.

Amanda went to bed. She switched the light out and lay there, wondering. What if they seized everyone's private assets, like their money in banks as a capital levy, like they did after WWI and after WWII, to achieve stability?

If so, what did all this have to do with the Foundation? Definitely, she'd have to talk to Dave about this. What were all those numbers meaning?

∞

At the office Amanda had been sent another report. She examined the narrative, and found it to be a recent official and scholarly finding.

The UN Framework Climate Change Convention cites a concentration of greenhouse gases applicable for the elimination of anthropogenic impact on the climate. There has never been a consensus that man is to blame for global warming among the experts at the Intergovernmental Panel on Climate Change. Especially if you consider recent global growth of birth-populations.

The basis of the argument, she knew, came from the Kioto meeting of World Leaders at Copenhagen where the reference point came from pre-industrial era. World leaders agreed to do everything not to exceed this level by more than two degrees. Such an assertion, she knew, even if implicit, presumed that man was the cause of warming.

 Not that it made much difference in the order of things. Except that nations had set high political standards for Environmental emissions and regulations. Some said, enough to bankrupt entire economies in the world of free trade and competition.

Their argument was that if you abided by those rules -- which some nations did not –you could not be competitive on a global scale.

In the United States, as she well knew, such unfunded mandates by a liberal Washington encouraged writing up Regulations at will.

Some said, it amounted to manipulative chaos by purpose.

Others were critics of the basic assumptions...

None of this helped anything.

Moreover, she wasn't sure how she felt about such complicated issues. Hardly her specialty since she couldn't fix a light bulb if she had to. Nor did she want her shores polluted or her cities choking.

But then again, as a trained anthropologist, she knew the danger signals of an ailing society when she saw them.

So she looked closely at the report.

One call was coming from Russia, recently the center of fires and storms that threatened to choke the air in Moscow.

And then there was something else...she'd look at later, she decided.

But for now Russia drew her attention.

Apparently, from some studies done by Borisenkov and Pasetsky, climate conditions do *not* draw on the conclusions that man makes any difference.

They cited chronicles from Russia and Greenland ice, citing the width of the annual tree trunk rings, and various other indicators that expressed fluctuations over several millennia.

She noted that in their work, the warmest period in Europe was between 1150 and 1300. They asserted that while between 900 and 1300, one or two droughts occurred every hundred years, in the 14th and 15th centuries there were 11 or 12 droughts and eight to 13 floods in each century.

Further, they said, in the late 1500s, heat was replaced with cold and the average temperature dropped by 1.5-2C. The period has been called the "minor ice age". It came to the Russian plain in about 1560 with the cold peaking in 1645-1675. Warming resumed from 1900 and has continued.

Ok, she thought. But honestly. Grapes in the tundra in December? Give me a break!

Then again, their recent fires had caused serious damage. Above all, they were balking at the cost of environmentalism. And their economy had enough challenges as it was.

So how do you rule in favor of policies that are, to say the very least, are unsustainable by the locals?

"Hi Babs. How was your vacation?"

It was almost ten minutes before Barbara finished talking. But it was early in the morning at the office, and Amanda was still nursing her first cup of coffee.

Finally Amanda gave her list of requirements for office work. Amongst them a number of request for further information, data points and contacts. Then came a list of tasks for the upcoming month's events. And finally, some follow-ups and data gathering for the assembled parties attending the Foundation Conference prior to the Annual Meeting.

"Anything else?" asked Barbara. "Dave tells me you had him take his daughter down to the beach for the weekend?"

Amanda laughed. "Yes. They had fun." She thought about asking her next question then said

"One more thing Barbara. Find out what the latest is from the IMF on some figures coming out of Europe these days..."

"As in...?"

"GDP and present figures of ECB policy."

"I'm   not   sure   I   get   what   you   mean?" "What do you know about a capital levy?" said Amanda.

"Umm. Not much. But err... if you need to know, I'll find out!"

Amanda turned to other matters, other than the phone ringing off the hook, and the receptionist "Sorry...But he said it was urgent and needed to talk with you!"

At four o'clock in the afternoon Barbara showed up at the Foundation and plonked her paraphernalia on the desk with a loud jingle of stuff. She stood there with her dark look, heavy shaded eye makeup, and skin-tight black clothes beneath leather boots, gloves and a hooded thread-trailing coat that resembled a wooly mammoth. Not exactly your New York's most prestigious look, but deceptively attractive, and, as Amanda knew her to be, a delightfully amusing and warm hearted soul with an incredible brain. Never mind that she needed three advance phone introductions before anyone let her into their corporate lobby, much less their IT centers!

Barbara was just Barbara. "So! You wanna know what brought me in?" she twanged in Brooklyn style.

"Tell me everything!" said Amanda leaning back into her chair. Barbara didn't pull attention-getting stunts for nothing. She waited.

"It's ain't exactly what you think. There's a big surprise coming for the Euro. Not the first time, either. So far, the Fed is keeping its distance, but with Washington playing politics, you never know what going to happen in the future"

"What are you saying?"

"Well. It's like this. Remember Cyprus...?"

"The financial crisis that gripped the government and forced the investors to take a haircut?"

"Well, it's like this. After WWII in Germany, during the Marshall Plan, that is the European Recovery Program where America gave economic support to help rebuild Europe – ostensibly to avoid the spread of Soviet Communism, the model was not too dissimilar to the Euro today. That is, remove trade barriers, modernize and upgrade things and allow for economic development. It was a rescue program. "

"And...?"

"It has come to be considered as the first element of European Integration. As you know, it worked, and put Europe on its feet. But some critics found that if funded and subsidized central governance rather than encourage independent business, as it was supposed to do. Especially since much of the money was to pay for American goods...Alan Greenspan, un his The Age of Turbulence credits Ludwig Erhard for the economic recovery, saying that Erhard's polices were the most important aspect of postwar Western Eruopean recovering, far outweigh the Marshall Plan. Erhard's reduction sin economic regulations made for Germany's miraculous recovery...etc. etc."

Amanda looked at Barbara who sat down now. She looked a little shaken, if unburdened by the information just delivered. Clearly, there was more coming.

Amanda waited.

"So, the list. As in err... the list of corporations that you gave me? I don't know what it means, but I'm guessing it's a couple of our donors? Well there's something unique about them. They all were part of this counterpart fund to circulate capital through Germany through this one big bank. All their borrowing is managed by this one management fund designed to aid sovereign debt. Well, they've all pulled out and putting their money elsewhere ...."

"Where?"

"Us!" said Barbara simply.

Amanda stared at her, trying to comprehend the meaning of her words, Barbara in all her garb and extreme looks was telling her something important.

"So, you're telling me that they are donating funds to us as a means of ...what, exactly?"

"I don't know for sure. But it sure like its flight of capital to a US entity, wouldn't you say?"

"I have no idea" she said. "I'm not an economist..." She was dialing Dave's office. He was an economic analyst at one of the world's most renown accounting firms representing their interests. Surely he would understand the full picture. He'd be back by now, and his trip overseas not scheduled for a couple of weeks, so he had said. "Yes. Hello. This is Amanda Wells calling for Dave Taylor. Is he in?" Amanda looked up at Barbara and did not like the expression on her face. "Yes. I am returning his call - a message rather, that he sent me this morning..." She was on hold again. "Oh. I see. Then could you tell him I called?"

Amanda put down the receiver. She looked at Barbara. "They haven't heard from him in a few days!"

"How come? He was at your place this weekend, right?"

Amanda dialed the number to her Aunt's house, a tinge of apprehension crossed her forehead. There was no answer.

Barbara got up. "I'm going home! And here's what you need to know. I was only mincing about the fringes with my questions. I'm glad I didn't show them our list. They would probably have thrown me out...It was getting hostile, like that. They're edgy as hell...In fact, Fumosa is something of a dirty word at the Economic Office of the IMF at the UN."

"Sorry I put you through that..." began Amanda.

"No. Nobody knew a damned thing. It was like, fresh information... I just happened to step in the dog shit!"

"Maybe they didn't like your leather boots!" twinkled Amanda.

"Maybe they didn't like opening their account books!"

"I don't see why not. We are one of their best clients."

They almost made it to the door when they heard the office phone ring. It would have been perfectly acceptable to ignore it, the lights and even security system had been switched on for the night. "Shit!" said Barbara "Leave it!"

Amanda took a step or two forward in concordance with that sentiment. Never one able to just walk away from things, she hesitated. The call persisted. Barbara threw down her arms in frustration. "Run! I'll switch off the security alarms from down here!"

When Amanda returned she was unsteady and pale faced. She looked blankly at Barbara.

"What?"

"Dave's office. They said they just heard from his former wife. Dave Taylor is dead."

"*Huh?*"

"Traffic accident."

∞

The ship was at battle stations and on full alert.

"Fire!" said Captain Melison.

"Fire. Away. Sir!" came the response.

"Tube number two: Fire!"

"Tube number two. Fire. Away. Sir"

The missiles were launched in synchronous orbit with the oncoming delivery to the space capsule approaching the Shuttle.

They waited, the ship shuddering like an obedient horse delivering her burden.

God, if these was ever a need for the real warheads...

Nobody said anything.

The time passed quickly.

"Mission Executed!" said the Captain.

Finally Trevor tapped the Captain on the back, perspiration down the back of his shirt.

"Well Done, Captain!"

He straightened up...

"And now we wait" said the Captain.

"Thank you Gentlemen" he said to his surrounding officers.

He surveyed the face of each one in turn with a nod. They started to breath again.

"How do we know it's a kill?" asked Trevor.

"The KW does not carry any high explosive. Hit-to-Kill technology relies on the kinetic energy released in high-speed collisions, such as between the KW and the target. The energy from the impact has been calculated to be in excess of 125 mega joules...."

He stepped down from his command post.

"Besides, the Americans will tell us if the Shuttle gets shot at" said Captain Melison . "Our duty is done"

He went to the communications station.

∞

"So where is she now?" asked Amanda on the cell phone.

"Up in the tree house with Susie. They're having an afternoon tea. I had to procure nothing but the best cups for those two, a tablecloth, the proper silverware and all but my best china!" said Alice DeBuerlin.

"You've always been a sweetie with children Aunt Alice. And I can tell that she's in good hands..."

"They've been inseparable those two, you'd think the girl had never had a girl friend to play with! They're like salt and pepper those two, one carrying on about houses in trees, the other about gardens in the woods..." She giggled.

Amanda smiled, listening. "She's lit up, animated, sleeping well, and eating like a horse. She and her father had a blast together at the beach. But with Susie waiting at the gate for her, she didn't flinch when he said he had to go back to New York for a day or two...Yes. I know. I know, it was just for the weekend right? But honestly Amanda, what's a week down here! You know how it goes in the summertime. The place is presently empty and I'm equipped like a hotel..."

"So, you are sure you're OK with that?"

"Yes. Yes. Yes. Charity always begins at home in this family as you know. So, I'll stick to my promise, act normally, alter nothing, and wait for her mother to pick her up."

"Yes. And I'll be down this weekend to give you a hand. She should be back soon, her attorney tells us."

"Umm"

"Well, that's what Barbara says when she called up" explained Amanda "They're making the funeral arrangements now, and of course we will attend. I told the attorney where Twinkle was, and he said he had left word for the mother. She's out sailing in the Lesser Antilles with her boyfriend apparently. Communications are not the best...So, we'll wait and see and do what we can to help. Are you absolutely sure you're ok with the situation?"

"Yes. Yes. Really. I've got the bridge club coming in this afternoon, and a small buffet following for the hubbies. Twinkle will be with us and around us. I'm sorry, of course. He seemed like a very nice man. He enjoyed himself here. But there it is, life for you. I do understand, and please offer my sincere condolences..."

"I will Aunt Alice. I'll call you tomorrow " said Amanda, ending the call. *Thank God for Aunt Alice!*

She was frustrated as hell. She dialed Barbara. "Any word yet?"

There was several items accounted for. Finally Amanda said "Ok. So for now let's inform Mr. Bates that Twinkle is still at my Aunts, and seems to be fine and safe. He is welcome to send someone if he wishes, but they must be announced in advance, with full identification with the Sherriff's office. Meantime, Aunt Alice is watching over her, has told her nothing, and waiting for instructions. She can be considered a friend of the family. I'll be down there this weekend, too. Ask again about the whereabouts of the mother, will you? We should make a daily effort to enquire. Even if it's fruitless. Those damned sailing cruises can take weeks, especially if they are out of ship-to-shore range. Which I suspect is no accident, considering her haste to leave Dave with the child and go. Still. Keep asking. Please!"

∞

Chapter 7

Amanda did not expect to be wined and dined by Commander Lloyd of the US Navy.

In fact, she would have said no altogether. Except that she had been asked to keep herself informed by her superiors. And Lloyd was most definitely a man most informed.

Surprisingly, there was nothing more fun than a spin about the city on the back of a Harley Davidson. Especially in the middle of December.

They had alternated between hard liquor and hot coffee bars all night.

"I know this one place..." Amanda said finally "In Brooklyn. Open 24-7, where they make fresh baked bread that comes out at midnight!"

"Now that I'd like to see!" said Lloyd.

"Only in New York" she laughed. "Come on. Let's go!"

"And later..." he was saying in her hair on the ride "You free?"

Amanda did not realize what a long night it would be. Because once they entered the bakery, they started to talk.

Lloyd, evidently, had quite a history. And yes, he was an astronaut

Oddly enough, it was his cell phone that ended it all. He read his message.

BOTTLED MESSAGES AWAY. SEARCHING FOR A HOME, NOW "I've got to go" he said abruptly.

He had a trailer, he said, parked at Newark Airport. He'd insert his bike and have it driven back to Washington, he explained. Meantime, he would hop a flight into D.C.

Amanda felt a little dazed.

"So... If there is anything more you know about this guy, this is where to reach me" he was saying about Salim "We need to find him. We need to stop him!"

She looked up at him, blank. *And the evening?*

He leaned down, blue eyes and all. "And after we do, I shall come to the Hamptons..."

Another text followed on his cell.

It was pre-dawn. Yes, she was fine, she said. Err...she would take a cab home, thank you!"

What she didn't expect was a police siren to appear and escort Lloyd as he revved up his bike. They followed him out.

Some date. Good thing they weren't in bed.

∞

The data sheets in her hand definitely were sent to her by Dave. He even had a note at the bottom.

> *"Amanda,*
>
> *Before Fumosa sends me on some forlorn trip for his priorities, I wanted to mail you some information that you showed an interest in. It's not strong drink, but even on the rocks, this could give the IRS cause for inspection. Take a look. keep it safe!*
>
> *Best, Dave."*

Fortunately, there had been no questions or legacy legends to add to Dave's cards of condolences. Being y honest, she was glad the envelope arrived in the mail several days after his funeral. That way, it could remain in her inbox without anyone asking her if she heard from Dave.

Kept it safe! What was that about? Since when was there anything suspicious about their donors? True, they valued all their contacts - and kept them private as a matter of office policy. Yet he was concerned. Writing this note was one of the last things he did before he died. It was addressed to her in a brown manila envelope with data sheets folded inside.

She put it in her purse.

At home, she studied the contents.

She called her Aunt. No word today, either. Maybe tomorrow, she said.

Amanda felt suddenly irritated. There was nothing here out of the ordinary. Everything here was in good order. All were good donors with solid standing.

She took a long breath. Neither was Dave a man of riddles nor was he an alarmist. So what was unusual here?

She went to the fridge, poured herself a glass of lemonade, added a slice of lemon, pushed it under the icemaker and returned to the computer.

She checked for any updates of the donors by their websites, examined first their CEOs; their contact and their Annual reports. She examined their Mission Statements and found them to be older companies with a long history of corporate charity donations. Most were global companies; some tech and the rest in industries of mining, transportation and communication.

The phone rang. It was Mrs Simpson, Dave's neighbor. She was told to call Amanda about any questions regarding Dave. They chatted.

Amanda talked about Dave as a friend and advisor to the Foundation. Mrs Simpson did most of the talking. She wanted to know if she could send a Note of condolence to his family - he talked often about them. The last day she saw him she said, he was in a big hurry loading up his car. Then there was the time when *she* got locked out and Dave came over.

It was a good fifteen minutes before the call ended, and Amanda felt hot. She reached for her drink and downed a long gulp, Dave's list still before her.

She sat back, stared at the companies on her screen, still without a clue. She felt tired.

What was she looking for anyway?

Were it not from Dave, she would not ordinary have been surveying this stuff. Maybe if she added up the numbers of the donations? Would that be what he was talking about? She put down her drink. She opened another spread sheet. Now all the donors were on his list logged in.

Nothing. Nothing strange there.

She reached for the drink which left a ring on the envelope. That's when she noticed.

Condensation from the icy drink had dissipated into the bottom edge of the envelope leaving a moist ring over a soggy protrusion. Like a metal rivet.

She dove inside the envelope and it lay there, a small metal strip that had been dropped in, stuck in the bottom corner of the envelope. So tightly lodged was it cornered at the bottom of the fold that not even a see-through inspection would have shown up anything. It looked like a button to an electronic device.

It surprised her, and she felt like she was being invasive. She inspected the back of the last data sheet. Evidently, there had been a piece of tape attached, Dave had tried to tape it, but it fell loose and must have fallen astray.

She got up and made her way into the kitchen. She felt hungry and reheated some dinner, thinking.

Later, she circled the desk and sat staring at the thing - this time with a real drink on the rocks.

Finally she came to one conclusion. Dave was in haste, and he was being secretive. *Why?*

What in the world was Dave doing with such concealment? Nothing they did was clandestine, and nothing they worked on needed secrecy. That is, aside from exercising routine administrative care.

This was different. What in the world was he doing? She thought about calling Barbara. She could ask Fumosa. Or she could even call Dave 's office. She thought about it. None seemed appropriate.

He had sent her this note, clearly appealing to her sense of discretion. But why? What would accountants have to hide in records anyway?

Button nothing. It was a flash drive.

It took her all night to make a decision about a flash drive sent to her by Dave. Couldn't he have just forwarder her documents? Or an inter-office courier delivering a package of data? No. He chose a flash drive, period.

She inserted the device into her laptop. She opened the drive.

The images that come up on her screen looked like spiders. Spiders, spiders, spiders.

She looked closely and saw that they revealed networks. Each hub represent a source from which lines emanated. They revealed bracketed names and numbers. Each cluster by itself was not unusual, nor the numbers. But each developed into further hubs, and further networks of numbers.

Amanda stared at her spread sheet. Nearly all the names had links to the corporations making donations.

Sometimes executives, board members, even just employees. But all were entrenched in a company making donations.

Next, she turned to the ends of the lines - obviously account numbers.

Many were corporate accounts in various repositories. Often repetitive, they interlinked, and multiplied. Then another image of more spiders, lines and more numbers. There was at least ten spread sheets emanating from one center. As data points they could be reconfigured. She would compile them into datasets.

So preoccupied with the lines and where they led, that Amanda almost overlooked the center from where the lines all sourced. She zoomed in. She suddenly sat upright.

Expecting to see more clients donating to their non-profit foundation, she was unprepared for what she saw.

The data was encrypted, and revealed each hub as an Intelligence source. The IRS. The CIA. The NSA. MI5. These were unauthorized lists of...of... *surveillance?*

"Hello! You alright?" asked Mrs. Watson as Amanda walked into the office. "You look a little tired dear!" The voice grated.

Amanda was exhausted. She had been up all night. She was tense and uneasy about what Dave tossed into her lap. Did Fumosa know or not know about this?

Dave was trying to warn her.

All account numbers were in banks accounts related to their donors: That she figured out. It had been long hours of study. Bank accounts were being watched by the authorities. *Why?*

Did that mean that now *they* were the subject of some kind of computer investigation – perhaps recipients of money... from those donors?

She calmed down.

Well no! The money was just pledged. Not actually transacted. So far so good. So that made everything just for future information, right?

But the questions were baffling. What on earth was Dave doing? Why send something like that to her? Where was Fumosa on all this...?

After all, these were not sovereign agencies, right? The numbers were individuals or corporations with bank accounts? What did all that mean? And what was she to do with all this now? Report it to whom, exactly?

"Your marching orders!" announced Barbara, handing her an email from the general Admin Inbox with instructions from Fumosa. "You will get your own email, I'm sure!"

She was to travel for the Foundation. A trip to Rome, first for the Annual Meeting, followed by a field survey for the inspection of environmental compliance. A Research Report, he said... A request from the US Government.

She muttered to Barbara about it. They had lunch together. Then she realized she had uttered not one word about the data still sitting on her laptop at home! She would go to the Hamptons for the Weekend, is what she said. That would relax things. Besides, there was the child to worry about - still unclaimed by her mother yet!

Jesus!

No. She would not, she decided. Many reasons came up, but in the end, she would not expose them! Yes. She was a liability now. *What the hell* Dave? She was furious. Why drop this on her?

But as the day wore on, she realized that going overseas was not such a bad idea, perhaps. She listened to Barbara prepare things; the travel itinerary and paperwork.

Finally, the day came. She gathered documents, packed, gave her Landlord details of her absence, and walked herself onto the flight to Rome...

Dave's list was in her bank safe! That's the best she could do. End of story.

Damn it!

∞

They called him The Defender. It was his way to speak easily to the public and thus work his way into the infrastructure of European Central Bank governance. Swiss by birth, his family had lived in Belgium since the war.

His father sent him to America for his University training in the 1960s after which he served as an economist both at a renown East Coast University and then in Washington on the staff of the World Bank. There, he had travelled extensively, discovering that what international politics could not solve, money could.

In large measure, it was his hand that brought about the solutions in multiple countries, including India and Korea. By the time he was examining Serbia, he had gained a reputation for solving irreconcilable cultural divides.

But it was for Ireland's conflicts, that he developed the name of Defender. There, he not only sweetened the pie for internal conflicts, but encouraged the kind of Swiss-minded liberalism to financial transacting.

It brought the ECB down upon them with more than a few scorching words of reprimand. Had there not been such a surprising defense of Ireland made by the British, the ECB would never have backed off.

It might have had to do with bailout opportunities attractive to the British. But he knew he had to do more than offer money. So to Ireland, he introduced Apple.

Now, to Syria he introduced Arms dealing. But he was no longer with the World Bank, the ECB or even the financial trading culture. He was on his own. Still, as The Defender, he had a reputation.

Aside from his recognizable egotistical good looks, even as a middle aged gentleman with a trimmed beard and sun lined face, he was a creature of politics. Thus he showed up for the occasional high-visibility events at the Kennedy Center in Washington DC, or the Metropolitan Opera in New York, or other high visibility Charity Events. But it was clear he liked being noticed, exposing himself as a generous philanthropist.

He claimed to manage a Fund. In fact, he managed a network of IT specialists divided by firewalls and national boundaries, if not international laws and Reform banking. His work was cleverly masked.

What the Fed meant for good, especially following the 2008 banking collapse, he could translate for private gain. If Greenspan wrote *"The Age of Uncertainty,"* he surely could write *"The Age of Recession"* for social progress.

He patterned himself, he said, after the richest men of the nineteenth century who gave a damn about politics, but could control a nation with money, as if he were a Kenneth Gailbraith deciding for Keynsian economics.

"Give me the management of a nation's finance, and I care not who governs!" was his favorite quotation at many a cocktail party, bringing down the house with laughter.

What he specialized in were Reactionary social impulses. What he studied were the anomalies, the computer trends that spoke of deeper human tendencies, not by individuals, necessarily, but by groups, or cultures, or politics. He noticed for example how once policies like the Marshall Plan had left its indelible mark on American industrial expansion; capital markets; corporate leverages, and social programs, both East and West. Here was such a fabric of interlocking behavioral patterns lessons from the World Bank about societies needing assistance...and the data that turned them into societies dependent on Systems. Especially those with cash, like Europe.

No trend that stood out with any measurable amount of money went unnoticed. No research of spending, credit, investment or banking bubble went without deep analysis. Congress would yearn for his data bases, such that they could write policy and earn themselves the next elections.

But no! Let the elections run amok!

His staff was loyal. They uttered not a word, lived quietly in Brussels, and did his computing.

The collapse of Europe, they knew in advance. The bailout of Cypress was a foregone conclusion. The Americans were malleable. He could surely help himself to half their investor's portfolios' overseas. He could create a run; reverse a flow of cash, or garner fees from each.

One client particularly intrigued him. Not for his strength of cash, far from it. But for his strength of world vision. For him, he would insert another place into the framework of the UN, and he knew just the Foundation to do it.

Except for one spy, it seemed. An Accountant who was theorizing on what he was seeing. Someone who had an uncanny way of following the numbers, and more significantly, what they meant. His accounts, after all, were saying a lot. Besides predicting demographic shifts; changing economies; local wars and unsettled weather, there was a world of opportunity out there to shape.

Actually, the spy, or his "problem" would not be tracking his numbers any further. Apparently he had come to his demise, they said.

"Just the same!" he told his Administrators in Brussels on his way out the door that evening. "Keep an eye out for anyone else looking..."

He left. He and his wife were entertaining at their home in Waterloo that evening.

What his staff did not know were his reasons for tracking "Reactionary social impulses" as he put it.

"Trends!" said one enlightened techy.

They had all laughed.

"Geo-political metrics?" volunteered another.

"Triggers..." he enlightened them, the glint of admonishment in his handsome face. They loved it. He was nothing less than an icon.

Today however, was a serious day. For the soiree at their home, he and his wife were resplendent in white tie and formal attire.

They made a stunning couple.

The chateau at Waterloo was a Dutch colonial on Rue de La Mont, located outside the city and not far from the War Memorial park of Napoleon's famed battlefield. It was accessed from one of Belgium's magnificent Boulevards. Ancient trees and perambulating parks punctuated by statues; benches, and green lawns marked the roads of Waterloo, just outside Brussels.

When gathered in Brussels for the formation of the European Commonwealth in the 1970's, many recalled the ignoble denial of Admission to Great Britain not once, but multiple times by the ambitious General DeGaule. Yet much had changed since then. Here, only the well-financed or leaders of governments lived.

Glossy cars appeared up the chateau driveway, valets opening their doors. Out stepped a tall athletic man in his late thirties, wearing a dark suit with a crimson dinner tie. A formally dressed woman unfolded from the car and stood at his side. They approached the grand entrance where stood the host and his wife to greet guests.

"May I come in?" he said, in theatrical hesitation, "Or does the Great Defender pose a threat to those who enter his castle?"

They roared with laughter.

"Mays pas du tout!" said the host, extending his hand "I am honored to have you as our guest tonight. Entrez, please, Mr. DePhillip."

∞

Amanda was back at her Report again with a coffee on her table.

She needed to answer Barbara's request for environmental air quality in the region.

"Tell me if you see anything unusual" said Barbara "It's part of the broader scope of things that must be included in this damned Report I'm struggling with..."

"The data on greenhouse concentrations are interesting" said Amanda.

Barbara looked at her, puzzled.

"If their concentration reaches about 180-200 molecules per million molecules of air, the ice age on the earth will set in!" she explained, grinning. Barbara sat across the office from her.

"And what does that mean, in now-terms?"

"Ok. In 1900, the figure was 280 molecules per million. Today it is 380 mm. For the sake of comparison, when the temperature on the planet was 10-12C higher than today, that figure was 4,000-6,000 molecules.

"Scientifically speaking, we are closer to an ice age but we are drifting away from that boundary: True, cycles last thousands of years and if the geologists are right, an ice age will occur in the distant future while a sharp temperature rise is already happening."

"Really? ...Err. Any coffee left?" said Barbara.

Amanda poured out two cups and returned to her reading.

"Russia is vast and climate change will affect its different parts in various ways. In some it will be welcome and in others it will be harmful. For example, water is a vital issue...." Amanda's voice faded somewhat.

Barbara cleared her throat to intonate she was still there.

"On much of the territory – in the north and northwest, in the Volga, Non-Black Soil, the Urals areas and in most of Siberia.." said Amanda in distinct volume "the amount of water will increase, while in the Belgorod and Kursk regions, the Stavropol and Krasnodar regions and Kalmykia there will be a serious decline in water. Water will become a key problem. .."

"Oh?" said Barbara, again.

Amanda was getting the feeling that this was not going to be easy to read.

"In agriculture, everything will depend on rainfall and droughts. On the whole, grain crops are expected to drop by 10-13pc in the Black Soil area, by 25pc in southern Siberia while they will grow by 10-20pc in the Non-Black Soil area. If warming continues, the boundaries of warm-climate crops will move north and the areas under these crops (beetroot, soybeans, sunflowers, etc) will increase. In some southern regions, subtropical farming will become possible. At the same time agricultural pests, especially locusts, will become more of a problem."

She stopped reading.

"The err...locusts, you were saying?" quizzed Barbara, sensing some alarm. "Is there a problem?"

"One key climatic plus for Russia is the northward shift of the area that is suitable for human habitation. The southern boundary of extreme discomfort close to the boundary of the far north will move 60km in the area of Komi, Arkhangelsk, 150km in Khanty-Mansiisk and Evenkia, 250km in the republic of Sakha, the Irkutsk and

Khabarovsk regions. The country's centre and south will grow hotter. Temperature swings will happen more frequently, harming people's health. High temperature, among other things, contributes to the spread of infectious and parasite-borne diseases..."

"Amanda? Something the matter?"

"I don't like these predictions" said Amanda, and she swallowed another gulp of cold coffee.

"By the mid-century the permafrost zone, which occupies about 60pc of our country's territory, will move north by as much as 200km in western Siberia. This will have a negative impact on the numerous pipelines that deliver oil and gas from Siberia to Europe, and on the structure of buildings. Some experts believe that an increase of the average annual temperature by 2C diminishes the strength of foundations on piles by 30pc."
"Oh?"

Amanda put down the technical journal.

"Barbara?" she said "What do you know about Russia?"

"Very little. Why do you ask?"

"More than a quarter of houses built in Yakutsk, Vorkuta and Tiksi in 1950-1970 may be destroyed. In Norilsk in the last 20 years, the surface has been melting a whole meter deeper during the warm period, which has already caused foundations to sag. What will happen if global warming hits the area with full force?"

Barbara was listening. "Why?"

"...There will be more precipitation on Russian territory, it will increase by an average 10pc between 2000 and 2050. The biggest growth will happen in winter, especially in the eastern and northern regions. By contrast, in most of the European Russia, in the south and southwest, there will be less precipitation".

Amanda stopped. A thought struck her like a stake in the heart.

"What is it?"

"Who knows anything about accelerated melt down?"

"That Geek downstairs. He's got doomsday things to say about everything!"

"I need to talk to him" said Amanda tearing away from her desk. "Something here *isn't* right!"

"Amanda!" called Barbara "I need something to give them for a discussion..."

"How about a crisis!" came back Amanda's reply.

"What?"

She couldn't find Barbara's Geek downstairs. But that's when she got her call from Fumosa.

"Darling" he said, as always. "I was wondering if you could do me a gigantic favor?"

Shit, she thought. "What do you need Dr. Fumosa?"

"I'm presenting a paper in Australia next week. And I wondered if you could take my place? I'll send you my data and you can present it in your name if you wish..."

"No need for that..." she began, about to find an excuse for saying no. But he pre-empted her "...Also, if you stop in Karachi on the way there. There is a delivery shipment that needs to be directed inland to a Relief Area when it arrives. I want you to oversee that it arrives safely at the dock; secure it and then then redirect it inland. You will be our Representative on location to receive the Disaster Relief Shipment..."

He paused. "Then by all means proceed on to Australia for the Adelaide Conference on Drought Management..."

She would have liked a chance to respond, let alone say something intelligent. But he was gone before she could stop him.

∞

The Constitutional Hall in Milan was where most government meetings were held. Especially Hearing about Working agreements; planning and strategic policy.

The Finance Ministers were gathered to find ways to prevent the consequences of an uncertain market and wave of volatile currency. They must stave off a financial collapse that would not only take out most of their commercial credit, but more damagingly, hurt their viable new industries...

In fact, if the rest of southern Europe was to be counted, Italy - for all its celebrated scandals; corruption and socialist governments represented the most viable country in new business development. Or rather, the most liquid.

But only by the hand of one man, an economist called up two years ago to fix the deplorable state of their national budget - not as a politician, but as an academic. Today, he stood amongst his colleagues.

There was much to be pleased with. The country had not only taken a haircut, but assisted its neighbors. They in turn had become customers for products and manufacture, and opened up new global opportunities for further growth. Infrastructure had been well spent, and transportation was free and open for yet smaller industries. Even housing was starting up.

 That is, until the jobs dried up. Suddenly, the only traffic free and full were the roads of incoming and illegal immigrants fleeing despoliation and military riot at home.

It could not have happened at a worse time. Global collapse had found a way of contagion.

For them to resort to Nationalistic thinking was entirely unacceptable. Yet some choices had to be made! It was a matter of choosing between crisis management, and despair of all hope for decent governance...

What the Ministers were most concerned about were the events that could lead to total civil breakdown and riot.

Present were bankers, all of them citing a run on their accounts; low reserves and little option but to close the doors before Regulators of International Banking withdrew their authorizations.

"The first thing we do, is cease to mingle the accounts of our customers with the accounts of our investors!" began the Minister.

"Eh! Eh! Eh Bene!" objected the first. "We are not Cyprus!"

"Not yet!" he proceeded. "Nor are we the United States. But the Volker Rule will come to apply universally in due course, so we may as well jump on it as a means to start solving our insolvency. That's first!"

They all looked at him, shocked. This was perhaps the only man who was privy to the complete picture of national finances available in their Treasury. What he knew mattered. It was a question of how severe was the crisis. They waited for more information.

"Unless we wish to degenerate into the situation seen in Egypt, and, as you well know, it is not an easy thing to keep the Treasury free of political dipping ...Then we must severely look at ways to cut our national expenditures..."

"How will our government agree?"

"Frankly, we are past that point of agreements. They have no choice!" he said. "Gentlemen, believe me when I tell you that we are in a crisis. I look forward to the day when this is fixed, and I can go home..."

Nobody spoke.

"So we have work to do!" he said.

The result was a near total shut-down of government. Except for policing and some military defense to preserve law and order. It took him all day to hammer out a consensus. But only with such a plan could he approach the European Central Bank for printing more money to lend to their country. It was that simple.

He told the assembly of Ministers that just yesterday, over the phone with his ECB principles in Brussels - including one investor the Defender, that there had been a plan endorsed...But it was an ultimatum!

Finally, the Agreements were signed. But it was a somber moment of consent.

What they feared the most was one small outbreak of crisis, or emergency disaster that would induce total breakdown and civil disorder.

But who could anticipate such an event..?

∞

The Secretary's office at the United Nations was busy today. Not often did the Secretary of State take her place at a the General Meeting to state the position of the United States, but to admonish others to rediscover order! Spain had shown unnecessary violence in a skirmish at the Basque hills along the Spanish border.

The speech was long and hotly delivered, never once acknowledging the receipt of a written apology by the Spanish government for overzealous policing, nor even the incident that set off the violence. Most of all was the awful gap in what was not said. A terrorist cell was deeply embedded in the Basque Hills. And clearly, it was not for the Spanish to engage... The situation was one for action only to be taken by the United States.

The requisite number of votes were predictably noted, including one objection coming from the Soviet Union who knew better than what was being presented for public dissemination. But it made for good media copy, and allowed for some assertions of control and victory by top key leadership in an endless war against terrorism.

Finished with her speech, the US Secretary of State was photographed with her allies, then attended an official luncheon. She later spend some time on the phone talking with various senators and congressmen to advise them of her progress, and finally she made some personal calls on her cell phone.

By the time she strode into her office, they were ready for her, and gave her a small round of private applause. She smiled, and thanked them. But she was far from pleased. If anything, she was fatigued looking and irritable. They knew why.

The only time Washington's administration came boiling up to New York to deliver some politically correct speech was to garner public support and election votes. It made for happy liberal copy.

But she was anything but happy.

In the limousine to La Guardia Airport, she was alone with her thoughts. No, she would *not* retire to her home in New York but fly back to Washington directly where she knew there was much more going on. Never one to miss a party, she wanted to be at the center of it all. Especially in this upcoming election year. Campaigning – and financial contributions were important if you wanted to win elections. But even if you're political Party failed to win, then surely your political sphere of influence would make you attractive any new administration, and keep you on...

She called into her Assistant. "Emily, tell the staff to concentrate on a second round of discussion next month, there is much to be made of this situation, even as it dies down..."

"Yes Ma'am."

"It was an incendiary situation... and send me all the Reviews before I come up again. And yes, well done today. You set up a good speech! I'll want another from you..."

"Will the Senator be joining you for the next round?"

It was a question that was reasonable, the senator being her husband who sat on the Foreign Relations Committees of Congress.

"Hell no! Besides, I want to talk to Fumosa and get the World Health involved with the drought of that region, and the famine that incited the rebellion. Plus, I have other things to talk to him about. Where is he now?"

"I'll check."

"Wait! Someone told me he was in Brussels, now I remember... Invite him to lunch with me in Washington DC at State, will you?"

"Yes Ma'am. Fumosa?"

"Yes. Fumosa."

"Oh, and Emily. Did you get me those financial reports I asked for two days ago from Treasury?"

∞

Barbara was frustrated. She had cramps all day; taken up with a pile of new work, and never got any jogging done. It was now raining, and the crowd at the Irish Pub tonight would just have to order their food without her there!

The Foundation Offices where she and Amanda worked were not far from the United Nations. They had support-contracts to fulfill and remained close by. Whenever a General Meeting occurred, Barbara was the one who went up to attend to the particular Speakers. It had been a long day.

By the time Barbara got back to the Foundation Offices, she was dripping wet. She tossed her raincoat on the hanger and her umbrella in the parasol-bin.

"I hope you appreciate my efforts up there!" muttered Barbara coming into Amanda's quarters.

Amanda appeased her with a fresh brew of coffee and a couple of biscotti left in the kitchen.

Barbara looked at her.

"You look pretty drained yourself kiddo. Have you been at this all day?""

"Umm" said Amanda, a cookie in her mouth. "Run and go! I know you want to join the others tonight..."

"Alright. But I learned something. Have you heard from Dave's office recently?"

"No. Why?"

"Nothing really. He is..*was* with the Accounting Firm responsible for producing the Reports on Fiscal Disbursements, right? He keeps a desk Uptown, as you know, and he's usually the one in and out of the Secretary's office with Annual Reports and Meetings up there..."

"I know. I know!" said Amanda, her mouth still full but her hand saying it all.

Barbara just looked.

"Ok. Guess who I ran into today – it was a big day today up there with the Secretary delivering her speech, all over the news. Anyway.. Emily!"

Amanda's look was fixed.

"So we had a little time out and I got the impression all hell's breaking lose. Amongst other things, they wanted accounts. Accounting and more accounting. But with Dave, well...gone, they were having a hell of time procuring the figures they needed from his Firm. Apparently, much of his stuff was buried in with IT who couldn't help much, and the Secretary wanted as much accounting info as she could get before going back to Washington. Emily was *pissed!*"

Barbara paused, both of them puzzled.

Then Barbara added "No. I mean she wanted to *leave*, like...the job! Who *leaves* jobs like that?"

After a while Amanda sighed. It was with a measure of understanding.

"I don't know Barbara... You need a special tolerance for that kind of game. Thank God we live in the world of the non-profit. Difficult, maybe, but honest and uncomplicated!"

Barbara looked down, searching for words of a specific kind. The kind that meant things without saying things. She was great at chatting. But she was on unsafe ground with real observations.

Amanda said "What's up?"

"Nothing. I'm just saying, because I'm not saying anything. But Emily says she doesn't like the lists and things she gives the Secretary because she feels...Well she feels like they're used for the wrong budgets."

"Maybe she's overworked"

"Or maybe she told me they take money for other things in that group. She wants to leave her job!"

"Emily threatens to leave her job every time there's a United Nations Meeting."

"No. I mean it. She means it. She's nervous she may have to answer questions or something. And she doesn't want to be implicated."

Amanda sat back. Emily was an office clerk, of sorts. With a mass of tangled curls, an open face and a short stature, it was easy to forget that Emily had a role that was more than clerk and office chores. She had a law degree. And she was smart. Everything she did was as much to advance her superiors as it was an investment in her own future career.

Something was wrong here, and she was seeing things that made her feel like a party to it. If it became a criminal investigation, perhaps later under a different administration...

"Let's call it a day Barbara! It's hard to know what's bothering her. You're terrific for observing, and for all the extra effort you got out of Dave's office. I shall have to appeal to her superiors for an official report."

Barbara almost reached the door then turned around. "Have you heard from Fumosa?"

"Yes" said Amanda. "I got my marching orders, as you put it. He now wants me in Australia..."

"Ewe!" exhaled Barbara. "How long? When do you leave...."

"A Conference. Don't worry. I'll be fine, and Australia is wonderful! Relax. Now go to dinner! We'll catch up later..."

Amanda wrapped up her day at the Foundation and went home. She made a decision and would spend the evening alone. After all, she liked to get her life in order before a trip, and there was much to do before the end of the week.

Perhaps going on a trip was a good idea. It would give her some fresh air to breath, some thoughts to untangle. She might find some explanations behind all these accounts, some links and viable answers...

It had become rather a puzzle: Why couldn't Dave have just gone to his superiors with this information? Or even to the authorities if he suspected foul play? No! He sent it to *her*. Not being able to crack this nut was taking up all her time. It had become really annoying.

Still, there was one more thing she wanted to examine, now that Barbara mentioned Emily's discomfort.

She polished off her meal , drained her wine and cleaned up. Then she took the time to prepare for a new day at work in the morning.

Instead of turning on a show to unwind, she turned on the lamp above her desk and switched on to her laptop to examine the data that Dave had put in her custody.

It took some searching, but she found the compiled lists of sources from which Dave received his data-points.

Many of them were government agencies that had clearly been hacked. Budget cuts; budget proposals, appropriations etc. etc..The numbers reeled off the screen like a tickertape cataloguing corporate earnings and stock transactions.

Since most of the large government agencies had budget offices and accounting platforms, mainly as a means of delivering their budget requests to Congress there were few surprises. Even the White House and the Executive Branches of government were listed as offering line items for which monies had been transferred from Treasury.

There is all lay. Nothing unusual. She wasn't sure what it was that she was searching for, really...

There was one agency she hadn't noticed. She typed Department of State.

Instead of an accounting of operating budgets and key players who made donations to the Foundations, she found a list of banks and agencies overseas. They were tallied differently. They showed large numbers, some equivalent to large government budgets. Mainly, they were ascribed to management. Management of accounting. Management of collections. Management of banking deposits. Management of Supervisors, Executors and Judicial offices administering the oversight of police departments.

Most of the tallies were different. They showed a ten percent kite-mark.

Enough! She felt tired and took a bath. About to turn in when something sent her back to the computer.

Then it dawned on her.

She pushed back on her chair, her hand flew to her mouth. Impossible!

Who did this stuff without democratic process? Surely, she got it all wrong...

Here was a list of a massive ten percent seizure of all banking assets, *everywhere*

So, what was Dave telling her? How did the Foundation have anything to do with this...?

Then she looked at the amounts of the donations, and the amounts of the tally sheets.

Their Foundation was being used as a... conduit?

What on earth did this mean?

Was the United States complicit? Presumably, that must mean significant danger was brewing internationally, right?

Perhaps they needed a Relief Fund or something...

She turned to the most recent economic reports issued by the World Bank.

The European Bank Crisis was getting worse, and in the balance was the question of sovereign sustainability. Obviously, neither could the banks save themselves nor could political leaders make the kinds of decisions that would solve fiscal shortfall....

Was that it?

Hence the entire system was about to be revamped with a massive capital levy on all assets across Europe!

Such ideas occurred only a few times in history. During war, or total collapse. The Marshall Plan was designed for Reconstruction and Rebuilding. Nationalization was a forever control tool to acquire people's assets. But here, even with steady subsidies coming from ECB's offering more printed money, there seemed to be a huge "takings."

That would require legal accounting conduits; proclamations at the global level, perhaps even at the United Nations...

But what about constitutional rights, legitimate democracy and the rule of law? Wouldn't there be process and debate and election...? Amanda was puzzled at the clandestine nature of this sweeping action. Surely at the very least, it would be open for public debate and explained in the Media?

Come to think about it, other than uncertainty about markets, there was little about what to do to solve these issues. In fact, there was little said about it anywhere. This was pretty sweeping stuff....surely there would be sanction...somewhere?

Without such checks and balances, Amanda knew, who was to say it would all be legitimate and properly reimbursed, let alone endorsed?

What if this was used by those with *less* than good intentions?

What if... the system was hijacked...?

Ridiculous!

Besides, how would you conceal such a ploy?

Or what if was all legitimate and working fine, but for one small anomaly able to toss the whole apple cart?

How to reconcile knowing all this...?

Distress Planning Contingency, that's what they called it. Emergency Preparedness, surely!

She thought about it. Of course. That was it.

 Dave must have known, he must have wanted to...Wait.

Dave? What happened to him? An Accident, right? She should take every precaution.

No! Now she was getting silly...

Dave had entrusted her with information nonetheless. She should put it in a secure repository where none of it should be discovered without purpose. For now, anyway. How would she hide this, in her bank vault?

Neither should she be irresponsible, nor should she allow it to cause harm...

She was supposed to be visiting her Aunt this weekend. There were still arrangements to be made pending decisions about Dave's affairs.

She picked up the phone and cancelled her plans with her Aunt. If there was one thing her Aunt could say was that Amanda never showed up. That way, she could enjoy absolute indemnification from having had any contact with Amanda or proffering opportunity to be "given" anything that might count as a liability.

Such were the bounds of trust amongst family at the beach house: There, there was an honored family tradition with regards to mail. If any mail arrived for anyone, it was left neatly in a box for them to pick up! It was never opened. Her brother once discovered a postcard at the house that was over a year old!

In the morning, decided Amanda, she would mail out a package. Then she would pack for the trip.

Barbara complained all the way to the airport. It was still raining. "Are you serious?...Australia? With a stop in Karachi as our 'Representative to receive the Disaster Relief Shipment'? What is he thinking, Fumosa? It's dangerous as hell..."

Amanda answered her buzzing cell.

∞

Karachi was not known for its cultural delicacies.

It was, Amanda felt, a vortex of humanity without destination.

If the city was ancient, the docks were new. And for good reason.

Just offshore was an industry that stripped, scrapped, recycled and resold ships in parts, pieces, pressed or processed. Ships were recycled for markets in the East; the West, and for every ocean in between.

Amanda felt hot, tired, dehydrated and... getting nowhere with the local officials who could not direct her to the docks, let alone a cargo.

For one thing, it had taken her two days and 18 hours of flying time to get there. For another, she had little to guide her through Fumosa's agenda. She received a short email about the cargo, an Invoice for information as to its size, weight and contents, and little valuation. By phone-message she was given a vague description of its intended destination – for victims of the quake in the hills of the Earthquake region, as he phrased it. "Under the auspices of the FAO..."

In a city of torpid bureaucracy where the heat was unbearable; communications limited and transportation almost non-existent, there was little she could do to receive UN cargo in any authorized way, let alone make arrangements for its warehousing and security. At the present moment, as far as she was concerned, the situation was almost beyond her.

A hotel, nearby, was her only haven.

Managed by a family of five, it offered the best she could find. Most importantly, it was not far from the docks. It had a clean room, shower facilities and a veranda. Accessible to the main highway populated by tourists from

Tour boats, there were a few shops and Restaurants nearby. Plus the proprietor spoke some English.

Most importantly, it did have battery charging capabilities, and an Internet uplink.

She set up her Laptop, electronic devices, notebook and files as her base of operations. But it was woefully inadequate, she knew.

She checked the locks and keys, and asked for a small vault to secure some paperwork. She sat down, and began calling down a list of contacts to local officials who would be handling the cargo. Thankfully, the Dock-master's Office had several English speaking individuals.

By the end of her second day, she started to relax. The Veranda was furnished with rattan seating and colorful cushions, and she came to appreciate the sunsets and the smells of the sea.

Sipping a tall lemonade, she decided that tomorrow, she would go for a stroll. In the meantime, she appreciated the Hotel air-conditioning and the dark shady spots from a searing sun outside. A Hotel service Attendant arrived to provision the room with fresh muslin sheets and linen. Amanda asked her if the local merchants accepted purchase payment from a credit card, VISA.

The Attendant nodded sweetly. *Yes.*

That night Amanda slept through the soft night echoes of Karachi - a world away from New York City, and she slept well.

Day three was altogether a different story. She was getting nowhere with the cargo delivery.

Even if her countless messages to New York; Rome and Australia were answered - which they were not - they could wait, she decided. She was exhausted...

Only on the next evening did she notice the bird song within the courtyard of the Hotel, and the fountain that kept them cool. Never mind that the fountain splashed onto the head of a Buddha and its many arms of Christna, now white with droppings. It had a calming effect.

She was the only one on this side of the house. The Veranda was a balcony that ran the length of the three story building. There, a small boy sat. She, evidently, was his job.

"What is your name?" she asked.

He grinned and nodded his head sideways.

"...Your name?" she said, with her hand to beckon.

"Harry!" he said.

"Harry?" she repeated, happy to find a handle with which to address him.

He pointed to the statue in the garden. "Hari Christna!" and with that all the birds fled the multi arms of the goddess.

By day five, black sweet tea with spiced food began to appeal to her. Especially enticing was the aroma of a charcoal tandoori-cooked chicken from street vendors not far away. The city began to reveal its charm.

Today was Thursday, she had to find some resolution to the cargo Fumosa had shipped. Being on the same continent, she would attempt to leave a message for Trevor MacDonnell at his Post in New Delhi, India.

Friday, her flight to Australia would take her to Canberra where she would attend the Conference intended for Fumosa, and present a paper to a University forum. Several emails had confirmed her attendance and schedule from Canberra. She opened the envelope containing her topic of discussion, and resealed it safely for travel. Only now the clock in her head started ticking.

By lunchtime she was frantic: The cargo was in dock, at last! But transportation for the cargo from the docks - once the cargo passed Customs Inspections, remained uncertain.

She left messages everywhere. She sent messages everywhere. Time for her was getting short!

By now the matter should have long been resolved and delivered.

∞

If the Russians denied any knowledge of a Sobra class satellite orbiting the earth, they won't mind losing it, decided NASA.

What the kill was, or wasn't with the deployment of SM3, remained to be seen. But they knew they got the satellite. At close range, it registered as a large burst with some debris. That was the last signal from the device at impact. Detonation was confirmed.

What they could not know was what it carried.

The explosion destroyed the satellite superstructure but might not destroy the payload in its makeshift containers.

Hours later, they discovered that a dispersion pattern had formed emanating from a substance released following the explosion.

Upon closer inspection, it was reflective, a powdery carbon-graphite that suspended in the vacuum of space, like a cool silvery cloud.

By itself, on the dark side of the earth, it was harmless. If the sun hit the suspended substance it would ignite in a process difficult to contain. The temperature would start to rise.

If the Shuttle was wrongly positioned to sustain such sudden jumps of temperature she would be met with a fire-burst of heat.

Presently, she was positioned on an incline, travelling through the heavens at 18,000 miles per hour, her Albating-

High-Resistant heat tiles facing the sun. This was taking shape on the opposite side.

∞

Trevor awoke to the bloodcurdling screech of a Peacock. Incessant, it ruled the roof of his official Residence. The big bird had taken to some flight, which was unusual. For strangers, such a noise took a lot of getting used to. For Trevor it was heaven on earth after his forced march across the Arctic Oceans, as he put it.

Silk sheets beneath him lured him back to snooze for another ten minutes. Finally, as the habits of his morning dress beckoned, he was glad to be surrounded by the familiar comforts of his Residence.

 He was back at his office in New Delhi, even if his position had changed. A new Ambassador had been assigned to the Post, Sir Henry Giles, presently taking a tour of the continent and meeting various officials before arriving as Head of Mission.

Trevor smiled, relieved. He had held the Post for eighteen months as a courtesy. He was Acting Minister. So he calculated that he had another month to go. And then he would hand over the position completely!

After that, it was six weeks off for him, and following a debriefing in London at the Home Office, he could return to his life back in Scotland where friends, colleagues and investors awaited for a variety of activities; banking decisions and civic obligations... That is, while dividing his time between there and London where he kept a house and could savor the delights of the city, as usual...

The heat here was almost unbearable, he decided.

Still, something was disturbing him. And it wasn't the peacock on his roof ruffling and strutting. Even as the lines of fatigue on his face drew sharp furrows, it was that there had been a frenetic call from Amanda Wells.

From *Karachi*? He would see to it first thing...

He stopped short. A communique came across his desk that left him dumbstruck. A military assault was planned on a village in Pakistan by the Americans!

He picked up the phone to the US Ambassador in New Delhi. She wasn't in. Her First Minister picked up.

An explanation came in full. The action was to stop the shipments of a toxic substance that was considered a threat to US missions...

What missions, he wanted to know.

It took some digging, but Trevor got to the bottom of it, mainly through other sources in New York...

The substance was identified as a source of hostile material used in atmospheric space. That is, according to a call from a trusted friend at NASA.

Worse. The village that produced the substance had just experienced an Earthquake. He was barely finished when a call came in from the Front Office.

The voice of the American Ambassador was unmistakable. She was outside.

∞

"Unfortunately, Attack Drones are not effective at high altitudes" she explained.

As if that told him anything, he thought. Besides, Trevor was still uncertain about the justification behind the mission.

He was pacing, his understanding not processing very well today. He rubbed his forehead. Whatever it was that NASA had recorded, he was told it was a success. Yet here was the Ambassador cheerfully telling a different story. He wasn't pleased.

Damn it to hell. He was a barrister, even if still suffering from jet lag. He knew the constitutional bounds of policy. So what was she pulling here? He had to be certain.

He marched her down the hallway, half steering her by the elbow as if she were a recalcitrant child needing to make some explanation. "And could someone bring me a decent cup of coffee, please!" he barked, rubbing his head again.

"How do you see the Justification for such an expeditionary use of force?" he demanded.

She skipped to keep up. He reached the Conference Room. For some reason, inviting her into the privacy of his office - Ambassador notwithstanding, was not something he wanted to do. It seemed...incongruous somehow. In fact, considering his friendship with the woman, downright inappropriate.

She looked up at him full face, her eyes true and blue. "Two bodies were identified as being killed within a hundred and seventy miles of the roadway there. One was an identified UN official - a USAID Administrator from Rome, Carina Rielli. The other, a US Naval Air Force Captain, Tim Martin. Both US Citizens. Both linked to the region in professional work, and both with ties to this ...this...Mining interest thing up there...some mineral or other " She turned on her heels.

Trevor looked at his watch. Less than twelve hours ago Amanda Wells had called his home from Karachi.

Why?

"I'll send you a complete brief..." the Ambassador was saying.

"Yes. Please do!" he said firmly.

Trevor had a scheduled lunch appointment with host-country ministers. On the way down to the driver waiting, he pressed the elevator to Level 2, and walked into the cable office to check for any Home Office directives. There were none.

∞

Dr. Sumptra had been sitting in the Lobby of his office waiting to see Mr. Trevor MacDonnell, his secretary told him.

It had been a particularly tiring day. He felt drained.

Dr. Sumptra had seen Amanda Wells at the Conference at the Empire Hotel *with* Trevor MacDonnell, she said. And she wanted to pass a message along from a mutual friend at the dinner party, explained Sandy.

"Who?"
"She didn't say from whom... just a friend using her as a conduit. Sir...are you alright?"

"Yes. I'm fine!"

"Dr. Sumptra added that she wanted to know about the casualties in the region, if we had any information..."

"Casualties?" asked Trevor.

"Yes. The village has been wiped out by a landslide..."

"God! Is that what she said?"

"Yes Sir. We have no reports whatsoever. She said if there was any need to reach her, she would leave her card."

Trevor turned to walk away. *God Amanda, what have you got yourself into now?*

His stomach lurched.

"Mr. McDonnell. Mr. McDonnell, Sir..." called a staffer

"Not now!" he bellowed, storming into his office, his head reeling.

Trevor discovered that Dr. Sumptra had also been to his Residence, apparently to leave a note. She wanted to know, the message said, if he knew of the whereabouts of Amanda Wells... The house staff had let her in, and there she had waited in the foyer. She had waited an hour.

Trevor decided to follow up.

What he did instead, was fall down.

By six o'clock that evening, Trevor was in bed being attended by his staff physician.

Dr. Draper was inspecting the Printout at the window. A nurse was affixing a bag of intravenous fluid to an apparatus.

Trevor's head felt was hurting, his tongue dry.

"Hello Trev... " Dr. Draper said cheerfully. "You're on an Intravenous drip of saline and glucose." He had been at the golf course.

"What happened...?"

"You passed out" said the nurse. "Twice!"

"So, don't ask questions. You're going to be sedated for a while now. And we won't have anything to worry about" said Draper.

"Worry about...?"

"Yup! You're going nowhere for a while. Dysentery can kill a man in three days! I've communicated with London. They want to know how you're doing in the morning. And you're on my watch now. So sweet dreams!" he said with unmoving determination.

"God..." muttered Trevor. That's all he needed. The rest was blank.

∞

It was Yusef who took the call.

Not often had he salvaged the phone from his boss's belongings to answer it. But he had a few years of loyalty to merit initiative under certain situations. This was one of them. With Trevor out cold, and Amanda Wells calling...

So when her number lighted up, he answered.

"Karachi?...Yes. Yes. I'll tell him..."

∞

The boy arrived with the birds. They always did come and go together, the one heralding the arrival of the other.

But on this occasion, he wasn't paying attention. He had a mission. And that was to retrieve Amanda from her quarters and inform her that a Gentleman from the Authorities had arrived to declare for the cargo.

And about bloody time!

She was close to panic and had a plane to catch in the morning... The taxi had been arranged, her luggage nearly fully packed with only a blouse and last-minute belongings still drying off on a hanger. The rest were toiletries, and few bits of jewelry bought locally and held out for adornment.

Having left messages everywhere that she was making an appointment to meet with the American Representative later in Karachi, mainly to deliver the cargo inland, she checked her mail once again. Everything had been slow.

In this part of the world, people paused for the sun to cross their sky at its zenith point. Temperatures could rise well over 100 degrees between Noon and 3PM. Even if the continent embraced Western habits of industry, air conditioners waged a losing battle during those hours.

Even the streets emptied, leaving an eerie quietness.

At home people took showers, changed their clothes wet with perspiration, or lingered in the shade. They rested in cool places before returning to work. Even the Hotel had been quiet.

It would have been easy to succumb to local habits in this heat. But Amanda had too much to lose if she lost her grip on her scheduling. She found the pace of activity frustrating and determined to work on her paper for Australia. It was saved on her laptop.

The docks, even with mechanical loading of ships rotating continuously, had paperwork... And local officials, she discovered, loved paperwork: An office was not an office without paperwork. In piles. On chairs. Up the walls. Tied in bundles with string if necessary to keep the overhead fans from twirling them about, but stacked nonetheless. It was a sign of authority.

So when the boy introduced Mr. Sing as having come from the docks to tell her of her cargo, she was all agog and willing to get on with it, paperwork doubtless waiting somewhere.

She would need to sign for the provisions now being unloaded, and she would need to get the approval of the Superintendent of the Docks to post a guard on the provisions. They had the blue insignia of the UN, but yes, she should go!

She hopped into the cab and left the boy at the curb, thanking him with a grin and happy hand wave. He waved back.

Wearing a leather handbag slung over her shoulder and a lose fitting chiffon dress, albeit lined with a soft cotton chemisol, she felt comfortable. Her sandals were flat leather and good for walking. In her bag was her Laptop - fully charged; Notebook and calendar. She sent off two quick messages from her cell, one to Barbara and one to Fumosa saying that finally, things were moving well.

That meant that a Transport Trucking company had been arranged to pick up the supply shipment and start its delivery journey inland. This she already confirmed previously.

In the heat, the cab was making good time down empty streets. No donkey carts; scooters and bicycles festooned with bells and tassels transporting tourists and businessmen across town...

One message came back, though cell tower reception was fading. Barbara: *"Thank God!"*

It wasn't that the cab was small, but the air conditioner, such as it was, had lost its effectiveness in the rear seat. And not until she was close to the River Streets did Amanda notice a difference.

Oddly, the thing she noticed first was the driver's hair. He was not a Sikh wearing a turban. His hair, beneath his turban, was short. Even neck close-cropped. He was no local.

Nor was Amanda going to the dock.

The cab had left the city.

∞

It was time to bring the ship home, they had said.

Even with all the dangers, as long as one crewman remained alive, the Shuttle would be brought home: All crew would be transferred to the adjoined ship - the rescue ship *Courageous*, then to re-enter the earth's atmosphere. That had been the plan. *Courageous* needed two weeks to prep.

But the closer they examined the question, the higher the risk. *Eagle* was losing her orbital integrity and she could not stay aloft. Her elliptical positioning was decaying; her fuel supply damaged. Even at the hands of an expert crew if the ship were viable, she might not survive the heat stress at re-entry.

What if *Courageous* were to see the same?

If either ship were not to land successfully it would be considered a failed mission, if not a dishonorable one. Airman Patterson - the sole survivor would be considered abandoned under orders of a poor command!

To lose one Shuttle was bad enough. To send up another in rescue and place it harms way had even less desirability. Or low odds, as the Chief of Staff put it.

As Washington was reminding them, this was not inexpensive hardware they were sending up: There was no replacements! Worse, Congress might consider this a waste of taxpayers' money with long term ramifications; public outrage and political fallout.

The decision was made not to launch *Courageous*.

∞

The journey North was not short.

What threw Amanda was that the Taxi was driving Southbound...

Finally, half way down the road, Amanda insisted the driver come to a halt.

He explained that the Government office of the Mr. Dari - the official from the Docks, was on the Manghopir Road.

She had to be shown it on the map, and found it impossible to digest that they would have to travel so far to get there.

A hundred miles was cheap at the price, he explained. But, he insisted, he had been paid in advance to bring her to the offices. Of course, it didn't help that mountains made road construction a long and circuitous route to anywhere the crow might fly.

Amanda held her tongue, chiefly to weigh her options and calculate her position.

They were out in the middle of nowhere, and she was alone in a car with a stranger. Her fingers began reaching for her cell phone...

Just as panic began to seize her, the Taxi stopped and both doors rear opened for two passengers. She was seated between them.

Whatever thrashing she had planned for the driver was quickly abated by the size and suits of the two men flanking her, both of them wearing baby blue colored turbans, Sikhs.

She kept her panic under wraps by offering a polite "hello" to which they responded with a few words to the driver, less by way of greeting, as by instruction.

The minute they spoke, Amanda recognized the Urdi tongue, and she knew her options were closing fast. This Taxi was on his way to the Punjab.

"Excuse me..." she began.

They sat distant from their co-passenger, looking resolutely ahead or out the open windows as thy jostled down the rough road.

There was little said, let alone understood. Immune to the prattling of a foreigner, she was ignored - the dusty road ahead of more interest... the windows blowing in hot air and the screeching sound of a rusty muffler. She might as well have been on a public bus going somewhere.

The only question remaining, then, was on what terms she was with them.

They did stop, not too far long into the journey. The driver pointed to a Restaurant and tourist stop for her convenience.

She went inside, her cell phone useless.

When she came out, she found the two men at the steps, waiting. She was frustrated beyond measure at the situation, uncertain as to its intentions as she walked towards the waiting car. She stopped and would not enter the taxi. She lashed out at the driver as if he could understand her language.

They all stood there, watching her, the driver seated inside, the other two standing nearby.

Then one of the two passengers spoke. "He doesn't understand you, Ms Wells."

"*What?* You speak Eng.. How do you know my name?"

"You are, Ms Wells, for all intents and purposes, our guest until you reach Lahore!"

"Excuse me...I have plans...a plane to catch..."

"Compliments, Madam...of the Government..."he added politely.

"I'm supposed to be meeting the official Mr. Dari about our cargo delivery from the United Nations!"

"Mr. Dari is waiting for you... and for the cargo...in Lahore, please, Madam" repeated the speaker with a polite bow, then stepped forward. "And it's no good using your cell phone. At this altitude you are well out of range. Not that we have Towers for a signal to begin with..."

"Please explain yourselves before I raise hell out here in public!" she blurted like an angry tourist.

"Lahore!" he repeated. "Please?" he said holding open the car door for her.

At least there was a connection?

But by the time they reached the Hyderabad Motorway, she knew she'd been had.

∞

Jim Oliver's quiet eyes searched the room for dissenters. He sipped at his coffee and waited, his eyes darting frequently to Lloyd.

Cappachutto had a question about the angle of approach to Edwards. Bennington, specialist for fuel consumption, was thumbing his pencil anxiously against his pad.

"I don't like those fuel charts. It's close. Too close. There's very little margin..." he said.

Oliver was waiting for this moment. He would impress them with an array of statistical data.

"Why argue with fuel efficiency and performance in flight when the calculations are flawless?" he said.

He waited before proceeding. "The *only* chance *Eagle* has is to land at Edwards Air Force Base."

"Look..." he said "the options of fuel limitations are dismal. A freefall over the Pacific would conserve fuel but compromise the ship. After you calculate the Cartesian coordinates, a gliding approach to Edwards can rely on some hydrodynamic uplifts. After all, she is a plane. She can fly!"

"Assuming you have two pilots onboard familiar with Emergency landings experience..." said Lloyd

"True. But remember. She's on remote control. So she's fine, her margins are wide, and that's where I come in: *Arianne* has no manned systems. The 'what- if' drills could go on endlessly. What if I fail to compensate for downdrafts? Port wing? Uplifts? And just plain on-board response failures etc. etc..."

The room fell silent. Then Cappachutto stepped in. "The truth is, we have a lot of probabilities here with a lot of unknowns. The best we can hope for is a salvage job."

Lloyd pushed back his chair, picked up his papers and left the room. Cappachutto joined him in the hallway.

"You're gnawing on your knuckles and it's not helping a bit..." he said trying to keep abreast of Lloyd's enormous strides.

"I don't like it. I don't like it one bit. There is something wrong with his attitude. The 'margins are wide?'...What does that mean? Immunity from screwing up because there's already a low probability of salvage? I say, treat it like it's the most important decision of the mission!"

"No wait just a minute, Lloyd. He has a lot of *Arianne* background..." said Cappachutto.

Lloyd paused. "He finds our program too easily dispensable Tom, *Arianne*-background or not. The Shuttle has m*aybe*... just *one* option... *One* shot at landing. That's it! Play with that and it's all over. And in full living color for the world to see on TV! I've got to check out some schematics. There may another way..."

"Damn to hell Lloyd you've been bitten by some personal bug on this mission. And there's no room for personal predilection here. I don't care whether you like Oliver's style or not. He comes from the *Arianne* space program that is familiar with higher orbits. So. He's calling the shots and he's the decision we defend no matter what." Cappachutto was red from the neck up.

"That's where you're wrong! His calculations are fine except for a few weightings...."

"That include Karen?"

"Yes that includes Karen! The *'oh she'll do fine'* - won't cut it. Especially from an outsider unfamiliar with our thresholds of precision."

"You don't *want* to trust him..."

"OK. So I don't trust him. Truth is, he knows no more than we do. There's a big difference Tom between Europe shooting up remote capsules and calling it a space program, and our delivering shuttles into space an re-landing them like a plane that's been on vacation for a week! We send humans into space. They send a rocket fuel into orbit! You may be willing to put all our hardware into his hands, but I'm not prepared to hand over Karen without being absolutely sure there is no other way."

"You know we've checked it over.... Don't push your demands..."

"and what? Lower my expectations?" Lloyd looked at him closely. "That's great coming from the man who redefined the US space program" Lloyd looked down at the sheets he was holding. He took a big breath.

"Look. All this was equally designed for deployment of military hardware on a national defense mission, right? So *use* it! Use our other resources out there, hell, even abuse it if necessary! Don't flinch at discovering that there is a failed system here. Even if we do find it to be flawed in design; contaminated or mismanaged whatever.... Don't hand over our system to someone else just 'cos you don't want the responsibility of failure...!"

"Now hold on..."

"Tell you what, have you thought of the possibility that something *is* wrong here. Perhaps even programmed to be used *against us.* So, handing the controls over to an outsider is just too...convenient! Even if all ends in a tragic embarrassment. Then it's our responsibility and ours alone!"

Cappachutto's red face resembled a volcano ready to deliver its load. But that didn't stop Lloyd. "Has it occurred to you that since we've lost *Eagle*, we have seen concomitant failures elsewhere? And we may be looking at sabotage?" Lloyd eyes turned to steel.

"'Some people..." said Cappachutto "think that maybe it's the surviving astronaut who is the one dysfunctional element! You're the only one prepared to hand over a 3 billion dollar piece of hardware to a woman who is clearly stressed out!"

"She's also a trained combat graduate officer from the United States Naval Academy!"

 It was Tim McDougal, Interim Flight Director, who came running down the hall.

"We're receiving our first signals Sir. She'll be wanting to hear your voice with instructions for re-entry." It was Lloyd's voice that had to be on the transmissions from CAPCOM.

"Right!" said Lloyd, and both men hurried into Cape Canaveral's Command Center.

"Besides, you don't have an option" jogged Cappachutto.

Lloyd did not need to be reminded that the *Eagle* could not sustain her orbit indefinitely. It would decay. The window of opportunity would close.

 Or Oliver would close it for them.

Chapter 8

"*Eagle* this is Mission Control. Come in"

The signal was weak and technicians adjusted for whatever amplifications they could receive. He repeated: "*Eagle*. This is Mission Control. Do you read? Come in"

Bleep:

"Hello Mission Control.....*Eagle hssssss...*"

They were overjoyed.

There was something about hearing Karen's voice that send a small shudder down Lloyd's spine. The kind of outpouring that comes from finding a lost child. Or a friendship. He shut his eyes and spoke words from his heart.

"*Eagle* this is Mission Control. Captain Jim Lloyd. It is good to hear your voice ... Over"

Pause.

Bleep:

"...Roger Mission Control....Computers won't let me play any games up here.... But.... me.......for company."

Lloyd was touched by her courage, imagining for a second the unutterable sense of hopelessness that she must be enduring now that *Courageous* was no longer viable. She had shown bravery.

In flight, he recalled her understanding of his decision to abandon her in space. God knows she had cause for despair. And now, they both knew that she had less than 40% probability of returning a damaged shuttle to earth. If that.

"*Eagle*. We read you nice and clear. You may be solo up there but down here you have a *huge* fan club of good looking guys..."

"Roger ... that... Out"

"*Eagle*, we have good news. We are going to bring you home!"

It took a second, but the thrill in her voice was unmistakable

"Roger, Control..."

"Standby"

"Roger. Instruct as to support systems and re-entry plan?" The signal was getting clearer, if short.

"*Eagle*..." Lloyd took off his head set and gripped the transmitter. "..There has been a change of plan. Support is limited. Repeat. Limited. You will be able to bring the ship home yourself with the help of computer codes 706. Stand by for transmission programming through de-orbit. TAEM to touchdown will be remote control. Computers will help you through. Do you copy, *Eagle*?"

 "..Roger"

There was something far away about her answer. Something dutifully honor-bound, regardless the reality. She was prepared to die, if necessary, as trained, and as smartly as any man, whatever the odds.

Lloyd paused, his thoughts reconciling the realities of re-entry. He looked down, and softly, a phrase came to him from his youth, words that would come to his rescue in the service of others by brave men and women. *Greater love has no man than ...to... lay down his life for his friends.*

"*Eagle*, I am going to walk you through from de-orbit to loss of signal..."

"Roger that..."

He paused, and looked up at Tom. "If not...Then you will be guided in by *Arianne* space program. Do you copy?"

There was no reply.

Lloyd looked up at Cappachutto and Oliver who were standing behind his console.

"Control. Repeat... name identification at CAPCOM. Over..."

"*Eagle*, Mission Specialist *Arianne*, Flight Director Jim Oliver - assisted in flight transmissions by Captain James Lloyd"

No reply.

"*Eagle*, this is Control. Do you copy?"

"Roger...!" was all they got, and Lloyd wondered what Karen was thinking. Perhaps she assumed that they were asking her to die smartly, and with her former Commanding Officer at the helm! Perhaps she was intimidated.

He was wrong. She came back loud and clear.

"Control. This is *Eagle*...Does he have a steady hand? Over"

They all laughed, except Lloyd. Of all the things to say when seconds counted. Why did she ask the question *Does he have a steady hand?*

Was she was actually asking something else. Could she trust the man?

Too late. The program roll had started.

"*Eagle*. Prepare for de-orbit" said Oliver, taking over the Flight Director's position.

Lloyd poured himself a cup of coffee.

He could see Karen now, floating around the flight deck. Mission and payload specialist posts were perhaps preparing for landing. She must be wondering if Control was joking. She would be staring at a bank of control panels designed for two highly trained flyers, she, alone in a shell of a ship trapped in an atmosphere of hostile electrons. Was CAPCOM Control playing with her? Did they want to see if the thing could land or not?

Lloyd remembered the hours they'd spend strapped into those seats just running through estimates together - none of them good.

She was greatly more informed than they knew!

Lloyd sipped on more coffee. Was he now getting paranoid? Or just nervous...

He regretted his harsh words to Tom, a man he truly respected. But really, had they given any thought to sabotage? Were there any directives *other* than technical advisors? Had they investigated *any* political strategic theories?

Dark thoughts...

Of course Karen would be going through the procedures to prepare for deorbit. She was too well trained not to follow instructions. The least he could do was to match her resolve.

He marched himself into the debriefing room, vaguely noticed the others. Suddenly his resolve was firm. He, for one, was not going to let her perish! If he failed to bring her in safely, he would never be the same man.

"Roger" Cappachutto and Oliver sighed gratefully with every response from *Eagle*. Malfunctions were to be expected. The ship had been severely stressed and damage control was their main option. They were prepared for the lowest odds.

"*Eagle*. Confirm APU prestart complete. Over"

"Roger, APU prestart complete, over"

"*Eagle*. Check Boiler N2 supply all three, boiler controller all three. Boiler power/heater all three position A. Over"

"Roger, Boiler N2 all three, boiler controller all three. Boiler power/heater all three position A. Check"

"*Eagle*. APU fuel tank valve switched all three Closed. Check"

There was no answer. Karen was either unable or unwilling to respond.

"*Eagle*. Repeat check APU fuel tanks."

"Control... Please reinstate Flight Director Captain Jim Lloyd"

"*Eagle*. We have Flight Directors Oliver and Cappachutto at your disposal."

Sssss

"Control. Please reinstate Flight Director Captain Jim Lloyd" was all she said without wavering.

She was beginning to panic.

Okay, thought Lloyd. That was her way of avoiding the issue. She was indulging them. Her overhead schematics said it all. Her fuel supply was non-existent. Her oxygen and nitrogen levels inadequate. Her burn would barely last 3 minutes, probably not enough to turn the ship around. Lloyd took the seat of the Flight Director

"*Eagle*. This is Captain Jim Lloyd. Onboard computer enter deorbit program 302"

"Roger, 302. Check"

Without a word she would execute the orders, knowing full well that those orders would not perform as anticipated, and probably kill her.

Lloyd wanted to say something relevant. He wanted to tell her how he admired her, how much like an officer she was behaving. *Now*, before she executed the order to commence her deorbit burn and consume, or be consumed, the last remaining fuel. This might well be her last chance of survival – if not a fiery furnace as she hit the earth's atmosphere. The room went silent.

How obediently could you plunge yourself into a nil option? Like a good soldier?

Like lamb that is led to the slaughter, and like a sheep that before its shearers is dumb, so he opened not his mouth..?

This was it! The Go/No-Go decision from Mission control and she was committed. One word, one last instruction. Cappachutto and Oliver came in closer. The Center fell silent.

Lloyd clutched the receiver, the words choking in his throat. He opened his mouth to execute the command. Cappachutto and Oliver were waiting, they turned to him. Something alarmed them. He was hesitating. They were moving in...

"*Eagle*, this is Mission Control..." he said, having come to a conclusion. He had made his own statistical probabilities and options.

"...Abort! Repeat. Abort de-orbit burn! It's a flyby. Orbit Repeat. Deploy Generator! Repeat. Deploy Generator! Over..."

Cappachutto lurched for the Transmission Control to *Eagle* but Lloyd anticipated his move and killed the link.

Oliver grabbed the back of his seat and shook the chair, "You damned fool!"

"Do you know what you've done?" barked Cappachutto.

∞

Amanda Wells had fallen asleep - to her appalling embarrassment.

With hours of roads unfurling their way inland in a Ford with windows down for warm humid air, her body had crumpled and succumbed to fatigue.

 At least she had leaned against the window, the rear seat now only occupied by one Sikh passenger. The other had put himself forward with the driver. He too had fallen asleep.

But the last words of their conversation sank in nonetheless, even as she sucked in her breath, her mouth dry for water.

"Your Country has put us at a severe disadvantage!" said the Sikh to her right.

She was about to respond when the car jolted to a sudden stop and the driver jumped out like a good Server. He opened the trunk, and came forward with four sealed bottles of Sanji Water.

They all drank.

"You see..." continued the one Sikh, wiping his mouth with his sleeve, "you have suggested that we are delivering toxic elements into the atmosphere!"

Nothing could have surprised her more. She resisted the temptation to say "*What...?*"

Evidently the utter blank on her face solicited more information.

"Allegedly from the *very* site to which you are sending *your* UN cargo!" he said smugly, another swig.

Frustration was taking its toll on her passengers, she knew. Civility was breaking down and was loosening the tongue.

The question was, how vulnerable was she? How dedicated to their mission could they be?...Or for how long? The veneer of social respect was very thin, she knew.

She shrugged innocently, and averted further provocation. The drinker searched her face for expression, then turned away out the window, bored.

That she was his captive was indisputable, she knew.

They had travelled for miles in this state of silent resignation. Yet he was clearly been mulling the situation in his head.

By the time the statement had awoken her from her sleep, he had weighed his options. So far, he was acting within his instructions. But he could go rogue.

If there was one thing Amanda understood about rogues was that it was a matter of time. And her mind was quickly calculating her possibilities. And the situation was not getting any easier in the car. She strained to sit straight, feeling stiff and sore in multiple places, if not windswept by an open window and caked with dirt and grime. They induced as much discomfort on her as they could.

It was less than an hour later that she began to notice increasing traffic on the highway - even buses with passengers. By the time she saw a school bus, she knew she was in a Metropolis.

They stopped for gas, briefly, and she was offered a sandwich of salted chicken, a bag of chips and a coke by the driver. She accepted them all, and entered the Hospitality Visitors Center to use the facilities.

She refreshed herself, if appalled at the paucity of her provisions, and refilled her bottle of water from the faucet. She dug for her cell phone, still without signal, and low on battery charge at that. More than anything else on her list of discomfort and anger was the stupidity with which she had let herself fall victim to this hijacking! How could she have not recognized such duplicity? When did the malfeasance begin? The instant she agreed to enter the taxi... or the moment the boy told her? The thoughts swirled through her head endlessly. The least she could do right now was to remain calm and be alert.

They re-entered the Taxi.

Somehow she knew that her patience would pay off. They became entangled in city traffic for further discussion. A road sign indicated Sukh Chayn Gardens, a housing community, and she started to hope for some kind of solution.

By the time they drove Downtown past a vibrant business district with pedestrians all about, and they circled Liberty Roundabout of Al-Falah Square, she felt like she could start breathing again.

The city of Lahore presented itself thick with distractions. Congested streets, bicycles, sirens, police, shoppers and people everywhere. It made her feel less like a hostage. Her two "escorts," she noticed were completely absorbed with the commotion around them. Especially the taxi driver who couldn't resist his share of rancor on the car horn.

By the time they drove passed the PIA in Lahore, she felt her anxiety lessen considerably. There were policemen about actually inspecting cars for anything suspicious.

She felt her hosts stiffen.

Still, even as the ancient city unfurled before her, she was too tense to notice. Or so she thought until she saw balconies trellised with ferns and terrain vine, hibiscus, bougainvillea and oleander...Ordinarily, she would consider such color resplendent. Now, she only yearned for liberty from the two thugs at her side.

Yet she was drawn into the nuances of a modern city revealing its cultural traditions. How she would have liked to soak it all up under more favorable circumstances... She cast a furtive glance at her captors. *Damn them!*

Suddenly the tax stopped.

"You may stay at this Hotel, Miss Wells, until we contact you!" said the first Sikh, stepping out.

It was a Clarion Hotel, located next to a Dunkin Donuts Restaurant.

Amanda dashed into the Lobby - mainly to avert any further restraints, and as she stood in the heart of a crowd, she resisted the temptation to look back.

Gone... Just like that!

Something put them off?   What?

She calmed down, the public place uneventful. She looked around, and decided to sit down on a divan rather than attract attention. Right now all she wanted to do was thaw her frayed nerves, and think...

"Can I help you?" said a delicate voice in a silk sari bordered with the Clarion insignia.

Amanda looked up, still gripping her bag.

"Yes! I err..." she stopped. Her appearance must have been frightful.

"Are you registered in the Hotel Madam?" persisted the young lady.

"No. Yes!" she recalled the words of the Sikh, *you may stay at this Hotel...*

For now, she would play it safe. "My name is Amanda Wells."

Nothing could have prepared her for the response.

"Yes. Miss Wells. We've been expecting you! Please come to the Front Desk. There is a message for you from a Dr. Fumosa?"

"Dr Fum...?" she stared.

She couldn't decide whether she to swoon with relief or roar with outrage. She picked herself off the seat with as much dignity as her dusty appearance would allow, and trailed the attendant to the Front Desk.

"Yes. Miss Wells. Your room is No. 232. If you will show us your identification, please?"

"Identification?" she spluttered, diving into her purse seeking less the requisite card than the answer to why they were asking, and on what ground she stood, whether as tourist, traveler or hostage.

She did have her purse at least, and produced her ID to the man behind the desk.

"Welcome Miss Wells! All your expenses are paid by the United Nations. And you are invited at any time to an open account at the Restaurant in the Hotel. Miss Siu will show you the way to your room. Do you have any luggage to be carried up?"

"No" she said, pleased at the return of normalcy.

Evidently, their complete ignorance of the conditions under which she had traveled presupposed notions of being a captive. Was it all in her head, she wondered.

So she followed the Ms Siu to Room 232 which she found to be ample in comfort and cleanliness, yes. Thank you.

Fumosa. *I'll kill him!*

"God!" she said, sitting on the bed.

She'd been totally diverted from her mission.

"Unbelievable!"

Chapter 9

Cappachutto was sitting at his desk. The phone buzzed. He pressed the button with the Speaker-On.

"Hi. It's me."

"Right."

He had been waiting. He was tense.

Cappachutto switched Off the Speaker, hung up and moved to another phone. He dialed and waited for two rings. They were on a secure line. "Yes Bill"

Stevenson was the point-man for the Oval Office, and God knew who else was "in" on the decision-making. Cappachutto didn't much care. His job was to carry out instructions, so he made his statement flatly. "We don't have confirmation that *Eagle* will be resolved within 16 hours. Solution will not be secured and cleared."

The answer came back without the slightest hesitation. "Twins will proceed at zero seventeen hundred. Trajectory coordinates at lame duck to flush clean the flock."

"Yes Sir!" was all Cappachutto said and he replaced the receiver.

Lloyd walked into his office and shut the door behind him.

"I'm sorry..." said Cappachutto.

Lloyd stood very still.

Cappachutto looked up at him. "Like you said. She had one option left. You just stole that option from her."

Lloyd knew that Cappachutto had just received his directive: *Code X20.000.*

In seventy two hours two nuclear warheads would detonate. The target was *Eagle.*

Cappachutto swallowed hard, sick at the thought. He turned to the window.

In all his 38 years with NASA and countless man-hours and human effort to redefine spaceflight, he never though he'd be blowing up one of his own shuttles!

He turned to Lloyd, his expression confounded.

"How long do I have?" said Lloyd.

"Twenty four... Make it short!"

∞

The SEC wasn't expecting a call from the Department of Agriculture. It usually came from the Treasury. Or the Internal Revenue Service. Even the Fed.

Paul Demuth was on his way up to his office on the 23rd floor of the New York City glass building, the sun beginning its decline on a Hudson river now shimmering with diamonds.

He was accustomed to hearing about who did what and why. He was accustomed to preparing or defending cases of illegal trading; insider information; insufficient capital thresholds misrepresentations... and every other trick of the trade that a stock exchange could unearth. Even he got calls from Banks themselves!   But the Department of Agriculture?   Who could steal crops?

Futures Trading perhaps? But that was usually the Chicago Board of Trade...

So let's see, he wondered, enumerating the possible infractions one could find in Futures Trades.

He was holding a Starbucks coffee in his left hand; his briefcase in his right, and had to put the envelope - containing his transcripts, in his teeth to the push the elevator button.

His transcripts. He wanted to see what grade he got for his Research Seminar at Columbia - That was his one escape from the daily grind as an SEC examination attorney. Evening classes.

He drained his coffee, situated himself comfortably at his desk, and then took the call.

"I'm with NASA on this..." said the caller from the Department of Agriculture. "Actually, an attorney at NASA and I thought that you should be the one to investigate this puppy...I just got the call about this a few days ago. And frankly, I don't know what to do with it!"

Paul rolled his eyes.

"Report Suspicious Activity" meant misplaced parcels; terrorist activity and quit-whining-about-Homeland-Security or the Transportation Safety Administration. DO NOT call your local *SEC* about someone making money on Wall Street. *Give me a break!*

"No" he sighed. "We have pretty limited guidelines for investigating these things. Can you be a little more specific? And... pardon my ignorance, but how does NASA have anything to do with the price of potatoes?"

They laughed. He crumpled his empty coffee cup from Starbucks and wanted to lob it across the room. That would be the end of it.

He listened.

Within minutes, he swiveled on his chair, sat up, and said he'd call back.

He was marching into his boss's office-floor on the twelfth floor, the glass door inscribed with the firm's name Prouse & Bertmutler, Associates besides a plastic potted tree.

"I'm here to see Mr. Prouse, please Susan. ASAP!"

Within twenty minutes of his meeting, he was back in his office and had Susan 'at his disposal" as she put it.

"Tammy wants you to block every trade made at the Chicago Board of Trade by these Exchange Desks and Traders for the last 24...

..."Plus a complete list of all their trades within the last six weeks...

..." And book me a flight into Washington err... let's see, tomorrow?" He was rooting across his desk for papers like a rabbit unearthing his den.

He stood straight, hoisted up his belt and faced Susan with his agenda requirements.

..."Arrange a day of meetings downtown with Interior. Then Agricultural and Commerce legal counsel" He looked up for her nod, taking notes. "And I want an appointment the day next with the Secretary of Commerce of the Russian Embassy. Got it?"

"Yes" she said, knowing when not to linger and make jokes. He was on a Panic Alert.

"Anything else?"

"Yes. Tell Tim and his staff to be here for a briefing session in my office at 4 pm. They can clear their desks of all else for the week: I'll need all the legal minds in the building..."

"Got it" she said. She went to the door and was about to exit.

"What's up?" she asked.

"46% of our cropland has been bought by foreign investors. By next month it'll be 56%"

"That's good" she began "...for winter wheat crops on the Futures..."

"I didn't say crops. I said cropland, with proprietary Rights of Title to the Assets!"

"Very funny!" she chuckled.

But he wasn't smiling.

∞

Onboard the shuttle, it was back to business as usual. The stress of processing what happened at the last exchange was enough to leave an astronaut in a state of turmoil. But turmoil was routine these days for Karen Patterson as she calculated the odds of her survival.

One thing was certain. Washington and NASA were having to make some drastic decisions, if not events she imagined. God, how she hated being the center of attention! Why had not the others survived? What if this were Cindy?

Which made her laugh, really, considering her own realities. So now it came down to when and where her predicament would be solved. The reasons behind the Flight Director's instruction to flyby and make another orbit were countless, by now. Still, at the end of the day, it was confidence in their need to exhaust every possibility - before playing with chance... that she must reconcile.

"Chance" she muttered. Now there's a good name for a baby!

At any rate, there was little she could do. Relax! Music. Eat. Sleep!

Karen proceeded with the business of heating a meal. Thermo-stabilized beef with barbeque sauce, freeze-dried cauliflower with cheese and beans with mushrooms, thermo-lemon pudding and pecan cookies in their natural form. She stuck a straw in the lemon drink and ate the pecan cookies. The lemonade hurt her lips now. She floated to the mid-deck and changed the air crystals. The cabin pressure remained stable. But she was getting dry.

She looked at herself in the mirror and saw a pale face, white lips raw from dryness and constant licking. Her eyes were bloodshot, dry, stinging and she blinked for moisture. But behind the eyes was fear. Increasingly in her mind all the permutations were coming to the same conclusion: There were nil options left. Reality was gaining its grip.

"Okay," began Karen in a matter of fact voice, "it doesn't look good. But the problem remains. And I have to face it."

She licked her lips and they stung. She covered her eyes with her parched hands and they were shaking. She clasped the left hand to stem the effects of prolonged spaceflight.

Hours bereft of feelings can be filled with silence. And silence speaks in echoes to amplify loneliness. Lloyd and Martin had come into her world, and gone. Now only one reality remained.

She floated to the flight console and strapped herself in. And there they were. Six little digits. That's all. Six little digits like six little games. Lloyd had transmitted the signal just before signing off. Anyway, she took a big breath.

She wanted air. That meant take a walk, as if that were possible. She unstrapped herself and put herself on the treadmill. She walked and panted, but the panting hurt her dry mouth. So she floated up to the porthole and looked out, a miniscule face peering out of a small ship, orbiting a vast universe.

She caught a glimpse of the blue earth. She saw the snowcapped Andes, like ancient white stories guarding a blue sphere and her secrets ... gently waiting for time to pass.

At the next sunrise - thanks to a fresh supply of carbon particles delivered by an unknown carrier, the US Shuttle *Eagle* would amplify ultraviolet sun rays through a concentrated hole in the ozone, causing more havoc below.

Now there was the irony. That they should somehow be expected to solve that problem! But as Lloyd said, if they could solve the problem, then who?

So where did that leave her?

Turmoil thrashed around in her mind and she was afraid of articulating her despair lest it ignite anger. Anger that sent humans out to the limits of endurance without understanding why. Decisions, they said.

She was a threat.

So, in her silence she contained her thoughts, and it took all her might not to scream out.

∞

The idea that Amanda had been captive for 15 hours of driving across 1300 kilometers under forced escort was disconcerting, if not downright horrific.

She was pacing. What, no phone-calling? No verifying. No warning? Who knew?

How could that have happened?

She walked to the window, refused to accommodate any view, and fiercely drew the curtains closed.

No!

She wanted to talk. Out loud with her thoughts... Who were these goddamned people anyway?

Her boss and his damned *persona* with his goddamned missions to nowhere to save the world? Where did that leave *her*?

She found the edge of the bed again and sat.

"Unbelievable!" she uttered.

Then she started to rethink.

If somehow this was pre-arranged by someone, then...Or, if she had been misinformed accidentally?

No! She had been *deliberately* misled, she decided.

But then again, it was entirely possible that they had neglected to explain the 'circumstances of her transport' as it were. Surely? - Not even Fumosa was capable of such callous neglect.

Or, that the local authorities simply assumed that *she* assumed that *they* assumed that...

And what about the boy? Crashing in to announce the arrival of her expected 'official.' And her - like a damned fool believing him! And how did he know *who* ...?

No.

So that left the Port Authorities themselves.

Where did they expect her to take possession of the cargo, exactly? Inland by 1500 miles, or upland by 20,000 ft.? Or what about $100,000 worth of mercantile goods on the black market?

If it came to that, why not just dispatch her and be done with it? After all, it was a morass of a city in which anybody could disappear!

Her two Sikh *escorts* could have made her disappear anywhere along the way up, of that she was certain. No scruples there.

There was more to this picture than she could figure out.

Like why... By whom? And when was the curtain going to rise on some enlightenment.

She took a shower, and tried to regain any vestige of dignity left in the paucity of her backpack - most of her luggage having been left in Karachi in preparation for travel...

Downstairs in the Lobby she noticed a couple of glossy shops and boutiques. She had a credit card, yes? She decided that she would take full advantage of the facilities at her disposal and reinstate herself with as much aplomb as the situation would allow.

That meant, first and foremost, some refreshment, food, recharge of her cell phone and Laptop which the hotel was able to provide for.

To her surprise, she discovered in the great lobby nothing less than a stylish shopping Mall, replete with every amenity and convenience a traveler could wish for. All interior spaces were air-conditioned, masking the astonishing outdoor heat and white hot glare of the city.

She purchased a few pretty toiletries and essentials from the pharmacist store. Boots, they called it. At least they accepted money on her credit cards.

The Mall was extensive and multi-storied. Balconies of specialized export furnishings; Asian artwork, galleries. On the second floor balcony were cafes, restaurants, salons, perfumeries...Even as shoeshine, repair and alteration services!

She walked. If this were her confines, then her captors had chosen well, she thought wryly.

The displays were fabulous. Jewelers encased gems of white gold filigree; porcelain of gossamer bone china; fabrics in colored silk and dyed wool; woven rugs... Electronics, hardware, software... Here was the center of trade for Importers from the West, she realized.

The indoor surroundings was park-like. Tropical fauna, wrought iron seating for weary tourists staying at the hotel, fountains...

What luxury was Lahore!

Before long she was able to replace her travelling baggage with new personal items, clothes, shoes and she even booked an airline ticket. Certainly, if she were under surveillance by her two thugs, they would want to know.

She would call Trevor later, tonight, which of course would give her his messaging service. Even if she were at a destination anywhere in India, Italy or New York, she knew. He was screened. But at least she was doing something that allowed her to reconnect and regain her orientation.

She rested in her room. Then went downstairs for a drink and dinner. She felt she had earned it.

She picked a Bistro in the main Mall not far from entrance fountain, cool and laid out as an au-giardin Restaurant of an Atrium. She picked a seat from which she could scope her surroundings and evaluate the contours of her boundary.

She could even see the main entrance including who was approaching the hotel front desk and who was leaving. When the hot humid air of the outdoors swished in from heavy brass entrance doors, she could get a glimpse of the outside – pedestrians, street traffic, passengers, tourists, hotel visitors and shoppers.

Of course. The tax service was there. This she observed.

Yes.

Always there. Waiting. Standing. Watching. One man, always the same driver. *Her driver!* Never really gone, never called away on duty for delivery, exactly. Just there. Waiting. Watching for *her*.

So. That was it then. She was being watched. Or was she the dust-bunny under scrutiny as it attracted more dust. Just who else were they waiting for, she wondered.

And what of that Mr. Dari she was supposed to meet?

That night in her bedroom she opened her Laptop, and finding her wireless and online capabilities recharged, she logged onto a saved site for travel arrangements and booked another airline ticket.

From New Delhi to Baghdad.

Who would book two flights simultaneously? It was worth the money if it fooled her pursuers! Plus the notations were hard to notice on her laptop because of pre-existing booking activity.

How she planned to get to New Delhi however, was another matter.

For the moment, she knew she was being watched and she would present no surprises.

Obvious options would be expected of her. Like calls to the local American offices; the Transportation Depot for incoming transit and cargo, even an enquiry as to the whereabouts of a Mr. Dari. For all intents and purposes, she was doing her job. This, at least was predictable. That is, as long as her Laptop remained serviceable.

One thing was certain. Someone, like a Barbara perhaps, had put her on the UN expense account. They had cited Dr. Fumosa at the desk. But Amanda found that suspicious: Fumosa was one for exaggeration and effusiveness. But he was not ignoble. It might be a ploy, a cover. She wasn't fooled, and she would take every precaution. And every opportunity...

This was a cat and mouse game: Three days was all she had... *if that*. Then she would worry about catching that flight.

She paused, recalling those moments in the Taxi:

Your Country has put us at a severe disadvantage!

What did he mean, exactly?

You see...you have suggested that we are delivering toxic elements into the atmosphere!

She lay on her bed thinking about it. Not entirely her line of work on climate controls. Perhaps it was meant as disparaging propaganda.

More than suspicion, there was actual malice in his voice

Allegedly from the very site to which you are sending your UN cargo!"

Even if true, how would he know to probe on these matters?

No.

 The situation was not good. Definitely not good, she decided.

Tomorrow she would park herself out in the coffee shop downstairs and make like a student tuned into her electronic devises for entertainment or homework. The best place to hide was out in the open.

Besides, laughable as it was, she actually did have work to do!

Later she would test the waters and go outside.

She changed her password and went to sleep.

∞

Karen proceeded with the business of heating a meal. Thermo-stabilized beef with barbeque sauce, freeze-dried cauliflower with cheese, and beans with mushrooms. Thermo-lemon pudding and pecan cookies in their natural form came next.

She stuck a straw in the lemon drink and ate the pecan cookies. The lemonade hurt her lips.

She pushed back and floated to the mid-deck to change air crystals. The cabin pressure remained stable.

She looked at herself in the mirror and saw a pale face; lips red almost raw from dryness and constant licking. Her eyes were bloodshot, dry. She blinked for moisture. Behind the eyes was fear... Increasingly, all the permutations were coming to the same hopeless conclusion. There were few options. It felt too crushing to think about them.

"O.k." began Karen speaking aloud. "It doesn't look good. But the problem remains..."

She licked her lips. They stung.

 She covered her eyes with parched hands, and she noticed they were shaking.

She paused, knowing what that meant. She clasped the left hand to stem the effects of prolonged spaceflight.

She turned to free-float, and sighed deeply. She felt alone.

Hours bereft of feelings can be filled with silence. And silence speaks in echoes to amplify loneliness. Lloyd and Martin had come into her world, and gone. Now only one reality remained, her only companion.

She floated to the flight console and strapped herself in. And there they were: Six little digits. That's all. Six little digits like six little games.

Lloyd had transmitted the signal just before signing off...
She took a long breath.

So, bad news is better than no news!

She wanted air...Green, fresh air, the kind that helps you
breath freely.

She unstrapped herself and put herself on the exercise
Treadmill.

She walked and panted, but the panting hurt her dry
mouth.

So she floated up to the porthole and looked out. She was
a miniscule face, peering out of a small ship orbiting a vast
universe.

She spotted a blue earth. She recognized the snowcapped
Andes, like an ancient symbol sitting upon a sphere
holding secrets of humanity.

At the next sunrise, thanks to a fresh supply of carbon
particles delivered to *Eagle*, she would amplify ultraviolet
sun rays through a hole in the ozone, causing more havoc
below.

And there was the irony. *That she should somehow be
expected to solve that problem!*

But as Lloyd said, if not them, then who?

So where did that leave her? She banged her fist at the
framework, a cell padded for insulation.

Turmoil roiled her emotions, and she was afraid of
articulating her despair lest it inflame with ferocious anger.
She turned away.

Nothing was any better when she awoke.

Six digits. At least she had the ETA of two nuclear warheads
from earth! Yes. *Eagle* was their target for solution. She
looked at the digits. She wasn't sure what stung her most.
Being blown up... or being betrayed!

17:80:30, and counting, the digits rolled.

"I've got to think" she said, strapping herself into the pilot's seat. "There must be something. For God's sake, don't fade out on me now like this...." her voice faded.

She waited.

What was is he had said?

She replayed the transmission "...abort deorbit burn! It's a flyby. Deploy generator!"

What was it? Martin and Lloyd had discussed the matter when onboard.

Think!

It was dry, hot.

She was trapped on *Eagle*, a sitting target for two oncoming nuclear warheads, breathing earthly air like a frog in a bubble orbiting a plant that was 93 million miles from the sun.

And what was the solution? Capcom's response to the disabled shuttle. Kill it!

On the other hand, there was a plan of some sort.

What was the plan?

What did they want her to do?

It was getting hard to focus. She gazed at the labyrinth of electronic switches, dials, and banks of buttons on the consoles. All five computers were silent now. They had engaged with Ground Control, talking back and forth to each other like commiserating Aunties. The first computer specializing in prelaunch and reentry data; the second in orbital flight systems and trajectory computations; the third little computer went to town and the fifth little piggy went to market...*Never had the universe been be so quiet.*

Did life stop when support systems failed or when there was no mission?

What was a *mission* other than to be useful to someone? It was very quiet in this peaceful mode, quiet without stress. Or without being needed by someone. Someone like Lloyd.

She wanted to sleep right now.

A fish came sailing out of the kitchen and smacked the floor at her feet where it slid. It landed there as a silver and glossy-finned creature, eyes wide and mouth agape.

Amanda gasped.

Behind her at the kitchen doors, a Waiter from whose tray the fish had flown, stood as wide-eyed as the fish on the floor, and it brought the café to a halt as everyone just stared. It lay there, as if the world had just defied gravity.

It was the German newlyweds who broke the silence. She, with her guttural voice and skinny jeans - and he, with his balloon eyes burst into exclamations of laughter and amazement.

"Look! A fish..." he pointed.

Amanda Wells was seated at the coffee bar, her *Command and Control Center* as she put it.

She had chosen that spot because from that spot she could purview pretty much all that occurred from the ground floor lobby on upwards. Safely seated under the protection of public view, sipping coffee and playing on the Laptop, she could wait. Especially useful were the nearby wall plugs for customers with Laptops and electronic devices.

There she was. Waiting like a cat with a hat. Or a fish...

She looked back.

The young waiter was a boy clearly inexperienced. He disappeared long before the full range of mirth was exhausted, bringing out the clean-up crew; the manager, then the Maître D of the Restaurant... who recognized Amanda from the previous evening. Even the service personnel at the Hotel Lobby stopped by to examine the excitement at the coffee bar of the Lobby. It was a coffee shop in the Hotel that flanked the kitchens - that place from where flowed streams of food for the Restaurant next door and the guest patrons of the Hotel calling for room service...

She turned back to her work. Even with her earplugs on, she could hear the commotion inside the kitchen where the young waiter was far from being let off the hook at the fish debacle.

His cry, in fact, was not only audible, but definable. And it occurred to Amanda that long after the affair was over, he would be persecuted by his Kitchen supervisor. She kept her eyes down.

Then suddenly a crash of pans followed by hollow pounding and a dull scream resulted in the youth rushing out of the kitchen in fright for his life. He navigated his way around a table or two, knocked over a chair, his eyes aflame and heading for the Front Lobby Desk where he presumed he might find safety, and he crouched under a luggage table, clutching his hand and rocking on his heels.

Amanda looked down, and saw a few drops of blood on the floor that trailed him.

The Kitchen Supervisor was an Indian with an impeccable English accent. He came striding out, his nostrils flaring with hot anger, searching...

"Excuse me!" said Amanda, leaning over to unplug her connection from the wall. She failed to disconnect it, and pulled instead at the plug long enough to distract him.

He was clearly incensed, but brought his wits in check soon enough to realize that he was meddling with a customer at the coffee bar and not in pursuit down a back alley. He diverted his eyes from the front desk and turned to her.

She smiled, peripherally aware that the boy was scurrying away.

 "I was wondering if I could place a lunch order?"

She felt as if she had inserted herself between a Bengal Tiger and his prey.

Would she ever learn to mind her own bloody business, she wondered. What was she thinking?

Whether he registered her or not was debatable. But the Manager from behind the Lobby Desk spotted him and raised his arm, averting the cook's fury by waving a gesture that begged for discretion now, if murder later...

"But of course!" he said with as much courtesy as he could muster. "I'll send the waiter..."

She ordered something under chicken, or over chicken, collected her personal belongings and strayed over to the Lobby Desk.

She saw the youth hiding behind the storage counter. She asked if the young man could show her the way to the Ladies Hair Salon? A stern look from the Manager defied him to resist, and out he came, nursing his wrist and limping as he led the way.

They approached the ascending elevator to the second tier of shops and Ladies Boutique. He was slowing down, and very pale. She stood behind him.

By the time he approached the Ladies Hair Salon, Amanda wondered if he were about the pass out.

It was then that she looked back and saw the Desk Clerk look up at them, gesticulating to a man as to their direction.

The man was the taxi driver.

She dodged to the left. Out of sight from points below, she thrust out her hand and grabbing the boy's elbow, steered him briskly passed the store and into the Pharmacy next door where she leaned over the counter and asked for immediate medical attention.

When the lad was presented, the Pharmacist pulled him inside immediately and into a back room where the boy crumbled into a seat.

"I'll be back later. See to him!" she said, unsure if he even spoke English.

He nodded, pulling out the boy's hand, now blue and full of blood. A deep gash reddened at his wrist, and a livid pink stain from above the wrist to the elbow showed where he had been burned.

She did go back later in the day. But Boots was closed. The Pharmacy was shuttered and dark.

Only after dinner, while waiting for the elevator to go up to her room did she hear words from a man who paused briefly at her side. "You saved the boy's life" he said sotto voce, and left.

It was the pharmacist.

∞

With Uri Pravda's testimony clearly on record, Tim Martin returned to CAPCOM.

"I thought you were dead!" said Lloyd.

"I was" grinned Tim. "Long story. Later" The propitious call came in not a minute too soon for Lloyd who wasted no time in re-establishing his credibility. Oliver and Cappachutto would be dealt with later.

The Shuttle was sabotaged. For now, they had to eliminate the imminent danger.

"*Eagle.* Now listen up! We *are* going to bring you home"

Karen shut her eyes. Did it really matter anymore? "Roger" was all she said.

"*Eagle*, standby to receive Code 712. Information for your analysis."

She was tired. She didn't want to work with Houston anymore. She didn't want to do anything. She was at that point in a state known to sailors at sea who welcomed death as an alternative to continued stress.

"*Eagle*, this is Control. Do you copy data?"

She let the computer run the code and she read. It was hard to focus. "Err...234...238..."

"Karen. This is Lloyd. Martin is with me. Now listen up!"

It took a minute. But she responded.

"Speak!" she said

"The particle crystal structure carbon that surrounds the ship. We must find a way to neutralize it before you de-orbit! Once known as 'space dust.'"

He waited.

"Roger."

"It has 60 molecules; hexagon in structure with various functions of form. Substance is formed in a vacuum..."

He waited.

"Roger"

"It can be dissipated by electrical impulse when heated and cooled suddenly. It changes form into a substance known as fullerene..."

He waited.

No answer.

"This is Control. Do you copy?"

"Sorta. Kinda."

"I'm copying you with instructions. Switch to code 712."

"Roger."

"*Eagle*, to change to fullerene it must be in a vacuum: Check...?"

Bleep.

"Second, it needs heat – Like an incendiary condition. Check...?"

Bleep.

"Third, it needs an electrical discharge: Check...?"

Bleep.

"Fourth, then cool, that is, return to space ambient temperature. Check?"

He waited.

Had anything registered with the pilot of the vessel? Was she viable?

Bleep.

"Control. How do you plan to introduce a bolt of lightning out here in space, gentlemen?"

Lloyd smiled. "*Eagle*, remember AIC No. 6 of our mission?"

"Roger. Experiment to test static discharges in space? The Electronic Pulse Generator Apparatus? That dumb thing!.."

"That's it!"

He waited.

"Control. First, setting up such a chain reaction is well-nigh impossible - even under normal operating procedures.

Second, with two nuclear warheads on their way I'm not exactly in total readiness for experiments here."

"*Eagle*. Stand by for data."

The computers came up with a nice bell shape curve.

"*Eagle*: Transmitting data. Energy release mark. Light mark. 0.76 second delay. Explosion here. Release of Pulse Generator on the spin table, equipped with three photo electric cells which will be triggered by the light. Delay 0.76. Release electrical impulse simultaneously"

"Roger. Over!"

Lloyd opened the microphone. "In other words, Karen, you can diffuse the whole damned cloud by changing its properties: One, heat from the nuclear explosions. Two, electrical charge from Pulse Generator"

"Control, that's crazy!"

Martin grabbed the speaker from Lloyd.

"Why not? Karen, listen to me. This is Martin. Time is of the *Essence*. It's a giant capacitor...It will discharge an electric bolt like lightening once ignited, sending an electrical discharge through this fullerene substance, which will quickly reduce to cold space ambient temperature and dissipate into harmless 'space dust'!"

"Nice dreamin' guys, but how do the nuclear bombs not blow me up?"

"We will disarm, for one thing..."

"Well that's a comfort Houston!"

"But...You'll get a swift kick in the ass and sent to fly in on slingshot elliptical!"

"And once I'm out of harm's way, how do I fuel up for reentry?"

She was resigned, and no amount of persuading was going to work.

Lloyd took the microphone back. "Karen. *My co-pilot* does it all the time! He likes to drive these babies home on a dead stick."

"Control I know you're all trying...and I appreciate the effort. But, Houston, you guys are crazy in the head..."

"That's what we are so proud of!"

They waited.

Bleep. "Roger. I'll give it a shot. If I die tryin'!"

It took some computing and precise triangulation on all five little piggy's – as Karen now called her computers - to position *Eagle* for the impact of two chain nuclear explosions. They would slingshot her into a higher elliptical orbit around the earth, yet an orbit that at one brief point might veer enough to penetrate the earth's atmosphere, manually and without fuel.

Lloyd transmitted the programs for a change in trajectories and elliptical orbits. The team worked with him.

It didn't take Karen long to realize what they were trying to do. She decided to give it everything she had. That's if she didn't stop breathing on the way.

"Do I have enough time to launch the generator for a good charge?" came her transmission.

"*Eagle*, do it now!"

Karen glanced at the digits: 14:40:25. There was a lot of work to do.

That left twelve hours to decompress. One EVA left. That gave her one hour and 40 minutes to work outside to preposition the generator. Then, if she survived the explosion, she'd be flung away from earth on an elliptical orbit, with enough momentum on the way back, to dead stick it home...

That is, provided her heat shields could penetrate the atmosphere. She shut her eyes. It was such a long shot. Okay, she decided.

Commence decompression mode. She called up LLoyd's programs and entered them into the computers.

Her next priority was to get on the Arm and put the generator on the spin table in the Bay hold.

Could she open the shuttle's bay doors?

The doors did respond, and the shuttle opened up like a blossom in space.

∞

"OMS Burn check" said Karen out loud. She steadied her trembling hand and engaged Program 602 Program.

"ENGAGE" flashed the computer.

"Karen was suited up and prepared, if sweating from her exertions as she watched two oncoming blips approach on the CRT2.

"Here they come," she muttered. "Fasten your seatbelts and do or die, girl!"

One detonation occurred.

Then another.

First light, then heat burst at impact, and the Orbiter rattled like a tumbling egg.

Then the giant capacitor's light cells set off a charge that, together with the explosions, ignited a million bright diamonds in a particle cloud surrounding the Orbiter.

It lasted a few seconds, discharging like a wicked summer thunderstorm and rearranging the molecular structure of the carbon into fullerene as it cooled fatally in the vacuum of ambient space.

From earth, Karen could hear "*Eagle*. Do you copy....ssss'

She was way out in space now, she knew.

∞

Chapter 10

It occurred to Amanda as she wrote her position paper on climate change that she was hardly in a position to make any assertions at all.

Chiefly, she could not access the supporting documentation that she needed.

Further, she was under duress from converging priorities that compromised her credibility as an official at the UN.

Here she sat, discussing and debating the qualifiers and equalizers of commerce based on assumptions that were deeply interwoven with other national priorities...Mostly to be complicated at best...

Worse, sitting at the Cafe and working on her Laptop, she could actually see the Taxi Driver standing outside the Hotel entrance. Clearly, she was under constant observation. Even if for unclear reasons, yet a captive nonetheless. These were conditions hardly conducive to objective thought for a professional paper.

Yet she must keep busy – a working professional, and a damned good analyst at that. She focused on the task and reviewed the policy analysis of climate change protocols.

Something had gone sideways in diplomacy.

Even without details, Amanda understood the dangers of rocking a boat that was positioned between two fiercely competitive nations, Pakistan and India - each with their own interests in climate regulation, and each with their own priorities: They were both emerging economies. And judging from Lahore, far advanced from destitution! They were both mature powers, each with a nuclear arsenal at their disposal.

However, even as both countries were trusted by the West, their inherent ascendant economies might pit their cultural values against materialist capitalism. This, many publications already asserted.

Amanda happened to disagree. Trade was trade. And they were each a lovely people. Except for the Mr. Dari's of the world.

So, concluded Amanda: Between global aspirants and local contenders in a geographically challenging environment with climate considerations at their center, they stood precariously on a ledge with commercial pressure nipping at internal stability.

How to help?

What priorities propelled them forward?

She took another sip of her cold coffee and looked around her.

∞

The youth was waiting for her.

Just like that, sitting off in the shadows of Palm fronds flanking an ornamental fountain. The potted plant cast streaks of afternoon sunlight across the marble mall.

Had she not seen him, he would have had to wait until the next morning where she normally she set up her Laptop at the Cafe of the Hotel.

She wandered over and sat on the edge of the pool. He did not move away.

"Are you alright?" she said.

He stayed mute as a statue, his hand wrapped in neutral colored bandaging, his services clearly no longer wanted in the kitchens.

"Family?" she asked, cradling by way of gesticulation, a baby.

He stared, unmoving. Then, still as a monk, four fingers straightened out from his wreath of bandaging.

She looked down.

She was about to open her pocket book for some change, then had a ridiculous idea.

"Can you sew?"

He didn't answer.

She threaded through the air with one sewing hand from the palm of the other, like this?

His eyes lit up.

"I'm going up to the Fabric store tomorrow... in the morning, and I need some dresses sewn up."

He got up, and ran off.

Well that went well, she thought, still sitting.

The next morning, she nearly decided not to bother. But she went anyway. Into the Fabric store she strode and picked out three textiles for some dresses. The shop was happy to have them sewn up for her. A Fitting was arranged. She paid up. She was a valuable customer.

It wasn't until she was passing the pool that she saw him again. Only he had a girl with him. She wore a gauze shift over Punjab pants and stood up, mutely, a wreath of a figure.

Suddenly Amanda understood.

"Come with me!" she announced and marched back into the Fabric store.

"I have a seamstress here whom I would like to *make* my dresses..."

They weren't too pleased. The Supervisor was called over.

"And since I'm in such a hurry, can she please make them up here in the shop... until I pick them up? They are simple shifts..."

The supervisor barked a few harsh words. He was the cook's brother, decided Amanda.

"And I'd like to add another outfit, as sari...Yes, that blue color cloth. That will do. I'll take that now, thank you!"

Outside, Amanda gave the blue cloth to the girl. "Tomorrow, you wear that. Nice and clean, you come. You sew. Yes?"

She nodded demurely. They both ran out of the hotel together.

Nobody saw a thing.

∞

With Amanda at her side, Dr. Sumptra hailed a cab, and there was no drama.

Amanda was beginning to think that her captors existed only in her head. Neither the "Taxi" nor the two assailants were visible.

Together, they entered the popular outdoor Coco's Café and sat at a table where the scent of jasmine and spiced foods filled the air.

For Amanda it was a real treat to be outside the confines of the Hotel, dinning alfresco, regardless.

"There is definitely an aberration going in on that region" said Saphira. "Look at it this way, here is this mountain culture that has existed along the margins for generations" she positioned the salt container. "And here" she plunked the pepper "is this mine operation - next to it, and then Bam! Everyone gets sick, leaves... or is killed."

"Something ain't right!" said Amanda, her mouth full of food.

"You're darned right something ain't right" repeated Saphira. "Only, for one reason or another, I can't add up the statistics as to what's causing the collapse of the community."

"Where exactly is this place you're referring to?" asked Amanda, her drink safely aloft from either the salt or the pepper.

"Well you see. That's the thing. I can't exactly put my finger on it. It's in the Shoehire Pass. It's like this rural landscape, with animals grazing all over the mountain side. Is it the water...?" she went on, forking her salad.

Amanda looked up. "Um"

Saphira continued. "If so, which source do they ingest? Is it the grazing animals they slaughter for food? Is it a toxin of some kind...Or contagion? The possibilities are endless..."

Amanda dove into her cloth bag bought at the hotel, and brought out her handy map, which was as wrinkled as the cloth. So she un-crumpled it and smoothed out the Punjab region.

"Over .....Here" circled the wayward fork in Saphira's hand before it land on a spot of brown mountain and green earth with a stab.

Amanda flinched.

"Is there any 'Help' going their way... to investigate? What if they need food or medicine? Or provisions. Like at the site of the reported quake..." she asked.

Saphira just stared at her with her eyebrow cocked. She almost laughed.

Amanda realized the ludicrous nature of such a feat at such high and rugged altitudes. No wonder there was no Mr. Dari!

The notion was one of these Western responses that had no relevance to the locals.

Amanda wondered. What of the cargo of supplies destined to aid the village stricken by disaster?

"Forget it!" said Saphira. "Mudslides and road blockages all over the place...Impossible!"

Saphira smiled at her, tucking away her table napkin.

Amanda groaned inwardly at her own ineptness in being so easily sidetracked from her mission to direct UN Aid to a village arriving in Karachi.

It probably would have helped to have direction from Fumosa, she thought. After all, he sent her an email. *That was it!* No points of contact. No outline. No mission targets. No authorizing oversight memos. No policy or insurance. Hell, not even a ship's manifest of the cargo!

Either he had extreme confidence in her abilities to execute the task, or she was on her own. She paused. Or he had no authority...*Surely not?*And she had been *duped*?

She swallowed her wine.

Saphira's thoughts were elsewhere.

Amanda knew there was no thwarting this woman. One thing was emerging. The village in question - and the site of the earthquake were not far distant from each other evidently.

Finally the conversation veered towards Amanda's position at the Hotel in Lahore. "They've got me in their sights at all times...As you can see over there!" she added, spotting one blue turban in the shadows.

Saphira surprised her. "What can I do to help get them off your back?"

Amanda sighed. "I'm not sure, really. I guess I'm on hold till they get the goods..."

"The *goods*?"

"You know, the supply and provisions from the UN for the village that had the earthquake. I'm the key to the loot!"

Now Saphira did laugh out loud. "But of course! It's good business. In fact *great* business up in these parts. But clearly, something is wrong..."

"How so?"

"Well, for one thing. There was no earthquake damage listed as a casualty site for medical attention. "

"What?"

"I would know! I'm on the Emergency Preparedness Commission. So that leaves the tacit understanding that it was a military assault of some kind. That - being the local vernacular for aid-for-assaults-programs!"

"What do you mean...?"

"It's how we negotiate our unholy alliances with the West when we host the terrorists they want in our mountains..."

Amanda put down her fork and stopped eating her gateau. "And I thought I was out here on a climate conference!"

"You are! But just don't ask too many questions. Besides, it's the medical assistance I'm interested in. So. We have this close-by village that is reporting distress - which as you can imagine in these altitudes is not an easy thing to survive in – Why don't we collaborate?"

Amanda stared at her, still trying to make all the pieces fit. All that Aid Assistance ...What had she got herself into?

"Look" said the doctor "Maybe we can help each other: I'll get you OUT, if you get me IN so to speak." Down went her wine.

The doctor finished chewing and presented her case.

"Perhaps I can get at the reason for your detention up here, and say that I am the medical recipient of the Aid for the err..*subjects*?"

"Well yes..." began Amanda, not exactly sure where this was going. Then it occurred to her that all this was without any fixed geographic location.

"Where is this village exactly?"

"That's what I'll find out. And besides, there is someone I want you to meet!"

Amanda was returned to the Hotel, and she re-entered the Lobby, wondering at the transformation that had occurred. If not entirely a free woman quite yet, there had been progress!

Her mind had strayed. She had been working on her Paper. Yet by concentrating on other matters, it cleared the mind for pragmatism, and suddenly she had recall of words written to her in a letter in New York.

If you are ever in Lahore, look me up!

That's exactly what the letter said from Dr. Saphira Sumptra. At the time she wrote down the phone number on her working calendar as a Contact. In her Hotel room that night, she went online and opened her account.

"I'm not exactly free to roam the country" said Amanda to Saphira on the phone. "But I'm at the Hotel Clarion and very comfortable..." she said gamely, if feeling broken.

∞

"Over here, Amanda!" admonished Dr. Saphira, glittering in sequins and jewels "I want you to meet someone"

They were at the Hospital Fundraising Event.

A band of musicians played an assortment of instruments, dulcet sounds from both West and East.

The party was glamorous. Women wore silk colored saris, and men stood tall in starched turbans with embossed folds of national significance. Others, like Amanda were in a standard cocktail dress.

Hospital staff came and went, some on-call.

Nobody could have prepared Amanda for Dr. Saphira's surprise. She led Amanda away from the party a man of some height, dark hair and deep eyes.

He was of Indian descent, the face familiar...

He was wearing a white dinner jacket, black tie, something that made him easily recognizable in this crowd, if not strikingly good-looking.

He took her hand with a deep bow, Edwardian style. He waited, smiling.

Of course! The young Village Elder.

She remembered. At the conference. Seated to her left. Salim...

But suddenly the memory of another visit back home made her stare at him in disbelieve: He was the subject of investigation by Lloyd in New York!

The look of surprise on her face must have betrayed her.

He waited and offered her a glass of Champaign from a passing bearer. "I see you've decided I'm a terrorist" he said, nonchalantly.

"No. Not exactly" said Amanda.

Another waiter in purple Punjab uniform offered a tray of hors d'oevres. She picked salmon and capers, happy for the distraction to collect her thoughts.

"But you don't know exactly, for sure, who I am?" he proceeded.

"It's just that I didn't recognize you" admitted Amanda. "Not then. And certainly not now!"

"Well that's understandable. I wear many hats..."

"Or turbans, you mean" said Amanda now sipping her drink with a twinkle.

"Yes. Yes!" he laughed, nodding sideways as was the local custom. "But what I think you should know is that I am *not* the enemy!" he insisted. "Well. That's a comfort! Then you won't mind telling me why you are of such interest to the Government?"

He held back, observing her, or meditating, for all she knew.

"Well no! That depends on which Government you mean..."

God!

Amanda was tiring of all this:

Detained at a hotel – well, *delivered* from Karachi under forced escort and watched, if not shadowed. Here entertained by a doctor of little acquaintance from Lahore. Socializing with a 'wanted man' in New York and armed only with an Academic Paper to deliver in Australia!

Where, she wondered, was the closest door to the American Embassy? More importantly, would she end up with the Sing Sing brothers again in their blue turbans?

She looked down.

"I can sense your frustration" he said suddenly. "Would you mind very much if I took you out to see something tomorrow?"

"Well that depends...err" she began, wondering who was friend and who was foe.

"I'm supposed to be meeting with a Mr Dari when my Cargo arrives from Karachi"

Not that it made any difference since Amanda knew that Dari was a fact of fiction here. And her cargo was in New Guinea or New Delhi for all she knew.

"What if I tell you that you're being followed by two thugs from Karachi who want to get their hands on your Aid from the UN for the black market?"

She held her breath. So, he knew her predicament! Truth at last! But still...how to explain New York?

"Amanda!" shrieked Dr. Sumptra "Come over here!"

Someone else was on her list.

Crazy as it was, it felt wonderful to be out. And she did enjoy meeting people.

But later that night she emptied out her bag and laid out the map that had done duty for Saphira at their lunch together.

X-marks-the-spot is where the fork landed. She looked at the map closely.

In small print she read the cartological designations: Topographical contours showed several black lines in tight proximity and converging, meaning steep drops and high altitudes.

The Shoehire Pass

Not that far, really. But almost unassailable.

∞

The data from the Sarbo deliveries were too clear to disqualify as a simple mistake. Telemetry and trajectory were coming in on different spectra. There was hardly room for speculation.

The mission had a saboteur. That would be for another Review board.

Cappachutto was debriefing a planning session. He excused himself to take a call at the secretary's desk.

The report had been long.

They had not heard any transmission from *Eagle*. And a contingency failure was assumed.

 Lloyd told them of Martin's expeditionary escape. And it was included in the report.

But it was what he omitted to say that he was particularly careful about. Something that he, as a former trained Marine and officer of the Elite corps had planned at the Pentagon. A mission to be executed in silence and on a special assignment. Already, as they spoke, a surveillance team was making its way in advance through the mountains.

Harvey, Vallentine and the others gave their report as to what might have happened.

That left Oliver.

Officially, until they heard from the *Eagle*, or found confirmation, they should provide information for a solution that worked.

 Oliver was still there on authority from the *Arianne* Project. Angry as hell, he said, and having delivered a scathing report to the Administration in Washington and the European Space Program about NASA and two "incompetent engineers" who should be relieved of the Command, if not investigated for irresponsible malfeasance. He stopped short of citing Cappachutto. But that hardly ingratiated him with the rest of the Assessment Team.

Cappachutto returned.

Nothing could be worse than the pall of the loss of a ship. Even as they made plans for the contingency. It tugged deep within the soul of every man present. The challenge was to remain focused on the present.

For now, what it came down to, decided Lloyd, was a comparison of two scenarios: Ship's certain failure at earth's re-entry managed by Oliver, or failure at their own crazy scheme to sustain the orbit. Either way, it was a failed Shuttle mission. Odds or not.

The repercussions would come later, they all knew.

For now, Cappachutto was Director of the Mission.

The charts before them showed critical path items that had been unpredicted. Period. It was a sobering and horrible reality for NASA's management. All they could do was wait and watch it happen.

"So. What else could we have missed?" asked a desultory Cappachutto.

When does the re-entry silence commence.

"In 8 hours, Sir. One more orbit to go. Then we put her on Remote Control coming in..."

"I suggest we all get a 10 minute shut-eye, think about responsible responses to the Media; and contemplate years of retirement as the team that blew it!" he said, preparing to stand up. "I've got work to do. Washington wants to be briefed at every step...For better or for worse, this day will come to an end. Gentlemen."

A fierce knocking belted the door.

"Jesus!" he burst out, his nerves frayed to the limit.

Bill popped his head in the door, his face red with a big grin.

"You're not going to believe this Sir, but your Shuttle is coming home fast and furious!"

They stared. It was too unexpected to believe.

Dropping everything, they filled into the Command Center.

Eagle blipped up the screens at Cape Canaveral as if she had never disappeared.

Bleep "CAPCOM..." said a voice

"*Eagle!*" exclaimed Cappachutto.

Bleep "You're not going to believe this...*hsssss*. I'm a little busy up here .... Plan to re-enter the earth's atmosphere at the following fix. Transmitting data now..."

It took perhaps point two seconds to receive.

Harvey and Valentine were obtaining input from six sources at once.

"She won't make it!" said Valentine abruptly.

Cappachutto acted quickly. He was to make the final decision. "Even if her ablating materials are still up...she's coming in too fast to sustain..."

He picked up the Speaker and was about to direct her to complete the second orbit to allow for some deceleration.

Lloyd put his face in front of Cappachutto "Let her use the atmosphere to slalom. It'll slow her down. Then she can re-enter!"

CAPCOM

They huddled. The room became a confessional where nothing was repeated outside its walls.

Cappachutto wanted to hear all options.

Tim was the first to speak the unspeakable.

"She has no fuel supply, and she'd have to dead stick re-entry on a glide most of the way to keep the nose up. Her underbelly Aft-albating tiles would be the only real protection she has, like waterskiing. And that would take the skill of a killer jet jock nursed on throttles!"

"She's a capable individual..." insisted Lloyd.

"But fatigued - malnourished and severely impaired at this point" added the Medical Adviser.

"To say nothing of her cabin pressure. Once she's entered the atmosphere, anything below 20,000 psi is zip!"

Cappachutto looked down at his note pad. "I doubt she's in any condition to survive the reentry let alone the ship's damage post explosion. We must assume the ship is compromised and we have no idea what the skin of the orbiter can take without temperature data..."

He paused.

"Gentlemen...It's been a long flight. God knows we've agonized and suffered enough loss. True, we have an investigation ahead of us, since sabotage is clearly evident. But please bear with me through to the bitter end...ok? This may not be elegant. But we see it through!"

They all nodded.

"May God help Patterson. God help us all"

He got up "Back to work. Anticipate a catastrophic failure. Ready?"

They nodded.

"Let's go" he said, and opened the door to Control and Command Center.

∞

At the Pentagon the situation was quite different.

Far from assessing the capabilities of a rescue mission in which two thermonuclear bombs had been detonated, it was a thrashing session of who should bear the blame: The Navy's incompetent training of astronauts or NASA's design.

So it came right down to assessing the pilot, a woman. That she should be flying one of the country's most expensive hardware galled every military leader in the room. Karen Patterson with "the training of a sailor and the experience of an administrative assistant" said Colonel Jeffrey of the Marine Corps.

"Well, not exactly. She's a reliable commissioned officer Sir" began the Naval Personnel Officer.

As far as the White House was concerned, in the event that the ship landed, they wanted nothing said about the possibility of climate tampering, if that was implied with the stratosphere dispersions and deflections of concentrated heat through the ozone.

That would cause damage beyond repair, insisted Stevenson, not until we have a handle on this, he told Cappachutto.

∞

"*Eagle*. This is Control. We read you. Standby for elliptical orbital coordinates. Edwards on standby. We read trajectory fix on orbital swing. Transmit life support data. Standby. Atmosphere blackout in two minutes. Good luck Captain Patterson! You're on your own now. We'll see you on the other side. Over"

High ablating shields had to hold out through penetration of the atmosphere. The question was, was the shuttle able to achieve enough protection to penetrate the atmosphere at precisely the correct angle? Otherwise, it was an inferno.

Back to Oliver, thought Lloyd.

She was close. *So close* to making it.

They monitored her fuel supply; drag and resistance which came up with astonished speed on computers.

"Come on, Karen! *Conserve* and *up* on the nose. C'mon!" they muttered, some in prayer, some in disbelief.

∞

Lloyd was amused by her last transmission:

"I may not be the officer you think I should be, nor the Flier. But I shall fly this goddamned bucket of bolts to your doorstep Houston! 'Cos I'm tired. And I'm pissed. And you should have more than one goddamned shuttle - built!"

Her words brought grown men to their feet, weeping.

Transmission silence during re-entry was endless. "God she's got courage!" said one.

They waited.

Then some were growing uncomfortable. It went on too long, the silence. Perhaps the inevitable was obvious.

Still, they waited.

Audible transmission came in with a rush "*Hsss....*"

Bleep "Edwards. This is *Eagle*...

"*Hsss*...

"... I've lost a few ceramic teeth....But I'm coming in ready or not. Over."

∞

Trevor found the cargo.

With some effort to get on board the vessel, and with the right paperwork, he got the authority to poke around.

In the hold of a ship that had carried it across the India Ocean was a Ziggurat of containerized cargo emblazoned with the insignia of the United Nations Relief Aid.

 He made arrangements to get the boxcars lifted off the ship and onto the docks.

Opened with crowbars, the provisions were wrapped in plastic cloth and stacked in behemoth squares weighing several tons each.

Forklifts entered the palettes of the tightly packed loads and cranes hoisted them off the docks and onto vehicular transports for distribution.

Or so it was supposed to be. There was no transportation to distribute them to the Interior.

The operation that should have occurred two weeks and would now take several hours. And only if paperwork preparations made in advance might take effect - which by some miracle, had occurred. But not physically, and not immediately. Who made those early arrangements was not easily answered, Trevor noticed.

 In any event, not having the requisite 'Transports' in place required them to make temporary quarters at the docks for the sitting cargo.

They cordoned off the area with an erected fence, and they posted guards around the perimeter. Guards - *thank God*, who had accompanied the cargo as a contingent of Italian Carabinieri sent by the FAO in Rome. In fact, it was their white boots that gave them away, standing around at the docks, waiting for their intended transports that gave Trevor his leads.

Otherwise, without security, the cargo would have been picked clean in under two hours, they said.

That night, only two shots were fired, reported the Guards. But without speedy arrangements to move it all soon, they knew their authority over the cargo could easily be overwhelmed. They were probably being watched... Besides, their assigned time on station with this cargo was limited.

Trevor understood.

On this Asian continent these were difficult times. Following several natural disasters, the areas around Karachi were resource- depleted in the extreme. Supply of any kind was fair game for the hungry and desperate.

Plus this was precious cargo. On the black market, it could fetch a fortune. And a dangerous business. Trevor had to act fast.

 He should have been in Germany on his transit home by now, he had vacated the premises of his posting officially. But then made alternate arrangements.

He would stop in Karachi with Yusef, his personal assistant. A salutary visit to the Consulate offices of the Government, if asked. Routine, and informal like...

 Yusef had promised the doctor to keep a sharp eye over him. So with that, they stole out of New Delhi under cover of night, before anyone could raise any question.

 Amanda Wells was the reason. And Karachi, he discovered, was not without its deficiencies.

He came upon a solution for 'Transports' in a desperate sort of a way. Of all the bedfellows, he wanted to say.

Instead, he shook hands with the Commandant of the Seventh Transport Patrol of the Second Division of the Russian Army quartered in Karachi, and drank the rest of his tea. Together, they would transport the cargo to his destination.

It was choice he had to make. At least it was subscribed by their corresponding governments on site. Not that Karachi received much attention from any government really. But the only other option for delivery services that might have any availability were the Australians. And they were seaborne, standing just off shore by way of escort for one of their Navy carriers. No boots on the ground.

So, the Russians it was!

 Three days to deploy. That was, prepare to load up, garage in quarters, and then form a Convoy of Troop Transports into the Interior of the Country: to reach the destination of disaster relief.

It was all Trevor could do to keep the affairs rolling: His communications were ongoing with his Home Office; his host at the Consulate informed; and his feet, if unsteady, were still beneath him considering every footstep was fanning a fever and serious dehydration.

And then there was Yusef, whose comments he had to ignore most of the time. Comments about this being this being very serious business...

∞

"Yes, sir" said Cappachutto to the White House "She's a highly trained offer. One of the best in the United States Navy, and we're proud she's flying our Shuttle, sir. Thank you, Sir. Her name is Karen Patterson. *Officer* Karen Patterson, United States Navy, Sir!"

Cappachutto, Lloyd and Martin all looked at each other and sighed. The crisis was over.

"So where are you going now?" asked Cappachutto, later.

"I'm going to find out whose messing with us" said Lloyd leaving the room.

He went to his quarters, packed his bags, and booked a flight to Pakistan.

"Don't worry. I'm pre-positioned with a plan!"

"Good thing I didn't have you arrested!" muttered Cappachutto.

"So. That's why..." laughed Lloyd "I made a plan!"

"Right."

∞

Yusef found the hotel.

He and Trevor went inside, and while it was clear the management did not like to show the rooms of absent guests, enough sway was brought upon the situation to prevail.

The room was cleared, as Trevor expected it would be. But it was the boy outside who provided them with enough information to paint a clear picture.

Amanda had been alerted that the cargo had arrived. A man from the docks showed up. They left in the Taxi together, and that was the last the management had seen of her. Three days passed, and the owner of the hotel bagged her belongings and rented out the room to new tourists.

Trevor looked about, his head moving from side to side. And he examined her belongings. He saw her personal effects bundled together, clearly abandoned. He thought about her.

Amanda was a cautious traveler and meticulous organizer packed and ready. Hers was not a profession at the UN for much decorative dressing these days, he knew. But her essentials had not been gathered. She had walked out with an unsuspecting mind and a heart full of trust, he could tell. Prime candidate for a hostage.

At the very least, it was known that Amanda Wells never flew to Australia. This Fumosa confirmed.

At most, it was also known in New York that she remained away from her desk. And short of alarming her family and next of kin, it was clear that the New York City police had little time for cases about people who failed to show up for work.

So that left Trevor with little recourse other than to inform the American Offices locally that one of their citizens had gone missing from Karachi. Something he hated to do either as an official with little authority locally, nor as a friend - with only a suspicion to offer. But Amanda deserved that at least, he thought.

He left messages on her every device, including desk and contact-bases, almost like beacons. Sensing her frustration at his unavailability and hoping that word of his enquiry would reach her, he wanted to reach her.

Privately, he was anxious. He and Yusef both.

All this, while superficially smiling their way into planning for transportation into the Interior of Pakistan on a convoy carrying UN Aid Supplies. At least he did had that authority to do...

 Without saying a word, he and Yusef examined every clue for a trail that might lead to

Amanda's whereabouts.

That is, if she was ever there. And still alive.

The moment finally arrived. They climbed aboard diesel lorries that the Russians used as transports, showing no objection that they were on military troop-carriers used for ammunition supply, complete with machine gun and armed personnel.

Instead, he and Yusef took their seat up front with the Russian Commanding Officer, Gregor, and said nothing.

∞

The convoy came to a halt.

Trevor did not like the Check Point at the mountain pass. It was heavily guarded, with few faces glad to see them. They were asked for papers.

It was an unnecessary procedure inside a national boundary, Trevor knew. But this was tribal country, clearly. And many an Occupation Force had resulted in occupation-resistance by local tribal leaders.

He and Yusef were the only Westerner civilians on this convoy. All others on this Russian military in troop combat uniform. Not that the Russian language was entirely alien to Trevor, but he was definitely sitting on the margins of a potentially growing problem: A fully laden cargo-load of supplies that could be interpreted in a dozen different ways, depending on whose side you were on, holding which gun, and defending which territory.

Checkpoints in these mountains, he knew, could be anything from an Army hold-outs to a terrorist cell, if not a Taliban stronghold looking for loot...

So. If the Russian Commander did not maintain authority, they could be sold out in a second.

Yusef, he could see, was getting nervous.

Trevor gave him a look to steady his nerves. And he waited, saying little, with every deference to Gregor of the convoy.

One thing was certain. They needed petrol, food and water for the troops in the trucks carrying cargo. They were on Empty. Trevor knew that even the reserve tanks were depleted.

His underlying concern however, he kept to himself.

Amanda had gone missing. And for all intents and purposes, he was on the lookout for the confirmation of a casualty up here.

However, the situation could deteriorate rapidly, he knew. As did Yusef.

Uri Pravda was cornered in a room with an office light above a desk, his hands in handcuffs.

Judging from the sanitation of the room and the gloss off the windows he knew that he was being interrogated by Administration officials. Thank God! This was no torture chamber.

He would tell them, he decided.

To hell with the scum work he'd done for De Phillpe and his man, Villas. Those Latino thugs were dealers... like anyone else - Castro Regime or not. And they had little respect for Americans.

Pravda looked at his interrogators. If these FBI Agents thought that was the *only* story, then they were naïve...

He was an American. And like a Roman Soldier, that was something to be proud of.

"So" said the voice from the shadows. "Mr Pravda. Do you have anything further you would like to add to your Statement, for the record?"

"Yes" he said.

To hell with bargaining. By the time he was finished, he'd have enough attorneys to line a block.

Fraud on Wall Street was not without its intricacies. Especially when it came to market manipulation of minerals; commodities and illegal licensing, let alone free trade.

The question he got however, surprised him.

"And will you identify the location of the source of graphite. The location of the mine?"

He nodded. "I will"

Within hours, the information was transmitted to a field camp posing as mountain climbers.

They had their target.

∞

"Trevor…" she had said, "I don't know if you will get this message. Or when. But its Tuesday the 18th of the month…"

She paused. What do you say to the only connection you *hope* is still a viable option? Hope, more than anything, for someone to care about your whereabouts…

"…But I am in Lahore. It's a long story. Look. I wanted you to know that I'm on my way to the Shoehire Pass in the Punjab. I'm with a Dr Saphira and someone I met at the Conference in New Delhi, Salim…"

God, she didn't even know if he was a Friendly – especially after Lt Commander James Lloyd came calling on her. And how to say it all on a phone message? *You can't fit a stable full of muck into a five pound bag ...*

"I was in Karachi, supposedly delivering UN supplies to the village of Sunijab that got hit with the earthquake. I got misled, ok? But...so, um, it's in the Shoehire Pass. So, that's where I'm going!"

She had paused then. "If you get this message, please pass along my report, I've been out of touch...Cmdr James Lloyd, NASA... "

Then she added hastily "Trevor. I'm so alone up here! And so scared. Where are you when I need you? I *so* wish these were the Welsh mountains...and I ...."

Click.

The call had been over thirty seconds ago. She had been monitored. There was no more signal.

That was her last communication.

She was up here in a mess she had walked into like an idiot and no exit in sight.

God!

Still. She had made the call. And to Trevor.

∞

The call showed up on the message grid almost instantaneously. It was picked up as an Intercepted message that related to the operation and into the IT monitoring system of the communications traffic, quickly routed to the command and control center of the mission on the ground.

The code was encrypted, then on a broadband reserved only for military personnel, the officer at the post was immediately tele-transmitting the message into the field zone, a base camp of mountain climbers...

The word that was flagged was the destination point for the incoming force and a drone was to target a zone of suspicious activities producing minerals from an unsanctioned mine. It was registered as a carbon-rock and crushing operation producing high-concentrations of graphite, mined as a rare earth element.

The Shoehire Pass in the Punjab.

The message to the field for Captain James Lloyd was an intercept placed on a need-to-know list. He asked to have the subjects and content identified and forwarded in full. He needed to know who the players were.

He got it within fifteen, and it was disquieting intelligence. Perhaps a coincidence. Perhaps a tribesman with nothing more than poor timing or promotion. Civilians, he knew, could complicated military missions.

But the cell phone call that had been intercepted was specific with a name he knew. The Shorehire Pass. Trevor. Amanda Wells.

Lloyd looked down.

Where was "Trevor"?

∞

Salim was neither in his dinner jacket nor in a Sikh's turban as in the photograph that Lloyd had shown to Amanda in the Hamptons.

He was in full military garb, rifle and ammo belt beneath a tribal cloak. Nor was he alone. In fact, in the gathering of tribesmen, she might have missed him altogether. Except that he stepped forward when Saphira opened the door of the Jeep.

How they survived the four-hour journey from Lahore up and down rugged mountain paths in a four wheel car astounded even Amanda.

One thing was certain. Dr. Saphira was more than a physician carrying a Socratic oath. She was carrying - after the sweat, dust and disheveling induced by her calloused driver who stopped only to resupply fuel from onboard tanks, a semi-automatic weapon! And judging from her fast jabbing tongue and oaths as the miles and discomfort stretched out... she could use it.

 Conversely, the further distance they traveled from Lahore, the more silent Amanda became.

By the time Salim stepped forward, Amanda knew she was their hostage. No question.

∞

The dinner was altogether uncomfortable for Trevor.

Seated between Gregor and his Lieutenant was hardly a treat. But then again, he wasn't a diplomat for nothing. Broken English was more or less the rule, since neither the Russians nor the Pakistani Guard were fluent in each other's language.

The conversation flowed, such as it was, with food coming and going in thick dishes of rice, spiced meats and strong drink, clearly the best the Pakistani Border Guard mess could muster.

What mattered most however, were the negotiations at hand. For some odd reason, Trevor felt an uncomfortable link with the Russians; one trying to pull against the other in veiled and not so veiled attempts to show a united front.

Something was afoot. This Yusef asserted to Trevor. But Trevor was unable to fathom the full situation.

For one thing, he had managed to remain dry while the others drank liberally. For another, turns of give-and-take were intermittently heated and loud, less with opportunities to negotiate than to mitigate...

Further, it became obvious that this was a game to which he was not necessarily invited. In fact, he was downright *shushed* at one point by the Russians, perhaps for his own protection. Especially as the Pakistani Border Guard, now emboldened by drink, were increasing their demands.

Clearly, the Russians were losing ground.

Worse. Even as their balance of superiority was being eroded, the cargo was the object of interest to the Guard. This even Trevor observed.

Finally, Trevor was invited to retire for the night - in the local barracks - for the journey "to resume in the morning."

Trevor waited two hours before Gregor passed his quarters and damned near knocked him out, his knuckles white and choking at the collar. "What the hell are you doing?"

Being drunk, Gregor was half way laughing. But he made a sign of hush to the lips, and Trevor released his hold. "I've agree to give them...some cargo" he answered

"*What?*"

"In exchange for ...how shall I put it, our lives? And for something else. Tomorrow. We see!"

Trevor had to live with trust. Trust for the Russian Commander who had agreed to deliver the UN Cargo Relief Aid...

God!

He disliked the position he was in. He suspected that the Russian did too. But what he disliked even more, was the disposition of Gregor's own Lieutenant...How had *that* element played into the bargain?

For now, he would sit still. But the questions lurked in his head for another day of driving. Especially when they were led off the track with the entire Troop Transport Convoy.

He and Yusef were still together. And alive. But the Lieutenant was absent.

It wasn't until dusk that he understood what it was that Gregor had bargained for.

 And he couldn't believe his eyes.

∞

The wedding was a festive occasion. The groom was his brother, Salim explained.

It was an unexpected stop at a village center. The young woman was wearing a yellow Shalwar Qamees, made of shimmering and floral design, and clearly enjoying a bridal shower, as Amanda saw it.

The bride's hair was thick and darkly shiny. On her arm where bracelets, gana-flowered garlands, bangles and rings adorned her hands... Gifts from the grooms mother and sisters.

"The Tael Mehndi Ceremony" explained Saphira, "they apply Oil and Henna to the bride to be. And the event is participated by both families in the arranged marriage."

If this was an arranged marriage, thought Amanda, then the girl evidently felt as if she had landed a catch. And a catch he was, when she saw him.

Tall, slender and earlier introduced to her as Salim's youngest brother, this boy was downright handsome.

 "The ritual of an arranged marriage" said Dr. Saphira. "... Is an ancient custom. But don't worry about those two kids. They've know each other for years. They went to University together! It's how we are, here, today."

The evening was a welcome stop from their relentless driving. Amanda was a houseguest of an attending family.

Tomorrow they would press on, said Salim. But this could not wait.

Amongst those who served at the tables was a young woman who stood off to the side, waiting. Amanda noticed her because of her Western dress. She was pacing a little, waiting for someone, evidently. Soon enough a young man showed up, kissing her with heartfelt passion.

She wept. He walked away. He had turned around, and was now presenting himself to the same family hosting the ceremonies for the bride. He spoke in Urdi, and bowed to the head of the Household.

Dr. Saphira led Amanda from the room and they stood outside. Salim walked in to join the young lad.

"There is a law in Pakistan that allows a man to have a second wife...He is that man, and making arrangements to take the second daughter of the household to wife..."

"*Second...?*" Amanda could hardly believe her ears.

Her eyes went to the girl outside, still pacing.

"That girl...is his first wife?"

Amanda did not need to say anything. The distress was obvious.

"Why?"

"Because she is infertile"

"*Infert...* How old is she?"
"21. She has been married to him three years. He must have... offspring."

"But look at her! She is heartbroken. And she's still young!"

"And so is he!" said a voice from behind her. It was Salim. "He is my middle brother..."

Singing and music took over the household, and the young bride was being shown the marriage contract that she was to sign, the Nikaah, as Amanda was told.

Even as the Ubtan ointment was applied to her arm by the groom's mother as a beautification process, Amanda could tell that the girls were submitting to ritual only temporarily, for in their ears were pierced earrings, and in their hearts were western ways. With jobs in the city.

Which made the girl outside the greatest tragedy of all.

"What's up with the ritual? That must be hell on that girl?" asked Amanda, pleadingly.

Dr. Sumptra faced her.

"It's the whole village. Everybody in it is *infertile*. There have been no children for three years. And now we're reverting to ancient ritual and old beliefs to break the cycle..."

"But the girls are...are...modern city girls!" protested Amanda.

Salim stared at her. Up here he was King, and Amanda would be best to show care with her judgments. He seemed to understand that she spoke from the heart, about things that mattered and were universal amongst young girls.

"These are the sorrows and pains we pay as a culture, if necessary, and in private!"

"By why? Think of the impact on the err... the first wife. How is she supposed to be normal and well-adjusted and compete with a polygamous marriage in today's global economy?"

"And what about my brother?" asked Salim. "To be infertile up here is tantamount to being a failed enterprise. Good for nothing! Besides, the allotted wedding is set for another year. I insisted on it. Maybe she can have offspring before then, and then the whole arrangement is off!"

Amanda looked down. She had no business interfering. They left her alone to process the ways of the ancients.

Only later, with the household quiet, and the village at rest did the three of them talk over a soft candlelight and bottle of cognac.

It was Salim who came to the rescue of Western thinking in a quiet discourse over cultural conflicts and differences. He explained the deeper questions that had been so difficult to attain since 9/11...

"You can't imagine the conflict that broods amongst the young in this part of the world. Easily misunderstood, and considered too alien to embrace by the West...

"... But after a decade of the likes of Mushareff who promised change, progress, development, and an end to corruption we find that nothing has changed for a young, vibrant population...

"...Even the icon of rock and roll music in Pakistan, Junoon has turned away: He reported that he, like so many others, had hopes to open up independent media and reduce the gap between rich and poor. He found, he said, emergency rule, closed media, muzzled dissent and judicial dismantling..."

Dr. Saphira continued "Many question the difference between democracy and dictatorship. The young identify *first* with being a Muslin, and *secondly* with being a National. It's the challenge they must face."

"I don't mean to take sides," said Amanda "but ...didn't it take more than one day to build Rome?"

"True" he laughed. "And don't worry, we can be highly competitive. In fact, we plan to run circles around you Americans!"

"Is there no recourse... for the young?" asked Amanda. "We in the West convolute over politics constantly. It's not pretty... nor perfect, but we have our means of redress..."

"Yes. And we have our crisis..." he began

"...Right now, frankly, it's a medical crisis. All the men here have become infertile" said Dr. Saphira.

"And we think we know why... So I'm here to shut this damned mine down!"

"What mine?"

"The one you plan to visit with your damned rescue package..."

"*What?* You think...there's a connection?"

"Of course!" said Salim rising to leave the room "I plan to blow it up. Good night, ladies!"

My God, thought Amanda, what have I walked into?

∞

The barrels were endless.

Round, three-tiered steel drums, sealed. Each containing stamped markings, now faded, Hazardous Materials. Corrugated tin and rusted roofing served for cover on the dozen or so sitting outside on palettes. Others had tent cloth for covering, long torn out, bleached by weather and flailing in the wind. Forty five barrels in all.

"Nerve gas!" announced the Russian. "I promised to haul it off..."

The barrels were still intact, if badly eroded. They belong to "the last war..." he tried to explain, the load of them rattling like a line of carnival cans in the back of the Troop Transport. But Trevor wasn't listening. He looked at Yusef, stiffly holding on and almost in shock.

It didn't much matter who provided them. Nor which side, and for whom. Both Trevor and the Russian knew the futility and damage of wars that had taken place in Afghanistan. A cachet of abandoned 'Supplies' delivered by unknown Arms Dealers across the border in Pakistan... for *whoever* would take them!

Certainly it was time to remove them from the landscape!

On that they were, at least, both in agreement. But now? Where to? Like this?

At any rate, the canisters and containers were all on board. Both Trevor and Gregor were reconciled.

Even with most of the UN Relief Supplies still onboard, loaded into two trucks behind them in the supply convoy line. Emergency provisions for the Shoehire Pass, crawling in convoy over the rugged mountain terrain like a war train with hazardous materials, already seeping.

The mountain climb was not easy for the convoy.

Trevor was showing signs of fatigue by the second day. And he informed Yusef that if he approached him one more time to admonish him about ill-advised positions, he'd scream at him!

So when Yusef, now at the wheel of a truck himself, drove up alongside the lead vehicle to ask for a Halt, it annoyed Trevor beyond measure and solicited a blistering oath from the Russian who swiveled the front tire of their ten-ton-semi to meet with a boulder, sending them all against the roof.

They stopped.

"What *is it* Yusef?" roared Trevor, dirt, dust and an aroma of gasoline encrusted to his clothes as he walked up to the window of Yusef's truck.

"Amanda Wells. I got a signal on my cell. She's going to the Shorehire Pass!"

∞

Chapter 11

They had travelled another twenty miles up the Pass.

They worked 18 hours straight to patch up the damage from the Tremors that quaked the mountain. And they did reinstate some semblance of quarters for those most in need. Not that the damage had entirely wiped out the village. It was just that some sectors had been blocked up by falling rubble. Remarkably, few had perished.

Again and again, Amanda thought that it would have meant so much to these people to have relief supplies.

It was a miner's village. A mountainside settlement of dwellings carved out of the slopes by humans centuries ago, now nicely escalated with huts, stone-ramped steps flanked by stone balustrades, walkways, sheep pens, and even tiered gardens for blossoms and herbs.

Small terracotta chimneys served as furnaces for baking, and heat circulated nicely amongst the grotto-styled escapements, each entrance providing ample privacy and separate quarters for every group. Some were entire families with children. But mostly it was men. Men who came up to work, then return down the mountain in the off season.

Amanda was amazed by the efficacy of the community.

The hamlet was embedded into the mountain like a delicate latticework of shapes and grottos. It was self-sustaining. A stone silo served to cure goat cheese and milk. A grassy terrace was in-filled with soil for vines.

Natural rock outcrops and hand chiseled walls were lined with grainy plaster. Overhead timbers, hewn and carved appeared hospitable. Terracotta tiles lay over cleared parterres reminiscent of architectural predilections from Eastern medieval times far exceeding the basic needs of survival.

Supplies were ample. Food, spices and textiles were in abundance. Even if carried up the paths by beasts of burden to the hamlet for the last mile where the road to the mine came closest.

Cisterns fed by mountain streams and melting snow supplied water, and fuel and electrical power was evidently in abundance from the mine. Even antenna and a small tower betrayed TV sets and wireless communications.

Only at the mine had roads been dynamited out of the mountain side. Pathways, just above the ledge elevation, connected the community to their place of their work with electric lighting, mainly to thread a pathway through weather in winter. Otherwise, goats kept the footpaths clear of snow and ice with their hoofs scraping the surface, often there to graze.

Amanda looked up and could hardly believe her surroundings. Above the tree line, they were surrounded by mountains much higher. Blue hued peaks capped with snow where shrouded by clouds. Yet flowers lingered at every hospitable crevice in the rock-face, bobbing and blowing in the wind. Only between the mountains did valleys betray gorges of extreme descent and melting ferocity, many perhaps uncharted.

It was a world from another planet thought Amanda.

"The biggest problem normally" Saphira was saying in her heavy parka "are sheep! They tend to freeze if caught out in the wind, often a wind that blows over the summits to freeze of a sudden weather-front."

Amanda stared at her, trying to imagine the prospect of a landscape of frozen sheep. Saphira laughed at her. "Makes for a fresh slaughter of good meat!"

They finished, having seen to all of the injured and dispensed anti-biotic quite liberally. Especially with the men. That night, tucked into their warm bunks with embers glowing still from a central brazen that conducted heat through the cave walls, they chatted for hours.

"I know what it is!" said the Doctor. "Some show signs of progressive lead poisoning..." she paused "No Board of Safety Regulation and hygiene here!"

"Then... why do they stay?"

"It's work. Money for their family on a seasonal basis" said the doctor, settling into her bedding. "Besides, the Corporation that owns this mine is foreign owned and probably lives in the tropics...offering some revenue to the State in return!"

"Is that good or bad?" asked Amanda.

Dr. Saphira was already asleep. And it wasn't long before Amanda's eyes closed.

The heat would be replenished by their house attendant, she knew, a lady who had already furnished them with fresh baked bread and lamb stew for supper.

But she awoke early. In fact, it was hard to tell whether the sun was up yet in a mountainside house without windows. Only in the receiving rooms did they exist. And small at that, chiefly to minimize exposure to the elements.

Saphira was already up and gone. Evidently tending her patients in the next structures.

So Amanda washed in a warm and softly lit bathroom within a square terracotta bathtub where fresh mountain water had been heated by natural fires. Stoked by the heat within the caves yet vented by chimneys, water was then flushed away into deep mountain crevasses with waterfalls, rock and melting snow. It might well have been called paradise on earth by some, mused Amanda.

It was still dark. So Amanda decided to retrieve her laptop from her gear in the front receiving room. And that's when she heard him.

In English, citing latitude, longitude, altitude and weather. He was taking notes, and talking into a navigational transponder.

"Nineteen hundred hours Zulu. Roger. Out!"

Through the tiny window portal she peered and saw the back of his head. The Map was clearly marked with a circle.

It was Salim on a cell phone.

She backed away.

∞

"Amanda!"

The call echoed around the mountain cliffs like a ghostly fog.

Amanda had her parka on and was zipping up the vest when she heard the call again.

"Amanda!"

She approached the front entrance of their hamlet and stepped outside. With the sun well over the mountain peak, she could see Saphira rushing down the rock steps circling the stone silo. A gust of wind surged so alarmingly that she had to pause and hold onto the flank stone wall that safeguarded a sheer drop. The drop was at least 300 ft. vertical.

The wind passed, her words lost, but her arm was flailing happily with a message. She got up, steadied herself and proceeded down.

"Your cargo... It's coming!" she sang out.

"*Yes?*"

"I got a message from my hospital in New Delhi. Apparently a call came in asking if I had seen you, and that your friend Trevor MacDonald is on his way here with the UN cargo intended for the victims of the quake!"

Amanda could hardly believe her ears.

She was both elated and stunned that such an event had occurred. First because it meant material much needed to aid the village. Second... Second because she, he, that is... she, no, *Trevor* ...God!

She turned to face the wind and could hardly reconcile her feelings just now.

What? Where was he...? A thousand miles away, almost like a thousand years away. Oh God. Trevor was coming...And with her supplies! Could that be true?

She wanted to cry. Her hair was a medusa's mess in the torrents of winds, whipping her face, her tears, her thoughts in this tangled... disastrous condition! It was a whirlwind.

Trevor had come through. And on her behalf...

And just then, she and Saphira looked up to see a helicopter, two of them now, lifting off over the ledge to depart the mountain. In one was Salim.

"How wonderful..." she started to say to Saphira as they ran for shelter from the downdraft "I'm thrilled to hear it..."

Saphira was enumerating the medical supplies needed to solve her problems, the patients, the repairs, the reserves, the reports... Yes, they would *all* need to be transported down the mountain. And thank God she said. All of them away from this wretched place...Just days away!"

Amanda acknowledged her. But there was something else on her mind.

It was all Amanda could do to get her attention. And it took some convincing.

"Saphira" Amanda said. "Salim has betrayed us!"

"What do you mean...betrayed us?"

"He plans to have the mine demolished!"

"Impossible! What are you suggesting, exactly?"

"*His* mission is not ours! He wants this place shut down. The mine, I mean. Yes. I heard him giving away our coordinates...in English. He's left, hasn't he?"

"You can't be serious..." began Saphira. "Why his own brothers are..." she turned pale.

"Gone!"

It did not need to be said that if the mine was to be demolished, then they too would all perish.

She and Saphira started packing and loading the patients, supplies and provisions for two hours before they heard the cry from one of the villagers outside.

∞

The Army had arrived to wipe them out.

He was standing there, this man, not far from the ledge, his sheepskin and fur-lined hat fluttering in a relentless wind, pointing to the road that approached the mine. An Army troop transport was behind him.

"Quick..." screamed Amanda. "Are there any defensive weapons in the mine itself?"

Saphira was just staring in disbelief. She barked to the villager.

"A short range rocket launcher, he said...Amanda, what are you saying?"

"If we don't use it. We're all dead. Period."

Saphira barked at the man once again. "Yes. He said he knows how to use it. He was trained for the security of the mine."

"Good!" said Amanda. "Get everybody over in the far end of the village. Tell him to target that oncoming convoy. Now! Have him damage the road. Then the convoy itself. Got it?"

Amanda found a pair of binoculars in the room that held the desk and equipment where Salim had been.

Russian!

Well I'll be damned, she thought. Polish the place off with a Russian convoy, no less!"

The gun turret atop the driver's cap revealed a man.

 She too was being surveyed in his sights.

∞

The volley that hit the road a hundred feet in front of them tore right through the ledge and exploded into the side of the mountain.

Trevor shot out of the vehicle. The Russian was jolted out of the seat and circled the rear of the truck to alert the soldiers to take shelter. His voice carried with alarm.

Trevor ran forward and squatted behind a boulder to survey the situation. From above, evidently, not far from the antenna at the top of the ledge had come the salvo.

He ran back inside the truck and grabbed both the map and the binoculars that splayed across the dash.

A moment of calm elapsed.

Clearly they were in someone's sights. He heard the troops descend out of the trucks and make for shelter in the slopes behind the trucks. He looked up, and a refraction from the sunlight caught the person training on him. A stand-off of some sorts had occurred.

The Russians were already signaling for defensive measures and a few men started to spread out, rifles slung behind their heavy coats. They would flank the village and ascend from behind.

Trevor stuck out his head. And he nearly lost it in a shell that shattered the rocks behind him.

He lay down, and inched across to ferns and brush from which he looked again through his binoculars.

A man, holding a rocket launcher was visible. Beside him was...

No! Beside him was...*Impossible*!

Amanda Wells?

"Don't shoot!" he yelled, to no avail in the torrent of wind. And too late.

The Russians were moving into position, he knew. They would take out the lot of them in a manner of minutes.

He watched her move sideways, talk to someone else, then return to the man with the rocket launcher. She raised her field glasses once again. And that's when Trevor made his decision.

He hoped she would see him. He stood up. Walked forward and raised his arms.

"Amanda! It's me!"

It took her some thirty seconds to process the situation. And Trevor knew he had to make sure this didn't escalate.

She at least had the sense to talk to the man holding the rocket launcher. He laid it down, and retreated.

She lifted her arms.

"Trev...." She seemed to have called.

He waived.

∞

New York

Indictments were handed out at the Chicago Board of Trade for Futures Trading and the New York Stock Exchange was issued with warnings as well as safeguards.

Many were brought to account with the SEC and a draft agreement was drawn to rescind all legal transactions of title transfer to parties unidentified within the last two months.

Gottlieb lost his Bar License, and two Trading brokers filed for bankruptcy proceedings.

"What about the Russians and Chinese brokers?" asked his boss at Prouse & Bertmutler, Associates.

"Their Embassies struck a deal in Washington. They would be dealt with at home, apparently. That's all I'm informed about."

"I see"

Paul Demuth hated the way Prouse could grill him with that expression. He could just sit there, leaning back in his chair on two legs, staring and waiting for the next inquisition. Especially with the room full of other partners and associates. It was a large Law Firm. One he had been so excited about joining. And it was a large board room. Damn them all, sitting there, watching him.

For sure, he'd be getting another job, never mind that he'd been through two weeks of hell.

Prouse surprised him.

"Well" he said, landing back down on the four legs of his chair.

"I'd say you've done an excellent job, then. Washington thanks us! Well done! Case closed..." He got up, and left the board room.

Which was hardly the truth. It would take two months to tie off the ends, Paul knew. But it wasn't until everybody filed out of the board roam, many shaking his hands with a terse "Congratulation buddy!" that it all sank in.

Finally his secretary approached him. "Looks like you survived. Here's work!"

"Right" he said, still numb.

∞

Trevor was stunned. He barely got out of the truck at the top of the road where it ended and froze.

Amanda stood at the path leading to the hamlet.

She approached with the resolve of a bear. She was carrying a large stick.

"Don't you dare... you sonnofabitch!" she screamed. "We came here in peace to aid these people, and your bring an ...an...arsenal?"

If she could she would have slugged him. But she stopped short at the sight of him. Bearded, bundled up, roughly redheaded and badly dehydrated in clothes too small for his body and inadequate for body warmth. He was barely standing.

"What?" he asked in a broken voice. "I've come to bring you the Aid..."

She would have raised her stick, he sensed, in utter frustration. She stood there, her nostrils flaring. Saphira came to her side.

He walked to the rear of the Truck, personnel having dismounted and opened the rear gate. He mounted the cargo platform, and with a tire iron pried open a crate. It fell away with a bang, its nails jarred and bent open.

Cellophane wrapped supplies gleamed in the sunlight. He tore open a section and threw her a bag of cotton swabs.

It wasn't until she and Saphira actually saw the supplies that she became coherent.

"I thought you were out to demolish the mine and take out the village..." she said.

He stood there.

She turned to him. "It's been scheduled for... a demolition assault of some kind, the man who was here..."

"I know."

She stared at him, unbelieving.

"I was mad as hell that he bailed out and left us...he left us to perish in what was an impending ..." She stopped "What? You *knew*. What do you mean, you *know*?"

"Who is doing this..." he said.

"Who?"

"Us!" he said quietly. "A US Team is preparing to take out the mine!"

She took a step back, almost ready to raise her stick, her eyes fierce, the full picture eluding her.

He waited.

"When?"

"Daybreak the 28th..."

"Let's get inside and shelter from this weather, all of us!" admonished Saphira, taking charge.

Amanda glowered. "What's in that other truck...back there, waiting?"

"You don't want to know" he said. "It's not what you think. But it is a long story. So feed these soldiers. They've come a long way. They have some work to do, and will make camp about twenty miles away. Then we load up the passengers. And we're out of here by dark tomorrow. Get it?"

"What *everyone*?"

"Yes"

"Why?"

"Because for now, those are my Orders!"

Yusef came forward.

They embraced with relief. "He came here for you!" he said to Amanda.

Later, when Saphira joined her, and both were settling into their bunks she said something completely out of the blue. "You love him, don't you?"

The silence echoed like a chamber of secrets. Amanda struggled for the answer.

"He looks exhausted" she answered finally.

"He's had a condition, evidently, that is sapping him clean..." affirmed Saphira. "He needs two weeks of rest in the sun with good food"

Amanda thought of the Hamptons. "I have just the place!"

"Yes" said Saphira. "You love him!"

∞

The Jeep came in handy. She had delivered Trevor to JFK Airport in a cheery return to normal, music blaring from the radio and a bandana for a hat. He looked like he had just been to the vet for his shot.

The laughter put a big grin on Trevor's face. They approached the Gate for flights to London.

He took her into his arms. "So?"

"Are you sure about this?"

"I am!"

She paused. "I have to catch-up on a few loose ends. Clear away some things at work..."

"Clear **Out** some things at work..." he corrected "Then, it's to London with you, right?"

"Right!" she said.

They hugged. Nothing felt more right.

∞

It was two weeks later when Amanda got a call.

It was Dr. Saphira. Long distance "...and I want you to know Amanda, that Salim says I'm to tell you that his brother is to be a father ...Yes! The truth is, when they were both medically examined, he was the one with low motility. Now they are willing to consider A.I."

The line was full of static.

"... Meanwhile, I persuaded them to leave the region for a while together, and to adopt a baby of their liking! They are thrilled."

Amanda was smiling.

"Don't forget to buy your dresses from my seamstress in Lahore!"

"I won't" said Saphira before hanging up.

She was still smiling when she read her email. James Lloyd and another party was coming to town. Could they arrange a meeting?

They met for dinner at the Grand Hyatt Hotel of downtown New York.

"I want you to meet someone special, Ms Wells. Astronaut Karen Patterson" said Lloyd.

Karen Patterson was recognizable anywhere she went. She was an advocate for the sciences, and had toured many high schools to encourage students into the sciences. Especially women. She was the slogan for an Air Force recruitment campaign.

And she was very human, decided Amanda.

"We can't go into details of our flight sequence up there" Lloyd was saying, but we know you had your share of ordeals in the Mountains Ms Wells."

Amanda looked at them both.

"We did. Thank You! They are good people, you know. They mean well...caught between traditions of the east and the west..."

"I know. I know" interrupted Lloyd "But they are a nuclear power nonetheless. And with that comes serious responsibility and serious accountability, which they acknowledge. So we've made amends, and plan to move forward with them as they progress with their growing economy..."

"Anyway, Amanda" said Karen squarely facing her. "I wanted to personally thank you for your efforts. I shall send you a confidential briefing report on what was going on. It explains a lot. And don't get too mad at your boss Fumosa. He was being yanked every which way, with some loss to his staff unfortunately. But you did great! Thank you!"

"So. Here's to the ladies of the world!" said Lloyd with a toast.

"Thank you, both..." said Amanda. "But I do have one question: Salim, the subject of your enquiry the last time you were here?"

"Oh Yes" said Lloyd. "Sorry. I forgot to say. He collaborated with our mission. Made some hard bargains mind you, but is considered a Friendly."

"Cheers!" said Amanda raising her glass as the waiter presented a feast fit for a king.

Facing her wild Alaska salmon, steak and rice pilaf, Amanda enjoyed a meal in the company of an astronaut and a NASA Commander with tales that ranged from the sea to the sky. She added her own stories about her visit to the Himalayan Mountains, and it passed the evening away.

"So. Back to work in New York?" asked Lloyd helping her on with her coat.

"No. Actually. I'm leaving New York" she looked at them both "I'm going to London!"

They looked at each other but were too polite to ask.

She continued "But err... I know of a midnight cafe for you two downtown New York where they serve fresh baked bread and French coffee at about this hour..."

They laughed.

"Keep in touch with us Amanda. We may need you in Washington!" said Lloyd as she entered her taxi.

Yes, she decided. She had made her decision.

It was London.

END